HIDDEN IN PLAIN SIGHT

HIDDEN *in* PLAIN SIGHT

WWII, Mussolini, and the
Plight of Internment Camps
in Southern Italy

CARMINE VITTORIA

TABLE OF CONTENTS

HIDDEN IN PLAIN SIGHT

WWII, MUSSOLINI, AND THE PLIGHT OF INTERNMENT CAMPS IN SOUTHERN ITALY

By Carmine Vittoria

First Edition
Copyright © 2023 by Carmine Vittoria

Published by
Munn Avenue Press
300 Main Street, Ste 21
Madison, NJ 07940
MunnAvenuePress.com

For permission requests, contact MunnAvenuePress.com

Paperback ISBN # 978-1-960299-05-5

Printed in the United States of America

Once again, reginella mia, my wife Rie, has come to my rescue.

She has encouraged me and helped in editing the book.
Thank you.

PROLOGUE

I once asked my friend, Virgilio, "How is it that you lived within a couple of miles of an internment camp in Calabria, during WWII, and you and your family were never aware of, or heard of, it then?" His reply shocked me. How could he not have seen Jewish internees living within a stone's throw from his house? After recovering my composure, I further asked him, "How is it that you never heard of the Ndrangheta Mafia until the 1970s?" His insistence that he was oblivious to the circumstances which encompassed the outside world only incentivized me to explore and investigate my friend's unexpected narratives. My findings revealed that the political decisions of the "high and mighty" affected not only the lives of individuals in remote and isolated towns as well as the lives of Jewish people who were interned there. A special kind of empathetic connection was fostered between these two communities, as their lives became unexpectedly entangled during the War. As such, the lives of these Jewish internees and Italian townies became intertwined for the sole purpose of surviving the War at their doorsteps. Hence, a more realistic and humane view evolved in these small towns of Southern Italy during the war period. The characters presented in this book are based upon stories passed down from preceding generations. These accounts are essentially factual and relevant to that period in history. However, their names have been changed to protect their privacy.

For the most part, the history of warfare has been chronicled by the victors, dwelling on military strategies, politics, armaments, army officers, etc. This book is about the poor souls who found themselves caught in the crossfire of warring armies in their native home of

Southern Italy. As was often the case, there were more ordinary people than soldiers in such perilous situations. Yet very little is known or reported about them. The purpose of this book is to delve into their choices, fears, and intentions while they experienced first-hand violence and utter chaos. Straying from the norm, *"Hidden in Plain Sight"* seeks to tell history, not from the dated pages of our history books, but from the lens of real people telling their stories.

As WWI was coming to an end, an invisible enemy, the Spanish Flu, appeared on the scene in 1918 Europe. The plague did not recognize any border and, therefore, killed indiscriminately, accumulating a death toll of over fifty million. At the same time, internment camps sprang up in Russia and elsewhere. One did not have to necessarily commit a crime to find themselves in these camps. It must have been beyond comprehension for someone to be interned for no legitimate reason after surviving both WWI and the deadliest of plagues. Soon enough, internments served very different purposes, depending on where in Europe they were located. The times were, in fact, dark. To add insult to injury, inflation was so rampant that it took a barrel of money to buy a loaf of bread. It was cheaper to eat the money. People were desperate for deliverance from all that misery and believed that things could not get any worse. They were looking for "angels" to turn things around for the better. Instead, three magi appeared on the scene, riding the wave of political success all the way to totalitarianism: Mussolini, Stalin, and Hitler. They represented the incarnation of evil on earth. Those three oppressors pitted groups and countries against each other to further their ambitions, egos, and psychotic behaviors. In short, they became among the worst despots in the history of mankind. Here is a story about how the human spirit overcame evil.

ONE

Trains Ran On Time

It is late in the 1920s. World War I, the Spanish flu, and economic and political upheavals still lingered in people's minds. Is Benito Mussolini the one to take people out of their misery? The general feeling among the people of Avella at that time was that, at least, he got the trains running on time. Those were the underlying thoughts among the peasants and gentry in the town of Avella at the time. It was well known that he was running around with mistresses and was corrupt as hell but, so what, if they felt that his heart was with the people. That was the hope. As it turned out, belief and hope superseded realities then and after.

Avella, Italy, is an ancient town and is proud of its history. It dates to the Paleolithic age (2.5 to 0.2 million years ago), the Old Stone Age. Archeological remains have shown human presence along the Clanio Creek. Water in the creek flows from the top of Monte Avella to the valley below and to the town of Avella. The valley extends from the sweeping foothills of the Apennine mountains to Naples and is sometimes referred to as Naples' backyard, see photo below.

In ancient times, the name of the town was Abella due to the abundance of hazelnuts there. The Abella hazelnut is one of eighteen species. The town of Abella was under the heavy influence of the Etruscans and Greeks who had settled in Paestum and Neapolis (Naples) in the 8th century BC, as well as the fierce Samnite tribes of the Apennine mountains. There is strong evidence that the Samnites were natives of the area.

3

The common denominator between the descendants of the Stone Age and Samnites was that they were nomads, hunters, and shepherds. To our knowledge, there is no evidence linking the two groups to modern-day shepherds. In the 3rd century BC, Abella became a principality of Rome while also being surrounded by Samnite settlements. As such, the town was rewarded with an amphitheater by the Roman Emperor Sulla in 89 BC, when the Romans invaded and conquered the valley.

View of the valley and Mount Vesuvius from the top of Monte Avella. The town of Avella is at the foothill below. Courtesy of Piero Busiello.

An antique map of the region may be seen in the Vatican Museum in which the name "Abella" can be discerned, although the year is not displayed. However, by the turn of the fifteenth century, the name of the town changed to Avella. As in most towns in Southern Italy, Avella, in the 1920s, was split into two distinct classes of people: the gentry and the peasants. This description of the classes is well documented in Carlo Levi's book, *"Christ Stopped at Eboli"*. Suffice it to say, these two classes of people in Avella did not mingle very well, and they lived in different parts of town. The gentry lived mostly in the center of town, usually surrounding a Piazza (main square), and the peasants lived in the periphery, toward the foothills of the mountains. As in Aliano, where Carlo Levi was exiled, the gentry in Avella may be described in terms of the establishment, like the Carabinieri (policemen), mayor, City Hall workers, artisans, landowners, etc. Farmhands, shepherds, and unskilled workers made up the peasant class. The clash between the "haves and have-nots" is as old as time itself and is universal.

The shepherds took their sheep to graze on the fields of Monte Avella as far as the Calabria region, commonly known as the "boot" portion of Italy. It was arduous work. The reward was the bountiful food supply along the many trails on the mountains, and the ability to sell dairy products and wool at the farmer's market. Farmers toiled the land of rich landlords, who resided in cities like Naples and Rome. Life was unfair to the peasants, but that was what it was. The central government in Rome only catered to the gentry. As for the peasants, they didn't exist in the eyes of "Rome". Thus, the division and resentment between the two classes grew with time, culminating in the delay of civilization in small and remote towns like Aliano and Avella. It didn't affect the gentry, however, because they had the opportunity to visit civilized cities like London, Paris, Rome, etc.

In the 1920s, the economic and political situations were rather dire in Italy and there was no one to take charge and clean up the corruption within Rome. Food was outrageously expensive and there was not much of it to go around. Butchers in Avella displayed cat meat as rabbit meat, selling it for 100 lire per pound (equivalent to $10). Red meat was exorbitantly expensive and sparingly available as well. Unemployment was high while politicians bickered among themselves as to who to blame. It didn't affect the shepherds that much, since they foraged for food up on the mountains where the wild boars and other animals roamed. The shepherds were taught to hunt when they were children. Mountains were their insurance against all perils, from invasions to inept administrations in Rome. In some sense, this explains the survival of the

Samnites, or shepherds, since the Paleolithic times, despite all the turmoil in the valley.

With the outbreak of WWI, shepherds withdrew to the mountains of Avella, as did their ancestors in other wars. Sergio Cortone was drafted into the Italian Army as a "Bersagliere" (soldier in the Mountain Army division deployed in the Alps). As a child, he fantasized about himself in the uniform of a Bersagliere with that plumed helmet. He saw those soldiers, when they visited Avella on their recruitment tour of Southern Italy. They ran up and down the street blowing trumpets and bobbing the side of their helmets to side, somewhat theatrically, enough to impress a little boy. He soon was cured of his fantasies once having served duty on the frozen tundra of the Alps. In his wake, he left behind a pregnant wife, Imalda, who had been his soulmate since kindergarten. They shepherded together, helping their parent's search for grassland on the mountains. It was inevitable that the two would get married. In those days, one married within their respective class. For example, a shepherd most likely married a shepherdess. Of course, they were some exceptions, but not many. Marriages were not arranged per se, but it was understood that one married within one's social stratum. Furthermore, women's rights didn't exist as they do today.

Soon after WWI, the second wave of the Spanish Flu caused the most deaths in Army hospitals. The flu claimed the lives of 100-150 people in the town of Avella. Sergio was lucky to be alive since he had contracted the flu one month before the end of WWI in October of 1918. Frankly, it was not clear at that time whether a particular army group or the flu won the battle in the final push by the Italian Army toward Venice in 1918. He was placed in a military hospital for one month during his recovery. Hospitalization gave him plenty of time to think about his imminent future as a shepherd. By then, he was exposed to the world of the gentry and felt comfortable with the thought of doing something else. The only problem was his wife, Imalda, the matriarch of the shepherd community in Avella. As such, Imalda exercised power and demanded respect as leader of the shepherd community. She adjudicated quarrels among shepherds, and, most importantly, she was the sale representative of all things produced by the shepherds at the Farmer's Markets. On one hand, most of the shepherdesses were still in the stone age, but on the other hand, they were well ahead of their time with respect to other countries, with Imalda as their matriarch. Her mother relinquished her mantle, with the consent of the shepherd community to Imalda after WWI.

In those days, it was not easy for a shepherd to change his "career" as the average shepherd lacked the education to do so. Even less chance for a shepherdess. In fact, no chance! However, in comparison with other shepherds, Sergio's credentials looked good. He and Imalda finished elementary school, which was more than what most did. Nevertheless, he was not deterred from his dream of becoming a Guardia di Finanza (finance officer). These mountain policemen are employed in airports, train stations, department stores, mountains and any place where money transactions are involved.

By the mid-1920s, a new leader, Benito Mussolini, often referred to as Il Duce, appeared on the horizon as Prime Minister and things appeared to be stable. It was important to the people of Avella to have access to a train station, because that was their only contact with the outside world and civilization, where most jobs were located. In those days the Fascist government provided many perks to relieve the misery of people. For example, stipends were awarded to families with children. In addition, army veterans had preferential treatment for government jobs. Sergio took advantage of being an army veteran when he enrolled at the Police Academy in Naples to train as a "Guardia di Finanza" specializing as a mountain policeman. This allowed him the luxury of distancing himself from the drudgeries of shepherding while still maintaining his friendship with the shepherds up on the mountains.

The previous mountain policeman, who retired, was not a shepherd and therefore had no sympathy for, or understanding of, the hardships shepherds faced. He was involved in a shady auction on a parcel of land in the mountains whereby he was the only person bidding on it. No one else was informed of the auction. The owner of the land emigrated to the USA in order to avoid conscription in the Italian Army before WWI. That episode created much animosity and confrontation between the former policeman and the shepherds because the parcel of fertile and rentable land was located near the shepherd's neighborhood. Thus, the shepherds were short-changed twice, short and long-term.

Sergio was intent on reducing the confrontational tone of previous interactions. After all, he was one of them. His wife was just as happy for him to become involved with issues that concerned her as well, being a matriarch. Promptly at 8:11 in the morning, Sergio boarded the Circumvesuviana train station in Avella and arrived in Naples an hour later. He then walked to the Police Academy in the Posillipo district. Classes were from 10 am to 4 pm and returned home at about 6 pm. He did that for a year even though he struggled with the handbooks detailing police rules and procedures. The evening was a family affair with daughter Sofia and son Paolo trying to explain to Sergio the contents of the handbooks. Sergio had a dream, and he was not about to let go. His children admired the passion and intensity constantly billowing out of him.

Sergio's family lived in an apartment in an old building with a front porton (large door). Inside the building, there was a semi-circular court-yard overlooking a large field of grass. The property was handed down from generation to generation by shepherd descendants. It was located at the edge of town next to a business farm that cultivated hazelnuts and green olives. It is interesting to note that the owner of the farm was able to hide a Roman amphitheater for an exceedingly long time by placing foliage, shrubbery, and trees next to it. He could not divulge the existence of the amphitheater for fear of losing the farm to the State. Across the street from Sergio's building, his family cultivated a beautiful garden consisting of fruit trees, grapevines and flowers. Sergio's neighbor in the courtyard, Don Nicola, lived next to his apartment. Abutting Don Nicola's apartment was a music studio. In the winter, Sergio rented the field to shepherds so they could feed their sheep at a minimal cost. Snowstorms are quite common at that time of the year up on the mountains.

Upon graduation from the Academy, Sergio was issued a uniform. He rose at 6 am and proudly put on the uniform each day. Shortly thereafter, he was ready to leave at 7 am for his inspection tour as a mountain policeman. He would exit the portone and quickly turn right, heading uphill toward Monte Avella, the tallest mountain in the range of mountains running from East to West, toward the Tyrrhenian Sea. As always, he met Ciccio, a local shepherd, riding his donkey loaded with warm ricotta cheese in a large twine basket that was covered with fig leaves to keep it warm. Ciccio was on his way to sell ricotta in the neighborhood and deliver hard cheese to Imalda for her to sell at the Farmer's Market. Sergio could not get his mojo going unless he started his day with the warm ricotta. Ciccio would roll the fig leaf into the shape of a cone, fill it with warm ricotta and proudly hand it to Sergio. Once the chit-chat with Ciccio was over, Sergio headed straight to the open-air aqueduct line that led water downstream to fountains in town. The water line was no deeper than a shallow trench or ditch about one to two feet deep. There were constant complaints in town regarding farmers who could easily re-direct the water from the trench to their farms. Sergio's tasks were to repair the trench and cite the poachers. It wasn't difficult to determine who the culprits were. The detoured water flow direction "pointed the finger."

The next checkpoint was to ensure that the same trench water line extended to the Roman aqueduct. The Roman aqueduct was built in ancient times to extend from the top of the mountains to the water fountains in town. However, during the 1920s, most of it was either destroyed or had simply eroded. Nevertheless, part of it was still functional enough to connect to a modern water reservoir, on higher ground, to the water line in the trenches. Often, the Roman aqueduct leaked, and Sergio was required to inform City Hall officials to have it repaired. Otherwise, city water stopped flowing into town. From the water reservoir location, Sergio was staring straight up at the peak of Monte Avella. After an arduous three-hour climb, he reached the camp where shepherds had gathered before starting their trek in search of grassland. Sergio's route uphill was along Clanio Creek.

The terrain was nasty and thick with underbrush, ravines, and deep gorges. In the spring, rainwater gushed down to the creek forming a river that flooded the town. In some places, it looked more like a canyon than a deep ravine. A wooden bridge facilitated the crossing of the creek at a critical junction of the climb. If possible, he would try to repair the bridge when needed. Otherwise, it would have been close to impossible to climb to the top, especially when it rained. The most dangerous part of the trek was chance encounters with wolves, wild boars and poisonous snakes, such as vipers. Wild boars are fearless and courageous, a bad combination for hunters. Sometimes, the best defense against a rushing boar was to climb the nearest tree. The bear population had diminished long before Sergio appeared on the scene. If he spotted one, he noted the location. The population of black bears was nearly extinct in the mountains of Avella since people living near the foothills hunted bears that encroached in their neighborhood for food. Eventually, bears were wiped out entirely from the low hills. Few could still be found on the high mountains. The Guardia di Finanza put in place a program to protect the bears by monitoring their whereabouts.

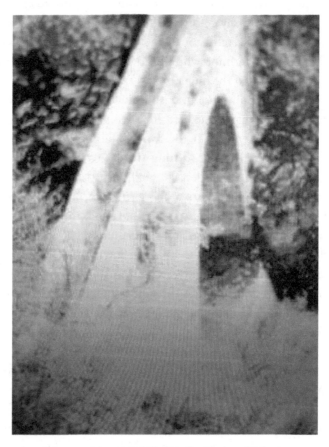

Roman aqueduct in the hills of Avella. Courtesy of Salvatore Morelli.

Once in the company of his fellow shepherds, he felt at home. Sergio stayed for lunch and talked about the good old times when he trekked to the grassland fields. He then gently reminded the shepherds about the due dates for tax payments on their land. Those payments came due every thirty years. Essentially, he discussed with them a convenient time schedule for them

The Clanio Creek flowing down from Monte Avella. Courtesy of Irpinia Avventura Club.

to make payments, while also never reporting late payments. After a lengthy accounting of payment schedules, he would rest at the camp for the night and walk along a narrow path to the National Park which was ten miles away. At the Park, there was a lake that drained small amounts of water which flowed in Clanio Creek. No sheep were allowed to graze there. Sergio was gentle in reminding shepherds about the park's rules and gave no citations. Also, he let it be known when he would return to inspect the National Park.

Homeward bound, the Bay of Naples and Mount Vesuvius view was stunning. The setting was unbelievably beautiful, with a bounty of wild berries and sights one could hardly fathom. Strawberries were the size of a fingernail, but so sweet in taste. In addition, wild porcini mushrooms, asparagus, and other vegetables, as well as snails were there for the taking. He was aware of which mushrooms were poisonous. He had been taught that since childhood. During Sunday family dinners, he would prepare the macaroni dish with porcini mushrooms and grated goat cheese. Of course, his friend and family neighbor, Don Nicola, and his children were always invited.

Signed monthly reports must be delivered personally at the Police Academy auditorium in Naples. There were one hundred or so Finanzieri di Guardia mountain policemen from all around the valley waiting to submit their reports in alphabetic order to a magistrate. The magistrate sat on the stage behind a desk overlooking the policemen below waiting for their turns to sign and hand in their reports. The whole scene was somewhat theatrical, as their reports were never read. Unfortunately for Sergio, it was an all-day affair, which swayed his allegiance toward the shepherds over the establishment, when confirming the substance of the report.

His wife, Imalda, was the fiery one and a go-getter. When she was barely ten years old, she and her sister were helping their parents with shepherding tasks on the high mountains. Often, they were left alone with the sheep, as their parents were on the hunt for wild boars and grassland. While her sister was afraid to be left alone, Imalda took charge and loved the opportunity to impress her parents by taking take care of things around the camp and the sheep. Arming herself with a special heavy wooden stick, she was ready to take on the wolves. Most marriages in the shepherd community were arranged by the parents. They were based on how many sheep each of the families could bring to the marriage. In the case of Imalda, she had had her eye on Sergio since when they both left their school in fifth grade. As far as shepherds were concerned, third grade was usually good enough for them to be able to sign their names on documents or on ballots during election times. Sergio, however, was no blooming flower ready to be picked. He was just as wild and proud as Imalda. It was only natural that the two of them would eventually get married. Their parents, in this case, had no choice but to let love take over.

The shepherd community recognized Imalda as their leader, choosing her to represent them in the business of interfacing with the gentry in the valley. Besides settling disputes among shepherds, she was basically the sales representative of all products produced by the community: goat cheeses, wool, milk, wooden utensils, etc. Imalda sold their wares mostly at the Farmer's Market in Avella every Monday, and in Nola on Wednesdays. She would display her cheese at the most advantageous spot in the marketplace and nobody dared to challenge her. She would shush away little children from her spot, because they behaved like little mice, especially around cheese. There was no tenderness when it came to business, although she was very soft-hearted with family and friends. The market at Nola featured a much larger crowd. The town was about ten kilometers west of Avella (toward Naples), accessible by train. Sergio and another shepherd helped her load goods on the train to transport them to market and back. The train usually arrived punctually at 8:11 in the morning and stopped for only five minutes. However, on Wednesdays, the train master made an exception for Imalda. He allowed extra time for her to load all her produce onto the train. He was too intimidated by Imalda to enforce the five-minute rule. The train master made up time by speeding faster between stations.

Don Nicola was a cellist employed by the San Carlo opera house in Naples. He was proud to have learned to play the organ on his own, as opera composer Puccini did. He met Giacomo Puccini at the San Carlo opera house, when the opera, La Boheme, was presented to a Neapolitan audience for the first time. At that time, Puccini was still revising his opera, although it had premiered much earlier in Turin, Italy. The sudden death of Puccini in 1924 shocked Don Nicola as well as the rest of Italy and the opera world. It was claimed later by some journalists that the composer was a Fascist. Being a socialist at heart and versed in the doctrines of Karl Marx, Don Nicola knew better, as he and the composer shared similar views of Italian politics.

Don Nicola's family consisted of himself, his son Nicola and his daughter Flora. His wife, Gelina, died of the Spanish flu, as did about 150 others in Avella. Don Nicola fervently wanted his son, Nicola, to follow in his footsteps as a musician, but his son's sole interest was in painting. Nicola was a young adult and was already an accomplished artist. He was beginning to attract the attention of churches that needed restoring old paintings. Somehow, he escaped the wave of impressionist art, exceedingly popular at that time, and concentrated on classical paintings, which was a rarity then. Don Nicola realized that his son was a talented artist already recognized by others at a very young age and was truly proud of him. Flora was Papa's favorite and attended his music studio. She was a mezzo-soprano and specialized in singing light operas, like Puccini's and Mozart's.

There was love and respect between Sergio's and Don Nicola's families, despite that their backgrounds were as different as night and day. Their children referred to the elders as "uncles". Sergio admired Don Nicola's political passion and intellect, although he was apolitical. Returning the sentiment, Don Nicola admired Sergio's common-sense approach to life and that "spirit of a goat" which was earthbound and proud. Whereas Sergio's descendants were local (Samnites), Don Nicola's were the invaders (Romans). To be precise, Roman Jews who resided in Rome around 100 BC migrated to Abella, since Abella, Pompei, and Naples (Pozzuoli) were then the only towns allied with Rome. Don Nicola's descendants came from that migration of Jews to Abella. Their personalities complemented each other. Like Sergio, Don Nicola was drafted into the Italian Army in WWI. His duties were far removed from the fighting fronts near the Alps Mountain ranges (Dolomites). His duty was to rally support for the War locally. He was a conductor of the Army band traveling from town to town playing military marching music. Being a socialist at heart, Don Nicola innately detested those duties. The Socialist party was against Italy entering the War. Nonetheless, he didn't have a choice unless he neglected his duties.

The neighborhood where Don Nicola and Sergio lived was located on the edge of the foothills, the eastern periphery of town, where mostly shepherds and farmers lived. That is, except for Alvaro, who was a lawyer and an accountant, and Don Nicola, whom both lived there and came from families who were well-to-do professionals and respected in town. Alvaro's family lived across the street from the building where Sergio and Don Nicola both resided. Alvaro's job, shortly after WWI, was that of a Public Notary at the post office. He was a jack of all trades, as recognized by all in town. He represented people in court, managed accounts of the wealthiest people in town, notarized important documents, assured people delivery of mail without delay, and signed off on immigration papers for those emigrating.

The name Alvaro is derived from the Spanish name Alvarez. He was a descendant of the Jewish denizens who left Sicily during the infamous Inquisition of the 1500s. A royal decree was approved in 1492 by Queen Isabel and King Ferdinand II which aimed to expel from Spain any free Jewish person who did not convert to Catholicism. Over 200,000 Jews were converted and about 100,000 were expelled. The ones who were expelled emigrated to Italy, Greece, and other countries in the Mediterranean Sea basin. They took surnames based on the towns they were sent to.

At roughly the same time, Sicily was ruled by the Spanish King Ferdinand II of Aragon. Most likely, the Jewish people who lived in Sicily were descendants of the ones expelled by Emperor Pompey in the sacking of Jerusalem in 63 BC. The Jewish population reached 30,000 - 40,000 in Sicily and they assimilated very well into the framework of contemporary society. For instance, they matriculated in philosophy, medicine, artisan pursuits, and farming. As in Spain, the Inquisition decree forced free Jews to convert or be expelled. Some of the expelled chose to move inland to the Calabria and Naples areas. Alvaro's last name, Da Alia, is derived from the town in Sicily from which his descendants came, Alia. Alvaro's family included his wife Felicia, son Mario and twin daughters, Serafina and Filomena.

During WWI, the Italian Army consisted mostly of conscripted peasants who were malnourished while fighting for a cause few could understand. About 470,000 conscripts resisted call-up and 300,000 deserted. Alvaro was the lawyer representing two shepherd brothers hiding in the mountains of Avella the entire time during Italy's conscription since Alvaro was well known in the shepherd community. He lived in their neighborhood. Other shepherds emigrated to the USA to avoid it. This was nothing new, as shepherds have often avoided wars generated by the gentry. Fortunately for the brothers, there was a national amnesty for all deserters in 1920. In Avella, being a small town, no secret remained a secret for long. Alvaro's reputation came to the attention of the only royalty in town, the family of Garcia Alavarez de Toledo. He descended from a Spanish royal family dating back to the 1500s. Garcia's son, Ramiro, employed Alvaro as an accountant for their global financial affairs.

The relationship between Garcia Alvarez, head of the family, and Alvaro Da Alia was like that of father and son, especially when Garcia discovered Alvaro's Spanish background. They would converse in Spanish in Garcia's library study where Alvaro worked one day a week storing accounting files. It is ironic that Garcia's descendants eventually chased the Da Alia's descendants out of Sicily. For now, both lived in the same town in harmony. Garcia was proud of the fact that his ancestor, Ferdinando, was the conquistador who, for the first time, captured Naples in 1555 for the Spanish Crown. As a reward, the King of Spain appointed Ferdinando the Viceroy of Naples. Alvaro was quick to remind Garcia that his ancestors arrived in Naples' backyard well before Ferdinando established the first Jewish-Spanish settlement. In a strange turn of events, Alvaro and Garcia were both thankful that their ancestors settled in the same town of Avella. They both got a big chuckle out of that bout of irony. Spanish influence in the area was and remains strong to this day. The Neapolitan dialect, cultivated food, and architecture are just some examples.

Once a year, children of the Palazzo Barone workers, including Alvaro's, were allowed to swim in the only pool in Avella, located in the garden adjacent to the palace. The palace was built in the sixteenth century by the 3rd Duke of Alba, Ferdinando Alvarez de Toledo when he was Viceroy of Naples. The garden was dedicated to Princess Livia Colonna as a token of love from her husband, Fernando Alvarez de Toledo, Count of Caltabellotta. The Colonna family had been a powerful one going back to the 12th century. It has produced six popes, was one of the wealthiest families in the world, and exerts tremendous political influence even to this day. In 1880, Livia married her long-distance cousin, the Alvarez dynasty.

Their two grandsons Ramiro and Alvaro were mayors of Avella during the early days of fascism. In the mid-1920s, the Fascist government abolished elections. The perfect in each province appointed mayors with the approval of the Interior Minister in Rome, who was a Fascist. However, the perfect might does not have necessarily been a Fascist, as was the case in Avellino (Avella being in that province). The perfect is a public servant and is the State's representative in a province. The office is called Prefettura, a position created in ancient Rome. Alvaro Alvarez married Anna Maria Dupont. The Dupont family founded Dupont Chemical Company which is in Delaware (USA) and today it boasts factories all over the world producing chemical products for the electronic industry and consumer products. Their children, Fabrizio, Ferrante, and Francesca-Chantal sold the palace to the Municipality of Avella in 1989 for 800 million Lire (about 1-2 million dollars). The city of Avella has converted the palace into a museum. The three offspring now reside near Rome where they currently manage an agro-tourism farm.

Palazzo Barone, Avella. Residence of the Alvarez family since the 1700s. Courtesy of Salvatore Morelli.

During those hopeful and happy times, Mario, and his twin sisters, Serafina and Filomena, Alvaro's children, were schoolmates of Sofia and Paolo, Sergio's children. Living next to each other, it was convenient to walk to school together. The private school was located downtown, and it fostered a bond between the children. Mario and Sofia were the elders. Kindergarten and elementary schools were managed by the nuns. Even at a very young age, Sofia was fiercely independent and proud, much like her mother Imalda, and protective of her brother Paolo. Her hair was blondish-brown and curly, like the painting of Ginevra Benci by Leonardo Da Vinci. Initially, these two groups of children didn't get along. They bickered on the way to school. Their parents not only insisted that they get along but also protect each other.

Mario was a serious student who excelled in Greek and Roman history. He admired the art of Greek mythology. The nuns favored him to lead school presentations to outsiders. That did not sit well with Sofia. She was forever competing with Mario. In due time, the two arrived at an impasse. They ignored each other. After school, Sofia, Serafina and Filomena apprenticed at a seamstress shop managed by two sisters who specialized in dressmaking. Much was expected of them if they stayed with it. The seamstress shop was one block from school, near the main piazza. Sofia took the responsibility of taking the twins to and from there. Mario took Paolo home after school so they could study together. Today, Mario would be considered a nerd, as he was often invited by other parents of school children to study together at their homes.

Sofia attended "Scuola Media" in Nola only to be able to compete with Mario and the rest of the group. However, the real reason was that she was infatuated with Mario. It was more than a scholastic competition; something else was brewing. Their understanding was no secret. The parents allowed their indiscreet understanding to go on. For one thing, Sergio and Imalda liked the influence Mario had on Sofia. As for Felicia and Alvaro, there was much to admire in Sofia's tenacity and wild, shepherd-like spirit. The parents thought that they were a perfect match. The attitude was one of "Che sera sera", what will be will be.

Felicia attended Don Nicola's studio where she took up piano lessons. The name Felicia translates to "happiness", and that she was.

Blessed with a beautiful family, she had much to be grateful for. She was an accomplished pianist who specialized mostly in Chopin's piano music. In the fall, when the harvest season was in full swing, Sergio would invite "The three Musketeer" families (Don Nicola, Alvaro and Ramiro) to help themselves in picking Moscato grapes in the garden and to partake in a typical shepherd dinner that included wild boar, lamb, and porcini mushrooms. At these social get-togethers, it was a smorgasbord gathering of the classes: shepherds, socialists, lawyers, royal family and musicians.

Usually, after dinner at one of the get-togethers in the garden, Sergio would invite the guests to visit his private museum, a collection of antique Roman statues, Greek vases, painting frescos, etc. The guests knew the origin of these artifacts since the area surrounding Avella was full of them. Sergio knew all the burial grounds of Etruscan, Roman, and Greek art treasures. The garden abutted the farm where the owner had been hiding the Roman amphitheater for many years. Sergio must have been aware of the amphitheater as well. Today the site has been discovered and turned into a museum site. The whole town may become a museum one day, like Pompei, as archaeological digs have been discovered with complete town settings below the farms' grounds. What a wonder that is. That Antique Greek, Etruscan and Roman settlements have been discovered. It is amazing that these treasures had been able to be hidden by farmers for millennia. It seemed that Sergio must have been aware of those treasures long before anyone else. Yes, those were happy times. The worst of times were just around the corner, and they were embodied by a terrible countenance: Fascism.

After WWI, the Italian government was inept at solving the economic woes of the country. Inflation threatened the livelihood of many on fixed incomes, administrative workers and industrial workers. By the mid-1920s, there was no longer infighting among political parties. Mussolini saw to it that there was to be no competition from other parties in parliament. He killed them off. King Vittorio Emanuele III thought that he could handcuff Mussolini by tying him up with parliamentary maneuvers. Even so, he could have dismissed Mussolini at any time with the consent of Parliament. However, Mussolini made sure that 75% of Parliament was under his personal control. The King was checkmated by Mussolini at every turn.

Under Fascism, inflation was under control and there were fewer labor strikes in the industrial North. People were aware of or at least suspicious of Mussolini's escapades with women, his political flip-flops and the nefarious way he handled political dissidents. People did have an odd feeling about the man, but what the heck, the trains did run on time. They didn't trust him, yet it was better than anything else before. They wanted so badly to believe in the man's doing good for the country. The threat of civil war or revolution subsided. People were raised in a tradition of gradual social change and respect for the existing system. For once in ten years, people were contemplating the future, not dwelling on miseries. However, it didn't take very long before Mussolini gained absolute power in the 1930s. Thereafter, it was pure hell. So much for belief and hope.

As for small towns like Avella, politics was controlled by the prefect, mostly career civil servants, who retained their traditional dominance over local governments, and the new Podestas (Fascist mayors). The Podestas consisted mainly of landowners, retired army officers or influential persons in local politics rather than Fascist enthusiasts. The prefect in Avellino appointed Ramiro as mayor of Avella, since the Fascist Party was not sufficiently organized in small towns like Avella to mount an objection to the appointment. To the peasants, shepherds and, in general, the people of Avella, Rome might as well have been in some remote place on the moon, where all decisions were made. It had nothing to do with their lives. In effect, Ramiro became a Podesta by default, ultimately in name only but not in spirit. The first appointment that Ramiro made was to put his friend, Alvaro Da Alia, as Chief administrator of City Hall. The job entailed the issuance of birth certificates, payroll, immigration issues, public school administration, issuance of licenses and ordinances, etc. Ramiro wanted to eradicate corruption at City Hall, as the outgoing and retiring chief was embroiled in suspicion of bribery charges involving the issuance of licenses. He wanted someone there whom he could trust.

For the first time school children in Avella dressed in uniforms, like boy scouts, which was popular in the USA at about that time. But children in Avella were required to wear a black shirt, a special uniform designed by Mussolini. Furthermore, children started the morning with exercise, interrupting normal school patterns. In each classroom, a picture of Mussolini hung on the wall. Clearly, Mussolini's intent was to indoctrinate the minds of adolescents early in life. The adults, on the other hand, were too stubborn in their traditional ways to change their minds. These new edicts were adopted even in private schools, like the ones managed by the nuns. In Avella, there was no resistance to this movement. To add insult to injury, the populace was encouraged, more like forced, to donate gold items to the state to enrich the banks in the name of patriotism. The gentry of Avella had no choice in the matter. They towed the Fascist line or else. The shepherds had seen this pattern in other dictators before, but this one was far more sinister according to the elders. They wanted no part of it. Once again, they returned to the mountains.

In the early 1930s, Don Nicola, Alvaro, and Ramiro's families were aware of where Fascism was headed. Their hope was that the bad dream was going to be over soon so they could resume their lives. In effect, they put their lives in a holding pattern until better times. As for Sergio, it made no difference to him; his family could always retreat to the mountains. Alvaro and Ramiro were immersed in global business ventures, almost immune from Fascist interference. Don Nicola did not like what was happening in Avella and the rest of Italy. He was a purebred Socialist. He detested Fascism. The other three families were afraid for his life because of his outspoken views on Fascism, as Fascist thugs were beginning to roam the streets of Avella. Fortunately for Don Nicola, many in town empathized with his views.

TWO
The Making of a Delusional Dictator

History teaches us that leaders in government who reign for more than eight years become corrupt. It doesn't matter what their good intentions were, to begin with. Of course, there may be a few exceptions to the rule, for example, Queen Elizabeth II being an ideal leader throughout her reign. In the case of Mussolini, he was always corrupt and a Machiavellian in politics, even before taking over the Italian government. What made him different from other corrupt leaders over the millennia was that he became delusional while in power obsessing over the idea of wanting to be acclaimed as the Caesar of modern times. How ironical! As a young man, he studied the works of Plato, Nietzsche, Machiavelli, Georges, and Pareto, and all his adult life he tried to emulate Caesar. Yet, the personalities, characters, and military philosophies of the two men were as different as night and day.

Historical facts may be compared with grapes on a vine. One must squeeze the grapes in order to obtain the character of the wine. Similarly, one must mesh or "squeeze" together historical events to deduce, as in this book, a mosaic of Mussolini's character or persona. Why bother? That is because Mussolini was at the center of a man-made global storm called WWII. His ambitions and actions cast a huge shadow over people's lives from the 1920s onward.

Italy won the War against Austria and Germany in the Dolomite mountains by default. The German Army was decimated by the Allies in the trenches of France. The Spanish Flu claimed more deaths than the actual fighting in WWI. The cost of the War with Italy was huge: some 600,000 dead, 950,000 wounded, and a legacy of bitterness and division. In today's value, it cost the Italian government about 600 billion dollars. Peasants in Avella and especially in Southern Italy wanted nothing to do with WWI because they did not understand what the fuss was all about. Shepherds moved to the mountains; some others emigrated to the USA but most of them disappeared from the sight of the Carabinieri (policemen) in the valley. As for the ones unlucky enough to be conscripted into the army, they deserted. Few shepherds fought for their country. Most of them, if not all, didn't even know what country Italy was fighting and the rationale for it. Simply put, they were divorced from any decision-making in Rome, as usual. Due to their poor schooling, they couldn't even place the warring countries on a map. They were of the mindset that if Rome wanted a war, then the "bastards" in Rome should fight it. The wealthy ones were able to buy themselves out of it. The Italian flag became a symbol of division and hatred. War memorials were contested all over the peninsula. These divisions greatly weakened the postwar political regime and fractured the identity of Italian society.

To add insult to injury, the Spanish flu broke out at the end of WWI. The earliest flu cases appeared in March 1918 in the USA. Soldiers in US General John J. Pershing's army exported the flu to the trenches of France and, soon after, it spread to all battle fronts. There were four waves of the Spanish flu. The second wave claimed the most deaths. An estimated 500 million people had been infected resulting in 50 million to possibly 100 million deaths. In Italy, as many as 500,000 died from the pandemic. Variants of the Spanish Flu can be traced to this day.

By 1920 infections from the Spanish flu subsided considerably while political and economic miseries appeared to climax at just about the same time, including in Italy. The Italian wartime government printed money to pay for the war, as inflation increased out of control. It threatened the livelihood of many of those on fixed incomes, especially pensioners, administrative workers, and other laborers not able to organize as effectively as industrial workers. The price of bread and pasta increased tenfold. Savings did not keep up with inflation. Unemployment rose to three million in a country of forty million. Unemployed workers seized land for themselves, especially in Southern Italy. The armament industries were too slow in re-tooling for a peacetime economy. As such, some of them went bankrupt. Trade unions in the North pressed for higher wages, and strikes became routine, including those in public services. A series of stoppages paralyzed the railroads, as well as postal and telegraph services. To say that Italy was in a mess economically is being charitable.

In big industrial cities like Milan and Turin, union workers seized control of factories. They did it under Socialist Party leadership and to the accompaniment of much talk in newspapers about a revolution like the earlier Russian Revolution. In contrast, the Christian-Democratic parliamentarians were advocating traditional social changes consistent with the economic system prior to WWI. Their attitude was "Let's go back to a time when things were functional. They had no solution to the economic crisis, for sure, they didn't want any revolution to change the system of the government of the past. The difference between the two parties was insurmountable. The government was inept and powerless to keep prices from rising or to satisfy the demands of the unions. Nor was there any attempt at serious reforms of the State or the economy. Some of the Socialist leaders, including the journalist, Benito Mussolini, talked as though they were in earnest about a revolution and some people believed them.

The divide between Northern and Southern Italy dates as far back as when Caesar crossed the Rubicon River to invade, called then, the Italian territory. Historians credit Caesar for the quote in 47BC in a battle in Turkey: "Veni, vedi, vici", meaning: "I came, I saw, I conquered". However, most Southern Italians believe that sentiment must have been expressed much earlier, in 49 BC at the crossing of the Rubicon and imposed the will of Northerners on the South. The Rubicon episode marked the beginning of the deep divide between Northern, and Southern Italy. People in small towns like Avella in Southern Italy had no sympathy for labor strikes and turmoil in Milan, Turin, etc., because they could not relate to it. There were no industries in the South big enough to be of concern. According to Don Nicola, even if the strikes or revolution were to be successful, it would not have affected the lives of people in the South. Hence, he was against any revolution by the Socialist party.

Furthermore, City Hall in Avella was immune to any form of government decision in Rome. If anything, local politicians distanced themselves from Rome, since the population was made up mostly of shepherds and farmers. Artisans and professionals provided the vital link to a big city, Naples, and the news media. As for the peasants, Rome seemed to be a place up in the North. Given a choice, they preferred to be ignorant of what was happening in Rome. Even then, there was mutual distrust and dislike between people living in the two regions of Italy. In Avella, access to news from Rome was rather limited, since few had a radio or a telephone. The peasant class did not keep up with newspaper stories. Most of them couldn't read. In contrast, Don Nicola was in constant touch with the literati and the news media, in Naples. Many of his friends shared his concerns about events in Rome and they were up to date.

Clearly, Italy needed a reprieve from that misery. People were looking for anything or anybody to get them out of the mess they were in. They were not too choosy, just anyone. Among the opportunists was the editor of a Milan newspaper, a man by the name of Benito Mussolini. One day during the short time the workers were on strike in Milan, the editor left his Socialist newspaper office to visit the nearby general headquarters of the workers. He assured their leader that he, Benito Mussolini, was with them, inciting a Socialist revolution. It soon became apparent that there wasn't going to be one.

Socialist labor leaders at the industrial site had no idea how to conduct a revolt and didn't want one anyway. They were mostly individuals raised in a tradition of gradual social change and respect for the existing system. They were as afraid of a revolution as anyone else and never called for an uprising. Southern Italians would not have followed along for the simple fact that they would have gained nothing. The workers quit the factories, order was restored without bloodshed, and the Socialist movement went into decline. If there ever was danger of a revolution in Italy, it disappeared from that moment on. Italian Socialist members in the North did not want to revisit the Bolshevik revolution. They wanted a slow evolution to a Socialist-Democratic government.

That same newspaper editor, Mussolini, was among the first ones to recognize that the revolution was not going to happen. He also saw an opportunity to profit from it politically. Only a few weeks earlier he had offered his support for Socialism and revolution but, suddenly, he switched course, as he loudly proclaimed that Socialism was Italy's greatest menace. He sallied boldly to the attack. Mussolini was playing on the element of fear. He was, indeed, a re-incarnation of Machiavelli's way of manipulating a political situation, a very conniving and dangerous man. Also, he followed Cicero's political dictum: tell people what they want to hear! He had allegiance to only himself. The middle class, the industrialists, and a good many members of the younger generation lived in fear. To guarantee against the Socialist revolution, they swung their support behind the newborn Fascist movement and its promises of law and order. Finally, the people of Italy got their guiding and saving Angel, except he was a disciple of the Angel Lucifer, by the name of Mussolini.

The ideological basis for Fascism came from a number of sources. Mussolini utilized the works of philosophers Plato and Nietzsche, politicians Machiavelli, Cicero, and Georges, and economist Vilfredo Pareto, to develop Fascism. Mussolini admired Plato's *The Republic*, which he often read for inspiration. *The Republic* expounded a number of ideas that Fascism promoted, such as rule by the elite, promoting the State as the ultimate end, opposition to Democracy, protecting the class system and promoting class collaboration, rejection of egalitarianism, promoting the militarization of a nation by creating a class of warriors, demanding that citizens perform civic duties in the interest of the State, and utilizing State intervention in education to promote the development of warriors and future rulers of the state. Plato was an idealist focused on achieving justice and morality, while Mussolini and Fascism were realists focused on achieving political gifts for themselves.

Organized militias began to attract support across Italy in an anti-Bolshevik crusade that united various social and political sectors and organizations. Local Fascist groups were busy not only on breaking up strikes but also dismantling Socialist and Catholic labor unions and peasants' cooperatives and, often with police collusion, overthrowing newly elected local councils. Fascist squads, dressed in black-shirted uniforms and often financed by landowners or industrialists, used systematic violence to destroy these organizations. Thousands of people were beaten, killed, or forced to drink castor oil and run out of town. Hundreds of union offices, employment centers, and party newspapers were looted or burnt down. Socialist and Catholic deputies were run out of parliament or had their houses destroyed. These new phenomena were mostly localized in the big cities. They never reached Avella. The people of Avella heard about it through Don Nicola's protestations to his friends.

Bloodshed between Fascist thugs on the one hand and Socialists, Communists, and Christian Democrats on the other was a daily occurrence. The Fascists, often with the help of the Central government in Rome, had gained control of many local governments throughout Italy. They felt that the time had come to threaten a violent seizure of power; it would at least be worth seeing what would happen. At Mussolini's call, therefore, the armed forces of the Fascist party converged in Rome in October 1922. On the night between 27 and 28 October 1922, about 30,000 Fascist "Blackshirts" gathered in Rome to demand the resignation of the Prime Minister, Luigi Facta. He, himself "marched" from Milan in the comfort of a sleeping car. Outside the city, they set up an awful clamor, shooting off their guns and generally feigning the threat of attack. Inside the City of Rome were units of the regular Army probably strong enough to disperse the Fascist forces if the word had been given by the King of Italy, Vittorio Emanuele III.

On the morning of 28 October, the King handed over power to Mussolini (who had stayed in his headquarters in Milan during the talks) by asking him to form a new government, hoping to tame him by Constitutional means in Parliament. His hope was that he, the King, could fire Mussolini anytime. It was a comforting feeling, but it didn't pan out that way. The King's controversial decision has been explained by historians as a combination of delusion and fear. Mussolini enjoyed wide support in the military, among the industrialists and agrarian elites. The King and the conservative establishment were afraid of a possible civil war and ultimately thought they could use Mussolini to restore law and order in the country but failed to foresee the danger of a totalitarian revolution.

CORRUPTION PERIOD

Mussolini headed a coalition government that included nationalists, two Fascist ministers, Liberals, and even two Catholic ministers from the Popular Party. For 18 months, he ruled via the usual government machinery, pursuing a policy of "normalization," and gradually concentrated power into his own hands. The Fascist squads (thugs) were incorporated into an official Voluntary Militia for National Security. Ordinary middle-class job seekers flooded into the Fascist Party, making it more respectable and amenable. The nationalists also merged their organization into it, bringing with them much respectable backing in the South. In 1923 the electoral law was changed once more so that a group of parties with the largest vote—even if only 25 percent of the total—would receive an absolute majority of the seats. This enabled the Fascists to attract most of the old Liberal deputies into a "national alliance." In April 1924, elections were held under this system. In a climate of violence and threats, the Fascist-dominated bloc won 64 percent of the votes and 374 seats, doing particularly well in the south. The opposition parties—by now including the Popular Party— remained divided but won a majority of the votes in Northern Italy. The Socialists had by this time split again and the left now consisted of three rival parties, which spent much time criticizing one another: the Communists, the Socialists, and the reformist Socialists.

Mussolini had no hesitation in killing political opposition. He portrayed an image of a man at peace, detached from the daily occurrences of his thugs in the streets. He even wore a specially designed white uniform to symbolize the image of purity and peace. What a con man. Being a journalist, he knew firsthand the power of the visual. He was meticulous in cultivating that image. All the while, for example, he planned the assassination of Giacomo Matteotti, a Socialist Parliamentarian. Matteotti had requested that the elections of 1924 be annulled because of irregularities, provoking a momentary crisis in Mussolini's government. Mussolini ordered a cover-up, but witnesses saw the car that transported Matteotti's body parked outside Matteotti's residence, which linked Amerigo Dumini to the murder. Dumini was imprisoned for two years. He was an assistant in the press office for Mussolini. On his release, Dumini allegedly told people that Mussolini was responsible, for which he served further prison time. Mussolini ordered Fascist fanatics to track down Socialist opposition leaders like Italian journalist Piero Gobetti and Italian journalist, professor, and politician Giovanni Amendola in Paris and Cannes, France, and had them killed. Gobetti became a symbol of liberal anti-Fascism, inspiring intellectuals like the author Carlo Levi.

The opposition parties responded weakly or were generally unresponsive. Afterward, Mussolini justified, in a speech, his responsibility for violence in the streets implying that he was maintaining law and order. That was sheer hypocrisy, but it was not challenged by anyone, including the King. The King was short in stature and intellect. He liked to tell dignitaries that he was Mussolini's boss. His only interests or concerns were to make appointments in the Armed Forces and in the Royal House. At this time, Mussolini could have removed the King from power, since there was no danger of the King dismissing him. He had a majority in Parliament. As such, Parliament could not act on a request for the King's dismissal. So, the King was handcuffed by him. However, it would have been foolish of Mussolini to do so, since the King was more popular than he was, especially among the peasants in small towns.

Mussolini's relative successes in Italy served as an incentive for other aspiring world leaders in other countries to follow. He had a secret admirer named Adolf Hitler. Hitler thought that he could replicate Mussolini's success in Rome with one of his own marches in Munich, Germany. He attempted a coup in 1923 to take over the Bavarian government. It is interesting to note that all three dictators, Joseph Stalin, Benito Mussolini, and Adolf Hitler, organized riots to topple their governments. Mussolini succeeded in 1922, Stalin in 1924 (after doing away with Lenin), and Hitler in 1925. Mussolini modeled his "march" on the Bolshevik Revolution and Hitler after Mussolini's. Obviously, the Nazi group at the "Beer Hall Putsch" was smaller than the Fascist one in Rome and considerably less than the Bolshevik one. It failed and Hitler was sentenced to five years imprisonment. He was released after one year. Even then, his hatred for the Jewish people was evident from his failures as an artist painter. There are many theories to explain his warped behavior. Suffice it to say, Hitler was a flawed man, uneducated, and a mediocre artist. As such, he was easily influenced and manipulated by others, like Nazi Party founder Dietrich Eckart.

During the next two years, there was no more pretense. Mussolini disbanded most of Italy's constitutional and conventional safeguards against government autocracy. Elections and free speech were abolished. The Fascist government dissolved opposition parties and unions. At the local level, appointed Podestas replaced elected mayors and councils. A Special Tribunal for the Defense of the State, run by militia and Army officers, was set up to bring to trial anti-Fascist "subversives". It imprisoned or exiled to remote islands and remote locations in Southern Italy, thousands of political opponents (including Carlo Levi to Aliano, Basilicata). It imposed 31 death penalties. Other opposition leaders, such as the Liberals Piero Gobetti and Giovanni Amendola, were assassinated at the hands of Fascist thugs. His true nature came out, ruthless and unforgiving. He mercilessly pursued political opposition.

The Fascist party itself was soon swamped by more than a million job seekers and clerical workers, replacing thousands of the original Fascist workers. The party and the militia, who soon had little to do, became engaged in propaganda and parades. The Fascist regime was mostly run by the elite in the military and civilian bureaucracy which were linked to landowners and Fascist judges. That said, it was much more authoritarian, nationalistic, and interventionist than it had been before. By the 1930s the Fascist Party dominated all aspects of daily life, from the workplace to schools and leisure activities. However, many of the regime's opponents merely went along superficially with the Fascists to procure space for protest and underground activity.

DELUSIONAL PERIOD

By the beginning of the 1930s, the period of political corruption and assassination of the political opposition was ebbing, since there was no need for it. They were either dead, exiled to other countries, or remained silent until better times in Italy. Mussolini entered a new period in his life, one of blissful delusion and obsession. The focus of his vision was to forge a new Roman Empire. Apparently, he didn't bother to look at himself in the mirror or look up historical facts about Caesar. He became paranoid in controlling all aspects of people's lives. He made himself head of seven departments including the premiership so that he could achieve his goal. He even fired his son-in-law, Galeazzo Ciano, as Foreign Minister, because Ciano did not agree with Mussolini's vision of himself and of the world. The alliance between Italy and Germany was an unnatural one from the beginning. Ciano told him as much. Also, Ciano, according to his diary, reminded Mussolini many times that the people of Italy were against such an alliance. The French ambassador warned Ciano that Italy would regret this alliance. People like Don Nicola and his Socialists friends asked themselves repeatedly: "Whom was he kidding? If Caesar were alive, he would have told him that it was an unnatural alliance. Teutonic warriors played an insignificant-to-no role in Caesar's Centurion Armies.

So why did the alliance occur? It was an alliance only between the two of them, Hitler and Mussolini. Hitler was looking for a partner in Europe for appearance's sake. No major European country wanted anything to do with him, because it was clear where he was headed. Mussolini gave him some respectability and no southern front to worry about in case of a war, by allying Italy with Germany. This was a typical Mussolini ruse. As a Machiavellian, he kept his main adversary (Hitler) closer than anyone else, including his family. Ever the con artist, he was looking for another sucker by reassuring and adulating Hitler, putting him at ease. Mussolini wanted to expand his colonies in order to fulfill his dream and was hoping for a short war. Hitler would then be discarded soon after, just as he had discarded in a wastebasket a postcard that he received from an admirer in 1922, Hitler. From his days as a journalist, he learned how to discard mistresses and causes (the Socialist Party) routinely in order to place himself at an advantage. To say that he was a disloyal person is an understatement. Ruthless is a better word. Thus, given his past behavior, that was his intent all along. Hitler charged ahead to wars without provocation and Mussolini rode on his back to benefit from it. By then, the German Army had already marched into Austria and Czechoslovakia without firing a single shot. Mussolini hoped to capture crumbs in future annexations of war by Hitler. The people of Italy, as well as the rest of the world, paid a heavy price for

Mussolini's delusion and obsession. The alliance was the root cause of all that misery in the world thereafter, WWII.

In the early 1920s, Hitler looked up to Mussolini, who was six years his senior, for guidance. Initially, Mussolini considered himself a small-time politician with few members in the Nazi party. He treated him more like a nuisance than an equal. It was a strangely personal relationship that lasted for more than twenty years. In the beginning, Mussolini was the main cog in their relationship. In the end, according to Ciano's diary, Mussolini played second fiddle to Hitler. Lucifer's disciple, Mussolini, was playing with another Angel of Satan and eventually lost everything that he hoped to gain in the relationship. He was dealing with a much more ruthless man. During the heydays of those two, much happened in Avella, mostly not good, but somehow, the human spirit prevailed over the evil deeds of those two arch friends.

THREE
Demagoguery Rule in Southern Italy

After a four-year stint, Podesta (Mayor) Ramiro was replaced by his brother, Alvaro Alvarez, as appointed by the same perfect. In the new Administration, Alvaro Da Alia, in turn, was appointed Chief Magistrate of City Hall, again in charge of everyday civil affairs. Thus, not much changed at City Hall. However, the same could not be said about the safety in the streets of Avella. By then, everyone in town was aware of the Black Shirt members of the Fascist Party. These thugs were the eyes and ears of the Fascist party in the streets, looking for political dissidents, Socialists, and especially Communist agitators. People ventured into the streets only for emergency situations. The social evening walk (passegiata) was a thing of the past, as some of these thugs were unruly, festering for a confrontation. Their purpose was to intimidate the citizenry into submission or make their presence felt.

Whenever a Fascist dignitary visited the town, black-shirt Fascists organized adults and school children for a rally along the streets, with boys dressed in special Boy Scout uniforms and adults waving flags and exhibiting the Fascist salute. All the while, the thugs kept a watchful eye on who skipped the parade. The focus of the parade and its propaganda was to influence the young ones. It was hopeless to convert the old ones to fascism. The peasant class was mostly apolitical or Communist. The gentry couldn't care less if they were left alone to do their thing; they flip-flopped depending on where the benefits resided. The thugs consisted of army veterans, former or retired Carabinieri (policemen) and unemployed bullies. They were employed and paid by the Fascist Party headquartered in Rome.

Before Fascism showed its face in Avella, the gentry and the peasants tended to be apolitical. With Fascism on the horizon, they split up into various party affiliations. The peasant class itself was divided between the apolitical shepherds and farmers on one side and the unskilled laborers (independent workers in cafes, farms, and odd jobs who sympathized with Communism) on the other. Similarly, the gentry was split between the professionals, mostly Socialists, and the very wealthy Monarchists. The shepherds, in general, were too proud to be intimidated by those Fascists roaming the streets. They disappeared into the mountains, waiting for better days to return to the valley. Professionals and Socialists detested the Fascist thugs as well as the Communists. There was no happiness in the streets of Avella.

The main purpose of the thugs was to quell any local insurrection against the regime and to keep tabs on anyone who acted too aggressively against the regime. In some sense, the locals have held prisoners of these street Fascists. People could not speak their minds. There was no love lost between Don Nicola and the Fascist bullies. His friends were forever warning him to keep his distance from them. The thugs knew very well about Don Nicola's Socialist diatribes against fascism. They were forever goading him whenever they met in the streets and would have loved nothing better than to have him incarcerated. Don Nicola was a marked man. He had to be more selective in unloading his diatribes on the people in Avella. However, he did have an outlet; musicians at the opera house in Naples, where Don Nicola played the cello in the orchestra, were all anti-Fascist.

For the first time, there was traffic on the main street of Avella. Shepherds, who had emigrated to the USA in order to avoid conscription during WWI, returned home a little richer. A few shepherds bought cars and started new building construction in the shepherd neighborhoods towards the east of town. After all those years, Carabinieri was still looking for those Americans who skipped conscription, unaware of the general amnesty granted in the early 1920s.

Italian Americans were influenced to return home by Fascist propaganda reaching the USA. The onset of depression in the USA made the return more appealing. The main street of Avella, Corso Vittorio Emanuele, runs east to west; Nola and Naples are west and southwest, relative to the street, respectively. At the east end, toward the foothills, the neighborhood consisted mostly of shepherds and few professionals. The few political ones tended to be Socialists. They advocated social changes within the framework of a democratic government - no revolution. As Main Street wound west, artisan stores appeared more and more, as did tailors, convenience stores, cafes, bakeries, pharmacies, professional offices, etc. City Hall and the main Piazza were located roughly halfway through Main Street. Well-to-do families, industrialists, landowners, medical doctor's offices, politicians, and elitists lived there. At the other end of Main Street, the west end, lived mostly farmhands, and unskilled workers whose allegiance was toward the Communist Party. They also advocated social changes but, through a revolution of the classes, much like the Bolshevik revolution.

There was no love lost among the Communists, the shepherd community, and the Socialists. Whereas shepherds were apolitical but fiercely independent, not depending on anyone for a living, the West end crowd was forever expounding the virtues of a revolution. They believed that only through a revolution could the upper class and the church be forced to share their wealth. To say that they loathed each other is an understatement. The role of the Fascist Blackshirts was basically to separate these two groups of people from each other, as they cordoned off the riff-raffs on either side of the Piazza. The Blackshirts Fascists were protecting the industrialists, landowners, and other wealthy people who financially supported their movement in the early stages.

Don Nicola's criticism was directed at Fascism as a result of union workers not being allowed to strike, a Socialist political issue since the 1920s. It was not about ethnic laws in Italy. In the early 1930s, Mussolini regarded Italian Jews as Italians. Italian Jews were part of the establishment. On several occasions, Mussolini spoke favorably about Jewish contribution to Italian society in general and the Zionist movement. Italian Jews occupied important jobs in Fascist courts, police departments, and Armed forces in big cities and small towns. For example, Da Alia was chief of City Hall. Don Nicola and Da Alia's families never felt threatened by the Fascist government. Nevertheless, Don Nicola had to be very selective as to whom he addressed his diatribes against fascism. It was not until the late 1930s that Hitler prevailed on Mussolini to introduce racial laws in Italy. As for the shepherds and farmers, it made no difference what imposition the Fascist government put on them. They were going to do things their way and that was the end of it. As for the artisans, professionals, and the gentry in general, they were a threat to fascism. They had the means and, perhaps, the incentives to rebel against fascism. In short, the bullies did not want Don Nicola to wake a sleeping giant.

One thing the thugs could not prevent was the gossip in the streets of Avella about Mussolini's love life. The rumor at that time was about Mussolini's new mistress, Clara Petacci. She was in her mid-twenties when she met Mussolini, who was in his mid-forties. They met at a beach resort in Ostia, east of Rome, as Mussolini's car was part of a caravan on his way to give a speech about the Pontine Marsh project, south of Anzio. The caravan stopped as several people were cheering and waving along the side of the road. Mussolini, forever looking for adulation and his next conquest, was mesmerized by Clara's blonde hair and her exuberance to meet "Il Duce", the leader.

He did oblige, especially in the sight of this beautiful woman supporter. Her mother was also equally an avid supporter and admirer of Mussolini. In fact, Petacci arranged for her mother to meet Il Duce. Mussolini did not discriminate between young and old, if they adored him. The next meeting with Clara was in his huge office located in Piazza Venezia. There he seduced her on the carpeted floor. Gossip about the new mistress was running wild in local newspapers and popular magazines. It was perplexing that those stories appeared publicly, in view of censorship. In fact, he secretly handpicked the editors of national newspapers and magazines. Perhaps, it was an occasion to show off his white uniform in newspapers and magazines.

Clara Petacci kept a detailed account of the time she spent with Il Duce in a personal diary which was seized by Italian authorities in 1949 and was released for public viewing only in 2009. It is now considered an important record of the private life of the dictator and sheds light on a side of his character that was long unexplored by historians. Her records conform to his image as a man of power and physical daring, which was central to the 'virile' cult of fascism. However, it also exposes the fact that he was a boastful man who often needed others to pamper his ego by telling him how handsome or virile he looked, how much women and the Italian people loved him, and how he was a genius much like Napoleon and Caesar. Interestingly, it was Petacci who recorded how dull a conjugal life Mussolini had with his wife Rachele and how he kept up to five lovers at a time when he was younger.

Claretta Petacci was born on February 28, 1912, in Rome, Italy, to Dr. Francesco Saverio Petacci and his wife Giuseppina Persichetti Petacci. Her father was a primary physician of Pope Pius XI. She was 'genteelly reared' in an upper-class Catholic family and, as a child, studied music with violinist Corrado Archibugi, a family friend. By the time she became romantically involved with Benito Mussolini in 1932, she was engaged to a man named Riccardo Federici, a lieutenant in the Air Force. Her family reportedly supported her affair with the dictator to climb the social ladder. She married Federici in 1934, but they separated soon after.

There is a myriad of history attached to Mussolini's love life. For one thing, people in town did not want to praise Fascism because they knew that it was corrupt. Castigating the man or the Fascist government would have landed that person in jail. Thus, by default, the safest thing to talk about was the love life of "Il Duce." One could just imagine the rumor mill in those days in Avella and other small towns. Any political conversations would have had repercussions. One favorite topic of conversation then was the emotional state of Mussolini's wife, Donna Rachele. His previous marriage to Ida Dalser produced a son whom he never acknowledged. When he became prime minister, Ida and their son were incarcerated. Other love affairs included the ones with a Russian Jewish emigre,

Angelica Balabanoff, and a married woman, Fernanda Facchinelli. He then married his first mistress Rachele Guidi and they had five children, two girls and three boys. Thereafter, Mussolini had several mistresses and brief sexual escapades with female political supporters. In the end, he died in the arms of Clara Petacci. It is amazing that the

Blackshirt Fascists acquiesced to the rumor mill in Avella and even partook in the gossip.

The people of Avella, as well as the rest of Italy, viewed Mussolini as vain and corrupt, and their patience was running out. In order to counter this mood, the Fascist government instituted a program in which it financially subsidized large families. However, the real intent was to reach an artificial goal of a population of sixty million. Only then could Italy support a viable army large enough to fight in Europe, as argued by Il Duce. The population then was forty million. Il Duce also argued for people to donate their gold wedding rings, necklaces, earrings, jewelry, etc. to the government. Thus, the Fascist government gave in one hand and received in the other. People were fed up and had no choice but to wait and see if improvements in living conditions were to be forthcoming from the regime. The other choice was to spend time in jail or be publicly ostracized by the thugs. It is not clear at what stage submission entered the mindset of people.

By this time, Sofia and Mario were a couple, not yet engaged, but it was a foregone conclusion that they would be married one day. Obviously, Sofia was not shy and knew who she liked. The families regarded it as "how cute." As a teenager, she was strikingly beautiful. Teenagers volunteered to carry Sofia's and Mario's twin sisters' books to and from the seamstress shop. She was popular with everyone in the neighborhood but timid and shy with strangers.

By the 1930s, Sofia and Mario's sisters, Filomena and Serafina, had completed their studies at the Lyceum school in Nola, specializing in classical literature in Greek and Latin. By then, the girls completed thirteen years of schooling. The level of coursework was slightly above that in American High Schools. That was unusual in the sense that in those days girls were not encouraged to attend high-level academic schooling, especially teenage girls from the shepherd community. That proved the power of love. It was a way for Mario and Sofia to see each other regularly on the way to and back from school in Nola. After graduation, their dalliance became more of a family affair.

On Sunday evenings most people in town took their "passeggiata" after dinner. The passeggiata usually extended from the east end of Main Street to the Piazza. Beyond that, it was somewhat risky as Fascist thugs and Communist agitators often confronted each other on the other side of the Piazza. The thugs would barge into bars and/or cafes in the West end to break up any large gathering of people and, usually, resulted in brawls spilling out onto Main Street. Usually, one of the parents and Mario's twin sisters served as chaperones to Mario and Sofia. Of course, not all dalliances in those days followed the same ritual, but that was the accepted protocol for such relationships. Nowadays, that practice is no longer in vogue. After a while, only the sisters chaperoned the two lovers to give an appearance to the locals that things were done properly.

The two sisters were two years younger than Mario, but they were not expected to attend the University as their brother did. The Lyceum school degree was sufficient for where they were headed. Sofia and the twins apprenticed at the seamstress shop for about ten years. All three were becoming proficient at dressmaking. More than anything, Serafina and Filomena wanted to have their own seamstress shop and, of course, also wanted Sofia to be an equal partner. In those days, there weren't that many business ownerships by women. Much like her mother, Imalda, up on that mountain with her sister, Sofia took up the challenge of making the dress shop a viable business enterprise. That fiery drive to succeed was busting out of her. Alvaro and Felicia agreed to help them financially, but the girls refused help from their parents. They rented a one-room space from Ramiro Alvarez in the middle of the Piazza. However, Ramiro stipulated that he would rent the space only with the proviso that the girls pay rent after the shop was solvent. Clearly, their papas (Sergio and Alvaro) had something to do with the business arrangement.

The timing for a new shop in the middle of town couldn't have been better. Sofia and the sisters were ecstatic at the prospect of launching careers of their own.

Initially, they were going to concentrate on knitting sweaters and making dress uniforms for school children. For one thing, Imalda no longer had to sell wool in Nola. Now, she would let Sofia sell her wool in the girls' shop to locals, meaning that Sofia could tap into Imalda's clients. Imalda envisioned that someday Sofia would take over from her, representing the shepherd's goods at the market.

At that time, new fashion styles were appearing in newspapers and magazines. The jitterbug era appeared on the scene globally sporting new chic styles for both men and women. For one thing, dresses and swimsuits were a lot shorter. There was a revolution in the fashion of women's apparel in sports and formal dress. The girls envisioned an opportunity to get involved with the new trends in fashion. Before the fashion revolution, there was barely enough business to support two dress shops in Avella, the girls' and one other shop owned by their mentor. After the fashion revolution, the two shops would be in a cooperative mold rather than a competitive one, working under the same umbrella.

Mario went on to the University of Naples studying to become a "ragioniere," and avvocato, a combination of lawyer and accountant, equivalent to a CPA in the USA. Four days a week, Mario would get on the train at 8:11 am to go to Naples. He either walked to the University, near the Vomero district or rode the tram. He attended every lecture, although it was not required. The only thing that mattered was whether a student passed one exam administered at the end of the year. Upon completion of university studies, there was a comprehensive exam to pass in order to qualify as a ragioniere. A student could take the comprehensive however many times until he passed it. Mario passed the exam the first time. He was looking forward to starting a family. However, he still had obligatory military service to fulfill. For sure, he did not want to serve in the army as he heard an earful from Don Nicola about the army, mostly bad. It was infiltrated by Fascist fanatics. Hence, he decided that he would enroll in the Naval Military Station in Naples, and he and Sofia would reside there with his new family on the Navy base.

Don Nicola and Mario would often take the 8:11 am train together to Naples. Don Nicola would head to the opera house for rehearsal and Mario to the University.

However, Mario was getting more than a university education. He was being indoctrinated by Don Nicola about politics, Socialism versus Fascism. For a change, Don Nicola didn't have to worry about being confronted by the thugs. Mario admired Don Nicola for his insightful observations of the political upheavals in Europe and Italy. Don Nicola advised Mario to enroll in the Navy to make up for his obligatory military service. The Italian Navy was not yet infiltrated by Fascists. At the Naples train station, the two splits to go their separate ways. At the university, Mario would attend a lecture or take a final exam that had been scheduled well ahead of time. As for Don Nicola, he went straight to rehearsal at the opera house. The university was within walking distance of the opera house. When Mario finished with schoolwork or attending lectures and Don Nicola had no evening performance at the opera house, they would return home together. Again, politics was on the agenda.

At that time something very special was happening at rehearsals. Composer and pianist Franco Alfano was commissioned to complete Giacomo Puccini's opera, *Turandot*. Puccini died while composing it. Don Nicola was too modest to claim any part of it other than participating in the rehearsal. Usually, after an evening performance, Don Nicola found overnight accommodation at the opera house. At the train station the next day in Avella, Don Nicola would stop by Erminio's winery, located next to the station, and have lunch there. They had known each other for a long, long time. Erminio was in the army band when Don Nicola was the leader of it during WWI. As always, after lunch, Erminio would share the best white or spumante wine in the house with him and discuss the politics of the day. That was the only outlet of his views in town without being incriminated by the thugs.

Being the fiery one, Sofia was impatient with the protocol of the chaperones anytime she was in town with Mario. She wanted Mario to herself. The town was full of gossip as to who was chaperoned during the passeggiata. That was all people wanted to talk about, "did you see so and so?" Sofia insisted that her mother, Imalda, take her along to Nola's Farmers Market in order to help her load produce on the train. Imalda was no fool. She knew that Sofia was after Mario. That was how she, herself, had corralled Sergio. Her daughter was no different. As

expected, Mario showed up at the train station in Avella to help both ladies. After unloading in Nola, the two lovers continued onto Naples. Yes, Imalda acquiesced. How could she get in the way of love? The two of them walked together all over Naples. Sofia was radiantly happy, and it showed. Naples gave them the privacy that they didn't have in Avella. They loved Naples and the Bay area. Their favorite district was Posillipo for good reason; both were aficionados of Greek Mythology and the famous Roman summer resort of ancient times. There is no better place to observe those splendors of antiquity.

Posillipo is the most picturesque district of Naples. There are two bays. One is confined mostly by the Sorrentine peninsula in the East and Posillipo in the West. The other smaller bay is bounded by Posillipo in the East and the town of Baia in the west. Of the two bays, most tourists visit the former. However, tourists don't seem to differentiate between the two bays and refer to both as simply as the Bay of Naples. The Islands of Capri and Ischia are within five to fifteen nautical miles of Posillipo, reachable by ferry boats. The smaller bay is about to literally explode at any time, as there are volcanos and earthquake fault lines below seawater and in the surrounding areas. The first violent eruption occurred about forty thousand years ago. It was so violent that the volcano itself exploded and vanished into the sea, giving rise to the smaller bay. Remnants of antique Roman villas are buried underwater. This area is often referred to as the Campi Flegrei (Phlegraean Fields). Further west, the islands of Procida and Ischia are part of the volcanic system surrounding the area.

Of course, imperial Romans were aware of Vesuvius but not of any volcanoes in the smaller bay. Nevertheless, Romans vacationed there. For sea air, Romans vacationed in the smaller Bay. For mountain air, they visited towns like Abella. Empress Agrippa, Julius Caesar, Nero, Hadrian, Augustus, Cicero, etc. all had villas in the smaller Bay, at a town called Baiae then. Also, at Baiae, the most ancient hot spring complex was built for the richest Romans. A few miles north of Baiae, the Greek colony at Cumae was established, where the main Greek prophet, Sibyl, resided. There were other Sybils, but the one at Cumae was the leading prophetess. The Cumean Sybil was the priestess or prophetess presiding over the Apollonian oracle of Greek mythology, as related to the Greek God Apollo. Being trained in Greek and Roman classics, Mario was comfortable visiting the area surrounding Posillipo.

He visited there often enough with his family during summer vacations in his younger days. Sofia was looking forward to the day when she didn't have to share Mario with others and have him alone guide her through all those magnificent sites at Baia. For him, it was like coming home. As for Sofia, she was also thinking of home but in a different sort of way. Forever the down-to-earth woman, she was thinking more about where to settle in Posillipo, when Mario would be stationed at the Naval Military station nearby, studying to be a naval officer, and that was even before she was married.

The two would stroll all along Posillipo Drive and around the Bay stopping here and there like tourists. "Uncle" Don Nicola would sometimes stop by and join them for dinner at a favorite fish restaurant or after an opera performance. Don Nicola was an excellent guide to all the interesting historical sites, restaurants, and nooks in the area. He wanted to spoil them because he had an inkling that war was brewing not too far on the horizon.

Back in Avella, it was an exciting time for the girls. But what was more exciting for them was Sofia's decision to convert to Judaism. Obviously, Sofia was marrying into a Jewish family, and she wanted to be part of them. She wanted to remove any personal barriers between families and adopted uncles because her effervescent personality would not allow it to be otherwise. Serafina and Filomena were more than willing to teach Sofia and walk with her to the Synagogue in Baiano, only half a kilometer away or five minutes by train. The two sisters introduced Sofia to Rabbi Ugo Zolla, an elderly man who knew the Da Alia family very well. If there was any conversion to Judaism, he would sponsor it. Above all the qualities in a person, sincerity was paramount in being sponsored, declared Rabbi Zolla. The Rabbi, being a clever and understanding man, asked Sofia, straight out, if the reason for the conversion had something to do with marrying Mario. She answered yes. That was the right answer, according to the Rabbi. He then handed her a book to read about the history of Judaism and the scriptures and told her to be prepared to answer questions once a month until he was satisfied with her answers. Filomena and Serafina went to work and would quiz Sofia from time to time about the Torah, Jewish beliefs, history, rituals and some simple Hebrew expressions. Sofia enthusiastically took up the challenge and, after a while, was at ease with the scriptures. Rabbi Zolla finally did sponsor Sofia. Mario, meanwhile, was not aware of Sofia's pending conversion.

It was springtime; violets on the highlands were already blooming. Everyone was looking forward to a Da Alia family dinner invitation to celebrate the Passover Seder/dinner. The invitation list included the usual clan: Don Camillo, the Sergio and Alvarez families, and Rabbi Ugo Zolla. Traditionally, families and friends gather in the evening of the Seder to read the text of the Haggadah. The Haggadah tells the story of the exodus of the Jews from Egypt and is recited each year as a reminder. Half is read before the meal and the other half, is read after the meal, and is usually accompanied by songs, sung by all, appropriate to the holiday. The Seder is a commonly celebrated Jewish ritual, performed by Jews all over the world. Each attendee reads a portion of the Haggadah in rotation, either in Hebrew, the local language, or a combination. In many homes, each participant at the Seder table will recite at least critical parts of the Haggadah in the original Hebrew and Aramaic. Usually, a learned Jew will interrupt the reading only to discuss different points or to offer a Torah insight into the meaning or interpretation of the words.

Early in the morning of the day of Seder, Mario, in a formal suit, visited Sergio and Imalda. Imalda was all smiles, as she knew what that was all about. He formally asked Sergio's permission to marry his daughter, Sofia. It was no surprise to Sofia as she and Mario's sisters watched the spectacle through a slit in the kitchen door. Sergio tried to appear as proud as a goat, stern and indifferent, but he acted as gentle as a lamb. Of course, Sergio granted permission. All the women knew ahead of time that Mario was arriving that morning. They all came out of hiding in a burst of joy. As for the men, they tried hard to keep their manly images, distant from the whole affair. This called for celebration, a drink of Marsala All'uovo. This concoction of Marsala dessert wine, egg yolk, and sugar is a favorite morning drink of shepherds, usually around Christmas time.

The Da Alia family members took time to read from the Haggadah in Hebrew. Then the biggest surprise came when Sofia took her turn to read in Hebrew. Mario's reaction was one of awe, as he had no idea that she knew Hebrew. He was so proud of her and was eager to marry her. Rabbi Zolla added that Sofia was an excellent student in her conversion to Judaism, thanks to Serafina's and Filomena's help. Sofia and Mario were finally left alone as the elders finished the dinner. The two went out for a walk, or passeggiata, without the chaperones. That was their way of announcing their engagement to the town.

The wedding was organized by Felicia, who was well acquainted with the processional and recessional protocols of a Jewish wedding. Sergio's garden was a natural place for setting up a chuppah, a traditional "ceiling" over the couple. Alvaro, Felicia, Sergio, and Imalda held the four poles attached to the linen sheet which made the chuppah. The processional part took place prior to the wedding and the recessional thereafter. During the ceremony, the Cantor sang in Latin to appeal to the Christian guests, and "Yerushalaym Shel Zahavk" ("Jerusalem of gold") in Hebrew for the Jewish audience. After stomping on glass and sealing it with a kiss, traditional Horah music was played for all audiences to enjoy. The breaking of the glass symbolizes the frailty of human relationships as well as hopes that their love will last as long as it takes for the broken pieces of glass to become whole again. On their honeymoon, they went to Posillipo, their favorite place to visit. They loved their parents, but now they were on their own, yet close enough to Avella. In those days one did not travel too far from home to carve out a new life.

FOUR
Hidden in Plain Sight

The future looked bright for Mario. As a ragioniere (lawyer/accountant), he could always work as an accountant at City Hall or as a public lawyer, but Mario was enthusiastic about enrolling in the Naval Military Station. He would train as a Naval Officer for a year or two to meet his military obligation, which he had delayed since attending the University of Naples. He and his bride would live at the Station near Posillipo. Mario took Don Nicola's advice and had no plans for a career in the Navy or in the Fascist Party. That was the right decision, as the Italian Navy became vulnerable in the Mediterranean with the invention of radar in Britain and the USA, and the demise of fascism. The downfall of fascism was just about to begin, as Mussolini was blustering about the Italian Army to intimidate the Ethiopian regime.

A border incident between Ethiopia and Italian Somaliland in December of 1934 gave Benito Mussolini an excuse to intervene. Rejecting all arbitration offers, the Italian Army invaded Ethiopia on October 3, 1935. Under General Rodolfo Graziani and General Pietro Badoglio, Italian invading forces steadily pushed back the ill-armed and poorly trained Ethiopian Army, winning major victories and taking the capital, Addis Ababa, on May 5, 1936. The nation's leader, Emperor Haile Selassie, went into exile. In Rome, Mussolini proclaimed Italy's King Victor Emmanuel III as emperor of Ethiopia and appointed Badoglio to rule as Viceroy. The war demonstrated the ineffectiveness of the League of Nations when the League decisions were not supported by the "great powers." The atrocities committed by the Italian Army were enough for people like Mario, Don Nicola, Carlo Levi, and those like them, to be ashamed to be Italian citizens.

There were four leaders who concocted the invasion: Mussolini, King Victor Emanuele III, Badoglio, and Graziani. They were scheming how to get ahead in their careers. Mussolini was forever the con artist, planting the idea in the King's mind that the King ought to be Emperor of Ethiopia, thus conniving the King into believing that he was Emperor material, not Mussolini. The King adored royal titles and to become an emperor would make up for his short stature, which was a little over five feet. Badoglio wanted the King to bestow royal titles on his children. Graziani was bucking for a promotion to Field Marshal. There was no shame in his many atrocities. Ethiopians and Eritreans tried many times to kill him to avenge the atrocities he committed.

Mario was caught in the middle of the war as a Navy ensign (junior officer) on a troop carrier. The ship, Doria, made stops in Genoa, Livorno, Naples, and Palermo, carrying troops and arms to Benghazi, Libya. Libya was the closest port to Ethiopia and had a lot shorter trip than sailing around Cape Town. By 1935, radar was discovered in Britain. However, it was not deployed in the Mediterranean Sea to intercede with Italian ships, although Britain had colonies in East Africa. Every other month Italian troops or arms were transported to Benghazi. The only time Mario saw Sofia was when Doria docked in Naples for two to three days. She was pregnant with their first child, and soon after the war, Sofia gave birth to daughter

Lena, is named after Mario's grandmother. Finally, the nightmare was over, as Mario was discharged from his military obligation soon after the war.

It is interesting to note that Carlo Levi, Communist agitators, and political dissidents were exiled to Aliano, Basilicata, and to other towns in remote regions of Southern Italy in 1935. These towns were so isolated that civilization hadn't reached there yet. Hence, the title of Levi's book, *Christ Stopped at Eboli*. That was a common saying in Aliano, implying that civilization stopped at Eboli. Since the last train stop was in Eboli, Christ and, therefore, civilization stopped in Eboli.

The divide between the peasant and the gentry classes in Aliano was even deeper than in Avella. Political exiles there endured a secluded, harsh life in a mosquito-infested region; no different than being incarcerated. As a journalist, Mussolini knew firsthand the power of the visual: out of sight, out of mind. He did not want to draw attention to the plight of political dissidents by putting them in places easily accessible to outsiders. He wanted to convey to the Italian people that there were no dissidents and that everything was fine with Fascism in Italy. He succeeded to some extent. The only escape from one of these God-forbidden places occurred in 1929.

Carlo Rosselli, a Socialist, was exiled to the island of Lipari, about ten miles north of Sicily. Lipari was so remote that escape was considered impossible. Carlo escaped by boat to Tunisia and on to France. He and his brother, Nello, were later killed by Fascist thugs in 1937. Certainly, the rest of Italy was not aware of those remote places. Mussolini learned that he was successful in hiding political dissidents from the rest of Italy and the world and, with the icing on the cake, there was no need to pay for jails, guards and maintenance. He applied the lesson learned in 1935 with the creation of internment "towns" in 1940. internment camps or towns in Southern Italy were exemplified by the town of Aliano. Not even people in towns bordering the so-called internment "town" were aware of the internees. More importantly, Mussolini wanted to convey to Hitler that Italy also had internment camps, just like Germany. So, what if he mislabeled towns as camps. Just a small lie. The effect in Hitler's mind was more important than the lie, forever *messing with people's minds*. However, "camps" in Germany were extermination camps. The ones in Southern Italy were not. In fact, not a single Jewish person or political dissident died there during WWII, except naturally occurring illnesses. Those internment towns were liberated by the Allied Army in late 1943. In Northern Italy, the Nazis raided the internment camps, as well as towns, and deported its occupants or internees to extermination camps in Germany and elsewhere.

The war in Abyssinia dampened and delayed the plans of the newly married couple, Sofia and Mario, but not their spirit to live life to the fullest. They put their married life on hold, as Mario was assigned by the Italian Navy on a transport ship. When the ship was away, Sofia returned home because she did not feel safe living among all the sailors. She moved into an apartment made available to the couple by her parents in the building they owned. The building was old and surrounded by a courtyard with a lot of empty apartments which, at one time, housed shepherd families. In very cold weather, some apartments housed sheep. However, Sofia welcomed Mario with open arms at the Navy Station when he was on furlough. They were in a hurry to make up for a lost time. The couple still had Posillipo in their dreams and, for their three-day get-togethers, they romped all over Posillipo and visited Roman and Greek sites along the coastline of the smaller bay.

Mario had total confidence in his mother-in-law Imalda delivering their baby. She delivered thousands of babies in the shepherd community as well as in the general neighborhood. Mario planned to be home at the time of delivery since his discharge from military duties would have coincided with the delivery. Whenever Imalda performed the procedure, she took on the persona of a Field Marshal. Everything had to be in order: hot water, towels, people in proper places, and no distractions. Children were chased out of the room. Windows were wide open for fresh air. This time she demanded no less. She requested, demanded, that Sofia move into another room where there were three windows. She was meticulous in the delivery of her first grandchild. The only thing that she could not plan for was the sex of the baby. In those days, there was no technology in acoustic equipment to do so. But it didn't prevent Imalda from predicting the sex of the baby correctly 90% of the time. She never revealed her secret but predicted a baby girl for Sofia.

Serafina and Filomena initiated a new trend in women's fashion design besides knitted sweaters. The new changes in fashion caught the fancy of the world, including Avella. However, few in town could afford the new dresses except, perhaps, residents of the Piazza neighborhood, royal families, and members of the Fascist hierarchy. Like her mother, maternity was not going to hold Sofia from expanding the pool of customers. She had collected a list of potential clients from the days when she and Mario frolicked around Posillipo, meeting neighbors near the Naval Station and visiting Don Nicola at the San Carlo opera house. These were customers who could afford the high-end fashion designs. Alvaro and Felicia, the twin sisters' parents, we're proud to inform Don

Garcia that the girls were able to pay rent. It took only about six months to reach that milestone. In fact, Ramiro Alvarez' wife ordered three dresses, each in different pastel colors, and all in the same style. The former seamstress shop where the twins and Sofia apprenticed, assisted each other when overloaded with work. In effect, the two shops had a monopoly on dressmaking, since they were the only two shops in town and they shared the patterns of the new fashions. Both shops developed the fine art of modifying the original patterns to fit the sizes and shapes of their customers. The girls were aware of Uncle" Don Nicola's scorn for Fascists in town, but they had no choice but to serve the wives of important Fascists. Otherwise, the thugs would find a way to shut down the shop.

Mario's discharge from the Navy occurred on June 1, 1936. The war in Abyssinia ended about a month earlier. On the same day, Mario hurried to pack things at the Naval Station, return home to his wife, and be present at the birth. Remarkably, on the same morning, Zio (uncle) Don Nicola, huffing and puffing, was knocking on the door of Mario's apartment. By the intensity of the knocking, Mario surmised for a split second that Sofia was at the door. So, he purposely delayed opening it. He hurried to pack heavy items, as he didn't want Sofia to pack anything, knowing that she was in no condition to do so. By now, Zi Nicola was frantically shouting, "Open the fucking door! Sofia is going to have the baby soon! Mario looked at his watch and there were 12 minutes before the next departure of the train from Naples to Avella. Usually, he would take the tram just to enjoy the scenery of the neighborhood, but not this time. He ran to the station and arrived in Avella one hour later. Don Nicola trailed with all the packed suitcases on the next train. He didn't mind as he knew that it was for a good cause.

From the station in Avella, Mario took the dirt road through Erminio's winery and farm, a shortcut to home. As a schoolboy in Nola, he would often stop there to climb a fig tree, but not this time. The farm consisted of a small parcel of land dedicated to fruit trees and the rest to grapevines. In early fall, Erminio produced a variety of wines, but his specialty was Prosecco. He was the first one to introduce a motorized grape crusher to make wines. In the old days, either it was manual labor, or a donkey was tied to a rotating wooden rod to crush the grapes.

When Mario arrived at Sergio's house, Alvaro's and Sergio's families were waiting for him outside the locked door where Imalda was delivering the baby. He knocked on the door, but Imalda refused to open it. He then got on his knees to peek through the keyhole to observe the birth of his child.

Zi Nicola arrived at the station in Avella later and asked Erminio about Mario's whereabouts. It seemed that the whole town knew about the impending arrival of Sofia's baby. Erminio, without hesitation, offered to drive Don Nicola to Sergio's house. He could see that Don Nicola was exhausted from all those suitcases. As in any other small town, few things remain a secret for long. By the time they arrived, a crowd had already gathered to celebrate the birth. Erminio came prepared. He brought bottles of Spumante wine (Italian Champagne) to add to the happy occasion.

Fortunately, Mario left the Navy just in time to avoid being recruited to serve in the same capacity as before, in transporting Italian troops to fight in the Spanish Civil War. Naval transport was vital to Italian participation in the war in Spain. Mario received an inquiry from the Navy, as to whether he was interested in re-enlisting as a Lieutenant Commander (third in rank after that Captain), a promotion from the previous assignment. Zio Nicola advised Mario to be careful with how to refuse the Navy and that he should reply in terms of doing greater good to fascism by assisting the Fascist government in Avella. Of course, that was an outright lie. He had no desire to work in the local Fascist government or to teach at a public elementary school, for which he qualified. However, the Italian Navy didn't need much of a convincing story, since they operated almost independent of Fascist's directives. Mussolini was embroiled in the Spanish Civil War in which the Republicans, Communists, and Socialists were pitted against the Nationalists and Spanish Fascists. One hundred thousand Italian troops were transported to fight in Spain to help Francisco Franco, who eventually became the Fascist leader of Spain.

Mario really wanted to get involved in the world of music but still stay within his specialty, ragioniere (lawyer/accountant). This decision had a lot to do with Zi Nicola. Of course, he exposed Mario to the idea of seeking that job. Zi Nicola just wanted company on those long rides to Naples and back with someone he knew and liked, and, besides that, Mario was the most qualified of the candidates applying for the job. During the little time spent at the Naval Station, Mario was relentless in pursuing the job at the opera house's business office and he became a good friend of its General Manager. Mario cultivated the art of being charming and unyielding when he needed to be. This time, it paid off. To strangers, Mario appeared distant and devoid of emotions. However, mentally, he was as active as a volcano, especially on things that mattered to him. He was relentless about his dream of one day settling in Posillipo. Mario became the main accountant/lawyer at the San Carlo opera house with Zi Nicola leading interference in his getting the job. Of course, Zi Nicola was ecstatic. Now, they could travel together to Naples, taking the 8:11 train from Avella.

The San Carlo opera house lost money each year during the 1930s. The ticket office generated only forty-five percent of its budget. Few of the so-called upper class and/or nobility were able to donate, and that wasn't enough to make up the difference. In 1835, Alexandre Dumas, who spent time in Naples, described the upper class thusly: "Four families enjoyed great fortunes; twenty lived comfortably and the rest had to struggle to make ends meet. It mattered to them to have a well-painted carriage harnessed up to a couple of old horses and a private box at the San Carlo. They lived in their carriages or in the theatre, but their houses were barred to visitors." This was a facade of wealth prior to WWII, but more so during the War.

Management tried to squeeze the salary of orchestra players or reduce the size of the orchestra, but not that of the singers. Mario came up with a brilliant idea. Instead of expecting people from the valley to travel to Naples in order to attend a performance, he suggested that performers visit small towns to stage operas. Mario concluded that such performances did not have to be first class. The entry fee would be commensurate with the quality of the performers. Singers had not been in the habit of taking a pay cut even when performing in a small town. However, orchestra players could be recruited locally. Churches, schools, and civic centers provided the acceptable outlets for staging an opera. Relatively speaking, the availability of places to stage an opera in the valley far outnumbered the number of performers. This meant that

Zio Nicola's music studios needed to produce many more performers to cover all those outlets in the valley. Not an easy task. Don Nicola saw an opportunity to expand his studio. In addition to his accounting job, Mario started a talent agency in collaboration with Zi Nicola. Whereas Don Nicola trained new performers, Mario represented promising talent to San Carlo as well as to other opera houses in Europe.

Don Nicola staged the opera, La Boheme, in Saint Peter Church in the east end of Main Street in Avella for the first time. He conducted the orchestra and directed the performers. The orchestra consisted of musicians from the local band. He recruited popular local singers, who were known for singing Neapolitan songs, and trained them to be adequate opera singers. For a successful performance of La Boheme, a good bass/baritone voice is necessary. One of his students volunteered for the role. To the audience, it made no difference. They were starved for opera music. It was hard work, but he believed in the cause and knew very well that the locals would be humming those tunes long after. His hope was to neutralize all that gossip about "Il Duce's love life" on Main Street and have people concentrate on the overthrow of fascism. The opera in Avella succeeded beyond expectations. The Communists boycotted the opera because it was staged inside a church and their credo was anti-Christ, at least for that moment, although their wives attended the performance.

Between 1934 and 1938, the relationship between Mussolini and Hitler changed in a dramatic fashion. It changed from Mussolini being scornful of Hitler (almost to the point of contempt) to one where he played second fiddle to him. The turning point in their relationship occurred in September 1937. Mussolini paid a state visit to Germany, where he reviewed a long parade of troops, artillery, and other military equipment. He recognized for the first time that Germany had built a powerful Army with advanced weapons. This German buildup would not work under the peace agreement of Versailles in 1919. These Army demonstrations of strength were obviously intended to impress the Italian leader, Il Duce, and they did. Hitler was the mastermind behind the rebuild. Mussolini realized, then, that Hitler would go to any lengths and means to achieve his goal. Also, it was clear to him what the goal was. Thus, their relationship went through a transformation. Being a schemer, Mussolini envisioned an opportunity for himself (as always). He decided to play second fiddle, only because there was something to be gained. He would "ride his back" and benefit from "crumbs" (colonies) left by Hitler after a war.

The final coup d'etat in their relationship occurred when Hitler occupied Austria, although Italy was Austria's protectorate as of March 1938. Austria and Italy signed a treaty in which Italy would protect Austrian territory against foreign invaders. Also, in 1938, Il Duce assisted Hitler in fooling Prime Minister Neville Chamberlain of Britain to accede Sudetenland to Germany in a "peace" meeting in Munich. Il Duce served as a translator at the meeting! By that time, Hitler could have placed a collar around Mussolini's neck and led him around like a puppy. The flip-flopping on the part of Mussolini in less than a year showed his unscrupulous Character.

On May 4, 1938, Hitler visited Naples to review the Italian Fleet, not too far from the Naval Military Station where Mario had trained. There was a large crowd there along the coastal road organized by the Fascist Blackshirts. Mario and Don Nicola wanted to see the "madman" up close, since the Station was within walking distance from the opera house at San Carlo. They noticed that Hitler was doing all the talking while Mussolini looked away, rolling his eyes as if to ask, "When will he stop talking?" Hitler's entourage mostly snickered at the poor condition of the Italian Fleet. At that time, Nazi Germany had an operational radar system and kept it a secret from their supposed ally. It was obvious to anyone there that the two countries were marching to a different beat. Germany was marching to war and Italy was not. The arrogance and body language of the Nazi entourage seemed to say as much. Mario and Don Nicola walked away with a lot of questions, one of which was: "Why was Il Duce so subservient to Hitler and the rest of them?" Clearly, this was not an equal partnership. The only thing that Il Duce didn't do was kneel in Hitler's presence. They worried that something terrible was brewing in which Mussolini had no clue as to the real intent of his guests. They questioned, *who was fooling whom*? Mario and Zi Nicola felt uneasy andapprehensive but couldn't put the finger on what disturbed them the most.

It wasn't long before bad news made its way to Italy. There was a special proclamation exported from Germany. On July 14, 1938, Mussolini embraced the "Manifesto of the Racial Scientist. Between September 2, 1938, and November 17, 1938, Italy enacted a series of racial laws, only to appease Hitler. The gist of these laws included the following: foreign Jews were forbidden to settle in Italy; Italian Jews were banned from jobs in the government, banking, insurance, education, the entertainment industry, and the practice of law. The Manifesto was shocking to all Italians, especially when, a few years back, Mussolini declared that the Italian Jews were the "glue" that bound the Italian Society together. Either Il Duce was a hypocrite or didn't believe in anything he had said, much like in Milan in the early 1920s. However, the real reason was that Hitler needed Mussolini's support for the new laws, since the rest of the world though it was an abomination to a civilized society. Thus, Mussolini acquiesced to Hitler's demands only to foster his delusion!

It was no surprise that the racial laws in Italy pretty much reflected the ones in Germany, enacted exactly four years earlier. On 15 September 1935, two laws were enacted in Nazi Germany (referred to as the Nuremberg Laws). Jews were no longer permitted to work in the civil service or government-regulated professions such as medicine and education. Many middle-class business owners and professionals were forced to take menial employment. Emigration was problematic, as Jews were required to remit up to 90% of their wealth as a tax when leaving the country. By 1938, it was almost impossible for potential Jewish emigrants to find a country willing to take them. The only country in Europe that did not require an entry Visa was Italy. Whereas before, Mario and Zi Nicola had some doubts about Mussolini's disposition, they now knew for certain that Mussolini was a puppet leader, abandoning all his previous convictions on racial laws. The man, Il Duce, sold his soul to the devil. If Italians were upset before, now they were more than livid. The laws went against the core of what most Italians believed.

With the issuance of the Manifesto, could no longer hope that things would get better under the Fascist regime. They would be lucky if it stayed the same as before the coming war! Suspicion ran rampant about Mussolini's motives. People began to talk openly about all the corruption in the regime. Most Italians followed their consciences and resisted the unjust treatment of Jews and did so at great personal risk to themselves and their families. This resistance took many forms. Some Italian Jews transferred businesses and other sources of wealth to trusted Christian friends for safekeeping. In addition, there were Jewish lawyers who continued servicing non-Jewish clients with the assistance of non-Jewish attorneys. Other examples of non-compliance included those bankers who overlooked or ignored Jewish bank accounts thereby protecting their assets from being confiscated. For example, before the outbreak of WWII, most countries in Europe required a visa to enter, except for Italy. As such, a Polish Jewish family decided to leave Warsaw just before the outbreak of WWII. They left much behind friends, family, a chocolate factory, a house, bank accounts, everything. They arrived at their usual summer vacation hotel in Florence, near the Ponte Vecchio bridge. The family explained their ordeal to the hotel owner, Giacomo. His answer was reassuring: "Non ti preoccupare, penso Io" "Don't worry, I will take care of it." The family enjoyed their stay while feeling assured. The hotel owner drove the family to the French Riviera and on to Paris. He refused a single Lira of payment and that included their stay in the hotel. Eventually, the Polish family emigrated to the USA. One member became an influential advisor to President Reagan on Russian affairs.

Not only was the populace unhappy with the racial laws, but so was the Catholic Church. As is common in the Catholic Church, their views are usually expressed by the Pope, but sometimes there are exceptions. And there was a serious exception prior to WWII. A chronology of events which took place in the Vatican before and after the publication of the racial laws in Italy follows:

May - June 1938

Pope Pius XI deliberately planned to be out of the city while Hitler was in Rome on May 3rd. On June 25th, he sought out the American Jesuit and priest journalist, John LaFarge, and summoned him to Castel

Gandolfo, the summer residence of the Pope near Rome. It is located on the Alban hills overlooking the Tyrrhenian Sea and Lake Nemi. The Pope told the Jesuit that he planned to write an encyclical denouncing racism, and asked LaFarge to help write it while swearing him to strict silence. The title of the encyclical was to be "Humani Generis Unitas" meaning, *The Unity of Humans.* A papal encyclical is one of the highest forms of communication by the Pope and usually deals with some aspect of Catholic teaching: clarifying, amplifying, condemning or promoting one or several issues. Historically, a papal encyclical is addressed to bishops and priests of a country or region, or to all clergy. LaFarge took up this task in secret in Paris, but the Jesuit Superior-General Wlodimir Ledóchowski promised the Pope and LaFarge that he would facilitate the encyclical's production. This proved to be a hindrance since Ledóchowski was privately an anti-Semite and conspired to block Lafarge's efforts whenever and wherever possible.

July 1938

Pius XI addressed the students at Propaganda Fide (faithful) with words that were to provoke Mussolini's wrath. "It has been forgotten that the human race, the entire human race, is a single, large, universal human race. The expression **human race** denotes, precisely, the human race... However, it cannot be denied that in this universal race, there is no room for special races or for a multitude of different variations or even many nationalities that are even more specialized... One might well ask why Italy ever needed to imitate Germany... We must call things by their name if we do not wish to incur grave dangers, including the risk of losing the name and even the notion of things".

September - 1938

On September 6, Pius XI received members of the Catholic Radio of Belgium on pilgrimage and gave a speech that has remained famous: "Listen carefully. Abraham is our patriarch; our forebear anti-Semitism is a hateful movement; We Christians must have nothing to do with it anti-Semitism is inadmissible. Spiritually we are all Semites.

On September 15, the Holy Father related to Fr. Tacchi Venturi (Vatican Ambassador to Italy): "But this is gross! I am ashamed... I am ashamed of being Italian. And you, Father, please tell Mussolini! Not as Pope but rather as an Italian, I am ashamed of myself! The Italian people have become a flock of stupid sheep.

In late September, LaFarge had finished his work and returned to Rome, where Ledóchowski welcomed him and promised to deliver the work to the Pope immediately. LaFarge was directed to return to the United States, while Ledóchowski concealed the draft from the Pope, who remained wholly unaware of what had transpired.

Fall - 1938

LaFarge realized that the Pope still had not received the draft and sent a letter to Pius XI where he implied that Ledóchowski had the document in his possession. Pius XI demanded that the draft be delivered to him but did not receive it until 21 January 1939 with a note from Ledóchowski, who warned that the draft's language was excessive and advised caution. Pius XI planned to issue the encyclical following his meeting with bishops on February 11, but he died one day before both the meeting and the encyclical's promulgation could have taken place. After Pius XI's death on February 10, 1939, Cardinal Eugenio Pacelli was elected his successor as Pope Pius XII in a short conclave on March 2. Pius XI's encyclical was returned to its authors by the new Pope. Yet, it took about fifty years for the encyclical to "see daylight".

1986

A copy of the encyclical was discovered in Paris, France. The book by George Passelecq and Bernard Suchecky and translated by Steven Rendall, *The Hidden Encyclical of Pius XI*, Copyright in 1997, Harcourt Brace & Company, New York, tells the story.

These episodes have raised several questions. How many copies and/or drafts were there of the encyclical and who had them? How was it possible that all were hidden for nearly fifty years? Whose draft or copy was discovered in 1986? Clearly, the unknown outweighs what is known. Could the publication of the encyclical in 1938-39 have changed the course of WWII? There have been many speculations about the medical condition of Pope Pius XI at the time of his death. Again, everything about it appears mysterious.

The implementation of the proclamation was applied unevenly by the Fascists, depending on where one lived in Italy. In big cities like Rome, where visibility was high, the Fascist government counted on appearance with the hope that the visual would be received and seen in Berlin. However, at the San Carlo opera house, the Jewish General Manager has fired as well as some Jewish members of the orchestra, including Don Nicola and Mario. The same was repeated at military installations, like the Naval Station in Naples. Whereas before the proclamations the Italian Navy was "divorced" from fascism, afterward, the Navy was forced to obey Mussolini's whim. In small towns like Avella, nothing changed. Alvaro still worked at City Hall. The Jewish community just ignored the proclamations, since the thugs did not have the authority to enforce them. Only the prefect could do that, but being apolitical, he was not about to.

The winter of 1939 in Avella brought brutal tornado-like winds. The cold and the snow flurries, for the first time in fifty years, felt like daggers to the bone. The weather matched the proclamation on posters of the racial laws being splattered all over town. The townspeople stayed indoors, but it didn't stop the Fascist thugs from putting up the posters. Still people did not want to come out, because they knew that Fascists were usually the bearers of bad news. Indeed, that was the case. The news traveled as fast as the wind. The town was dumbfounded. They were a homogenous society and comfortable with each other. Besides, their neighborhood had been established for millennia, long before Fascism. Hence, they looked at the proclamation with disdain, asking themselves, "Who are they talking about?" It never entered their minds about the distinction of any of their neighbors.

The Jewish community had contempt for the proclamation. They were part of the fabric of the town. It was inconceivable that this new movement of a few years, Fascism, was going to separate people and communities that had lived together for centuries and, sometimes, for millennia. The proclamation made no sense to them and others in town. The town rallied behind their friends and neighbors, since they made no distinction between anyone before, and they were not about to do that after. Don Nicola connected the proclamations to the German racial laws enacted four years earlier. However, he thought that the Italian people would not cooperate with them, or it would come to pass as had many other proclamations proposed by "Il Duce. By then, it confirmed what Don Nicola concluded after that infamous "charade" at the Naval Station in May 1938. The man, Il Duce, was a stool pigeon for Hitler.

Don Nicola and Mario were able to operate the studio and Mario's talent agency. Apparently, the San Carlo was still in the business of sponsoring opera performances in small towns in the valley. The new management at San Carlo didn't particularly care what happened in small towns, if opera was performed there. Good or bad performances didn't matter. Since Alvaro held on to the City Hall job, he relinquished the accounting part-time job at Alvarez's residence to Mario. The seamstress shop managed by Filomena, Serafina, and Sofia was unaffected by the proclamation. In effect, Avella has mostly stayed the same. Also, both Don Nicola and Mario realized that as soon as things quieted down, they could go back to San Carlo to resume their jobs.

In times of peril, Neapolitans have learned over the many years how to adapt in order to survive, "Ci arrangiamo. That motto has been ingrained in Neapolitans from the day they were born. Don Nicola and Mario felt the same. Being superstitious, like most Neapolitans, they had premonitions about the future. The year 1939 was the time for all those emotions. Something was brewing and the two of them "smelled a rat. An entry in Ciano's diary best summarized the feelings of most Neapolitans and the rest of Italy about Hitler. Ciano was the Italian Foreign Minister and the son-in-law of Mussolini. He married his older daughter, Edda. On August 11-12, he had conferences with his counterpart, von Ribbenthrop, and Hitler in Salzburg, Austria.

Ciano's Diary - August 13, 1939

"......I return to Rome completely disgusted with the Germans, with their leader, with their way of doing things. They have betrayed us and lied to us. Now they are dragging us into an adventure that we have not wanted, and which might compromise the regime and the country. The Italian people will boil over with horror when they know about the aggression against Poland and most probably will wish to fight the Germans. I don't know whether to wish Italy a victory or Germany a defeat. In any case, given the Germans' attitude, I think that our hands are free, and I propose that we act accordingly, declaring that we have no intention of participating in a war that we have neither wanted nor provoked.

Il Duce's reactions are varied. At first, he agrees with me. Then he says honor compels him to march with Germany. **Finally, he states that he wants his part of the booty in Croatia and Dalmatia.**

End of Diary

Don Nicola and Mario had every reason to worry about the future. Their Neapolitan intuition was right on the mark! WWII would take place within a few days. Germany invaded Poland on September 1, 1939.

FIVE
Three Memorable Days

The battle of Dunkirk has been studied, analyzed, and dissected by military officers, historians, and scholars of WWII and they all agree that it was crucial and a turning point in the War. However, there is one piece of the puzzle still missing in fully explaining that event. This book chronicles day by day for the first time, the background that precipitated Hitler's decision to pause the German Army for three days, allowing Allied soldiers to escape the encirclement at Dunkirk. There have been many explanations for the pause, allowing for the escape of British, Belgian, and French troops, by sea, across the English Channel. Books about WWII have already chronicled what led to the encirclement at Dunkirk.

The evacuation inspired Churchill's world-renowned speech that included, "We shall fight on the beaches. The evacuation at Dunkirk bought time with the hope that the day of reckoning would come. It did come at Stalingrad, El Alamein, Sicily, and at Normandy. It showed that the German Army was not invincible. More importantly, it gave people in small towns like Avella in Southern Italy, and the rest of the world, hope and the spirit to fight Fascism and Nazism in their inimical ways. Also, it set in motion partisans all over Europe to sabotage the war efforts of Nazis and Fascists. The situation at Dunkirk on May 21, 1940, may be summarized in the map below. As to how and why the British, French, and Belgian armies were trapped at Dunkirk, the reader is referred to these references.

German Army group (**A**) was commanded by General Gerd von Rundstedt and (**B**) by General Fedor von Bock. Group (**B**) attacked Belgium, while three panzer (tank) corps of the group (**A**) attacked south, toward the Ardennes forest, and then swung around to the English Channel. It trapped elements of the British Expeditionary Force (BEF) and the French and Belgian armies in Dunkirk and its vicinity. Paris is about one hundred miles south of Amiens. The French Maginot line of defense is about 100-150 miles East of Reims. The situation was rather dire for the Allied Armies, especially for the British Army. The British contingent at Dunkirk represented the best-trained troops and more than fifty percent of their active army. Even with the recovery of their troops, it affected their war strategies for the rest of the war. The British hierarchy was reluctant to commit British troops indiscriminately but prone to commit colonial troops in battles.

On May 22, 1940, Winston Churchill convened the War Cabinet to discuss the Dunkirk entrapment and what to do about it. After two days of intense discussions, on May 24th, War Cabinet members Neville Chamberlain and Edward Woods, the 1st Earl of Halifax, prevailed upon Churchill to contact the Italian Ambassador to Britain, Giuseppe Bastianini, in London for the purpose of mediating a peace conference, like the one in Munich, 1938, among the belligerents. By normal circumstances or by protocol, an ambassador reports an important message directly to his Foreign Minister. At that time, it would have been Mussolini's son-in-law, Ciano. By default, Bastianini must have contacted Mussolini, since Ciano was absent from Rome from May 22nd to the 25th. He was dispatched by Mussolini to Albania. According to Ciano's diary of May 21, 1940, he was reluctant to go to Albania, when the military situation in Dunkirk called for him to be in Rome. *Was it possible that Il Duce was up to no good?*

On May 26th, 1940, Ciano returned to Rome. According to Ciano's diary, Mussolini did not mention Bastianini's message; for that matter, Bastianini also did not report to Ciano about the call on May 24th. If Ciano had discovered the insubordination or Bastianini's disloyalty, he would have recalled Bastianini and sent him to jail. Bastianini's only choice was to not report information to anyone. Otherwise, he would have caught the wrath of Mussolini. Mussolini double-crossed him anyway, as he did with Dumini in the Matteotti affair (see chapter 2), not surprisingly. Quoting Ciano's diary of May 31st, 1941, "Bastianini was liquidated (terminated from his job) by Mussolini, who explained it by saying that his (immediate) family doesn't like him, and also reproached him for having built a villa at Rocca di Papa - a victim of the campaign started against him by Donna Rachele. Donna Rachele, by this time, ruled her household, including her husband, Mussolini.

That was unusual, to say the least! It was as if Ciano lived in a vacuum purposely created by Il Duce. Why? Given the fact that the two disagreed about the alliance between Italy and Germany, there was no incentive for Mussolini to inform Ciano, since there was no trust or agreement on anything between the two. Therefore, it is surmised that Mussolini must have contacted Hitler on the same day that Bastianini informed him of the call from London, May 24th, and advanced the idea of a peace conference as proposed by the British. It is claimed here that, on the same day, Il Duce urged Hitler to call for a halt, or a pause, in the German Army's advance to Dunkirk to show goodwill. Only Hitler had the power to stop the advance on Dunkirk. No General would have dared to challenge the Fuhrer.

It is argued that both Fascist and Nazi leaders had much to gain from a peace conference like the one in Munich in 1938. Remarkably, the same individuals who pushed for a peace conference in Munich, were the same ones, Lord Halifax and Chamberlain, who initiated another peace conference. Mussolini and Hitler recognized those "players" as weak and would deliver anything in the name of peace. Given Mussolini's personality and his deep desire to gain colonies at no cost and let the German Army be the conduit to his dream, he must have called soon after he received the message from Bastianini. Also, it would not have committed Italy to enter the War, since Il Duce was advised by the Italian General Staff that Italy was not ready for war until 1943.

As of today, there is no evidence of communications between Bastianini and Mussolini and between Mussolini and Hitler on the 24th. However, the communication between members of the British War Cabinet and Bastianini is reported in *McCarten's* book *Darkest*

Hour: How Churchill Brought England Back from the Brink. The order given to the German Army by Hitler is cited in many references. Thus, the common denominator of the two unknown communications is centered around Mussolini. We will never know, since Mussolini and others of that era are all deceased. Also, in those days, there was no recording of telephone conversations. Interestingly, Mussolini retrieved Giuseppe Bastianini from unemployment in the Fascist government by reinstating him as Foreign Minister, replacing Ciano in February of 1943. Effectively,

Mussolini acted like the Foreign Minister. Ciano was banished to the Vatican as Ambassador there. Could this appointment have been a payoff to Bastianini for keeping quiet for approximately three years about their conversation of May 24, 1940?

The pause lasted from May 24th to the late afternoon of the 27th of May, almost three and a half days. It saved many lives, see the plot below.

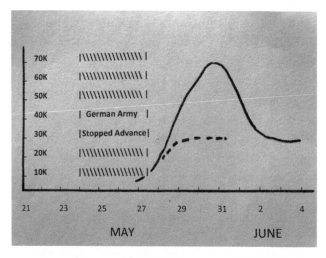

A personal drawing of the plot of soldiers rescued daily from the beach of Dunkirk in May-June of 1940. Data were obtained from actual reports of soldiers rescued. The dotted curve represents the estimate of soldiers rescued, if there was no pause in the German Army's advance toward Dunkirk.

The top curve indicates the number of soldiers rescued daily (in thousands) starting on May 27th. The evacuation peaked at about May 31st, and it ended on June 4th, when the German Army reached Dunkirk. The fact that Mussolini proposed to Hitler to enter the War on June 4th, according to Ciano's diary, demonstrated that he was aware of the end date when the German Army would arrive at Dunkirk. He was itching to get into the spoils of war and wanted to be first in line for the "crumbs".

Had there been no pause or halt, the German Army would have been at Dunkirk between May 31st and June 1 (see the dotted curve in the plot above). It is estimated that only 125,000 soldiers would have been evacuated instead of 338,226 as a result of the pause. No matter, Allied soldiers at Dunkirk lived for another day to return to the battle-fields of North Africa, Italy, France, and Germany. Political dissidents, like Mario and Zi Nicola and partisans, took to the streets and mountains to fight Fascists and Nazis throughout Italy.

Soon after the Dunkirk debacle, Mussolini entered the War on June 10, 1940, allied with Germany. In addition, he initiated the internment camps in Italy about that time, June 10th, only to impress the Fuhrer. His feverish drive to seize colonies was insane as was his willingness to knowingly follow a madman (see Ciano's diary). Clearly, the intent of Il Duce was to ride early in the good fortune of the German Army to reap the spoils of war. From the German hierarchy's perspective, they achieved much without the assistance of the Italian Army. Why is this "clown" coming around now? Thus, Hitler advised Mussolini to enter the war much later than the fourth. Clearly, Hitler did not want to share the spoils of war or the glory of marching on Champs-Elysees in Paris with him.

By then, Il Duce should have realized that they had had their last chance, and the Nazis knew it. As such, Hitler was onto his ruse. This was like a poker game in which the player with the high hand calls the bluff and wins it all. Yet, he did not walk away from the table and call it quits, i.e., walk away from the war. The question that begs to be asked is why he didn't walk away. It didn't make sense, since he would always have a poor hand. His army was not prepared for war until 1943, according to his General Staff. His logic made enough sense to kill a horse! It is a mystery to this day. Perhaps, madness! At this stage, Hitler could have told Mussolini to jump, and Mussolini would reply, "How high?" Thus, the persona changed from a con artist to a beggar. People in Avella and the rest of Italy didn't have to be told; they sensed that Mussolini exercised his will, not the people's.

The day after the arrival of German troops at Dunkirk, the German Army turned toward Paris, only about 100 miles South. The sixty remaining French divisions and the two British divisions in France made a determined stand on the Somme and Aisne but were defeated by the German combination of air superiority and armored mobility. German Armies outflanked the intact Maginot Line and pushed deeper into France, occupying Paris unopposed on 14 June. After the flight of the French government and the collapse of the French Army, German commanders met with French officials on June 18 to negotiate an end to hostilities.

On June 22, 1940, the Second Armistice at Compiègne was signed by France and Germany. The neutral Vichy government led by Marshal Philippe Pétain replaced the Third French Republic. German military occupation began along the French North Sea and Atlantic coasts and their hinterlands. The Vichy regime retained the free zone in the south. Following the Allied invasion of French Africa in November 1942, the Germans and Italians took control of the zone until it was liberated by the Allies in 1944.

Italy declared war on France and Britain on the evening of June 10, 1940, to take effect just after midnight. The two sides exchanged air raids on the first day of the war, but little transpired on the Alpine front at the border between France and Italy, since France and Italy had defensive strategies. There was some skirmishing between patrols and the French forts of the Ligne Alpine, exchanging fire with their Italian counterparts of the Vallo Alpino. On June 17, France announced that it would seek an armistice with Germany. On June 21, with a Franco-German armistice about to be signed, the Italians launched a general offensive along the Alpine front, the main attack coming in the northern sector and a secondary front advancing along the coast. The Italian offensive penetrated a few kilometers into French territory against strong resistance but stalled before its primary objectives could be attained; the coastal town of Menton, situated directly on the Italian border, was the most significant conquest.

On the evening of June 24, an armistice was signed in Rome. It came into effect just after midnight on June 25, at the same time as the armistice with Germany signed June 22. Italy was allowed to occupy the territory it had captured in the brief fighting. A demilitarized zone was created on the French side of the border, Italian economic control was extended into south-east France up to the Rhône and Italy obtained certain rights and concessions in French colonies. An armistice control commission, the *Commissione* certain *Italiana Francia* (CIAF), was set up in Turin to oversee compliance. Italy reclaimed the birthplace, Nice, of their famous hero of the Italian revolution of 1860, Giuseppe Garibaldi. Most historians regarded the invasion of Italy into France as a stab in the back of an old "friend. At that time, France was fighting for its life against the onslaught of the German Army near Paris. The world had never witnessed an army move so rapidly with their armored divisions. It came to be known as the "blitzkrieg. The Italian Army was not as powerful, it had amassed a huge Army merely to gain a few "inches" of territory. That was how much Mussolini was blindfolded by his ambition and *d'Armistizio con la* French delusion of himself. The Germans saw him as an opportunist at their expense.

The people of Avella were anxious about Italy entering another war against France, besides the ones started by Germany in Poland and France. They felt that they had tolerated Mussolini long enough. Now things were getting out of hand. The gossip in town was no longer about the love life of "Il Duce - The Clown", but when the next round of warfare would be. They didn't have to wait long. The town was in shock when they heard about the invasion of France. France and Britain were allies of Italy in WWI. If anything, their mindset was to repeat WWI on the side of France. Of course, Fascist thugs were parading up and down Main Street drumming up support for the war. If townies were anxious before, now they panicked, hiding their true feelings from the thugs about the War. Don Nicola could not help himself from draping the statue of Giuseppe Garibaldi in the Piazza with a black cloth, implying the death of Italy. It was prophetic. Garibaldi is to Italy what George Washington is to the USA. Fortunately for him, no one saw him doing it in the middle of the night. He was treading on dangerous grounds. He could not afford to antagonize Fascist thugs. They didn't need a reason to put him away. As usual, shepherds fled to the mountains, as they had done for centuries in times of war and turmoil in the valley.

SIX
Beginning of a Nightmare

Fascist extremists, like the Blackshirts, clamored for more war! They even went around Main Street putting up posters of Mussolini while singing the Fascist song "Faccetta Nera" (Black Face). People refused to look at the posters and it reached the point that they no longer took their *passeggiata* in the evenings. The consensus among the locals was that the less said and seen Mussolini the less likely they were to think about him. Now the town gossip was about the Ciano family (Mussolini's in-laws) profiting from the armament industries.

The Fascist government in Rome probably planted those stories with the consent of Mussolini. The Communists on the West end of Main Street would take the posters down or paint over them in the middle of the night. They were itching for a fight with the Fascist thugs since there was no popular support for any war, especially one allied with Germany. Their goal was to incite a riot, or at least a disturbance, at any cost. There was no peace in the streets. For a change, Communists instigated brawls with the Fascists. The Carabinieri kept peace between them by cordoning off the Piazza area from both groups. The well-to-do and middle class kept their distance from both groups of belligerents. The shepherds at the other end of Main Street appeared to be indifferent to all the commotion since they focused on ways to avoid both them and conscription. They didn't believe in wars or revolutions, seeing as it only led to more wars and revolutions.

In the fall of 1940, there was a lull in warfare in Europe. Germany and Russia occupied Poland. Germany gobbled up part of central Europe and Mussolini was rewarded with the "crumbs" - the Balkan countries and the French Alps, which he craved. World leaders did what they do best, nothing. They accentuated only the fears of renewing the war. Germany shipped raw materials (iron, nickel, metals, coal, wood, benzene, etc.) to Italy, which was needed to upgrade the armaments of the Italian Army. The consensus among the Italian General Staff was that the army was poorly equipped even with the addition of those raw materials from Germany. They needed to modernize their army to a much higher standard. Most of their weapons were from WWI. Their tanks were so small that British soldiers labeled them as "matchboxes." One rifle shot could blow them up. Also, the morale of the soldiers was rather low. According to Ciano's diary, Italians would have preferred to fight Germany, if at all. Hitler's intentions were clear to every country in Europe, war at any time and at any place.

The people of Europe, including those in Avella, hungered for peace and normalcy. They enjoyed whatever little peace they had at that moment rather than entertain the thought of another war. Trains ran on time. There were financial perks for having children. Men were at home, and Mussolini was welcome to bullshit all he wanted. Hence, no reason to complain. In the shepherd neighborhood of Avella, Imalda, and Felicia were basking in the winter sun caring for their granddaughter, Lena. By then, Lena was four years old and was chasing baby sheep all over the courtyard. Sergio was on his last inspection tour in the mountains before the winter snow. Sofia was pregnant, but it didn't stop her from working with Filomena and Serafina at the seamstress shop next to Alvarez' palace. Brothers, Ramiro and Alvaro Alvarez were no longer mayors, as they concentrated on their personal and global businesses. Alvaro Da Alia ran City Hall as before. Every Sunday afternoon, the four "musketeers" (Sergio, Alvaro, Don Nicola, and Ramiro) gathered to play cards under the shade of grapevines at Erminio's wine factory. Only Erminio was allowed to chit-chat with them. They wanted to put as much distance as possible between themselves and all that talk about the next war from customers at the winery. A bomb could have exploded next to them and they would not have budged one centimeter.

Life was beautiful, at least for that moment and at that place. The prefect, who had been in office long before Fascism, handpicked the new mayor. In effect, he acted as the liaison between the central government in Rome and the province. Similarly at this time, the office of the Questore (in ancient Rome Quaestor) linked the National police force, the Carabinieri, with the province. Sometimes these two offices acted more like a buffer between Rome and the province, as was the case in towns like Avella. In many towns in Southern Italy, peasants viewed Rome as the real enemy to be feared.

Like the Alvarez brothers, the new mayor was apolitical. This reflected the perfect. The other responsibility of the Questore, in consultation with the prefect, was to appoint the Chief of Police, *Maresciallo* of the Carabinieri, equivalent to the rank of Sergeant. The enforcement of law and order at the local level was thus "shared" between the Carabinieri who were, by and large, apolitical, and the black-shirt Fascists, who answered to the Fascist Interior Minister in Rome. The Questore trod a fine line between the two extremes of law enforcement at the local level, between the Carabinieri and the black shirt Fascists. The prefect had a free hand in appointing the mayor since the Fascist party abolished elections and the Interior Minister couldn't care less about the appointments. In addition, the perfect superseded a Fascist Judge's recommendation regarding the assignment of a political dissident to an internment town or camp, for example. All Judges were accountable to the prefect since Cicero's time.

Mario managed the accounting office for the Alvarez family at the palace. However, he practiced law out of his home, next to Sergio's apartment. Don Nicola was the local music impresario getting ready for the next opera performance in town. Both Mario and Don Nicola awaited word from the San Carlo about returning to the opera house. The racial laws prevented them from working in Naples, but not in Avella. Big cities were under the watchful eyes of Fascist Judges for violators of the law. That was Il Duce's way to impress the Nazi hierarchy with the implementation of Italian racial laws in big cities. Italian people sensed where he was headed and didn't like it one bit. More war.

Don Nicola rejoiced at the stalemate between the Communists and Fascists in the streets. He could speak his mind and not be afraid of being beaten up or sent to jail. But still, he had to be careful to pick the place and audience to exercise his newfound freedom. He was a loose cannon but dearly loved by his friends Sergio, Ramiro, and the Da Alia families. He represented everything that they believed in. How could they be angry with him? Don Nicola knew that war was imminent.

Mussolini claimed privately that the Italian people needed a "bloody nose" to toughen them up for the next round of wars! According to him, that was what it took for the Roman Empire to expand in Caesar's time. It took more than a "nosebleed" to build the Roman Empire. For one thing, it took powerful Centurion Armies and the backing of the Roman Senate to raise the money. Mussolini's war effort was short on both accounts. How could anyone listen to a such idiotic talk at that time? What made it more intolerable to the Italian people was his pledging allegiance to Germany. Once again, shepherds made plans to hide in the mountains. Their intent was to avoid conscription in the army, including hiding in caves or whatever in the mountains. In the last war, it took two years after the start of WWI before the Carabinieri searched for shepherds. Shepherds expected the same response this time from the Carabinieri. Besides, their friend, Sergio, would warn them about future raids. Sergio was privy to gossip in the Carabinieri's barrack, as he was the Mountain policeman sharing the same barrack. The Carabinieri purposely informed Sergio about any coming raid, since, like Sergio, half of the shepherd community was related to the Carabinieri.

The Fascist thugs rallied the people on Main Street to join the army. Italy was already on a warpath in Libya as the Fascist Army, under the leadership of Field Marshal Graziani, invaded Egypt. The next country on the list to invade was Greece. Mussolini upstaged Hitler for the first time. Prior to that, whatever invasion was planned in Europe by Italy required permission from Hitler, but not the other way around. In some sense, it was a "one-way street" relationship in which orders could only flow one way, from Hitler on down. The sad part of it all was that their personal relationship and one-upmanship games affected people's lives. It was incomprehensible but true.

Some in town signed up to join the army. Others donated gold wedding rings and jewelry to the war effort. It was no secret to the Black shirt Fascists as to what the shepherds were up to. They would reconnaissance the shepherd's neighborhood from time to time for unusual activities on the part of the shepherds toward the mountains. Regardless, shepherds were not going to sign up, period. The general feeling among them was contempt and disdain. Besides, they didn't want to catch the wrath of Imalda. She would warn them when to "hit" the mountains. For the shepherds who knew the infinite paths to the mountains like the palms of their hands, it was a trivial matter to avoid both the Carabinieri and the thugs. The two groups differed in their definitions of law and order. Whereas the Carabinieri would go through the motion of capturing young shepherds and find a myriad of ways to fail at that, the Fascists were earnest in trying to capture. As such, there was no cooperation whatsoever between the two police groups.

The upper class in the Piazza area couldn't care less whether Mussolini declared war. They bribed their way before and they would do it again in having their sons avoid enlistment or in obtaining special favors from the system. Their connections went all the way to Rome. Thus, the burden fell mostly on the middle class and the peasants of the West end (mostly Communists), and, yet they were the ones complaining the most about the war. There was no fairness on Main Street.

The declaration of another war would not have surprised Don Nicola or the Alvarez family. For one thing, the Alvarez family had nothing to do with City Hall or the Fascist Party. Don Nicola and his son were too old to be enlisted and Alvarez's two girls were ineligible for the army draft. Racial laws were a distance away from the time that they were enacted. Don Nicola regained his former position in the orchestra at the San Carlo opera house. The novelty of the Italian racial laws was beginning to ebb even in big cities. It was just a matter of time before Mario could resume his former position at the San Carlo. Even though there were fewer performances at the San Carlo, Don Nicola would find any occasion to snoop around for news about the war in Libya. He had direct access to the latest news of war events, as the port of Naples was located nearby. The port was the main one for transporting troops to and from Libya. He didn't trust the national newspapers, since editors needed Mussolini's approval.

In the meantime, Mario and his father were able to hold on to their jobs as lawyer/accountant and chief of City Hall, respectively. The main preoccupation of The Musketeers was to keep as far away as possible from the war, the Fascist party, and the Fascist thugs. As for Sofia, Sera-fina, and Filomena, their seamstress shop was still in business, and they catered mostly to the upper crust (elitists of the Fascist Party in Avella) of the Piazza crowd. Lena, Sofia's daughter, spent her time after kinder-garten between the two grandmothers, Imalda and Felicia. Sofia was looking forward to the birth of the next baby, a boy, as Imalda predicted this time.

Life did not wait for anyone. People in Avella were dealt a terrible hand. In sports, one could stop whatever action on the field by calling time out, but not in life. All were caught in a whirlpool of madness generated by Mussolini, and they couldn't get away from it. The locals were powerless to change things. They were simply resigned to what-ever. As such, people did the best they could under difficult circum-stances. Unfortunately, the nightmare lasted five more years. As in life, there are always happy moments, irrespective of the times. Exactly four years after the birth of Lena, on June 1, 1940, Sofia gave birth to a baby boy, Carlo, named after Sergio's grandfather. Again, Imalda delivered the baby, and this time Mario was there at birth.

To add insult to injury, Mussolini created internment camps in Italy starting on June 10, 1940, the day Italy declared war on France. Mussolini wanted to impress Hitler that he, too, had internment camps, but he intended to hide the camps from the Italian people. He adopted the same approach as he did in 1935, when he placed political dissidents in very isolated and mosquito-infested towns, away from large urban cities. These were the types of towns where civilization was slow to reach, and, therefore, time was irrelevant. Internees and locals had to put their lives on hold until the madness of war was over. Convents, monasteries, abandoned churches, castles, and old villas were all utilized to house internees. In some cases, internees were housed in regular run-down houses or apartments.

Internees could walk around town incognito since locals were too busy trying to survive a war to notice a stranger in town. To this day, some mayors of those "internment" towns in Southern Italy have denied or were not aware of the existence of internees in their midst during WWII.

In fairness to modern mayors, there were not many camps where internees were held behind barbed wires, fences, or walls so that the populace could notice them. Usually, internees mingled freely among the populace and carried on a normal life. Although locals may have been aware of internees in town, like them they were trying to survive the War. There was much empathy between the townies and the internees. The internees couldn't believe how backward the locals were, as they, themselves, were professionals and highly educated. They could see that life was hard for the locals who never tasted modern civilization as they had. The locals could not understand why these cultured people were in town and in the middle of a war. "Who put them here?" they would ask. But they had something in common – surviving the war. They helped each other as best they could.

The Fascist government in 1940 claimed that it needed internment camps in order to protect the country from both Italian and foreign-born dissidents who advocated opposition to the regime during wartime. The internment camps were classified into two categories: One was for foreign-born civilians who were detained according to war laws. Those who were detained for "public safety" reasons. The other type of internment camp forced the internee to live in barracked camps or, often, in a town designated by the prefect. For either category, one could be detained as "internamento libero" (free internment) which obligated the internee to remain in small towns, usually remotely located. The internee didn't report to anyone. He was free to move about town. However, the internee was responsible for his own food and lodging. If an internee lived in a barrack, the State provided for living quarters and financial subsidies. In the Calabria (the boot part of Italy) region, there was only one such internment camp, Ferramonti Di Tarsia. In most cases, internees were interned in small towns. As such, he was required to report on a regular basis to an official representative of the town, usually someone at the level of the local mayor or chief of police, Mares-ciallo. However, a magistrate or clerk of City Hall could also perform the duties of having the internee report to him and sign a certificate of attendance. The mayor, or Maresciallo, rarely got involved with the actual day-to-day administration of the internees. Hence, it was not a "free" type of internment.

In the summer of 1940, internment camps or towns populations included foreign Jews and those who had become stateless people, such as gypsies. Italian Jews were interned only if suspected of subversive political activities or those constituted a real threat to public order. Again, it was left to a Fascist Judge to interpret what constituted subversive political activities or a threat to public order. For example, if someone read Shakespeare, it might have been regarded by the Judge as being subversive, a totally subjective judgment. In the summer of 1940? bout 51,000 Jews resided in Italy: 41,300 of them Italian and 9,800 foreigners. In late 1940, there were about 6,800 non-Italian Jews in Italy, and 4,000 more would arrive. Also, Jews interned in territories controlled by Italy such as Libya, Slovenia, Dalmatia, Albania, and the Dodecanese, were transferred to camps in Italy. About 6,000 foreign Jews were interned and 400 Italians.

There were 48 internment camps located in Italy. About 44% were in the north, 24% in the central, and 32% in the south. Three camps were set up in Tuscany, six in the Marche, and one in the Umbria regions. As many as 19 camps were set up in the Abruzzo-Molise regions. Four camps were in Campania, and four were in the Puglia regions. In the Basilicata region, Potenza, Brienza, and Tito operated internment towns where internees were housed in antiquated apartments. In the Calabria region, an *ad-hoc barrack* camp was built in Ferramonti Di Tarsia in June 1940, holding the greatest number of Jewish prisoners, about 4,000. However, other camps or towns in Southern Italy were never accounted for, as they were well hidden from the public as well as from historians. It behooves this generation to keep searching.

Interned Jews were treated with much care and solidarity by the local populations and, occasionally, even by the authorities. There never was physical danger for Jews. The most critical aspect of internment was overcrowding, which worsened the already difficult hygienic and residential conditions, especially by dietary deficiencies, which, with the passage of time, would become ever more pressing. In the years 1942-1943, the scant government subsidy no longer sufficed to "cover even the most elementary needs." As the War became more and more of a burden to the Fascist government, in terms of food supplies to the troops, materials, casualties, etc., the subsidy to the internment camps diminished considerably to the point of becoming nothing. Most internees were on their own to support themselves. Indeed, that was exactly the situation during the Abyssinian War, when Dr. Carlo Levi was exiled to Aliano, Basilicata, in 1935. He had to pay for everything, including room and board and even medical supplies needed for the locals.

From 1940 to 1941, the German Army was forever bailing out the Italian Army in Greece and North Africa. The Italian Army was taking a shellacking from the smaller Greek Army. Hitler came to the rescue, and in doing so, he occupied the Balkan countries. He didn't leave any crumbs for Il Duce, because he was annoyed for taking the time to rescue Mussolini at the hands of the Greek Army. Hitler had to postpone his plans to invade Russia. Initially, the invasion of Russia was scheduled for the spring of 1941. It was delayed for two months. The delay turned out to be crucial in the defeat of the German Army in Russia.

The specter of Napoleon loomed larger and larger in the minds of Hitler and his staff of Generals as the war in Russia raged on and on. It had already lasted one year, and the German Army has stuck in a quagmire of wasteland in Russia, miles, and miles away from Moscow. The German Army Command predicted an eight-week campaign. The war situation in Russia served as an impetus for the two nemeses (the Communists and the Blackshirt Fascists) to be at each other's throats in the streets of Avella in the summer of 1942. Now, the roles were reversed. The Communist thugs were in pursuit of Fascist thugs. Partisan groups began to appear on the mountains of Avella-Baiano, free to move around. They consisted mostly of Communists, Socialists, former army conscripts, farmers, and shepherd youths. For the first time, Communists and shepherds joined forces to fight a common enemy, Fascists. They hid in mountain caves. Thus, the tide was turning not only at the local level but throughout Europe and North Africa. The shadow of Dunkirk loomed greater and greater over the minds of Nazis and Fascists as El Alamein and Stalingrad were just around the corner. The myth of an invincible army was about to hit the dust.

The need for more recruits to join the Fascist Army heightened to the point that the Carabinieri were forced by Fascists, into action looking for any male on two legs. The only potential source of new recruits was to be found in the shepherd community, and they had escaped to the mountains. It was no secret where to look – in the hidden mountain caves. The Carabinieri knew in their hearts the day of reckoning was coming and the Fascists would try to impose their will. However, they still went through the motion to appease the Fascists. Young shepherds seemed to be one step ahead of their search, thanks to Sergio's collaboration with the Carabinieri. During the time Italian troops were engaged in Stalingrad, there were no more recruits.

Many soldiers from Avella never made it back to their girlfriends, fiancés, wives, brothers, sisters, mothers, fathers, and friends. A handful came back home from the campaigns in North Africa. Only one soldier returned from Russia. There were about 50-100 deaths, and many others were injured. The sad part of it all was not knowing what was happening to loved ones in faraway lands. Letters from the front stopped coming soon after the soldiers arrived at their destinations. The people in town were emotionally drained. Those days were the saddest in the lives of the people of Avella. The hurt was truly unbearable. For some, the scar lasted a lifetime.

People sensed that Europe was on the verge of either catastrophe or liberation. As such, people were anxious and "sitting on pins and needles." Food was becoming more and more scarce. For example, coffee beans were replaced by dried chicory buds. The daily diet consisted mostly of polenta (grits) in the morning, noon, and evening. On Sunday, tomatoes were squeezed on polenta to give an appearance of a pasta dish. Butcher shops exhibited fewer meat varieties. There were no longer stray cats on the streets as now cat meat was sold as rabbit meat. Shops boarded windows to save glass or to discourage looting, even though there wasn't much in them. The Lira was worth next to nothing. Salt could be had at 150 lire per kilogram on the black market. Its original price was one lira. Little sugar was allowed and only one hundred milliliters of olive oil was allowed (3.4 ounces). Green vegetables, fruits, potatoes, milk, meat, fish, eggs, tea, and coffee were impossible to obtain except on the black market. Thank God for wine. It was still in abundance.

Shepherds didn't suffer as much, as the mountains provided all the food they needed. Hunting for wild boars was becoming profitable. Sergio made sure that the "clan" was taken care of in terms of food availability. Their main preoccupation was to avoid daily conflict in the streets between Communists (partisans) and Fascists. Don Nicola informed Mario that the management at the San Carlo would welcome him back to resume his former position, as soon as Mussolini disappeared from the scene. In the meantime, opera performances were curtailed for a short period of time. People were in no mood to be entertained.

Mario and his family were awakened early one morning by a loud knock on the door of their apartment. Flustered and bothered, Imalda was pleading: "Please help me, they have detained my nephew, Nino, in a raid in the cave of San Michele." Apparently, Blackshirt Fascists had raided the cave and apprehended a group of partisans including Nino. They did not inform the Carabinieri. Normally, the Fascists would request the Carabinieri to raid a specific location based on their intelligence, but not this time. Mario visited Nino the next day in jail. He learned that the Fascists also discovered Partisan literature, pamphlets, and posters advocating the overthrow of the Fascist State. At best, Nino would be sent to an internment camp. At worst, he could be shipped to Libya to join the Italian Army and become a casualty of war or be injured for life.

At the trial, a Fascist Judge presided over the court. Mario argued that Nino couldn't possibly have written the posters or anything else, since he could barely sign his name. Besides, Nino took refuge in the cave, as a violent rainstorm came down on the hills. Thereupon, the Judge asked Nino who was responsible for the literature. Nino declared that he needed the paperwork to start a fire. It was getting cold. Finally, Mario presented a doctor's testimony that Nino was handicapped. Nino's left toe had been bitten by a wolf and was mutilated. Hence, he argued that Nino would be exempt from army service. Mario invented a cock and bull story to diffuse the issue on hand that Nino was a partisan. It must have been exasperating for the Judge to decipher fact from fiction. Neapolitans love that type of talk. It is in their nature to take things with a grain of salt, when it does not involve life and death matters.

Mario's violation of the racial laws never came up during the trial, as he was Jewish and practicing law. The Fascist Judge purposely stayed away from bringing it up, since he would have been reprimanded by the local prefect and most likely whatever decision he made in that regard would have been annulled. The Judge then asked Mario if he was aware of the pamphlets hidden in the cave. Mario alluded that there were rumors in town about partisan activities in the foothills. Mario knew very well that Don Nicola might have written the posters. Thereupon, the Judge said, "Avella is a small town. There are no secrets here, so who did it?" Mario shrugged his shoulders and hands in a typical Neapolitan gesture, as if to ask, "Who knows?" The Judge sentenced both Nino and Mario to internment camps, Nino as a partisan saboteur against the State and Mario as a political dissident. Interestingly, Mario did not deny the charge, because he had much to hide and did not want to produce evidence against himself and others. His strategy was to keep the trial short and to the point, since the State did not produce any evidence against him or Don Nicola, other than the flimsy charge of a political sympathizer.

The trial had nothing to do with justice, but a search for potential threats to fascism. The Judge was amused by Nino's bullshitting. Neapolitans loved that and concluded that Nino was harmless. The Judge considered Mario the real danger to fascism in the future. Mario was a marked man, since he had submitted a letter to an obscure Naval Military Newsletter criticizing Fascist leadership on the poor condition of Navy ships - lack of radars He had alluded to corruption at the highest level, preventing modernization of Navy ships. The Judge must have read that article and felt that Mario represented a potential threat to Fascist rule.

The snooping into the Navy's magazine was nothing new by the Fascist' government agents, OVRA. OVRA were the watchdogs for any Italian institution which was not committed 100% to fascism, and the Navy was not. For one thing, the navy, in contrast to the army, was not an early supporter of fascism, although it was subordinate to the Fascist government by no other choice. During the Ethiopian war, political dissidents were sent to internment camps just based on what they wrote or read in personal letters. In one case [6-11], a prominent medical doctor extolled a book that he read about Socialism in a letter to a friend. The local mailman made the letter available to the Fascist agent for review of its content. The Fascist agent warned the doctor that there might be consequences in reading books of that nature. The implication of the threat was rather obvious. Mario's opinion was in the open literature and, therefore, more damaging to the Fascist State.

Sentencing of internment was the purview of the Fascist Judge, but the implementation of it fell to the local administration, the prefect. Thus, there was a way to soften the blow of the Judge. As such, the prefect had the option to consult with anyone he wished. At least, Nino avoided conscription in the army. It was a small price to pay for Mario. He believed the war was soon going to be over, and Fascism overthrown for good. His ace in the cards was his close connection to the Alvarez brothers and indirectly to the prefect, who was the final arbiter of his fate. Mario's family was not pleased with the outcome of the trial, regardless of where the internment camp was going to be. Sergio, Don Nicola, and Alvaro soon prevailed on Ramiro to intercede on behalf of Mario and his family.

The Judge recommended sending both Nino and Mario to the internment camp at Ferramonti di Tarsia in Calabria region (see appendix 1), an obscure mosquito-infested place, although he really had no jurisdiction to do this. He over-extended himself. The Alvarez family could not afford to turn over tons of paperwork to another accountant. They wanted to keep their finances private. Also, the family desperately needed Mario to be nearby and easily accessible. Ramiro Alvarez interceded on behalf of Mario by suggesting to the prefect where his dear friend and accountant, Mario, could be interned in order to alleviate pain to the family and to his global business. After all, this perfectly recommended Ramiro to be mayor at one time when Fascism was almost fashionable in Avella. Thus, the perfect owed Ramiro a favor.

Saint Michael cave. Courtesy of Rie Vittoria.

As Fascism became more and more of a nightmare to the people, Ramiro could take liberty with the prefect by suggesting a camp accessible by train from Avella. Some camps in Campania, Basilicata, Calabria, and Sicily regions were remotely located and not easily accessible (see Appendices 1 and 2). Towns like Campagna (Province of Salerno) and Ferramonti (Province of Cosenza) could only be reached by train to Eboli, then by bus, and, finally, by other means of transportation. The desired option would be for Mario's family to travel readily back and forth from Avella to the internment town by a single mode of transportation, preferably a train. As such, they could visit Mario on a regular basis, even though inconvenient to all concerned. It could have been worse. The only camp that satisfied Ramiro's criterion was the one at Tito near Potenza in the Basilicata region.

Whereas Ferramonti Di Tarsia gathered all the accolades as a premier internment camp by the Fascists, locals at Tito and nearby towns, like Potenza, weren't even aware of the internees or exiled people in their midst. Even fifty years later, the locals denied the existence of internees among them, (see appendix 2). However, Tito and Potenza were as different as night and day, although separated by only a couple of miles. Civilization arrived at Potenza, but not at Tito. Running water was common in houses in Potenza. Tito was located at the foothills of a mountain where water was secured from wells and fountains much as in Avella. Animals were still housed in one-room apartments by shepherds and farmers. Mario was looking forward to meeting the locals at Tito, but Sofia and the children were not. They loved to have their papa stay home. The only inconvenience was that an official representative, or a Carabiniere, was assigned to guard Mario when he traveled by train to Tito. The family could visit Mario any time. In Tito or any other internment town, he needed to report to a local Maresciallo. The perfect (via the Questore) made sure that a Carabiniere friendly to Sergio was given that assignment on the train to Tito. Yes, things were almost the same as before the trial with a slight encumbrance. It could have been much worse.

SEVEN
In the Middle of Nowhere

I n July of 1942, Mario reported to the Maresciallo's office in Avella for his internment in the town of Tito, Potenza Province. It was at that time that the invincible German Army was about to experience defeats for the first time at El Alamein, Egypt, and at Stalingrad, Russia. Tito is in the Basilicata region of Italy, about 50-60 miles from the Ionic (South) and the Tyrrhenian (West) seas. During the Middle Ages, Calabria and Basilicata (Lucania then) were under Byzantine rule, and the region was an important commercial center. The Jewish population then was estimated at about 12,000. It flourished and influenced the commercialization of the region. Some areas had a Jewish population of up to fifty percent. Many Jews were prosperous merchants dominating such industries as silk trading and cloth dyeing. Money lending was also an important source of revenue for them. However, by the 1940s, towns were poor, isolated, and usually rampant infested with malaria. Modern civilization had bypassed these towns since the Middle Ages. They were ideal remote small towns for the Fascist Regime to hide internees from the rest of Italy and the world.

Sofia dreaded this day. While the family wished so much for the time to linger after the trial, time seemed to fly. Mario was accompanied by a group of shepherds, his wife, and family, Don Camillo, his father's family, and friends. They clamored for the Maresciallo not to let Mario leave Avella. Avella, being a small town, everyone knew the circumstances under which Mario was being exiled. Fortunately, no Fascist thugs showed up anywhere nearby. Otherwise, it would have been like pouring gasoline on a fire; a riot would have ensued. Ramiro assured friends and concerned family members that Mario would be in good hands. His assurance went a long way in soothing the feelings of all there, but it was time to let him go.

The train connection from Avella to Tito made four transfers: Naples, Salerno, Eboli and Potenza. The train to Naples was unusually crowded, as farmers were on their way to the Farmer's Market in Nola. The Carabiniere accompanying Mario sat at the opposite end of the train compartment from him. Everybody could see that he was a guard, as he was wearing that black robe type of vestment. He kept his distance from Mario so as not to draw attention to Mario and regarded himself as more of a protector than a guard. He was a veteran of WWI who served in the army with Sergio. He and Sergio had spent their youth as shepherds up on those mountains. At Potenza, there would be a change of the guard, since Potenza was in the Basilicata Province, a different jurisdiction. The relationship between Mario and his first guard was very cordial and respectful. Certainly, Sergio gave him an earful, as to how to take care of Mario.

Farmers brought every imaginable kind of fruit and other produce to the Market: apricots, peaches, figs, oranges, cherries, hazelnuts, olives, canned tomatoes, etc. In addition, chickens, rabbits, pigeons, and other small animals were brought along. The farmers all recognized Mario as well as the guard, Giacomo, and offered them enough food to be stuffed. At Nola, farmers, shepherds, and vendors got off the train and the compartment looked like a barn, but it was a welcome relief. At Naples, Giacomo purchased the transfer tickets, as they changed trains. Mario soon learned that Giacomo paid for the tickets out of his own pocket. Giacomo had that swarthy appearance reflecting his descendants of millions of years ago and had a heart as big as Mount Avella. The Fascist State no longer subsidized internees for travel, food, and lodging! The government couldn't even feed its troops in Libya or any place else in Europe. The regime was bankrupt of money, soldiers, armaments, and soul, but still pretended everything was fine and under control.

However, the Fascist Regime running out of money was not really a new situation. The same occurred in the Ethiopian War. Mario didn't know what to expect once he arrived at Tito, but he trusted Ramiro that everything was going to be fine. At the train station in Potenza, two Carabinieri guards from the town of Tito, wearing the usual black robes and triangular hats, were waiting for the train to arrive. The two guards nodded, never greeting Mario or Giacomo or checking whether or not the right internee was handed over to them. Giacomo embraced Mario and planted two kisses on Mario's cheeks and said, "One kiss is from Sergio and the other from Imalda," and left to catch the next train home. Without uttering a single word, the two Carabinieri proceeded toward the train station in Potenza to catch the train to Tito. This time, Mario had to pay for his own transfer ticket.

As the train approached the station in Tito, Mario heard faint music. His first thought was that someone important must be on this train. Why the music and for whom? He recognized the song, "Parlame D'Amore, Mariu" ("Talk to me of love, Mariu") which was a popular Neapolitan song and the personal anthem of Mario and Sofia. Unbelievably, Ramiro, standing next to a three-piece band, waited on the platform, as one musician played the trumpet, another the clarinet and the third sang the song. Hidden behind big and jolly Ciccio was none other than Sofia! As Mario and Sofia ran to each other's arms, Ciccio sang his heart out the beautiful melody. As for the two, the song was too short. They wanted to stay in each other's arms forever. Mario was moved to tears. At the same time, he felt that he should never have doubted Ramiro and whispered to Sofia as much. He had learned an important lesson: faith and hope are important aspects of life. It was time to break up the party, and Mario thanked Ramiro for arranging to have Sofia surprise him when he arrived in Tito. However, Ramiro, forever the gentleman, said that the song was Sofia's idea and she organized it all. As always, he preferred to stay in the background letting others take the credit for his good deed.

Ramiro instructed Mario to meet him in front of the Palazzo Colonna, in the main Piazza, soon after Mario's visit to City Hall, which was located across Main Street from the Palazzo. Mario was required to register with the Magistrate at City Hall, and he appeared more upbeat and confident thanks to his warm welcoming party at the station. In the meantime, Ramiro needed to send the band back to Avella before the last train departed for Naples. Otherwise, it would have been a logistical nightmare for him and Mario. There were no hotels in Tito, and City Hall did not register ordinary citizens to living quarters arbitrarily as political dissidents without the consent of an owner. Mario recognized the members of the band. The short and heavy-set member, Vito, played the clarinet; the tall and slender one, Peppe, the trumpet, and the swarthy looking one, Ciccio, sang the song. Ciccio was the same man who had delivered warm ricotta to town early each morning on his donkey. Often, young lovers paid him to serenade their lady friends. This was a ritual of the times before the War. His repertoire was old Neapolitan love songs.

Ramiro sensed that Sofia was apprehensive about Mario being away from the family in a strange town. Then again, everything was topsy-turvy in small towns, like Avella and Tito. There were many questions running through Sofia's mind: Is it a jail? Is Mario going to be placed in a barrack? Will Mario have to do heavy work? It never entered Sofia's mind that he was going to be interned in someone's house or apartment or a monastery. She had to see for herself what was going on in Tito. Ramiro's intent was to remove all those lingering thoughts, assuring her that the family would have access to Mario at any time. He wanted to convey to her that everything was the same as before except he was required to be in Tito instead of Avella!

The two guards, who came for the ride from Potenza to Tito, scampered away during all that commotion. Apparently, they were not paid for the extra duty of accompanying Mario to City Hall. No official from City Hall showed up to receive Mario at the station. It puzzled Mario as to what to make of it. His first thought was, "Perhaps if I hurry, I could go back home with Ramiro and the band." No such luck. He could see, from the corner of his eye, a swarthy-looking man trudging toward the station. It looked as though he didn't want to fight the afternoon sun or that hot breeze blowing from the Sahara Desert of North Africa. "Signore Da Alia?" the man asked, approaching the station platform. The clerk was a short, heavy-set man wearing a typical "coppola" (cap) and a thin jacket. No doubt, the man was suffering from the heat.

The street to City Hall was equally torturous, straight uphill with oppressive air in that brutal summer heat. There were officially three towns near each other that housed internees or exiles: Potenza, Tito, and Brienza. Potenza housed about five hundred internees. Tito and Brienza together housed as many as three hundred internees. There may have been other internment towns, but we may never know.

There are no official records or books that have been written about other possible internment towns, especially in the Basilicata region. Some towns have been carved out of the mountains and are well hidden. As in Avella, there was no food to be found in these internment towns unless one went into the mountains scavenging for anything edible. Internees were in the same predicament as the townspeople. Locals had no time to be nosy about their neighbors or strangers coming to town. All their energy was spent on ways to scavenge for food, including the internees.

On the way to City Hall, conditions of the housing and the streets reminded Mario of the poor section in Avella toward the West end (Communist Section) of Main Street. Main Street in Avella became narrower and narrower, and the housing shabbier and shabbier, as it approached the Castle Longobardo on the hill. Tito was a carbon copy of Avella, except there were irregular-spaced steps every so often. It only made the climb to City Hall more tiring. There was something about the locals that he could not relate to, at least from his first impression. He was looking forward to meeting and engaging people in the streets of Tito. As in Avella, Main Street ran from East to West. Whereas in Avella, Main Street was paved and had sidewalks, in Tito, Main Street was a cobbled street with no sidewalks. The few locals who looked him over appeared to be suspicious, as if he were from a distant land. By then, Tito had many out-of-town internees. As Mario and the clerk walked up Main Street, they crossed paths with a herd of sheep heading for the hills. Mario thought that it was an unusual sight, unless the sheep were headed to a body of water to cool down. He knew that sheep headed to the hills in the early morning or headed back during evening hours. Then, immediately after that incident, a donkey loaded with farm equipment followed by a woman balancing something heavy on her head walked in the same direction. Mario was encouraged by what he saw. My kind of people, farmers, and shepherds, Mario surmised.

Stray chickens and goats roamed all over Main Street. A pudgy woman dressed in black vestments came out of her house, leaving her front door open, shouting to no one that someone stole her chicken. She walked from street to street raising a fuss. She didn't find her chicken. Someone must have needed that chicken more than the distraught woman. Obviously, food was also scarce in Tito. A quick glance into the woman's house revealed the makeup of her house: one room consisting of a bedroom, kitchen, and barn. No different from some shepherd homes in Mario's neighborhood. There were few young men to be seen in the streets.

The town of Tito (Basilicata) could relate to other nearby towns where internees were housed. The people's customs, lifestyles, and traditions in the Basilicata, Puglia, and Calabria regions have remained the same since the Middle Ages. In some sense, their behavior had been "frozen in time," or as if time stopped in those places. In comparison with other regions in Italy, the town, as well as many towns in the Basilicata region, were sheltered from modern civilization. Political internees, like Mario, in isolated towns like Tito placed their lives on hold until the War ended. In some sense, time was becoming irrelevant to internees and the locals. Interestingly, the great scientist, Albert Einstein, commented on the relevance of time, "...the distinction between past, present, and future is only a stubborn illusion." In other words, time is an illusion, as it was then for a lot of internees.

Finally, the clerk and Mario reached City Hall in the piazza, across from San Vito Church. The clerk was out of breath. He needed something to drink and rushed ahead to get some water at the fountain, near Palazzo Colonna. Duke Ferdinando (Fernando) Alvarez de Toledo, Ramiro's grandfather, married his long descendant cousin, Princess Livia Colonna. The Colonna family was a powerful family from the Middle Ages to modern times. They exerted tremendous political influence from Rome to Southern Italy including the Basilicata region.

Prince Colonna of Basilicata was the biggest landowner of the whole region and owner of the Palazzo Colonna, a relative of Ramiro through marriage.

In the Piazza facing Palazzo Colonna, there were tobacco, butcher, barber, and carpenter shops, a convenience store, and City Hall. In front of City Hall, a line of trees covered the entrance to a three-floor building. A concierge at the entrance to the building screened visitors and instructed them as to where to inquire on the second floor about the whereabouts of different offices. On the third floor was the mayor's office and that of the Magistrate of City Hall. The office of the Carabinieri and Maresciallo was located two blocks away on Main Street. At that time, the offices were half-staffed due to the attrition of young men because of the War.

The clerk directed Mario to the third floor to see the Magistrate. Normally, the clerk would direct an internee to either the mayor's or the Maresciallo's office, depending on who was available. Since Fascism was out of fashion with the locals and especially with shepherds in 1942-1943, these two town officials wanted no part of any Fascist program related to internment camps. They felt that whatever association, direct or indirect, with fascism could be detrimental to their political futures. In 1935-36, Fascism in Italy was on the rise as a result of the conquest of Ethiopia. So, every Maresciallo and mayor wanted to take credit for the success of fascism. They walked around town like peacocks trying to get attention from the populace and to exert their authority. Times changed and, as such, the mayor and the Maresciallo of Tito was sitting on the fence as to which way the political wind was blowing.

The Magistrate, Pasquale, was apolitical and he was clear about the rules of internment in Tito by which Mario had to follow: no government subsidy, signing of the register every morning at nine, no socializing with other internees, and staying within the confines of the town. Pasquale didn't define where the confines of town were located, since he did not want to pay for guard details stationed at the confines. When Mario entered the Magistrate's office, he had the feeling that everyone in that office, including the Magistrate, had a scornful look. He was shocked because he didn't know them. The Magistrate had a full dossier on Mario, and that framed him as a person on the other side of the fence, one of the gentries.

That attitude was somewhat hypocritical since the Magistrate represented the State and was, therefore, an emissary of the establishment in Rome. All that posturing between the two stopped once Mario inquired as to which shepherd to contact about food since it was clear that shepherds made up most of the population in Tito. Pasquale recognized, by the nature of the question, that Mario was acquainted with where to look. Mario explained to him that his mother-in-law was the matriarch of the shepherd community in Avella, and he was aware of their culture. Pasquale was impressed and was soon attentive to Mario's needs. It was clear from the ensuing conversations that both were anti-Fascist and sympathetic to the causes of peasants. There was a kindred spirit between the two.

Pasquale was raised in a shepherd family dating back millennia. Early in life, he had an aptitude for schooling. He was highly motivated in school, self-contained, and scorned trivial pursuits. He was mentally and physically more mature than most other children in school. Thus, he entered the world of wonderment, and knowledge. Being bottled up in the world of poverty and peasantry for all those years, Pasquale looked forward to turning the page over on the past. The family recognized as much and sacrificed to advance his education.

At the Lyceum school in Potenza, Pasquale majored in classical languages, Greek and Latin. He continued his studies at the University of Cosenza where he earned degrees in law and accounting, becoming a ragioniere. As with most ragionieri, he was unemployed for four years until the mayor of Tito, a Fascist friend of Pasquale at the University, appointed Pasquale as an errand clerk in the mayor's office, delivering mail to various offices. It only meant one thing to him, no turning back. From there, he moved to City Hall to distance himself from his Fascist friend.

The town of Tito consisted mostly of shepherds and farmers who represented the peasant class. The mayor, Maresciallo, government officials and representatives, bankers, landowners, etc. represented the gentry. As in Avella or any other town in Southern Italy, the eternal conflict between the haves and the have-nots or between the peasants and gentry dates back as far as time itself. The conflict between the classes is inherent in human nature. No legislative or political action can regulate this natural conflict. Rallying the lower class toward Socialism and/or Communism, as in the 1930s, would have generated only another lower class and it would have been back to square one, the eternal conflict. Thus, peasants in Southern Italy have masqueraded their animosity toward the local gentry under the pretense of complaining about rulings out of Rome. In their view, Rome had empowered the upper class to govern, subjugate and control for centuries the unskilled workers, farmers, shepherds, and peasants to do menial work and produce food to feed the country at measly compensation.

Due to the turn of events in North Africa and the Balkans, the mayor of Tito, a Fascist, was in a quandary as to which way the political wind was blowing, whether he should remain a Fascist or go through a conversion. He was sitting on the fence, forever procrastinating as to what to do. He minimized public exposure to hide his allegiance. The Maresciallo was too stupid to realize what political options lay ahead. Pasquale loathed both. However, Pasquale could not tip his hand, to Mario or anyone else, about his true allegiance. Mario surmised as much from his demeanor and body language. It was then a game of cat and mouse between officeholders in order to save themselves in those days.

By then, Mario was exhausted from all the traveling on that day. His life hung on a thread. Finally, he crossed Main Street to Palazzo Colonna, where he was to meet Ramiro. The Piazza was crowded with people. Old farmers and shepherds sat on benches, made of stones or of large rocks, smoking rolled cigarettes and staring at no one in particular. They seemed to enjoy the morning sun and retelling the same stories over and over. The gentry mostly stood in the middle of the piazza, indifferent to the peasants and vice versa. They behaved as if the ones sitting on stones came from some uncivilized world that had nothing to do with theirs. The topic of conversation among the gentry was to complain about other gentries. Their hatred of others ran deep. That was typical of the Piazza crowd, as in most small towns of Southern Italy then.

Ramiro and Sofia waited anxiously in front of the large fountain abutting the Palazzo. He asked Mario, "How did the bullshit go; sooner or later all those clowns are going to catch hell." "The mayor will be the first one on the way there,", replied to Mario. However, Mario wanted very much to clear the air while Sofia was there, as he knew there were some hard feelings between Sofia and her mother. He explained that the episode in court was unavoidable. It had nothing to do with Imalda and her nephew Nino. The Fascists wanted to stop Don Nicola from yapping away at them and others in the streets and printing those pamphlets. Then Mario added, "They used me to silence Don Nicola. They accused me of being a political dissident only because I represented Nino in court." He continued, "So, Sofia, please tell Don Nicola not to yap at the thugs, especially now. Sooner or later, they will get their due." The implication was that the Judge would have found any pretext, as in a kangaroo court, to send Mario to Tito.

As Ramiro and Mario entered the library in the Palazzo, Ramiro turned to Mario and said: "You may resume your accounting work here. This part of the Palazzo is usually inhabited by relatives of the Colonna family who are also my relatives, but, for now, they decided to live in a safer place. Pasquale has my consent for you to stay here. A courier will bring accounting papers from Avella from time to time. However, you may want to stay in the farmhouse during your internment." The farmhouse and the farm were located within the confines of the Palazzo. The farmer who managed the farm was thousands of miles away, and a soldier stationed north of Stalingrad, Russia. The German, Italian, and Romanian troops had been encircled at Stalingrad by the Russian Army for over three months. A custodian was left in charge of the Palazzo.

The farm within the Palazzo was not the only one devoid of its farmers. In fact, most farms in Southern Italy had not been cultivated for over two years. All, or most of the young and middle-aged farmers, were in faraway lands, from Libya to Russia, fighting wars. There were many broken-hearted women in small and big towns. These towns became women-dominated and past traditions, such as men's jealousy, honor, revenge, crimes of passion, etc., were forgotten/ignored.

The farmhouse was in the middle of nowhere. The town, also, was in the middle of nowhere, remotely carved into the hills in Basilicata. The Palazzo itself was separated from the farmhouse by a garden surrounding a swimming pool, like Sergio's or Ramiro's garden. Mario would have access only to the library. Thus, his world was confined to the farmhouse. The farmhouse was a typical one consisting of barns on the side of the house, but no animals at that time. On the ground floor, the kitchen and dining room were separated by a wall. The bedroom, with large windows, had a splendid view of the farm from the second floor. A wooden picnic table took up most of the patio outside the farmhouse. The only redeemable feature of the place was that he could walk to City Hall and sign the register every morning, maintaining his privacy among friends-to-be! He planned to get to know people in town. He had a feeling that he would like them since the neighborhood in Avella where he had lived got along very well with shepherds and farmers.

Politically, Main Street in Tito was more homogenized. Shepherds and farmers dominated both ends of Main Street. Communist and Fascist sympathizers were sprinkled here and there but never amounted to a "hill of beans" in many parts of town. They were not able to rally their respective troops, since were not enough of them to make a difference politically. Also, the War stretched Italy to the limit in terms of manpower and armaments. The well had run dry. People knew that, as the food was getting scarcer by the day. The few farmers around town had a bigger problem, no farmhands.

Finally, Sofia and Mario had a moment to themselves. After the exhaustive day, the two of them retired on the terrace, above the bedroom, and gazed at the stars. It was a lonely place in the middle of nowhere with no one around. The only pleasant visitor in the evenings was the cooling breeze from the Tyrrhenian Sea replacing that daytime hot, suffocating air from the Sahara Desert, referred to as the Sirocco of the Sahara Desert. When it rained, it deposited small sand particles from the Sahara Desert. Folklore stories of yesteryear told that this weather condition drove people to insanity. However, the sea breeze reverses the wind directions in the fall as the Siberian cold wind tries to warm up along the Southern shores of Italy. Mario and Sofia missed their children terribly as well as The Four Musketeers their family and friends. Sofia declared with vigor that she and the children were determined to visit every weekend to run the household.

The next morning, Mario accompanied Ramiro and Sofia to the train station in Tito. They embraced and parted. The occasion didn't call for much talking. They were left to their own thoughts. Mario thought: "The old man is a man of his word and a true sentimentalist." Sofia had peace of mind, since she knew Mario was in good hands locally due to Ramiro. As for the old man, he was happy to put the young couple at ease with the family situation. By and large, internment was not much of an encumbrance to Mario's family, but an inconvenience. He tried to imagine what the children or Sofia would say at the train station when they would arrive for the weekend. He had so many questions to ask and yet he was gone for only a couple of days. One pressing need was to secure some food before the family arrived. Mario contacted Pasquale the following morning when he went to City Hall to sign the register and inquired as to whom to see about food.

The Palazzo was separated from the farm by the garden with the pool. Courtesy of Salvatore Morelli.

Without hesitation, Pasquale suggested that he should see the local barber in the Piazza, known in town as Bambolone, meaning "big boy doll." Of course, everyone in town loved him. He got involved with everyone in town, from their love life to inconsequential things. The only problem with that was his house was across the Piazza where his wife had a good view of anyone coming and going from the shop. It raised havoc in his family. His wife was jealous of everyone, especially women, coming near him for consultation. However, Pasquale warned Mario not to call him Bambolone but Ottavio, short for Octavius. No one in town knew his real name. As a young man, Ottavio saw an opportunity to break away from the drudgeries of shepherding. He apprenticed in a barber shop as an assistant, since the barber's son wanted no part of the barbershop. Usually, apprenticeships were reserved for family members. In a way, Ottavio was lucky to latch on through this move briefly. derailed his plans to marry his fiancé, Carolina, whose mother, Strega, was the matriarch of their shepherd community. As a matriarch, she could not condone the marriage, since her first duty was to preserve and expand the community of shepherds. In cases like that, love always won over the personal obstacles of others. Eventually, they married and settled into the quarters above the shop.

Besides the normal day-to-day operation of the barbershop, Ottavio liked to gossip with his customers. The older men asked for a shave and the younger ones a haircut. There were no women clients. After a couple of years, he was drafted into the army and shipped to Libya to fight in the Ethiopian war. Most likely, Ottavio may have been transported there by one of the Naval ships in which Mario was a Naval officer. The army assigned Ottavio to one of the field hospitals where he learned the skills of a nurse. By the time he left the army, he had learned many skills and had become a true Figaro, skillful in many things but master of none.

At the time of Mario's time in Tito, the male population in the town was depleted, food was scarce, farms were unattended, and people were anxious for the next news about the war. The barbershop was becoming more of a psychology ward. Ottavio would console women whose boyfriends or husbands were away at war, American expatriates who made the mistake of returning to Tito, and people in general. He was a cheerleader and someone to lean on for comfort or sympathy. Besides performing barbershop chores, he was a matchmaker. Women would pass on messages to would-be suitors via Ottavio.

When Mario visited the barbershop, Ottavio already knew everything about him. The first thing he said to Mario was: "You can call me

Bambolone, but only you". He closed the shop and proceeded to walk Mario toward his mother-in-law Strega's house. She was still active as a matriarch. Her house consisted of two rooms: an all-purpose room on the ground floor and a bedroom one floor above. The downstairs room served as a kitchen and dining area and had an open fireplace where cheeses were made. The room was gloomy and the walls over the fireplace dark with soot. It looked more like a witch's hovel. Ottavio's family, which included his wife and two children, resided next to Strega's house. Whatever hard feelings there may have been between Ottavio and his mother-in-law in the past had evaporated away. On many occasions, Strega had to arbitrate arguments between Ottavio and his wife about women visiting the barbershop for consultations. She was happy to see Ottavio and it showed in their body language and in their manner of speaking with each other. Strega knew Mario was at her house in search of food. By then, Mario was the main topic of conversation in the shepherd community, as Pasquale's big mouth told Strega of Mario's special connection to the shepherd community in Avella. It was a small town. "What is the name of your mother-in-law? I can contact her. My people (shepherds) roam as far north as Avella," Strega blurted out. He realized that he needed the town's people more than they needed him, as he represented one more mouth to feed. Without the new friends he just met, he would go insane living in an isolated place like the Palazzo with no one around.

That Friday Mario went to the train station early in the morning knowing full well that Sofia and the children would not be there until around noon. He kept watching the clock above the train station entrance. In the meantime, he paced in and out of the station. Time became irrelevant as emotions took over. It seemed like an eternity for the train to arrive, but it finally did. Lena ran toward the platform and jumped into the arms of her papa. The little one, Carlo, trailed behind Lena and grabbed Papa's leg, wanting to be embraced as well, and Sofia stood stranded with the suitcases. They stood on that platform embracing each other, trying to make up for the lost time.

People waved and smiled, as the family walked on the cobbled street up to the Piazza. The locals were just as happy to see the family together. It completed, in their minds, their picture of Mario, like a dossier of the man. For them, the family was everything. News of the family's arrival spread up and down Main Street. At the entrance to the Palazzo, "Figaro" stood next to the circular fountain inviting himself to be with the family. He behaved like the acting mayor welcoming them since the locals hadn't seen the mayor in a while. It was a gesture to assure the family that Mario was in good hands. He informed Mario that some locals wanted to celebrate the arrival of the family so that all the children could frolic around the garden in the Palazzo. Permission from the Palazzo's custodian was secured for Sunday afternoon. How could Mario say no to such benevolence? Figaro was a mover and a shaker. When the family first arrived at the Palazzo, the children were excited to see the pool, the garden with grapevines and fruit trees, very similar to their grandfather Sergio's garden. Mario prepared a sumptuous lunch of macaroni with Porcini mushrooms and goat cheese and a side dish of snails. Watermelon, cherries, and apricots, just picked from the garden, were available for dessert. Sofia was impressed. Whatever concerns or worries about food evaporated in the hot and suffocating air from the Sahara. All four of them looked forward to the evening breeze and to gazing at the stars from the terrace.

Normally, the big meal in Italy is consumed right after noon. The hot air in Tito did not cooperate with the locals' natural inclinations or preferences. So, the big meal on Sunday was pushed to the evening hours, when the cool breeze would make its appearance. Ottavio, Pasquale, Strega, and a shepherd friend of Ottavio, Luigi, came to the farmhouse. They brought local wine, roasted rooster, all sorts of cooked vegetables, cheese, and their children. It was mind-boggling, given these times of hardship. There were children all over the place running around on the farm and in the garden. That was what the family needed, a feeling that things were normal.

Ottavio behaved like a master of ceremony. He loved to create happy occasions to dilute the sad period. At heart, the shepherd in him dominated his personality, he wanted to erase the War from people's minds and live as if war didn't exist. It reflected the mindset of most of the shepherds. He thought wars were meaningless and, therefore, he tried to create a beautiful atmosphere among people, right in the middle of town, isolated from the rest of the world. Ottavio was the ringmaster of the circus as well as the clown. In a toast to the hosts and guests, Pasquale invited Sofia and the children to visit Mario anytime, with no need to formally request permission through the perfect. He said with indignation, "You are one of us!" slamming his hand on the table. Pasquale assumed enormous responsibility which had no precedent then. They all drank to that.

With the coming of the fall season, dramatic news about the War broke out in the newspapers and radio throughout the world. British Field Marshal Bernard Montgomery stopped the invasion of German Field Marshal Erwin Rommel "The Desert Fox" into Egypt at the border with Libya, El Alamein. The combined Italian and German Armies were in full retreat to Tobruk, Libya. These two battles showed the world that the Axis armies were over-extended and beatable. There was a sigh of relief from the Allied Democracies. The specter of Dunkirk came back to haunt the German Army, just as Winston Churchill had envisioned.

The effect of these two battles had a tremendous impact on Fascists, especially in small towns. Now, Fascists could no longer "sit on the fence" and hope for the best, like the mayor or Maresciallo of Tito. Fascists became either more fanatic and died gallant and glorious deaths (according to their self-images), or they changed the shades of black on their shirts, to a more neutral color, politically, to confuse people of their former allegiances. Other Fascists took a hint from the results of the battles and left town altogether, to return in better times.

The Italian Army was in total shambles as the result of Stalingrad and El Alamein, with no hope of ever regaining its former strength, which was not that much to begin with. This meant that the populace in Italy took the brunt of the food shortage. Germany was not going to bail the Italian populace out of their misery. Germany had enough problems of its own. These turns of events produced dramatic changes at the local level. In one of the morning signing-ins, Pasquale informed Mario that, henceforth, he no longer needed to come to the registry every day. This type of internment was referred to as "Interno Libero," free internment.

Also, with the coming of early fall, the mindset of people in Tito and other small towns in Southern Italy was to prepare for the harvest. The problem at that time was that there weren't enough young farmhands to help with the harvest: corn, tomatoes, grapes, olives, apples, black cherries, hazelnuts, chestnuts, etc. Corn was probably the most important grain because the main diet of the people was three meals a day of polenta (corn grits). The absence of farmhands accentuated the shortage of food everywhere. Fortunately, there was not much to harvest in the farms inside Palazzo Colonna in Tito, or Palazzo Barone in Avella. Those farms were devoid of crops because no seeds had been planted in the spring, since no one was around. However, the grapes in the garden required harvesting.

This was a unique time in Fascist Italy. The top echelon leadership in government, either Fascist or traditional, were reluctant to make controversial decisions that may have affected their political careers in the future. Hence, they were just as happy having the underlings make those hard decisions. Pasquale understood that and so did Mario. Mario went through the motion of going through requests formally without expecting any response from City Hall. They operated in the usual Neapolitan way, with a nod and a wink. Mario desperately wanted to go home at harvest time to be with Sofia, his children, and his friends in Sergio's garden, just like in the old days.

He made a formal request to visit Avella with the purpose of helping with harvesting grapes on Sergio's "farm." Pasquale's reacted accordingly, "Can I come along?" They both laughed. "Of course," Pasquale replied and filed the request away so that no one could hope to find it in a waste basket. This way no one signed off on the request, as the staff at City Hall preferred. However, Mario was required to pay for the guard's extra duty, food, lodging, and travel costs. For him, it was a bargain, compared to the joy it would bring to his family and friends in Avella. Obviously, Pasquale learned a lot from Figaro. They were of the same kindred spirit, sentimentalists, softening the shock of internment, not only for Mario but also for other internees.

Word in town spread rapidly about Mario's coming home to visit. People welcomed any good news, especially after all those years of being careful of what to say publicly or being fearful of antagonizing the

Fascist regime. It was a new experience to be able to speak out. The Fascist thugs were no longer roaming the streets of Avella. Most of them had disappeared. Others did their best to cover their indiscretions of the past by leaving town. After the War, about 15,000 to 20,000 Fascists were hunted down by partisans/Communists and killed. Whatever minute administrative connection between Rome and small towns in the South ceased to exist. As such, these towns were on their own for survival. That also applied to internees residing in those towns. As far as the peasants, that was good news, because they felt that only bad news came from Rome. Not hearing anything from Rome was therefore a plus.

Emilio, Sofia and the children, The Four Musketeers, Mario's sisters, school friends, and some townspeople came to the train station in Avella to welcome Mario and the hired guard, who generously kept his distance. The guard didn't want to spoil the reception by intruding, portraying authority, or being an enforcer of Fascist rule; though those were what he was paid to do, he chose to present himself as a bystander. He was in no-man's-land, not here and not there. During the long train ride, he and Mario got along very well and arrived at the understanding that he would be out of sight of the towns' people. He would sleep in the Carabinieri's barracks. Normally, guards were required to be in full sight of a prisoner, even during sleep time.

The moment was magic. The grapes cried to be picked, but no one paid attention to them. The people in Sergio's garden were concentrating only on each other's company. Don Nicola was bubbling with emotions in wanting to tell Mario all about what had happened in town since his departure. Mario's parents were so proud of their son that they followed him wherever he went. Mario profusely thanked Ramiro for making his stay at Tito livable, with an opportunity to meet new friends. Sergio, the master of ceremony, was meticulous in arranging everything "just so." Imalda, forever the protector, had a watchful eye on the children, who were running all over the garden. The sisters and Sofia gathered in one corner to gossip. Erminio was as bubbly as his champagne served to the guests. All of them had one thought in mind, "When is Mussolini going away?" In fact, a short time later, King Victor Emanuel III declared, in Mussolini's presence, "You are the most hated person in Italy." The question then that continues to be asked to this day is: "Why promulgate internment camps, then, when Fascism and its creator were so discredited in 1942-1943? Where was the logic?" The only plausible answer was that the few ministers surrounding Il Duce were rabid fanatics who fought tenaciously for their survival and to hold on to their power or else!

After a sumptuous dinner, Don Nicola, Ramiro and Emilio stood on the dining table and sang the beautiful melody, "Parlame D'Amore, Mariu," "Talk to Me of Love, Mariu," a cappella in honor of Sofia and Mario. The trio put a lot of emotion into it, to the point of evoking some moist eyes. They had rehearsed the singing at Don Nicola's studio, in secret. As in life, all good or bad things come to an end. Mario and Sofia's good dreams were short-lived. Nightmares created by Il Duce seemed to go on forever, but the end appeared to be near. Mario had to return to Tito which was uncomfortable, with Sofia's visits with the children, made it tolerable.

The War in Libya reached a stalemate, localized between Tobruk and El Alamein. The Axis Armies were under the command of General Rommel and that the Allies under General Montgomery. Both Armies now lacked sufficient manpower or firepower to induce a breakthrough either way. After Dunkirk, the British Army was not in any position to dictate the pace of war in Libya but was still strong enough to repel Rommel at El Alamein. The German High Command treated the Libyan campaign as a secondary front, just to keep the Allied Army away from the European fronts. The purpose of the German Afrika Korps was to prevent the routing of the Italian Army by the British. The Italians were ill equipped for desert warfare.

Rommel strongly disagreed with the German General Staff about the Libyan strategy. He proposed that Berlin increase his Afrika Korps from three to twenty-five divisions. He planned to cut through Egypt to the Middle East on the way to Georgia, Russia, and open a front to relieve Stalingrad. According to Rommel, food and oil supplies were there for the taking and the weather was ideal for tank warfare. It was a bold plan but not a unique one. Alexander the Great had a similar plan but on the way to India. The plan was not approved for the simple fact that German troops were already tied down from Scandinavia to North

Africa (including Russia and the Balkans). However, it was just a matter of time before the curtain on the German and Italian Armies would be pulled down in Libya. The American Army, under the command of General George S. Patton, entered the fray, landing in Morocco. It took a "tank" man, Patton, to chase another one, Rommel, out of North Africa.

EIGHT

Plight of Internment Camps

On the same day that Italy declared war on the Western Democracies, June 10, 1940, the Fascist regime ordered the internment of anyone judged to be 'dangerous' for the nation, including political opponents, foreign Jews, nationals of 'enemy states,' gypsies and many others. About 350–400 gypsies were sent to internment camps in Southern Italy. The internment camps/towns were mainly located in Central and South of Italy. From a census taken by the Italian government in the spring of 1943 for the International Red Cross, of the 9,000 civilians who were interned at that time in Italy, 44.5% were in the North, 24.5% in Central, and 31% in the South of Italy. The census of 1943 could not possibly be accurate. By then, most internees in Southern Italy were not required to register at City Halls in view of the impending demise of Fascism. Hence, Magistrates destroyed whatever records that purported the existence of internees in their towns. Modern mayors have even denied their existence because no records of them were found at City Hall dating to 1943. Thus, the percentage assigned to Southern Italy may be an underestimate.

In 1938, about 51,000 Jews resided in Italy: 41,300 of them Italian and 9,800 foreigners. The number of foreign Jews, who risked expulsion, if they had not left Italy by March 12, 1939, increased to about 11,200. Approximately 10,000 foreign Jews were ordered to leave Italy. Most of them managed to leave the country, but just over 4,000 found themselves in Italy when the arrest warrants were issued in May 1940. European Jews soon fled from Nazism and arrived in the territories under Italian control (Yugoslavia, Greece, Albania and North Africa). Also, groups of people of other religions were placed in internment camps. In 1940, when the internment machine revved up, there were about 3,800 non-Italian Jews in Italy. Four thousand more would arrive when numerous groups had already been interned in territories controlled by Italy, such as in Libya, Slovenia, Dalmatia, Albania and the Dodecanese. In summary, about 8,000 foreign and 400 Italian Jews were interned throughout Italy.

On June 15, 1940, the Ministry of the Interior (a member of the Grand Council of Fascism) ordered the arrest of all German, Polish, Czechoslovakian, and stateless Jews between the ages of 18 and 60 and transferred them to internment camps. The women and children were to be removed from their places of residence and sent to remote small villages, where they were to be in "free internment" under police supervision. There is no proof of any discussions on record between the Italian and the German authorities about the disposition of those internment camps.

The affected people were taken from their quarters by the police, early in the morning, and brought to the Questura office of the Questore (chief of Police). Many hours passed before they were delivered to the local prison, where they were placed in proximity with each other as well as with common criminals. Frequently the cells were overcrowded, lacking the most basic sanitary facilities, and infested with lice and fleas. Probably most oppressive of all was the uncertainty about what the Italian authorities intended. Only during transport did many prisoners recognize that they were traveling south and not being deported to the German border. Prison was viewed as a very bad experience. In contrast, the ensuing internment meant a clarification, relief, and improvement of their situation.

The Italian "internment camps" for civilian internees were somewhat similar only in name to the German concentration camps. There was only one barrack camp built for internment, located at Ferramonti di Tarsia, North of Cosenza in the Calabria region. In all other instances, requisitioned or rented buildings were used: cloisters, hospices, camps, large movie houses, and empty villas that could accommodate from 30 to 200 people. In the months prior to liberation, only the Ferramonti-Tarsia camp contained more than 2,000 internees, including approximately 1,500 Jews. Documents from the Ministry of the Interior in March 1942 revealed the existence of 25 internment camps/towns where foreign Jews were held. Between 1940 and 1943 the total number of those camps never exceeded 40.

The internment towns located farthest south of Italy were Campagna in Salerno, Alberobello and Gioia del Colle in Bari, and Ferramonti di Tarsia (barrack camp), in Cosenza Provinces. Only in 12 places were Jews separated from other foreigners. There was a total of seven separate women's internment towns: Lanciano in Chieti, Pollenza, Treia, and Petriolo in Macerata, Vinchiaturo and Casacalenda in Campobasso, and Solofra in Avellino Provinces. They had been built in part to hold prostitutes, who were considered potentially guilty of espionage because of their association with the military. They also housed women who had been registered as politically unreliable in official dossiers. In the internment decree of 4 September 1940, it was expressly noted, "The internees are to be treated humanely and protected against offense and force." With few exceptions, this principle was followed, and there were no differences noticed in the treatment of Jews and non-Jews. Methodical atrocities and torture, common in the German concentration camps, were not known in Italy. There were, however, isolated individual instances of beating, kicking, and slapping, usually the result of a lack of self-control by Italian guards. Such behavior met the disapproval of the camp directors, who transferred personnel for such incidents.

The relationship of the camp commandants and guards with the Jews who had found refuge in Italy was relaxed, whereas their relationship with Yugoslavs, Greeks, and Corsicans, deported for political reasons, was harsher. Resistance by the latter was sometimes suppressed with force, or even using firearms. The internment decree also permitted the free practice of religion.

Nevertheless, internment meant severe restrictions on personal freedom, like a prison. People were separated from their families, apartments, and familiar social and occupational surroundings. They were arbitrarily put together, depending upon the capacity of the camp. The camps were guarded, though many had no barbed wire. Only for urgently needed medical treatment was an exit permit issued. Resistance to camp regulations usually led to transfer to a stricter camp for political prisoners on one of the islands off the Italian mainland, like the island of Lipari, twenty miles North of Sicily. That is the largest of a chain of islands in a volcanic archipelago situated between the well-known volcano of Vesuvius and Etna. As a rule, the internees were not permitted to work but received for their maintenance a daily allowance of 6.50 lire (about one dollar in today's value), an amount that was scaled to the needs of the poor rural populace and was increased several times to compensate for the progressive inflation. The allowance barely sufficed for food and left hardly anything for the replacement of worn-out clothing and other items of daily need. A priest in the Ferramonti internment camp would sometimes bring them money, which they used to buy goods on the black market. By late 1942, the subsidies were terminated in most Southern Italian camps.

The deplorable hygienic conditions and the shortage of heating in winter months frequently led to illness, and many internees suffered permanent damage to their health. Considering the monotony of camp life and the isolation from normal surroundings described in diaries and records of that time, the situation of the internees was miserable and humiliating. This can be confirmed, although many reports written later under the impact of news about the Nazi extermination camps make the Italian situation sound relatively bearable.

In October 1940, there were 2,412 foreign Jews in internment camps and in "free internment," while 1,365 still lived in their homes. According to reports by the prefects, by the end of 1942, the number of internees increased to 5,636 (2,139 in camps and 3,497 in villages). By the time of Mussolini's fall on 25 July 1943, the number reached almost 6,000 to which, in addition, more than 2,000 people living at home must be added. Only two days after the announcement of the Armistice on 8 September 1943, which included an agreement on the suspension of the internments, the Questore, in a telegram to the prefects, ordered the release of all aliens. They were given the choice of returning to their former place of residence in Italy or of remaining at the place of internment and continuing to accept a daily living allowance. During the general chaos, in conjunction with disarming the Italian Army, the telegram probably never reached all the prefectures and offices of the prefects. Most Jewish internees interned in Southern Italy decided to remain there since there was still a war in Northern Italy.

INTERNMENT IN THE TOWN OF CAMPAGNA

There were two camps in Campagna. The town is located about 30 km (20 miles) due east of the city of Salerno in the Picentine Hills of the Cilento area. It is about 5 miles north of Eboli. The criteria for the location of such camps were that the sites should be remote and, therefore, relatively isolated, not near ports, important roads, railway lines, airports, or munitions factories. Campagna met those criteria and the prefect of Salerno proposed two monasteries in the town to be inhabited by internees: the Convent of the *Osservanti dell'Immacolata Concezione* and the Dominican monastery of San Bartolomeo, both of which had already had some very non-clerical use in that they had been used as training facilities and barracks for officer candidates in the Italian Army. The San Bartolomeo monastery was built in the 1400s on a steep slope of the Girolo Hill in the valley near the Atri River. At the time, the building had three floors and sufficient room for 450 people plus guards. The *Concezione (conception) Convent* dates to the 1500s and was somewhat smaller than the monastery. The camps were for men only.

The internment camps were established in 1940. There were 430 internees captured in different parts of Italy. The number varied between 230 (February 1941) and 150 (September 1943). Most of them were Jewish refugees from Germany, Austria, Poland, Czechoslovakia, and Dalmatia. In the group, there were also some British citizens and a group of 40 French and Italian Jews. Internees were allowed to receive food parcels, and none of them was killed, subjected to violence, or deported to the infamous Nazi death camps in the North. Prisoners were allowed to organize a library, school, and theater. They could receive aid from DELASEM, Delegation for the Assistance of Jewish Emigrants. This was an Italian and Jewish resistance organization that worked in Italy between 1939 and 1947. It is estimated that during World War II, DELASEM was able to distribute more than $1,200,000 in aid, of which nearly $900,000 came from outside Italy.

The San Bartolomeo Church is immediately adjacent to residential buildings in what was (and still is) a small mountain town; prisoners were apparently at liberty to wander around and make friends with the populace and even accept hospitality, such as meals. Two inmates died of illness in three years and were buried in the local cemetery with Jewish rites. There were two rabbis among the detainees. A few inmates were also doctors who provided medical attention. Inmates had a soccer team that played against local amateur teams, and they had a camp bulletin. Also, a small synagogue was set up in San Bartolomeo church. For a while, a pianist among the prisoners played the organ for Christian services on Sundays.

While the Jewish internees did have a curfew to adhere to, they had the same rations as the local population. The camp was never a concentration camp in the German sense of the term. Internees were allowed to receive food parcels and visit sick relatives. In addition, there were no mail restrictions. None of the internees was killed or subjected to violence. In fact, the internees were constantly protected from deportation to Germany, as the Nazis often requested. Local Fascist authorities kept the activities hidden from the higher authorities. In September 1943 Italy capitulated. However, during the retreat of the German Army from Sicily in August of 1943, a German Major asked permission from Madre Superiore (Director of the Convent) to "inspect" the San Bartolomeo Convent, as possible quarters for German officers. The Major promised to be back the next day. That evening, all the internees fled to the mountains with the help of the guards, nuns and the locals. Upon inspection, the Major decided that the Convent was not suitable for officer quarters. That was not the last attempt by German troops to enter the convent. Days before the German Army retreated from Salerno, the same Major returned to the convent. But this time, he didn't ask for permission. Soldiers just forced their way into the convent.

For whatever reason, religious or woman's intuition, the nuns antici-
pated that the Major would return and prepared for it. The internees
came back from the hills, when the Germans finally retreated North.
The camp operated from June 16, 1940, to September 8, 1943. Thereafter, the guards walked away to join their families in town. The
internees were free to leave anytime, as there were no guards. Most of
them chose to stay put until the end of the War, which was still going on
north of the Alps.

Starting in 1942, Nazi Germany established extermination or death
camps for the sole purpose of carrying out the industrialized murder of
the Jews of Europe. These camps were established in occupied Poland
and Belarus. Millions of Jews would die in these extermination camps,
primarily by poison gas, usually in gas chambers, although many prisoners were killed in mass shootings and by other means. These death
camps, including Belzec, Sobibor, Treblinka, and Auschwitz-Birkenau
are commonly referred to as concentration camps, but scholars of the
Holocaust draw a distinction between concentration camps and death
camps. After 1942, many small sub-camps were set up near factories to
provide forced labor. In 1942, IG Farben established a synthetic rubber
plant at Auschwitz III (Monowitz), and other camps were set up near
airplane factories, coal mines, and rocket fuel factories. The conditions
were brutal, and prisoners were often sent to the gas chambers or killed
if they did not work fast enough.

INTERNMENT CAMP IN FERRAMONTI DI TARSIA

The only camp in Southern Italy for both men and women were located
in Ferramonti di Tarsia where, starting in late 1940, family barracks were
built, but these were not large enough to unite all families separated
during internment. Ferramonti was the largest internment camp in
Southern Italy established in the summer of 1940. They stretched over
an area of 16 acres and were made up of 92 shacks of various sizes, many
of them built in the classic "U" shape and equipped with kitchens,
latrines, and common sinks. The Italians began building Ferramonti on
June 4, less than a week before Italy entered World War II. The arrest of
Jews began on June 15, and prisoners began arriving at the camp on

June 20. From 1940 to 1943, over 3,800 Jews were imprisoned at the camp: 3,682 were foreign-born Jews, and 141 were Italians. In general, Italian-born Jews were not imprisoned unless they participated in anti-Fascist activities. At first, the physical conditions at the camp were not too bad. Prisoners slept on wooden planks in their designated barracks, and each was assigned a mattress, a pillow, two blankets, two sheets, and a towel upon arrival. The distribution of quinine – essential for the treatment of malaria – was prohibited, although this measure was later amended.

A study completed as early as 1941 in Ferramonti di Tarsia provides information about the nationality, native language, and religion of the internees. At that time, 38.5 percent were Germans and Austrians (the latter probably in the majority), 29.6 percent Poles, 22.4 percent stateless persons, 5.9 percent Czechs and Slovaks, and 3.6 percent other nationalities. Some 65.1 percent indicated German as their native language, 13.0 percent Yiddish, 10.1 percent Polish, and 11.7 percent specified a total of 11 other languages. Based on religious affiliation, there were 93.0 percent Jews, 6.2 percent Catholics, 0. 7 percent Protestants, and 0. 2 percent non-denominations.

The camp was located about twenty miles North of Cosenza, Calabria region of Southern Italy, the "boot." It had been erected on a swampy, mosquito-infested site near the Crati River. After heavy rain in winter and spring, the terrain turned into mud, and temperatures around 104 degrees F prevailed in the summer.

According to an American report written after liberation, from the time of the 124 arrival of the first internees in June 1940 to the end of 1943 there were 820 cases of malaria and 109 of jaundice. Fortunately, the type of malaria was not severe or fatal, so no deaths resulted, but it suffices to imagine that the feverish victims lay for weeks on their cots without having the necessary nourishment or sufficient medications. Altogether 37 persons died from illnesses, which was not much higher than the average among the local population.

Ferramonti was under the direction of a Police Chief (Questore), who was directly responsible to the Fascist Minister of the Interior in Rome. Under this supervision a self-governing system was developed by the internees which, as surprising as it may seem in a Fascist country, was based on democratic principles. A meeting of the barrack representatives was held to elect the camp spokesman and the people responsible for the various commissions such as those for health, school, and culture. The camp administration granted considerable latitude to prisoner self-government and was basically concerned (or fearful) that the Ministry of the Interior would intervene.

Gradually the internees set up a school, a kindergarten, a pharmacy, a medical station, three synagogues, one Catholic and one Greek-Orthodox chapel (for the deportees arriving from Greece after 1941). With donations from a private philanthropic relief organization in Milan, a concert grand piano was acquired. An active cultural life developed, with theatrical performances and musical events that were attended by police officials along with their wives and children. Five marriages were also celebrated in Ferramonti di Tarsia, frequently motivated in part by the wish to obtain one of the sought-after family barracks, and 25 children were born there.

With the increase in the number of internees and the presence of diverse groups in terms of language and religious orientation (there were Orthodox and Reform Jews), the Jewish community of the camp formed an internal parliament representing the members of the various barracks. Camp management supported the internal organization which provided significant cultural and sporting activities that helped to mitigate the extreme difficulties of life due to the presence of malaria and the scarcity of food.

However, as the situation of the Jews went downhill, so did the living conditions. Despite all this, Ferramonti was never a concentration camp like those that the Nazis ran. The relationship between the prisoners and camp staff was rather peaceful. The prisoners were not tortured or executed, and they were allowed to receive packages of food, visit sick relatives, and participate in cultural activities.

The prisoners at Ferramonti were released on September 4, 1943, six weeks after Mussolini was overthrown by his own Fascist Grand Council.

The year 1943 was the most difficult for Ferramonti, but also the one that saw its liberation. Between August and September 1943, the German Hermann Göring Army Division, retreating from Sicily, passed a few meters from the camp. To avoid danger, the guards ordered the evacuation of the Camp, and all the internees who could fled to the surrounding countryside and were hosted by the farmers of the territory of Tarsia. To avoid Nazi intrusion and to protect the ones who remained in the camp because they were too old or sick, a yellow flag was hoisted at the entrance of the Camp with the presence of a priest to explain to the Germans the presence of a typhus epidemic inside. Thanks to these stratagems, Ferramonti was unscathed by the retreating German troops.

Even though the Ferramonti camp was freed by the British in September 1943, many inmates remained there in the ensuing years. Chronologically, it was the first concentration camp for Jews to be freed and the last to be formally closed. A total of 38 Jews and 5 Gentiles lost their lives during the period spent in Ferramonti. Ironically, the only internees to die from machine gun fire were those from an Allied plane that flew over the camp and mistook it for a hostile military site. The aircraft fired on the occupants, killing four people and injuring 16 others at the end of August 1943. After September 8, the Italian guards left the camp, and, on the morning of September 14, 1943, the first British military trucks entered the camp. The camp was officially closed on December 11, 1945.

It was, perhaps, also Ferramonti's location in Italy's deep South, far away from Rome's radar, that kept people safe. People there were unaware of the atrocities happening in camps, such as Auschwitz in Poland. Though inmates went hungry, nobody starved. Being imprisoned at Ferramonti is also believed to have saved Jews from deportation to other camps, including Auschwitz.

INTERNMENT IN THE TOWNS OF
POTENZA/BRIENZA/TITO

There were three internment camps in the Potenza Province: Potenza itself, Tito, and Brienza. However, according to Elizabeth Bettina's book, *It Happened in Italy*, the mayor of Potenza denied the existence of an internment camp there, although there were as many as 450 internees in town. This is a huge problem in identifying internment camps in Southern Italy, especially in the Basilicata region. In fact, one former internee couldn't find any records of daily registration at the police barracks or in City Hall in Tito after the War. According to Bettina's book, birth certificates were the only proof that Jewish internees indeed lived among the populace of Potenza and Tito during the War. It is surmised that there may be more situations like Tito's in Southern Italy. The only record of Tito even existing in an internment camp is found in Bettina's book. The camps, more like internment towns, in the Basilicata region, were modeled after the town of Aliano, where Carlo Levi was interned. The internees paid their way for food and lodging in 1935. For the other internments mentioned here, the internees received subsidies from the state until 1942.

Most of the farmlands in the area near Potenza were owned by the Colonna family. Count Colonna di Stigliano (Don Prospero) was related, by marriage, to Ramiro Alvarez in Avella. Besides Potenza and Tito, the town of Brienza also hosted Jewish internees. However, there is even less information about Brienza. It is a small town in the province of Potenza, west of Tito and the city of Potenza. Whatever information previously gathered about the town; it was convoluted with the battle of Potenza in late September 1943. When the internees first arrived in Brienza, a policeman escorted them and even carried their bags into a small apartment. As in Tito, internees reported and registered at the police station or City Hall as required every day. Usually, after a couple of days, they were told not to come again and register! That may explain why there are no records of internees in that town.

The Germans came through Potenza, after the retreat of the German Army from Sicily on August 11, 1943. Italian men were forced to dig ditches and perform other manual labor. The main purpose of Germans being in Potenza was to protect the retreat of the German Army. Canadian troops captured Potenza in late September, coinciding with the invasion of Salerno by the Allies on September 9, 1943. Each time the Germans came through a town inhabited by internees, the internees fled to the mountains for about a week or so, or if the food lasted. They stayed in the loft of a barn with goats and other cattle beneath them, for example. Through all this turmoil, not one Italian informed on or spied on internees to the Germans. Internees made several Italian friends, including some prominent families. At this point, the locals began to tire of German occupation and let their guards down; however, it wasn't wise for some internees to ever speak German, since German soldiers were in town. At the time of the battle of Potenza, there were internees living in Potenza, Tito and Brienza, although there were German soldiers all around those towns. In one particular incident in Brienza, there was a non-Italian Jewish family interned in town and the daughter had long blond hair. She looked Germanic. One day, she and a friend were walking and two German officers commented on how Aryan she looked. They had to pretend that they were Italian and non-German-speaking so that no questions could be asked of them. However, there was a happy ending to this incident. The German officer's interest was only of the amorous kind. One of the girls and one of the German officers married after the War in Italy. It was a war report that revealed the existence of Jewish internees in Brienza. How many more internment towns were there like Brienza?

During the Salerno invasion by the Allied Armies, the British dropped a warning bomb, causing minor injuries. They also dropped leaflets to warn the citizens ahead of time of the impending Allied attack on Potenza. With the fall of Italy's Fascist regime coinciding with the invasion of Salerno by the Allies, the Italian Army surrendered to the Allies. Italian soldiers stationed in Southern Italy fought on the side of the Allied Army. The ones in the North or under German control declared neutrality, but die-hard Fascist soldiers fought alongside the German Army. Badoglio and the King of Italy never considered the plight of the Italian soldiers, spread all over Europe, when they signed the Armistice. They were short-sighted. They couldn't see past their noses. The occupation of Italy was divided into two regions. The North and Central part was occupied by the Germans under General Rommel, and the Southern part was occupied by the Allies. Internees, living in towns in Southern Italy, decided to remain there until the War was over because there was still a War North of the Alps. Nevertheless, they were free to emigrate anywhere in the world. Many of the prisoners in the North and Central regions did not have that option. They were shipped to extermination camps.

INTERNMENT CAMPS IN NORTHERN ITALY

According to the most recent research, 6,815 Jews were deported to extermination camps from Central and Northern Italy by the Nazis, of whom only 799 survived. The German occupation radically altered the situation for the remaining 43,000 Italian Jews living mostly in the northern half of the country. The Nazis quickly established an SS and police apparatus, in part to deport Italian as well as foreign Jewish internees to Auschwitz-Birkenau.

Deportations from Italy, 1943-1945

In October and November 1943, German authorities rounded up Jews in Rome, Milan, Genoa, Florence, Trieste, and other major cities in Northern Italy. They established police transit camps at Fossoli di Carpi, approximately 12 miles north of Modena, at Bolzano in northeastern Italy, and at Borgo San Dalmazzo, near the French border, to assemble internees in one location prior to deportation.

In general, these operations had limited success, due in part to advance warning given to the Jews by Italian authorities and local people, and in part to the unwillingness of many non-Jewish Italians, including Salò police authorities, to participate in or facilitate the roundups. Salo was the capital of the new Fascist government under

Mussolini. For example, of approximately 10,000 Jews in Rome, German authorities were able to deport less than 1,100. From the camps, the Germans deported 4,733 Jews to Auschwitz-Birkenau, of whom only 314 survived. Of the 45,000 Italian Jews counted in Mussolini's census in 1938, about 8,000 died in Nazi camps. About 7,000 managed to flee and 30,000 lived in hiding before being liberated by Allied troops.

SUMMARY

A woman internee said, during a question-and-answer period after her presentation to a Jewish audience in Ferramonti di Tarsia, "I would not be here in Ferramonti, if not for Italians." She then added, "An Italian woman hid me, an Italian priest put me in a convent where I wore a nun's habit, and an Italian boy risked his life to bring us food. These are the kinds of people you find in Southern Italy."

A man in the audience who said his family was interned in an Italian camp for several years, also stood to describe his experiences, saying, "If the Italians hadn't taken us to their internment camp, we would have been sent to the German extermination camp, and would have been killed."

Michele Sarfatti, the author of several books on Italian Fascist anti-Semitism, said a higher percentage of Italy's Jews survived the war than their counterparts in all other European countries. Italian culpability for the persecution of Jews remains relatively unknown, and largely unacknowledged by Italians. Professor Pavan said, "People were made destitute, and turned into ghostly non-entities in their own country. This is also true."

NINE
End of Fascism

P eople in Avella or Tito didn't have to read the newspapers to learn the status of the War in North Africa in early 1943. Food was becoming more and more scarce, dried chicory replaced coffee beans, not many dogs and cats roamed in the streets, farms were abandoned, no more passeggiata in the evenings, no more young men, etc. The mayor of Tito, a Fascist, left town never to return. No one knew his whereabouts. Terrible atrocities in German and Russian concentration camps were beginning to be reported, but not yet confirmed in newspapers and on the radio. Sofia's visits to Tito were becoming fewer and fewer, as train schedules were becoming more and more problematic due to daily bombing from Allied planes. She did go with the children for Christmas of 1942. Mario, with the help of Ottavio, put together a presepio (a nativity scene with small statuettes) for the children to see. Ottavio and two other shepherds played the bagpipes on Christmas day. Allied bombing loomed larger and larger on the minds of Mario and Sofia for, sooner or later, Sofia and the children had to return to Avella. The War was edging closer and closer to home.

The first two years of the War in North Africa were characterized by chronic supply shortages and transport problems spanning from Egypt to Tunisia. The coastline stretched for approximately 1300 miles with few ports to unload soldiers and supplies: Alexandria, Benghazi, Tobruk, and Tripoli. Hence, control of the central part of the coastline was contested by the British and Italian navies, which were equally matched and exerted a reciprocal constraint on supplies through those ports. As such, a stalemate between the warring armies was reached. With the entry of the US Army into the North African theater, the balance of supplies, armaments and soldiers swung over to the Allies. It was just a matter of time before the American soldiers adapted to desert warfare and could help the Allied efforts. The Americans had paid a heavy price for the lessons of war at the Kasserine Pass located between Algeria and Tunisia.

The German and Italian Armies were in full retreat to the port of Tunis, about 100 miles from Sicily. They were surrounded in Tunisia from the east by the British Eighth Army commanded by Field Marshal Bernard Montgomery and from the west by the US II Corps commanded by Lieutenant General Lloyd Frendendall. American soldiers were trained on "Simulated war games" back in the States. In February of 1943, they were confronted by a German Army consisting of soldiers from the Afrika Korps and the Russian Front, veterans of at least two years. Thus, it was a whole different scenario from home in the States. Field Marshal Erwin Rommel of the Afrika Korps saw an opportunity to seize the American supply depot at Tebessa, Algeria, near the Tunisian border. His objective was to consolidate their military position in Tunisia and expedite an orderly retreat to Sicily. To reach Tebessa, the Afrika Korps had to advance through a narrow corridor of about one mile wide (referred to as the Kasserine Pass) in the Atlas Mountains. It was such a bold move that it came under heavy scrutiny of the German General staff. One view expressed the concern that because of limited manpower and equipment it put the Afrika Korps at risk. General Rommel argued for raiding the American supply base in order to gain time for a measured and orderly retreat.

On February 14, 1943, armored units from General Erwin Rommel's Panzer Army Afrika Korps launched an offensive directed against the Kasserine Pass, lightly held by inexperienced American troops with some British and French support. On February 19, a veteran German-Italian assault group smashed into the U.S. troops holding the pass. The German Panzer IV and Tiger tanks were vastly superior to the U.S. M3 light tanks and light anti-tank guns, and soon the Americans were retreating along the pass in disarray. The American soldiers were unprepared for the Axis onslaught, and the American General's staff was also taken aback by the surprise attack. Once through the pass, the Axis forces continued their advance, but severe winter weather, increasingly mountainous terrain, and stiffening Allied resistance slowed progress. Simmering disagreements between Rommel and his superiors as to how the advance should proceed now came to a head, and on February 22 the "Desert Fox" (Rommel) called off the offensive. Two days later, after an intense U.S. air attack, Allied troops reoccupied the pass.

Soon after the battle of the Kasserine Pass, the leadership of the US II Corps changed hands, when Lieutenant General George S. Patton took over the command. The rationale of the American General's staff was that it would take a "tank" man like Patton to defeat another "tank" man like Rommel. However, Patton was more than a "tank" man. He was also a poet and a scholar of ancient Greek and Roman classics and history. He was overheard at the site of the Roman ruins in Tunisia saying, "I have been here. Oh, how much I love being here. I can see where the Roman and Carthaginian Armies lined up in the Punic wars." He was never there before. He went on to add, "I got him.:" Of course, he was referring to Rommel, as both must have been of the same mind set. After the battle, there was only one option for the Axis Armies, and that was to exit as quickly as possible through the port of Tunis with as many soldiers and as much equipment as possible. On May 13th, about 300,000 German and Italian soldiers were taken prisoner. According to our estimate, 2-3 German and 4-5 Italian Army divisions escaped to Sicily, where they regrouped to defend the island.

This turn of events in North Africa shattered Mussolini's dream of becoming a modern-day Caesar. He was no longer that cocky, arrogant, self-assured man making extravagant speeches in Piazza Venezia. For the first time in his career, he was forced to listen to others as to how to remedy his disasters. Doubts began to surface, from the King of Italy down to the people in the streets. Ciano, his son-in-law, and Mussolini no longer trusted each other and rarely spoke to each other. Ciano was demoted from the post of Foreign Minister to the Ambassadorship to the Vatican. He was replaced by Giuseppe Bastianini in early 1943, former Ambassador to Britain, as payment for the "Dunkirk" imbroglio (see chapter five). Conspiracies and accusations among Fascist Ministers mushroomed overnight. The council of Fascist Ministers was polarized, pro or against Il Duce. In Mussolini's household, Donna Rachele, his wife, was taking over as the main advisor and supporter of Benito. He trusted no one else. Still, he believed in his dream.

At least the situation on Main Street in small towns got better. No longer did Fascist thugs roam the streets, intimidating the populace. Most Fascists denied that they were affiliated with fascism. They no longer wore Blackshirts. Others left town. In Tito, the mayor was nowhere to be found. He saw the handwriting on the wall long before anyone else and took off. No one knew where. The Maresciallo came out of hiding to show some form of authority. After all, the Questura, the Carabinieri Administration, did not fall under the jurisdiction of the Fascist government. Especially at that time, no one in Tito listened to what Rome had to say regarding anything. It is somewhat of a paradox that the internment camps in Tito, Campagna, Brienza, Potenza, and Ferramonti were still in operation since the authorities in those towns paid no attention whatsoever to Fascist authorities locally or from Rome. The only logical explanation is that the hard-core Fascist fanatics surrounding Mussolini enjoyed intimidating people into submission. This implied that the prefect exercised more and more authority over the towns in each Province, as Fascism was ebbing.

In Avella, both the mayor and Maresciallo were apolitical. As such, they were safe from the growing Partisan and Communist activities in the hills. As in Tito, Fascist thugs seemed to have disappeared. However, a day of reckoning was not too far away. Communists and Partisans kept score as to whom to do away with after the War, trial or no trial. Some sort of normalcy returned to small towns, but, still, no food, no young men, no commercial activities, etc. When flowers bloomed all over the mountains in 1943, it reminded the shepherds to shear wool from the sheep and drop them in a pool of water to get rid of fleas and ticks. Town people as well as those from Naples headed to the foothills to scavenge for fruits in farms left abandoned by farmers, and chicory and other edible plants growing along dirt roads by the farms. Also, they searched for snails among partition walls built of rocks and stones. Wooden sticks were jammed into small openings in the wall to drive the snails out in the open. Wild boars and other wild animals roamed the high grounds of the mountains, usually accessed mostly by shepherds. Hence, the shepherds led, by example, the solution to the food crisis.

As for Sergio, he was oblivious to the War, although he sensed that it could soon arrive in Avella. He participated in WWI, and he had no room in his mind for those memories. The mountains defined his world. His hands were full of worry about poachers in the mountains. In peaceful times, two days per week, he would inspect the wooden bridges, water distribution to town, and water purity and would also warn shepherds about taxation schedules. With the shortage of food, he spent more time in the mountains looking for poachers. Poachers placed metal traps to capture any animal, including sheep. In order to prevent any incidents between shepherds and poachers, Sergio was up on those mountains daily to remove traps on grasslands owned by shepherds. In town, butchers were selling at exorbitant prices, anything that looked like meat, as the butcher told people what kind of meat he was selling. It came down to who had the money to buy and who wouldn't ask too many questions for fear of knowing what meat it was.

By that time, the country was in no mood for levity. High fashions were out of style, the movie industry was non-existent, most opera houses closed, and, for the first time, fewer Neapolitan songs were being composed. Sofia, Filomena and Serafina reverted to knitting sweaters, securing wool from Imalda. Sofia stopped taking the train to Tito for fear of the train being bombed. Rumors in town placed Allied planes circling around the Bay of Naples and as far north as Livorno, the two biggest Italian Naval ports on the Tyrrhenian Sea. The Four Musketeers still got together as often as they could, more to check on each other to see how the others were holding up, food-wise. The uncertainty in the next turn of events in the War kept everyone anxious, except for the shepherds. Throughout their history, they have witnessed catastrophes in the valley, but nothing like what was yet to come.

With the coming of the summer season, Mario was getting more and more worried, as he hadn't heard from or seen Sofia and the children for over five months. News about the War rarely reached Tito. In Avella, at least, Don Nicola kept abreast of the latest political news and the War in North Africa. Tito was isolated from civilization. Also, the picturesque scenery in the mountains just accentuated Mario's loneliness. For a social outing, he would visit Ottavio for a haircut and shave, getting the latest gossip about the Maresciallo and the mayor's whereabouts. But it was not enough to distract him from concerns about his family and friends in Avella. He had no inkling about the threat of War locally and the possibility of it reaching Tito or Avella.

Allied reconnaissance planes circled the island of Sicily in early July. On July 9, 1943, the Allied Army invaded Sicily, code named Husky, from south of the island on a two-pronged attack. The Eastern Task Force was led by Field Marshal Sir Bernard Montgomery and consisted of the British Eighth Army. The American Seventh Army commanded by General George S. Patton attacked the western side of Sicily. The two task force commanders reported to Alexander as Commander of the 15th Army Group. Altogether about 8-10 Army divisions were involved in the invasion. The aim of the invasion was to cut off the retreat of the German Army at Messina. The Italian Army stationed in Sicily presented no threat to the Allies.

Italian Americans were very helpful in the planning and execution of the invasion of Sicily. The Mafia was involved in assisting the U.S. war efforts. Associates of Mafia boss, Salvatore (Lucky) Luciano in New York City, contacted numerous Sicilians to help the Naval Intelligence in finding maps of the harbors of Sicily and old snapshots of the coastline. Vito Genovese, his underboss, offered his services to the U.S. Army and became an interpreter and advisor to the U.S. Army military government in Naples. His rank was that of a Sergeant. He quickly became the Army's most trusted employee and was instrumental in replacing Fascist mayors with his "recommendations" throughout southern Italy. In some sense, it was like foxes guarding the chicken coops. Through the Navy Intelligence's contacts from Operation Underworld, the names of Sicilian underworld personalities and friendly Sicilian natives, who could be trusted, were obtained and used in the Sicilian campaign. The Joint Staff Planners (JSP) for the US Joint Chiefs of Staff drafted a report titled Special Military Plan for Psychological Warfare in Sicily that recommended the "Establishment of contact and communications with the leaders of separatist nuclei, disaffected workers, and clandestine radical groups, e.g., the Mafia, and giving them every possible aid." The report was approved by the Joint Chiefs of Staff in Washington on April 15, 1943.

Sicilians are very proud people. Their culture dates before ancient Roman and Etruscan civilizations. Sicily is to Italy what California is to the USA, the fruit basket of their countries, and more. Their view of "continental" Italy is that of a junior partner. They consider any police and soldiers' presence in Sicily, ordered by Rome, as either an interference in their lives or an invasion. They felt that way when Italian soldiers were stationed in Sicily. To add insult to injury, the so-called Italian invaders were accompanied by German soldiers. The relationship between the Axis soldiers and the Sicilians was rather strained, to say the least. The German Army didn't have to call for curfews at night. The streets were deserted by evening hours. No woman dared to walk in the streets at any time. The men would have sacrificed their lives to defend the honor of their women. According to a soldier from Avella stationed there, Sicilians would not share their delicious farm bread with any of the invaders.

The island was defended by about 200,000 Italian, 32,000 German troops, and 30,000 *Luftwaffe* ground staff. The main German formations were one Panzer Division, *Hermann Göring*, and the 15th Panzergrenadier Division. By late July, the German units had been reinforced, principally by elements of the 1st Parachute Division, 29th Panzergrenadier Division, and the XIV Panzer Corps, bringing the number of German troops to around 70,000. The Axis Army plan was for the coastal formations to form a screen to receive the invasion and allow time for the field divisions further back to intervene, as needed.

The invasion of Sicily had a deep psychological impact on Mussolini. During the evening of July 24 and the early hours of the 25th, the Grand Council of Fascism (equivalent to a cabinet of Ministers) met to discuss the immediate future of Italy. By now, Donna Rachele was the major force in the family and "in charge" of the government. She advised

Mussolini not to attend the meeting because nothing good could come of it. He attended anyway. While all in attendance were jittery about countermanding their leader, they could see that Mussolini was sick, tired, and overwhelmed by the military reverses suffered by the Italian military. He seemed to be looking for a way out of power. Grand Council member Dino Grandi proposed a vote of no confidence in Mussolini as leader of the Council and the party. A vote was held on the night of July 24-25, 1943, and passed with 19 votes for, 8 against, and one abstention. Among the 19 votes of no confidence was that of Mussolini's son-in-law Galeazzo Ciano, who had been the former Minister of Foreign Affairs. At that time, he was Ambassador to the Vatican. The motion was passed, with Mussolini barely reacting. Some Fascist extremists balked and would later try to convince Mussolini to have those who voted with Grandi arrested. Il Duce was simply mentally paralyzed, unable to choose any course of action.

However, the next morning, the 25th, Donna Rachele advised her husband, to arrest those 19 council members and not to report to the King about the Council meeting. She warned Benito that the King would have him arrested. Mussolini scoffed at the idea of being arrested. Groggy and unshaven, he kept his routine of a 20-minute meeting with the King, during which he normally updated Victor Emanuele on the current situation. After the presentation, the King said that he, Mussolini, was the most hated person in Italy. Also, the King informed him that General Pietro Badoglio would assume the powers of the Prime Minister and that the War was all but lost. Mussolini offered no objection. Upon leaving the meeting, he was arrested by the Carabinieri, who had been secretly planning a pretext to remove the leader for quite some time. They now had the Council vote of "no confidence" as their formal allowance, since the Interior Minister voted for the dismissal. The perfect and Questore reported directly to the Interior Minister. To what extent the King was the mastermind of the Council's vote is not clear.

However, the King could not have arrested Mussolini without that vote. There was no other precedent prior to July 25th to arrest the man. When news of Mussolini's arrest was made public, relief seemed to be the prevailing mood among the conspirators. There was no attempt by fellow Fascists to rescue him. The only remaining question was whether Italy would continue to fight alongside Germany or surrender to the Allies.

Park in Villa Savoia (Villa Ada today) in Rome where Mussolini was arrested, July 25, 1943. Courtesy of JCestepario.

News of the incarceration traveled at the speed of light. Large crowds in small towns and big cities gathered in their main Piazzas to celebrate. They thought that the nightmare was over and The buffoon, Il Duce, got what he deserved. In Avella, for the first time, Communists, Partisans, Socialists, and Social Democrats gathered in town to celebrate in the Piazza. The crowd extended to side streets cheering all words politicians spoke, as politicians came out of the woodwork. Suddenly, every politician was anti-Fascist, but people didn't care what they said. For a change, they were happy. All was forgiven, except that the Communists were preparing a "hi list" of Fascists. In ancient Rome, it was called the proscription list to do away with political opponents. In two thousand years not much had changed. The same gatherings were happening in Tito. On one hand, Mario envisioned the end of the internment. On the other hand, there was a War not too far from where he was. His main preoccupation was, "How do I escape from both of them, the town and the War?"

From the day Mussolini was incarcerated on July 25th, to September 8th, 1943, when Italy surrendered unconditionally to the Allies, it was a confusing time for Italians. How was it possible to jail the leader of one form of Fascism and still fight along with a leader of another form of Fascism, Nazism? What about all those Italian soldiers dispersed from Russia to North Africa? Who thought this out? Obviously, the King and Badoglio couldn't see past their noses. They had fled to Brindisi, Puglia, which was occupied by the Allies. So, who oversaw Rome? It proved what peasants have thought about Rome for generations. "They are a bunch of useless strunzi." Local administrations in small towns didn't know how to proceed in those 45 days. It was like living in no-man's-land, a feeling of not overseeing their own destinies. In the meantime, the German Army was at their doorsteps, hovering over them! On the one hand, they were relieved, but on the other, so hopeless.

As the War was raging in Sicily, there was much disagreement between Montgomery and Patton as to the conduct of Operation Husky. There are many books written about their disagreements on the battlefield. It came down, basically, to a conflict of personalities. The upshot of it was that the bird escaped from the cage. More than 100,000 Axis troops escaped through Messina to mainland of Italy. Axis troops "rented" ferry boats to travel at night from Messina to Calabria. Countless Italian troops were taken prisoners by the German Army and loaded on trucks to be deported to Germany for forced labor. They would be part of the vanguard of a new workforce in German factories geared for armaments. Contrary to other historic reports, the first imprisonment of Italian soldiers by the German Army occurred on August 17th, 1943, not on September 10th, 1943, in Rome, when Germany occupied Rome.

The retreating route of the German Army is illustrated in orange. The internment camps are highlighted in yellow. Italian soldiers were rounded up and loaded onto trucks heading North along the old Roman Road (see map). In ancient times, Rome imported salt, wheat, corn, oranges and other farm products from Sicily. The road from Sicily splits into a fork at the town of Lamezia, one toward a coastal road, which had been the original road since the Roman days, and the other toward the mainland, which was a relatively newer road. Thus, from Sicily to Lamezia, the German Army was traveling on the old Roman road. Caesar must have turned over in his grave since, in his heyday, he would not have allowed barbarians near Rome or Sicily. But this modern-day Caesar did!

The pace of the convoy of vehicles traveling north was necessarily slow, because Allied planes strafed them randomly from time to time and from place to place, such as rail lines, main roads, industrial centers, and Army and Naval stations. In fact, the internment camp at Ferramonti, which was located within a stone's throw of the old Roman road, was strafed by an Allied plane. The camp was mistaken for an Italian Army base. Fortunately, the internees scampered to nearby hills with the help of the guards and the local people. However, there were four casualties and 15-20 injuries. The internees left the barracks as soon as they heard from the local Carabinieri about the German convoy heading their way. German troops did show up at the barracks and inquired about its nature and purpose. It would have been devastating if the German troops decided to accommodate themselves there. A "cock and bull" story about a yellow fever pandemic was concocted to drive them away and no internee was rounded up. Most of the convoy traveling was done at night due to extremely hot weather and the strafing by Allied planes during the day. The weather in mid-August can be excruciatingly hot and sticky in the Calabria region. The Sahara Desert is the main culprit. The beaches of Lamezia must have seemed very inviting to the troops. It was as though every soldier riding in a vehicle stopped on those beaches to cool down. The pattern was always the same. No matter what type of vehicle, soldiers would park on the beach, take off their clothes and run nude into the seawater.

The twin brothers, Dimitri and Vladimir, born in Ukraine, were part of the convoy as designated truck drivers. They joined the German Army in the battle of Kiev in Ukraine. The German Army recruited Russian farmers who were disgruntled with the economic system of collectivization. Russian farmers were poorer after the implementation of the Communist policy because there was no incentive to produce more wheat. Collectivization aimed to integrate individual landholdings into state-controlled farms in order to increase food production for the urban population. It resulted in more shortages of food for all. In that sense, they all starved equally, a Communist credo. In fact, according to Gareth Jones, a journalist who was an adviser to former British Prime Minister David Lloyd George after WWI, there was a famine in Ukraine and millions of people died of starvation. Wheat produced there was shipped to Moscow. Russian soldiers, recruited by the German Army, soon learned that whether people died of starvation in Ukraine or at Nazi extermination camps made no difference. Either way, the victims didn't receive proper burial! The logical conclusion was that both governments, Nazism under Hitler and Communism under Stalin, were equally bad. The two brothers desperately wanted out after being sent to Sicily as part of the reinforcement group to the Afrika Korps from the Russian front.

The two brothers were assigned to drive a truck loaded with Italian soldiers. In addition to them, three other German soldiers served on guard duty, riding in the back of the truck with the prisoners. When they arrived at Lamezia, the beach was too inviting to bypass.

The truck was parked near the beach and the road junction. No sooner had the truck approached the beach, but the clothes came off, and the three guards on duty ran nude toward the water. That was the brothers' intent all along, to entice the guards to leave their posts. Vladimir shouted at the astonished prisoners, "Fuori," "Out!" The prisoners scampered North, South, and East of the junction. The brothers knew exactly where the German convoy was headed because they had the map for the destination, Salerno, Naples, and further north (see map). Their best chance of avoiding capture was to keep their distance as much as possible from the pre-planned route of the convoy. This meant that they should proceed along the Roman coastal road to the town of Sapri and then pivot East toward the mainland, arriving in the hills near Potenza. From there, they would have the time to re-examine what to do next. The hope was that there would be no German troops in the area of Potenza. However, as it turned out, that was a miscalculation. The Germans deployed a small contingent of soldiers in Potenza to protect the flank of the retreating German Army traveling along the modern coastal road to Salerno. The German Army feared that the Allies could have approached Potenza from Taranto, on the Adriatic Sea. The two brothers arrived at Sapri well ahead of the convoy and turned into a secondary road, walking along the foothills, avoiding the town of Brienza. They still were wearing German Army fatigues covered with oil and grease and did not want to raise a commotion in town with their conspicuous presence. Besides, Brienza was too close for comfort to the convoy route. In late August, apples, pears, grapes, and figs are plentiful on farms. They helped themselves to the fruits along the way since farms and farmhouses were unattended. They entered an empty farmhouse and changed clothes. Their body frames were so big that the farmer's pants came only to above their ankles. The shirts looked more like pajamas barely covering the belly. By the time they reached the outskirts of Tito, they didn't care if it raised a commotion among the locals. They desperately needed water.

They rushed to the fountain in the Piazza. Ottavio could see from his barbershop that these strangers were no local farmers, too big of frame and too light complexioned! They walked, smelled and looked like deserters. How ironical a situation this was. These two deserters were looking for a remote place in the hills to hide and it happened to be the same place chosen by Mussolini in order to hide internees! Ottavio concluded that they were German soldiers, but the big question in his and the townspeople's minds in the Piazza was, "Where were the rest of them?" They knew that in the morning and afternoon Allied planes were buzzing around the area in the direction of the Tyrrhenian Sea.

They surmised that the German Army must not be too far away from Tito. It was useless for Ottavio to talk to the deserters in Italian to find out exactly where they had come from. He had to find out as soon as possible for time was of the essence. What to do? He was aware that Mario had attended the University of Naples and he thought that he might know some German. He was hell bent on reaching Mario, as if the very existence of the town depended on it. It was not desperation time yet, but not knowing what the hell was going on in the battlefield just miles away from Tito was tormenting everyone there in the Piazza.

Word spread like wildfire, as people drifted more and more toward the Piazza. At this critical time, they were looking for a leader, since the mayor left town or was in hiding. By default, Bambolone took charge of the situation. He inspired confidence and determination. To begin with, he decided to have Mario interview the deserters about their predicament and the German Army's location. There was a heated exchange between Ottavio and the Palazzo's custodian as Ottavio was trying to enter the Palazzo to see Mario. The Ukrainians could see that the custodian was being a pain in the ass. One of the brothers pulled a gun and put it to the custodian's head. That was an international message that the custodian understood very well. The fear of being captured weighed heavily in his mind. The four of them proceeded toward the farmhouse where Mario lived, with the custodian leading the way.

They didn't bother knocking on the door. The front door swung wide open, as Ottavio, the custodian, and the two brothers entered the room. Mario froze thinking, "Oh no, those bastards got me." He breathed a sigh of relief when Ottavio informed him that these two strangers were deserters. Unfortunately, Mario didn't know any German, although he was fluent in French and Greek. He attended a German class and dropped the course after two weeks. He'd learned a few words, not enough to translate anything that would be meaningful. At this point, panic started to set in but, as always, Bambolone was resilient.

The community of internees was not immune to the perilous situation. News from internment camps in Northern Europe was beginning to seep through to every part of the world. The atrocities were too horrendous to believe but why take a chance. Strega and her friend

Nanna Wolf, who was a Jew from Austria, walked together toward the water fountain to find out what the commotion was all about. They lived within a stone's throw of the water fountain, and they could see that something was brewing. But what? Finally, the Maresciallo showed up with two Carabinieri to calm things down in the Piazza. Strega was clutching Alice, Nanna's daughter as if to protect her from the crowd. Strega was the midwife who delivered Alice about a year earlier. Like Imalda in Avella, she delivered most of, if not all, the babies in Tito. Being the matriarch of the shepherd community, the shepherds in the Piazza cordoned the crowd away from Strega and Nanna.

The Wolf family resided in Vienna, Austria, before the War. The family included Father Ehrlich, Nanna, and three-year-old daughter Beatrice. As things got progressively worse in Austria, the family looked toward the Italian border to escape from Austria. Soon after Germany annexed Austria in 1938, their neighbor and cousin by the same last name vacationed in Italy but never stopped traveling until they reached Britain. Italy did not require a visa for anyone to emigrate there. After the invasion of France by the German Army, the Wolf family decided to make their escape to Italy because they perceived things were not going to get any better for them. However, it is clear now why things were better in Italy, since Italy was allied with Nazi Germany. The only explanation for the optimism could have been that the racial laws adopted in 1938 in Italy were not fully implemented in Italy as in Germany. They were aware of the difference, as the Wolf family traveled often in Italy. Before the War, they often traveled to Florence and Rimini for vacation. Each time they took train transportation via the Brenner pass. Their plan for escape was simple. They would arrive in Bolzano, Italy, by train, as they always did, and report to customs police there. The train ride from Innsbruck (Austria) to Bolzano was approximately two hours. Nazi Germany technically permitted emigration from the Reich until November 1941. Fortunately, at that time, the German Army didn't utilize the Brenner Pass for transporting arms, supplies, and soldiers into Italy until late 1943. After the start of the War, it was impossible to escape via the Brenner Pass. Germany annexed the Bolzano region.

There was no problem reaching Innsbruck, Austria, as the city is the favorite destination to the Alps for Austrians. As a precaution, they then switched their identity papers, as they boarded the train for Bolzano via the Brenner Pass. It must have been a very nostalgic trip to see those beautiful and picturesque views of the mountains. Once in Bolzano, they snapped out of that melancholy feeling and put on their survival mode mindset by turning themselves into the Italian custom police. The police quickly turned them over to the Maresciallo's barrack. This was a way for the Fascist government to wash their hands of the whole affair of interning Jewish emigres, although they were the architects of the racial laws (1938) and the policy of interning Jews (1940). The Fascist Interior Minister dumped most if not all, responsibilities of internment on the lap of the local prefect who in turn ordered the Questura or the local Carabinieri to transport new Jewish arrivals to various internment camps and towns throughout Italy. Besides Austrians Jews, others from Northern Europe somehow found their way to Nice, France, to avoid the Vichy Police and into Italy. The city of Trieste was also another destination for Jews from Eastern Europe. Obviously, Italy must have been the soft underbelly to take on all foreign emigres, including gypsies.

A priori, there was no organized pattern by Italian authorities as to where to assign new emigres to internment camps. The assignment depended on which old buildings, ancient castles, villas, old factories, schools, apartment buildings, convents, housing, etc. were uninhabited. It is surmised here that since the facility of barracks at Ferramonti di Tarsia (Calabria region, the "boot") was one of the earliest ones to be built by Mussolini, in June 1940, new emigres were initially transported there. It housed about 4,000 people with private beds and provided new arrivals with government subsidies. However, by early 1943, the subsidies stopped because the Fascist government went bankrupt, and, by and large, the onset of starvation throughout Italy was knocking on the door. In all, there were 48 locations evenly spread in Italy to accommodate new arrivals or expatriates. The common denominator in most of these facilities was that they were in somewhat remote places, away from busy streets. The Wolf family was escorted to the town of Tito (Basilicata region, next to Calabria) by a single Carabiniere. They boarded a train in Milan making stops in Florence, Rome, Naples, Salerno, Eboli, Potenza, and Tito. On the train, they had access to bathroom facilities, food, and whatever. It was a regular passenger train, not a cattle transport train. Most likely, at each stop, the new emigres were released to a waiting Carabiniere who in turn transported the new arrivals to a city hall for registration. However, each time the train crossed a Province, a new set of Carabinieri took over the escorting. It was a question of jurisdiction. For example, at the Potenza train station, the Carabiniere from Naples (Campania) was replaced by one from the Province of Potenza (Basilicata).

At Potenza, they boarded a local train which consisted of only two wagons full of farmers and shepherds returning to Tito from the Farmers Market in Potenza. All the seats were taken up. Compared to Vienna, it was like stepping back in time, an eerie feeling to say the least for the Wolfs. One old farmer got up from the seat and said, "Signora, per piacere," offering his seat. Then, an elderly woman put her arms around Beatrice and put the child in her lap offering a boiled egg. Ehrlich stood up next to both. The Carabiniere was no place to be seen. The woman next to Nanna held two roosters on her lap. A pig and a goat were running loose in the wagon. It was a madhouse, total chaos, but they were all happy to get home. By the time the Wolf family arrived at the Tito train station, they were exhausted and hungry. That wasn't so bad. The family was speechless when they arrived in what appeared to be a desolate place, asking themselves, "Where are we? It looks like modern civilization has yet to arrive here!" The station itself was a rundown small house. It had no signs on it. They were in total shock. Of course, they were comparing, in their minds, Vienna with Tito. "By the way, where is the Carabinieri?" asked Nanna.

As they got off the train, lucky for them, they were welcomed by Strega, as Pasquale at City Hall put her in charge of organizing lodging and financial assistance, depending on the family's financial needs. The first thing that Nanna inquired about was the whereabouts of a local doctor. Strega noticed that Nanna was pregnant. She said that there is no local doctor, but I have delivered all the babies in this town. That was the beginning of a beautiful friendship. The first thing that Strega did was to find housing for the Wolf family and make sure that it was close enough to her place in case of emergency. At least, Nanna could shout loud enough for Strega to hear. Yes, coming from Vienna was quite a shock for the family, especially when they discovered that there was no running water in the house. It was primitive living, but, at least, they were able to exercise their free will. No one around them imposed their ways on them. The people were friendly and extremely helpful. In effect, the townies and the new emigres were all in the same boat, whether they liked it or not.

Strega did deliver a baby boy, Werner, about four months after the arrival of the Wolf family. It was at three in the morning when Mr. Wolf knocked on the front door of Strega's house in full panic, as his wife was about to have a baby. By then, he learned enough Italian to adequately explain that Nanna was ready. Strega knew exactly what to do and calmly walked over to his house. She wanted to convey to Mr. Wolf that the people may be backward here but delivering a baby was as old as time itself and she was in charge. The Wolfs and Strega got along splendidly. Whenever there was an issue with food as it became less available, Strega came to the rescue. For example, Strega made available goat milk routinely for the baby, as she easily had access to it. She thought that whatever the reason was to exile the Wolf family to Tito must have been foolish because the Fascist government was foolish. Hence, there was no need for her to inquire about it. Nanna learned from Strega to cook local delicacies and often socialized together in a picnic set which also included Bombalone's family. Often Beatrice and Bambolone's children played with other children in the Piazza inventing new games every day. The War meant nothing to them. Fascist dignitaries stopped coming to schools in Tito and other small towns to indoctrinate young minds. People could see through the bullshit. As far as people were concerned, Fascism was finished by then.

The Wolf family interned in Tito for more than two years, and their baby son Werner was starting to walk. However, something was brewing not too far from Tito that was well beyond their control, a war. The German Army was retreating from Sicily toward their vicinity. They could see Allied planes overhead which was the usual sign that something was happening not too far away. One day in the late summer of 1943, as noted above, there was much excitement in the Piazza. It was not a typical Sunday morning crowd. Both Strega and Nanna could see from their houses that a crowd was gathering in front of the Palazzo, having seen Bambolone and two strangers enter the building. Nanna rushed over to Strega urging for the two to find out what the excitement was about. No sooner had Strega and Nanna reached the water fountain, when there emerged a distraught and worried Bambolone from the Palazzo, asking if someone knew some German. Nanna came forward. It was her turn to help the town instead, she felt.

Quickly, Bambolone, Nanna, and Strega hurried to the farmhouse, as Mario and the two deserters were waiting for Bambolone with the hope of him bringing back an interpreter since the chance was good with so many internees in town.! After much exchange between the deserters and Nanna, there emerged a bleak picture on hand. The deserters estimated that the German convoy was about 70-80 kilometers away (~ 50 miles) near the Tyrrhenian Sea. The Germans were retreating toward Salerno and Naples on their way to Rome. Their aim was to destroy the ports there. As standard practice by the German Army, the retreat would be covered by a flanking group of soldiers stretching to Potenza (near Tito) and Avellino (near Avella). As such, there was no place for people to hide, since Tito, sooner or later, would be in harm's way between warring armies. The best that they could hope for was to move all livestock (sheep, pigs, cows, etc.) to the high mountains, away from the German Army, because the town would need it later to survive starvation. The message was clear: grin and bear it for a short time and keep your mouth shut.

The brothers from Ukraine explained that there was no time to waste if they wanted to arrive in Salerno before the German convoy. Otherwise, they would be surrounded by German soldiers, a very perilous situation for the town and the people in it. Immediately, the custodian, Ottavio and Mario packed a suitcase full of bread, cheese and salami and Ottavio bid Mario goodbye for the last time. The two brothers changed into nice shirts and pants. The last parting words from Bambolone to Mario were, "In case the Germans arrive in Salerno before you, you may want to visit the church of San Bartolomeo in Campagna,", another internment camp.

Bambolone, Strega, Nanna, the brothers (Vladimir and Dimitri) and Mario emerged from the Palazzo. Bambolone delivered the bad news to the crowd in the Piazza which was nearly full. An eerie silence fell throughout the Piazza. They must have felt helpless in view of the imminent appearance of German troops in town. They felt helpless because the mayor left town and the Maresciallo was as useless as a tiz on a bull. Because their mayor had left, a surge of people came toward Bambolone proclaiming him as mayor and carried him on their shoulders. Strega followed with Nanna. Whereas before Bambolone's wife was jealous, now she was terrified of what the Germans could do to him. They carried Bambolone on their shoulders all the way to City Hall followed by the Maresciallo and the two Carabinieri. Forever an opportunist, Bambolone declared himself the new mayor and occupied the office in City Hall, declaring to Pasquale that henceforth to report to him. Of course, they were the best of friends and played a game of who can bullshit the most.

Now, he had a serious problem in his hand: how to keep German troops away from the limited supply of food in town when they showed up. Bambolone instructed Strega to put her community of shepherds on alert and start moving sheep to the high mountains. Similar instructions were given to the few farmers in town. However, she worried that German troops would not put up with any shenanigans from her husband. As for Nanna and the rest of the internees, they had confidence in Bambolone. They didn't feel an urgency to take special precautions any more than the locals, feeling that they were in it together to resist whatever came their way and support the new mayor.

Mario didn't have the time to say goodbye to all those well-wishers in the Piazza, including Pasquale and Bambolone, who waited outside the Palazzo for him. The trio had a train to catch to Potenza. As they arrived at the train station in Potenza, they saw, down a side street, two German soldiers patrolling Main Street. Quickly, they entered a house, scaring the family inside. Mario explained the situation and the woman offered to guide them in a round-about way to the train station. Finally, all three of them were sitting in the train on their way to Naples. However, when the train arrived at the station in Salerno they heard, over the public announcement speaker, that the railroad tracks between

Salerno and Pompei had been bombed by Allied planes. Fortunately, the convoy was at the outskirts of Salerno. What to do? The brothers knew the route that the convoy would follow. There was only one choice to get to Pompei and then on to Naples in order to avoid the convoy. And that was over the mountains that overlooked Amalfi. The convoy planned to travel later a road east of Amalfi, eight to ten miles away from where they were about to walk along the mountain pass.

The convoy arrived in Salerno a couple of hours later. Thus, they had a small window to get away and walk about ten miles to the foothills above Amalfi. It was a desperate situation for all. The problem was how to walk in the streets by the sea without drawing attention from the locals, especially when the brothers looked so conspicuous together. They decided to split up three ways so as not to draw any attention, crisscrossing the main streets and side streets every so often until they arrived at the foothills of Amalfi. After the convoy crossed the mountain pass, it split in two. One convoy circled left around Mount Vesuvius on the way to Pompei and Naples, and the other circled right toward Nola.

Both Naples and Nola represented communication and railway centers. From Naples, trains could reach as far north as Germany. The intent of the German Army in Naples was to create a collection center in which Italian soldiers, deserters, foreign and Italian Jews, Neapolitan residents, and gypsies were rounded up and transported north to Germany. Nola has always been a conduit to the Adriatic Sea via Avellino since Roman times. Telegraph, telephone and other forms of wireless communications have been routed through Nola. Roman statesmen, politicians, emperors, etc., traveled from Rome to Nola on the way to Brindisi on the Adriatic Sea. The destination was Greece or the Middle East. Emperor Octavius and his son Augustus settled in Nola. Thus, by occupying Rome and Nola, the German Army controlled all communications and railway centers heading to southern Italy. In addition, they had a direct escape route north from Naples.

By this time, news of the German retreat along the coastal road reached Avella. Sofia was anxious to know what was happening in Tito and about Mario. She prevailed on her father, Sergio, Alvaro and Don Nicola to intercede for her and ask Ramiro to find out about Mario.

Word came back that he had left Tito and was on his way to Avella with two surprise guests. Sofia was overjoyed. She started to hum her favorite song.

View of Amalfi atop the mountain on the way to Pompei. Courtesy of Aventura Irpinia.

There was no time to enjoy the scenery in and around Amalfi, although the two brothers fell in love with the area. After what they had been through, it was understandable why they let their guard down. Mario reminded them to stop gawking at the place. At the top of the hill, they stopped at the town of Ravello to purchase buffalo mozzarella at Mario's favorite deli. The Ukrainians thought that they were in heaven when they tasted a sandwich of mozzarella, salami, and tomatoes while overlooking the view below of Amalfi and the sea. In contrast, stale dark bread and marmalade were often fed to German troops. Again, Mario had to remind them that they were on a mission, and to get out of there alive. Mario's leadership as a Naval officer came in

handy. However, he behaved more like a mother hen than a military officer, protecting the two new friends like a hen to her chicks, except these
wandering chicks were a lot bigger than the hen. Mario wanted desperately to get home and count on Sergio and the shepherds to hide the two
brothers up in the mountains. He had a feeling that the brothers, being
of similar peasant stock, would be comfortable in the company of
shepherds.

TEN
Slow Boat to Naples

After an arduous climb from Amalfi, Mario, Vladimir, and Dimitri arrived on top of Mount Faito, where Mount Vesuvius and Pompei came into view. From their vantage point, they could see below that the two convoys toward Naples and Nola hadn't arrived yet. The descent down to the valley was rather steep and dangerous, but they made it safely to the train station in Pompeii. This railway system originates in Sorrento and runs through Naples on the way to Avella-Baiano, referred to as the Circumvesuviana, meaning that it circles around Mount Vesuvius. The plan was rather simple. Arrive at the train station in Naples before the convoy and then depart for Avella via the Circumvesuviana train. As the train approached Torre Del Greco (Greek Tower), the railway was elevated above the street level. The area was first colonized by Greek settlers. In Roman times, Torre del Greco was probably a suburb of Herculaneum, characterized by patrician (upper-class) villas. After the 79 AD eruption of Mount Vesuvius, two villages Sora and Calastroare, known to have existed in the area, were destroyed.

The famous Italian comedian, Toto, was among those who made Torre Del Greco their annual summer retreats. The reason for Torre Del Greco's popularity as a resort town was its fine beaches and the rural setting of lush farmlands and vineyards, as well as its proximity to Mount Vesuvius. As the town nearest Vesuvius, Torre Del Greco was the main starting point for tourists wanting to scale the mountain. This was facilitated by a funicular railway (Vesuvius Funicular) which took tourists to the crater from the town. During World War II, the Torre De Greco was used as an ammunition depot by the German Army and consequently suffered heavy bombing by the Allies.

View from the North Edge of Mount Faito. Amalfi is at the opposite end of the mountain. Pompei is just below in the valley and Mount Vesuvius is in the background. The coastal town of Torre Del Greco (Greek Tower) is on the West edge of Vesuvius, toward the coastline. Nola is on the north side of Vesuvius. There was no funicular railway, as seen on the left, at that time. Courtesy of Aventura Irpinia.

Coral art and jewelry remains a mainstay of the city's economy. Diving for coral has taken place in the Mediterranean Sea ever since Roman times, and in the 15th century Torre del Greco became known for its coral diving and harvesting of red coral. However, it was not until the 17th century that the first cameos were produced from shells. At present there are several hundred companies and several thousands of people employed in the manufacturing of coral and shell cameos. Coral is now mainly imported from Asia since, increasingly, areas in the Mediterranean are becoming protected. The total industry is estimated to have a turnover of around $225 million.

Like children, the three of them marveled at the majestic view of Vesuvius. Unbeknownst to them, the German convoy was traveling on the street below, in the same direction, on their way to Naples, a short distance from where they were sitting. The first one to notice the convoy was Vladimir and his face paled. Their elated feeling of safety vanished. All their effort, struggles, and planning may be for naught. Dreams of freedom had to be postponed. What to do? Panic? That was the worst thing to do! Mario had a plan, as he was very familiar with the area and the local fishermen. He often bought coral items for Sofia and the family when he was stationed in Naples during the Ethiopian War. He looked at the situation from a positive perspective. So far, they had traveled a long distance safely. The home was within their sight. He rationalized, "We have to travel only a short distance to be home." The glass was more than half full.

Torre Del Greco Coastline. The railway line is above the coastal road and Mount Vesuvius is in the background. Courtesy of Aventura Irpinia.

Mario and the two Ukrainians gingerly got off the train at the next stop in Torre Del Greco, and hid in the station until evening, pacing in and out, peeking every so often at the convoy from a concealed opening in the window. Soldiers in the convoy appeared exhausted and their faces were covered with sweat and sand. It appeared to them that the convoy was heading straight to Naples and beyond. Therefore, Torre Del Greco was not the convoy's destination or plans, at least for the time being. They decided to sit tight in the station until dark. Still, the remnants of the convoy were outside the station. They decided to roll the dice and head for Mount Vesuvius. The station master led them to a secret back door toward the foothills of Vesuvius, as the convoy was moving slowly along the road to Naples. Mario concluded that even if they were spotted by the soldiers, they would have been too exhausted to give chase. Halfway up on Mount Vesuvius, the trio camped. Naples looked so near, but so far. Mario could almost smell the home cooking from Sofia's kitchen in Avella. The panoramic views of the Bay of Naples, the Islands of Capri and Ischia, Sorrento, etc., was mesmerizing. It energized them to try harder to escape capture. So much beauty waiting for them to be free and enjoy. They were determined more than ever to get home free.

In their retreat, the German Army concentrated their troops in large cities (Salerno, Avellino to the east, and Caserta to the north), and in railway and communication centers, such as Naples and in Nola. Nola and Avellino were the gateways to the East. Thus, the main strategy of the German retreat was to create a safe escape north toward Rome. They stationed troops in Salerno in order to stop or delay the Allied advance from the south. They occupied Avellino for the sole purpose of protecting the flank of their retreat from Allied advances in the east and south. The city of Caserta provided the linkage to the supply line to Germany. This meant that German checkpoints controlled the only rail connection to Avella, at Naples and Nola. So, even if the trio were to bypass the train station in Naples, the German checkpoint at Nola or at other stations along the railway line would have stopped them on their way to Avella. So, they had to scrap the original plan. Traveling in the valley by daylight or at night was problematic. Sooner or later, the two Ukrainians would draw attention from Fascist sympathizers. There were still a few of those around. Mario decided that the best option was to forge ahead to Naples and wait until the Germans left, if they could ever get there. He felt that the Germans would not stay very long in Naples, as the Allies were chasing the German Army to Naples or anyplace north toward Rome.

In the meantime, the Germans were hell-bent on the way to Rome.

The German troops were led by "Smiling Al" General Albert Kesselring. He approached every military situation with a smile. He "inherited" remnants of the proud Afrika Korps. His main ambition as a General was to prove to Hitler that he was a better tactician in utilizing the Afrika Korps than the popular Field Marshal Erwin Rommel, who commanded the German Army in Northern Italy. Starting out as a Luftwaffe Officer didn't help his psyche. Hitler promoted "Smiling Al" Kesselring to Field Marshal and commander of Southern Italy on September 8, 1943. Once Kesselring's troops joined with Rommel's troops, he would have to relinquish his command and he was taking his time in doing so. Unfortunately, Southern Italians were caught in the middle of a deadly tug of war between two egotistical generals.

To Kesselring's credit, he was able to maneuver his Army in southern Italy to high grounds, forcing Allied soldiers to fight uphill, as in Salerno, Monte Cassino and Anzio. No general conquered ancient Rome by attacking from the south. Most successful invasions of Rome derived from the north. Due to the terrain in Southern Italy in the fall and winter, it is very difficult to climb steep mountains and fight an enemy while watching from the top. The mud is knee-deep in places, and it is an effort just to be able to trudge through it, let alone fight uphill. Apparently, Allied generals had not studied ancient Roman history regarding war tactics in southern Italy.

Only because of their superior firepower were the Allies able to forge ahead all the way to Rome. In Rome, some Allied generals took photos of themselves next to the statue of Emperor Aurelius to symbolize their conquest of Rome. Absurdity ruled over common sense then. The same generals justified all that devastation in southern Italy in terms of collateral damage. Certainly, the victims, Italian people and soldiers, didn't share that feeling. The battles of Salerno, Monte Cassino and Anzio resulted in enormous war casualties for all warring countries. Destruction from the bombing of towns and cities caused unimaginable misery, injuries and deaths to the civilian population. Some towns were bombed out of existence. This was an example of philosopher George Santayana's expression, "Those who cannot remember the past are condemned to repeat it," except at that time, the people who were doomed were civilians and soldiers, not the generals. Was there an alternative? Yes, of course, the reader is referred to the book *Bitter Chicory to Sweet Espresso*.

The only way to get to Naples from Torre Del Greco, without being discovered by German patrols, was by sea across the Bay of Naples. At four in the morning, everything was quiet at Torre Del Greco, as the three of them descended to the shoreline where fishermen gathered for their morning outing at sea. For part of the coastline at Torre del Greco, there is no beach. Large boulders take up most of the shoreline. The fishermen descended to a small clearing area next to the boulders where they tied their boats to a tree or a smaller boulder. Usually, fishermen started early in the morning for the sole purpose of fishing for octopus. Once an octopus is spotted by a fisherman on the boat, a flashlight is directed into its eyes, and it is picked up with a net. A dark background, as in early morning, enhances the capture of the octopus. At daybreak, the hunt for octopus is over.

Mario knew some of the fishermen there, as he bought octopus from them in Posillipo, Naples when he lived at the naval station. Also, he visited there with Sofia to purchase coral necklaces many times. He made an offer that they could not refuse. He offered them three times more money, compared to selling all their octopuses in Naples, if they could transport the three of them to the naval station across the Bay, about five to six miles away. All the fishermen there volunteered to take them over at no cost. Wow! The fishermen put two and two together and concluded that Mario's party was running away from the Germans. They made themselves available to help, knowing full well that they were endangering their lives. Mario was impressed by their contempt and disdain for the occupiers of Naples.

By the time the trio arrived at the naval station in Naples, the morning sun welcomed them. The station was demolished by the Allied bombing. Mario searched for his old apartment. It was barely livable. Later in the morning, scugnizzi came out of their hiding places: big and small buildings, storage rooms, garages, classrooms, auditoriums, etc. A scugnizzo was typically an orphan, due to the War, who roamed and hustled in the streets for food, stole anything that brought something in return, money or food and pimped their sisters or mothers. Their ages ranged from five to twenty years. Most times, the mothers threw them out of the house. One or fewer mouths to feed. Prostitution accounted for about 30% of business transactions. It didn't look like a Naval station anymore. Remnants of sunken ships drifted at sea near the harbor. All the food and utensils in the kitchen area were gone. Food existed only in their minds. Neapolitans scavenged anything that was edible in nearby farms and towns. It was a mess all around the neighborhood of the naval station, but a beautiful mess to hide from German soldiers patrolling the streets. The only recourse for the scugnizzi and the trio was to stay put. They made for a strange family.

The San Carlo Opera House was nearly intact, barely damaged by the Allied bombing. Opera performances there were intermittent at that time, which was a disappointment for few Neapolitans, but most welcomed the reprieve. Nevertheless, Mario moseyed over to the San Carlo Opera House to meet former colleagues. He hoped that, perhaps, Don Nicola would be there, knowing full well that Zio (uncle) was not about to go through two checkpoints at Nola and Naples. Of course, it was wishful thinking. Going forward, the routine was the same every day. He would go to the opera house and ask who was there. Most times, janitors and maintenance people were there. He looked for anyone who could pass a message to his family in Avella, but no luck. As for food, the Ukrainians went fishing every day catching enough to put food on the table. Scugnizzi traded jars of tomatoes for fish and a modus operandi was reached whereby each party did their share in the search for food. The biggest problem was the availability of drinking water. Scugnizzi took care of that by raiding gardens with small pools full of small non-edible fish. Fortunately, the rainy season was just around the corner.

On September 8, 1943, forty-five days after the arrest of Mussolini on July 25th, Italy announced unconditional surrender to the Allied Army and declared neutrality. There were quick knee-jerk reactions all around Italy as a result of the announcement. Many people in Italy wondered about their loved ones who were stranded in the middle of a war all over Europe. What's to become of them? Not a single word was uttered by the King or Badoglio about those poor souls! At least Italian soldiers stationed in Southern Italy had the option to go home (if they were local) or keep fighting on the side of the Allies. Even as the battles raged in Italy, the Germans persecuted Italy's Jewish population, executed partisans and even attacked their former ally, the Italian Army.

Badoglio's abandonment of his troops and his failure to order them immediately to fight the Germans resulted in the German capture of 600,000 Italian soldiers, including 22,000 officers, and a huge amount of war materiel, stretching from the Italian mainland to southern France, Yugoslavia, and the Greek islands. Italian soldiers were loaded into railroad cattle cars, taken to Germany and interned in slave labor camps in miserable conditions for the duration of the War. More than 7,000 Italian soldiers died when British bombers sank German ships transporting Italian soldiers from Crete to Greece and eventual internment. Those who did not drown, the Germans machine-gunned as they attempted to swim to safety, prompting Mussolini to send a message to a German garrison commander thanking him for "his kindness to Italian soldiers." He was, indeed, a sick man. German General Hubert Lanz received a 12-year sentence for the killing of the Italian soldiers in cold blood at the Nuremberg war crime tribunal in 1948, but he was released after five years.

An additional 600,000 Italian troops were either killed or taken prisoners, lingering in the tundra of Siberia. Only about 10,000 returned homes. Most of them vanished in the Russian Gulags. Others married and started families in Siberia. Most of them died in the battle of Stalingrad. Few of them were deported to Germany to work in armament factories. Similar stories can be recounted in other countries of Europe as well. It was doubtful that the King and Badoglio thought of these poor souls, when they signed the Armistice. It is safe to say that they were thinking of their political futures. It was a sad period for the soldiers, parents, wives, children, friends and women in waiting.

King Vittorio Emanuele III and family, the new prime minister (Badoglio) and other ministers escaped very early in the morning of September 9th through a German checkpoint at Tiburtina, Rome. To this day there is no satisfactory explanation as to how it was possible for them to escape the clutches of German guards at the checkpoint, when it was well known within the German hierarchy, that Hitler hated the King with a passion and vice versa. Hitler wanted their capture at all costs. Somehow, they made their way through the checkpoint on the way to the city of Pescara on the Adriatic Sea and headed directly south, along the coastline to the city of Brindisi, Province of Puglia, occupied by the Allies at that time.

On the same day, local administrations in Southern Italy abolished internment camps. Freedom at last for the internees! At Ferramonti, some chose to stay until the end of the War. Internees at Potenza, Tito and Brienza decided the same. The internees felt that the risk of traveling through parts of Northern Italy and Northern Europe, still under Nazi control, far outweighed the freedom and kindness of town's people that they enjoyed at those internment camps in Southern Italy. However, the Convent near the Church of San Bartolomeo at Campagna, near Salerno, where roughly 450 internees resided, felt eerie, since it was located near a large concentration of German troops. Government administrations in Northern Italy were caught off guard by the announcement of the surrender. As such, no decision on their internment camps was made. Besides, they had no control over their own destiny. The German Army occupied Northern Italy. They were forced to bite the bullet and smile.

Also, on the same day, the Allied Army invaded Salerno, September 9, 1943, code named Avalanche. The US Fifth Army (General Mark Clark), Canadian and British Armies spearheaded the attack at Salerno, while the British Eighth Army (General Bernard Montgomery) frolicked from Taranto toward Potenza (site of an internment camp). On September 10th, the German Army occupied Rome and rounded up Italian soldiers to be deported to Germany, deployed as laborers in factories. According to the book, *Bitter Chicory to Sweet Espresso*, the rounding up of Italian soldiers by German troops occurred much earlier, August 17th, in Sicily.

ELEVEN
German Occupation of Avella

While Mario, Dimitri, and Vladimir waited to extricate themselves from the clutches of the Nazi occupiers in Naples, the German Army paid an uninvited visit to Avella in the middle of the night. Townies became aware of their presence as the rumble of tanks and motorcycles scurried about town to the sound of the roosters coming up. The German Army occupied Avella from about September 1 to mid-October of 1943. News spread by word-of-mouth that German soldiers and tanks had arrived suddenly in Baiano from Nola; they traveled on the only asphalt road, Via Appia. According to the rumors, their tanks were headed, on the only dirt road from Baiano, toward Avella, but it didn't stop their motorcycle drivers from buzzing around the farms at the foothills and in the town itself. One purpose of those drivers was to announce their appearance, but most importantly, it was to strike fear in people's hearts. The Cemetery in Avella was located on this dirt road halfway between the two towns, one mile apart. The other connection between Baiano and Avella was via the railway line, the Circumvesuviana. Discussions in the Piazza centered on which farm the German soldiers might be camping, on and what their intentions could be. Speculations ran wild because no foreign Army (either in WWI or WWII) ever reached this far south of Italy and camped.

To add to their anxieties, confusion reigned as to whether Italy was still allied with Germany. Prime Minister Pietro Badoglio's declaration on July 25th was subject to anyone's interpretation. He declared then that Italy was still allied with Germany in the War. Hitler never believed him, as he made plans to occupy Italy, and forty-five days later, Italy was occupied by Germany, as the people of Avella attested. How could people of Avella or any other town nearby possibly know the mess created by Badoglio and the King? Not knowing the disposition of the German Army disturbed the locals more than anything else.

The locals were clueless as to the reason for the visit. They wondered why they were hosting those soldiers instead of at Baiano or Nola. The answer was simple. From the top of the hills of Avella, one could see the entire valley and the Bay of Naples. German soldiers of the 15th Panzer and Hermann Goring Divisions camped atop a hill next to two caves. The camps had a panoramic view of the valley below, including Avella, Baiano, Vesuvius, Caserta, and the Bay of Naples. Besides that, Baiano, Avella, and Avellino (nearby) formed the first line of defense against the Allied advance from the Adriatic Sea. It was vital for the German Army to have an uninterrupted escape route to Rome. Also, hiding in caves from bombing raids by Allied planes was essential in neutralizing the Allies' firepower. Obviously, the German General staff did their home-work in choosing the hills of Avella as their camp.

These two Divisions were part of the convoy that retreated from Sicily. Via Appia passed through Baiano, which served as the main supply line to Salerno and as an escape route to the North. A secondary road was built for quick access of the two Divisions to Via Appia from the two camps. This road was paved to avoid the dirt road, which could become muddy during the rainy season in October and November. After a couple of weeks of rest, these two divisions were committed to battle in Salerno. For military reasons, the Germans wanted to keep the location of the camps secret from the people of Avella. No one in town dared to try to find out the location. Of course, the shepherds knew, but they were not about to tell anyone. They were perched well above the hills, on the high mountains, and were not about to come down to the valley soon.

Vista from Mount Avella of the valley below, Mount Vesuvius, and the Bay of Naples. The hills and Avella are well below the high mountains. Castello Normanno is barely visible. Courtesy of Piero Busiello, 2019.

The valley has been invaded by every country surrounding the Mediterranean Sea and countries north of the Alps since Hannibal showed up in the valley in 217BC. It is not a question of specifically which country invaded there, but which one didn't. Even a group of gladiators led by Spartacus ransacked the valley and the town of Nola. In later years, religious crusaders built a castle (Castle Normanno) in Avella as an observation post during their crusades to the Middle East. An interesting statistical factoid stands out from these invasions. About everyone thousand years, a country or a combination of countries from North Africa have invaded the valley since 217 BC: Hannibal (217 BC), Saracens (900 AD), and French Expeditionary Force (1941). The French Expeditionary Force consisted of Moroccan, Algerian, and Tunisian soldiers. Could there be another invasion from a North African country in the year 3000?

The hope among diehard Fascists in town was that, perhaps, the Germans came to town to help ease the food shortage. That was delusional. All doubts and the few good vibes were removed when German motorcycles appeared unexpectedly, whizzing by and often aiming at people in willful acts of intimidation. German soldiers on heavy trucks, tanks, and motorcycles with side carriages arrived along the Cemetery dirt road to Avella. Tanks were so big that they took up the whole road. In order to get around them, one had to walk in a drainage ditch abutting the road. The soldiers moved about with purpose and looked busy putting up posters in the Piazza to declare a new order. Not friendly messages. Just orders. One word often repeated on the posters was "verbieten," meaning to forbid. The only things that they didn't "verbiet" were mosquitoes and gnats flying all over town.

The mood in town was somber. There was nothing friendly about these visitors. People didn't want to be caught in the streets with soldiers, especially when the soldiers were drunk, and that was most nights. Sometimes they would march from their camp to City Hall and back, with their guns at the ready, singing German marching songs in the middle of the night. The message was loud and clear, "Get off Main Street!" at any time of the day. It was frightening! The mood was beyond somber; it shocked the town into submission. One could not even breathe air from the mountains without having to share it with a German soldier. They didn't come to help, nor did they have regard for the plight of the people who were near starvation.

The worst feeling was not knowing what was coming next. The attitude was: to expect the unexpected and get out of their way. Most people in Avella locked the doors to their houses and didn't go outside once they realized that these soldiers would not hesitate to shoot anyone. Even seeing a medical doctor was an adventure in avoiding them in the street. People were afraid of being shot when venturing into farms and hills searching for anything edible because they didn't know how far into the farms they could go before encountering a German patrol or checkpoint. Sofia and the twin sisters shut down the dress shop in the Piazza. She hibernated with the children in one of Sergio's apartments. The whole Da Alia family also moved into another apartment in the courtyard where Don Nicola, Sergio, and Sofia families resided. Altogether, there were eleven extra people taking refuge there. At night, the portone to the courtyard was locked with steel bars.

Sergio no longer inspected the mountains for poachers because German patrols around the camps would not allow it, and he was not about to test their will. The camps were located on the hills near the east end of Main Street, about a couple of miles from Sergio's residence. Whatever little food was secured by the shepherds on the mountains for Imalda's family, Ciccio transported on a donkey, circumventing the camps. This meant that he had to travel along the edge of the high mountains an extra two or three miles in a westerly direction toward the Castello Normanno, and then, descend to Main Street toward Sergio's residence. That food went a long way in sustaining the bare minimum to satisfy the hunger of those four families in the courtyard. In the morning, soldiers were seen running nude in the streets surrounding Sergio's building toward their camps for their daily exercises. Sergio had to dart across the street just to enter his garden to secure any edible food. On the flip side, the four families bonded together like never before.

The mayor left town, running from the Germans. He was afraid that they would discover that he was a Podesta (Fascist mayor) in name only, since he was not affiliated with the Fascist Party. The apolitical Prefect appointed him. Again, he didn't want to be able to guess what they would do to him. Simply put, he did not want to give them the satisfaction of dictating orders to him. In general, many mayors in the area began to leave towns for that reason. As for Alvaro Da Alia, he left the Magistrate Office as soon as he heard that tanks were on the way to Avella. By then, news of atrocities at the German extermination camps was being reported globally. As for Don Nicola, he decided that the San Carlo Opera House didn't need a cello player after all, since it shut down. The War spread from Salerno to Naples. Neapolitans began to put up resistance to Hitler's demands to deport their few young men to Germany. The Alvarez and Colonna forebears had survived wars, revolutions, civil wars, and plagues for centuries. As such, the surprise visit by the Germany Army in Avella had no effect on Ramiro and his family. Interestingly, the very rich and the shepherds, the two extreme ends of the social class, seemed to be immune to social unrest and wars.

This period of time marked the end of Fascism governance and the beginning of lawlessness in Avella and in other small towns in the Naples area, since local authorities disappeared. The Maresciallo was useless in maintaining civil order in town. His main preoccupation was to hide or run away from German authorities because, sooner or later, he would have to be accountable to the locals. In the meantime, more and more deserters (not necessarily Italian) were showing up mysteriously in the mountains banding together with partisans. Some had good intentions as they became involved in sabotaging the German war machinery. Others were just brigands involved in the black market and thievery in towns.

Farms were raided for livestock, as the Germans needed horses to pull heavy equipment up the hills and for food. Even farms owned by the churches were raided. There were four to five wine stores in Avella. Fortunately for Erminio, his winery was located near the train station, sufficiently away from the camps to be noticed by German soldiers. Nevertheless, he too skipped town to a neighboring one on the Circumvesuviana line. Desperation was beginning to set in, and the true nature of the visitors' intent was clear to all: serve our needs or get out of the way. The problem was that there was nothing to give or serve, except for wine. The people of Avella were not aware of the debacle of the Italian Army in Sicily and there was no one to help them out of this mess. When there is no hope, desperation sets in. That was the situation in Avella as well as in other small towns.

Germans were not about to share any road with the locals, especially the escape roads to Via Appia in Baiano which led to Rome. From Avella, there were basically three roads that led to Via Appia, the dirt road in front of the Cemetery, the newly paved road, built by them behind the Cemetery, and another dirt road that led to a bridge over Clanio Creek. The first two roads were located on the east side of town and the bridge on the west. The bridge was bombed and destroyed by the partisans of the Baiano-Avella area operating in the high mountains which meant tanks could not traverse that part of town. As such, the two remaining roads were constantly patrolled by the Germans. Anyone from Avella or Baiano traveling on those roads would have drawn a lot of attention at checkpoints on the way to the Cemetery and were most likely detained for questioning.

German soldiers couldn't even leave dead people alone. Funeral processions on the way to the Cemetery were stopped at the checkpoint.

Often, soldiers would examine an opened casket. The priest would remind them each time that what they were doing was sacrilegious. Did they expect the dead to invade the camps? It made no sense and was just another way to intimidate the people.

At the foothills near where Sergio lived, there were five narrow dirt roads (2-3 yards wide) heading toward the hills and the high mountains and all were blocked by German checkpoints. Most likely, the German camps were located on one of those hills within sight of Sergio's building. Certainly, Sergio knew very well where the camps were located, but he was not about to share that with anyone in town. Ciccio volunteered that information only to Sergio. It was the type of information that didn't do anyone any good if the Germans caught wind of it. The location of the caves, where German soldiers hid during Allied bombing raids, was no secret either. There were only two caves in the foothills and every farmer knew their whereabouts. One other cave, San Michele cave, was located on the high mountains. The Germans surrounded the town and there was no way in or out or of running to the caves in case of Allied bombing.

Obviously, there was no recourse to complaining about the Germans' iron-clad encirclement of the town. Local Fascist officials had no leverage with the German occupiers. German soldiers did not trust anyone from the previous administration of City Hall, since the Mussolini debacle. Besides, there was no incentive for Alvaro to come out and confront the Germans. He would have been shot on the spot. It was such a helpless feeling to have German trucks, tanks, motorcycles, soldiers, etc. interrupt normal life in town. That special Neapolitan spirit, *Vivere senza malinconia,* meaning "to live life to the fullest," was snuffed out of them.

The occupation presented an immense problem for the Jewish community of Avella. News of extermination camps was beginning to filter through newspapers and radio, though details were scant. Whatever little news there was, was so horrendous that some found it hard to believe. Others believed it couldn't occur in Italy. However, what they didn't realize was that they themselves could be deported out of Italy to those extermination camps. Alvaro saw to it, before leaving City Hall, that all records were hidden in the cave of San Michele. Shepherds, with

Imalda's insistence, helped Alvaro hide the records in a deep, dry well. The cave is located halfway up to the top of Mount Avella. As for Don Nicola, he was vulnerable. The fear was that one of those Fascist thugs might be revengeful enough to turn him into the German authorities.

Of particular interest to the German Army in Avella was the capture of deserters who were to be sent to Germany to work in the armament industry. Apparently, the Gestapo police showed up much later in Avella to do the dirty work for them. However, they didn't need the Gestapo to flush out deserters. Former local Fascists pointed the finger at where to look. German security guards apprehended one deserter and immediately sent him to Germany. The only other deserter was never discovered. These types of searches were suspended soon after the Allies began to force the German Army from the beaches of Salerno. The small Jewish community of Avella breathed a sigh of relief.

All employees of City Hall also left their jobs. They didn't want to be accountable for the missing records. The Maresciallo pleaded ignorance (which fit him perfectly) of the records, since he had nothing to do with City Hall. Ramiro kept tabs on Italian and German authorities via gossip from the elites in town. Imalda (with Sergio's assistance) provided a liaison between the shepherd community in the mountains and the people in the neighborhoods, mostly shepherds. The consensus among The Four Musketeers was to lay low (especially Don Nicola) until more news came along in town.

With the demise of Fascism, there was no more singing of the Fascist song, "Faccetta nera," meaning "Black Face," and propaganda on radio. Newspapers splashed the report that the German Army was in full retreat at Potenza which was the back entry to Salerno. This implied that the Germans would soon leave the area. The feeling that they were leaving Avella was so overwhelming they forgot that they were hungry. Potenza and Tito, which still had about five hundred internees, were occupied in late September by the German Army with the aim of preventing Field Marshal Montgomery from entering Salerno from the Adriatic Sea. The Field Marshal never advanced within rifle shot range of attack, but a Canadian regiment did and relieved Potenza. However, the other internment camp at Campagna was weathering most of the attacks and counterattacks by both Armies. With Potenza in Allied hands, it was inevitable that the German Army would soon retreat from Salerno. As usual, the German Army controlled the pace of the retreat. As implied in the previous chapter, there was nothing abrupt about their retreat to Rome. Their retreat was methodically planned to stymie and pin down the Allied Army as long as possible in Italy and away from Germany. Basically, the Allies reacted to whatever defensive scheme was concocted by "smiley" General Albert Kesselring. As such, Kesselring chose the terrain and where the battles took place, always choosing the high ground. With the fall of Salerno, the handwriting was on the wall. The German Army had no other choice but to retreat North to Naples and eventually to Rome. In the meantime, they chose to make life miserable for all.

Back in Avella, the two German divisions camping on the hill were no longer there, as they were undoubtedly on the same convoy heading North. Everything began to quiet down in the streets as fewer and fewer soldiers appeared in town, but though enough to cause some concern within the Jewish community. When things appeared to be rosy with the news of Salerno, the Gestapo appeared in Avella near the end of September. Policemen in civilian clothes, most likely Gestapo policemen, abducted a teenager, his sister, and his mother from their house. They were carried away in the back of a truck. The father had died in Albania during the invasion by the Italian Army.

The people in Sergio's building realized that these belated actions were those of desperate Fascists before the curtain came down on them. There were old scores to settle between Don Nicola and Fascist fanatics who were willing to do terrible things to people who didn't agree with their political philosophy. Hence, The Four Musketeers moved fast for the sake of Don Nicola's and Alvaro's families. Obviously, the Gestapo must have had pertinent information about the teenager's family, since it was such a surgical operation. What worried The Four Musketeers was the precision and timing of the operation. So, where did the information come from? The four of them briefly considered having Don Nicola dress in a monk's garb but decided that would not work for he would be easily recognized by the Fascist thugs.

The only recourse was to find either a secluded place up on the high mountains or an isolated place among the many hills surrounding Avella. The first option was out of the question. Don Nicola or Alvaro or Felicia could not possibly climb up the high mountains, although, once there, shepherds would make a home for them. The old fox, Imalda, knew exactly the place not too far from town. There were still checkpoints toward the hills where the two German divisions left camps, as injured soldiers were left behind temporarily. Imalda had a plan as to exactly how to circumvent the checkpoints. She exuded confidence and the group of Don Nicola's and Alvaro's families would have followed her to the end of the world, if necessary. She wanted to impart confidence in them by saying, "If I can do this at my age, you can do better." Her stewardship was impeccable. She knew those hills like the back of her hand. There were no checkpoints on the way to the Castle, as Ciccio discovered, which was about two or three miles west of the checkpoints. Effectively, all the checkpoints were in the East end of town near Sergio's residence. The only possible problem was that, at the beginning of October, the rainy season commences and the Clanio Creek sometimes is flooded. Under those conditions, some in the group might not be able to cross Clanio Creek.

This meant that Imalda needed to move faster in implementing her plan. A group of eleven people saddled up and were ready to follow Imalda. It included seven of Don Nicola and Alvaro's families, Imalda, Sergio, Lena and Carlo. Sofia was left at home in case Mario would show up. Lena and Carlo stayed close to their grandmother. It was in the middle of the night. The mountain air was cool and refreshing in early October. The group walked with a herd of sheep down Main Street toward the Communist section of town, away from the five checkpoints, and turned right toward Clanio Creek. The only problem with that scenario was that sheep rarely were herded on Main Street and, especially, toward the West end of town. The high mountains are on the East side of town, at least the approach to climbing them. Sergio and Imalda were aware of that unusual situation. Their "radar" was at full alert for anyone in the street or peeking from a window. Sergio, Don Nicola, and Alvaro led the sheep crossing the creek. The water flow there was tolerable for everyone to either jump over or wade across. Behind the herd, the rest of the people followed, commanding the dogs to encircle the sheep. It looked like an authentic outing of a shepherd clan guiding sheep toward the mountains.

A sigh of relief could be seen on Imalda's face. The trickiest part of the trek was over. "Great, those bastards are sound asleep," Imalda said to herself, meaning those Fascist thugs. The uphill walk to the Castello was rather pleasant as Don Nicola and Alvaro enjoyed picking cactus pears along the way. It was more like a picnic setting rather than an impossible task of guiding the sheep. As in life, nothing ever goes according to plans 100% of the time. They encountered a fellow shepherd who was on the way to the high mountains with a team of guard dogs. However, Sergio recognized him and said, "You haven't seen anything." "That's right," he replied with a chuckle. The only two who knew how to guide the sheep were Imalda and Sergio, as they positioned themselves to control the sheep with the dogs. For the rest of them, it was fun just to experience the outing with real shepherds. Imalda warned the group not to sit on any big rock at the castle site but to keep going downhill on the other side. She went on to say that rattlesnakes might lie under the rocks. In her mind, being tired was not an option.

The "big" valley lies between Mount Vesuvius and Castello Normanno. The glen lies on the other side of the castle, hidden from the town of Avella. Courtesy of Rie Vittoria, 1988.

Imalda warned the group about the rattlesnakes and to just press on.

Coming down on the other side of the castle, there were farmlands and grasslands between the castle and the high mountains. Shepherds took their sheep to graze and did some farming there. It looked more like a glen than a valley. The glen was well hidden from townies who resided at ground level as well as the few German soldiers camped further away. Shepherds owned the huts and farmhouses, and they were loyal to Imalda, their matriarch. They were just as happy to get their sheep back from Imalda, who had "borrowed" them for the excursion. They sensed the urgency of the situation and were happy to oblige, provide shelter to the group, and make a home for her friends. She would have made a great field marshal.

Sergio waited for the next day to return home. Again, he traveled in darkness to avoid locals in the street. Sofia was full of questions: "How are the kids? Where is so and so staying? In the farmhouse, etc." The next morning, the same civilian policemen who apprehended the teenager, showed up at Don Nicola's apartment knocking on the entrance door down. They looked in and out of the apartment but there was no sign of him. By this time, Sergio and Sofia came out of their apartments into the courtyard, inquiring as to what the commotion was about. Shepherd neighbors also gathered at the entrance of the building wanting to know about the noise. One of the undercover policemen turned to Sergio asking if he had seen Signore Nicola Celeste recently. From the way, the policeman pronounced the word "signore," Sergio could tell that these policemen were not Italian or Fascist thugs, but Gestapo. For example, Neapolitans do not pronounce the ending, re, as in the word signore. Sergio then sent the policemen on a wild goose chase by answering, "Nicola left for Avellino yesterday because his daughter was in the Hospital of San Pellegrino with typhoid and his son worked in the Madonna Di Monte Vergine church in Avellino." With "tongue in cheek," he added, "Who shall I say is the one who damaged his door?". The policemen left in a huff. They were lucky to get out alive with all those shepherds in the courtyard.

The next day, German troops disappeared just as they had appeared six weeks earlier in Avella, suddenly and without notice. The nightmare was over. This called for a celebration, but Sofia was in no mood to celebrate until she was in Mario's arms humming their song.

TWELVE
Hope on The Way

Prior to the Allied invasion of Salerno (Code name Avalanche) there were many turns and twists by all sides: Hitler, the King of Italy, Badoglio, Churchill, General Eisenhower, etc. It is instructive in digressing to those events in Rome, as it sheds light on why it prompted the King and Badoglio to hightail to Brindisi in the middle of a war. On September 8th, Badoglio flip-flopped by declaring that Italy would fight on the side of the Allies. Forty-five days earlier he declared an alliance with Germany after the incarceration of Mussolini. Hitler countered by threatening to send tanks to Rome and arrest the King, the crown prince, government officials, and Badoglio. There were German troops stationed not far from Rome, and, evidently, that raised havoc in Badoglio's mind. General Dwight D. Eisenhower, Allied Commander in Europe, did not want to contend with Italian forces in mainland Italy. He wanted Italy to sign an unconditional surrender before the invasion of Salerno. In fact, General Giuseppe Castellano of the Italian Army signed a short surrender document on September 3 in Sicily. Badoglio still feared the Germans would execute him and wanted to delay the formal signing of the accord. By September 8, twenty-five German divisions poured over the Alps that Badoglio failed to defend.

In signing the Armistice, Badoglio and the King made a bold move to hold on to power at the expense of Italian soldiers out in the fields of battle. Thus, it was no surprise that the people of Italy hated Badoglio more than Mussolini. Italians felt that the King was being selfish in trying to form a government in which his son Umberto would eventually take over. Absurdity and chaos ran amok in the minds of these two. British Prime Minister Churchill promised them the "sky" just to alleviate Eisenhower's concerns of having to fight two foes instead of one in Salerno. Churchill moved a mountain to rescue more than 350,000 soldiers at Dunkirk. These two Italian clowns didn't lift a finger to save more than one million Italian soldiers at the mercy of the German Army, just to save their asses.

Within hours of the signing of the Armistice, the Allied Army invaded Salerno. The invasion of Salerno by the Allies had been planned soon after the signing of the Armistice. Badoglio (see *Bitter Chicory to Sweet Espresso*, by Carmine Vittoria) suggested that the 82nd U.S. Airborne Division seize Rome before the Allies invaded any other place in Italy. His main concern, and that of the King, was to escape the wrath of Hitler. Ultimately, General Dwight Eisenhower decided to call off the landing, at the last minute. That was a wise move because the US 82nd Airborne Division planned to land only one regiment of paratroopers north of Rome. Without reinforcements, it would have been suicidal. Hence, the dash to Brindisi by Badoglio and the King.

The day after the signing of the Armistice, a frightened Badoglio and the King fled to Brindisi without alerting his ministers and giving no instructions to his generals concerning the defense of Rome (see chapter 10). There was no bound to Hitler's wrath when he heard of the escape. In early September 1943, Princess Mafalda, daughter of King Victor Emanuel III, traveled to Bulgaria to attend the funeral of her brother-in-law, King Boris III. She was informed of Italy's surrender to the Allied Powers. On September 23rd, she received a telephone call from Major Karl Hass of the German High Command, who told her that he had an important message from her husband, who was imprisoned in Bavaria, Germany. On her arrival at the German embassy, Mafalda was arrested, ostensibly for subversive activities. She was transported to Munich for questioning, then to Berlin, and finally to Buchenwald concentration camp.

On August 24, 1944, the Allies bombed an ammunition factory inside Buchenwald. Some four hundred prisoners were killed, and Princess Mafalda was seriously wounded; she had been housed in a quarter adjacent to the bombed factory, and when the attack occurred, she was buried up to her neck in debris and suffered severe burns to her arm. The conditions of the labor camp caused her arm to become infected as a result, and the medical staff at the facility amputated it. She bled profusely during the operation and never regained consciousness. She died during the night of August 26-27, 1944. Her body was reburied after the War at Kronberg Castle in Hesse, next to her husband's grave.

The invasion of Salerno has been extensively studied and recorded in military history books. Our interest so far has been about the people interned in isolated towns and internment camps from 1940 to 1943 in Southern Italy: Campagna, Potenza, Tito, Brienza, and Ferramonti, and to a lesser extent in Northern Italy. What transpired in those towns is representative of what occurred in other places in Southern Italy as well.

Soldiers of the US 5th Army, under the leadership of General Mark Clark, cheered the news of the Italian surrender as the naval convoys approached the beaches of Salerno but were shocked by the speed and intensity of the German reaction to the landings. Four of the five German divisions in southern Italy were moved to Salerno to seal off and destroy the bridgehead. One of the German Army Divisions came from a camp in Avella, the Herman Goring Division. The battle hung in the balance for the next six days with little support from the 8th British Army led by Field Marshal Bernard Montgomery. The Germans had skillfully delayed the 8th Army with demolitions and a fighting with-drawal, though the British still managed an advance of 300 miles along the Adriatic Sea, 17 days, away from Salerno. The British official history claimed that transport problems and "administrative difficulties" hampered the 8th Army and were the real barrier to rapid advance. Few observers believe that transport problems were responsible for Mont-gomery's failure to press the advance toward Salerno with any sense of urgency. The Canadians (part of the British Airborne Division), there-fore, were ordered to turn inland and advance toward Potenza, a road and rail junction 50 miles east of Salerno.

It is interesting to quote directly from Norman Lewis' (soldier from a British Army outfit) diary about his experience during the invasion of Salerno. He was stationed on the beaches of Paestum, South of Salerno.

Not much was happening there until September 12th. From his diary of September 12, 1943: "Suddenly, today, the war arrived with a vengeance. We were sitting outside our farmhouse, reading, sunning ourselves, and trying to come to terms with the acrid-tasting wine, when we noticed that a rumble of distant cannonades, present from early morning, suddenly seemed to have come closer. Soon after, a line of American tanks went by, making for the battle, and hardly any time passed before they were back. There were fewer of them, and the wild and erratic way they were driven suggested panic. One stopped nearby, and the crew clambered out and fell into one another's arms, weeping. Shortly afterwards there were cries of 'gas," and we saw frantic figures wearing gas masks running in all directions.

Chaos and confusion broke out on all sides. The story was that there had been a breakthrough by the 16th Panzergrenadier Division, which struck suddenly in our direction down to Battipaglia Road, with the clear intention of reaching the sea at Paestum, wiping out the Fifth Army HQ, and cutting the beachhead in half. Rumors began to come in thick and fast, the most damaging one being that General Mark Clark was proposing to abandon the beachhead and had asked the Navy for the Fifth Army to be re-embarked. No one we spoke to believed that this operation was feasible, the feeling being that at the first signs of a withdrawal the Germans would simply roll forward and drive us into the sea." Thanks to the firepower of the US and British Navies, the German Army was prevented from closing in on the Fifth Army.

Potenza, the largest city in the region of Basilicata, was founded in pre-Roman times as a village on the slope of a south-facing ridge above the Basento River. The poor agricultural land had led to the depopulation of the rural areas. However, Potenza had developed as a regional center around its 12th-century cathedral. Beginning on Sept. 13, the Allied air forces began attacks on the city's railroad yards and road junctions. Potenza, crowded with refugees from the Salerno battle area, was targeted by Allied heavy bombers on six consecutive days and much of the city was destroyed in these attacks with heavy loss of life.

The first signs of a German withdrawal were noted on Sept. 17, but no one ordered the Allied air forces to cease attacking a town or the railway yards that the Allies would soon need.

The Germans had planned to hold Potenza with a regiment of the 1st Parachute Division and remnants of the 15th Panzer Division, which was partially camped in Avella. When the Canadians (the Royal 22nd Regiment) mounted an attack, using artillery, armor, and an additional infantry battalion, the German paratroopers withdrew. The Germans had already begun their withdrawal north, but they held onto Potenza with elements of the 1st Parachute Division. The battle for Potenza lasted until the afternoon of the 20th when the German Army withdrew to avoid being cut off. Canadian casualties at Potenza were very light compared to the standards of later battles: Six killed and 21 wounded. Canadian doctors treated 16 wounded Germans as well as Canadians. However, the real tragedy of Potenza was the number of civilian casualties, estimated at over 2,000, including several hundred dead in air raids directed against a town that functioned as a railway center and route for reinforcements. Yes, few internees suffered casualties in the bombing. One building where internees lived was demolished.

In Avella, rumbles from Vesuvius usually meant to the people in the valley that bad news was imminent, but not this time. Rumbles were due to cannon shots from Allied ships. People could hear the shelling off the Salerno coastline. They climbed rooftops to see what was happening on the other side of Vesuvius. They desperately wanted to confirm in their minds that indeed Allied ships were the ones shooting those cannon shots. American paratroopers landed all over the mountains of Avella, Cicciano and Avellino, 30 miles apart between those towns. The target for the drop was to have been in the city of Avellino in order to sabotage the German supply line to Salerno. From a military perspective, it was a failure, since most of the paratroopers were captured by German patrols. However, to the people in the valley, it was a huge success. The feeling that an American parachutist might land at their doorstep buoyed hopes immensely. If an American soldier knocked on the door of a house, a resident would have seen hope reincarnated being transformed in the form of two legs, two arms and a uniform, entering and, in an instant, misery and indignities of occupation would leave her or his state of mind. Hunger was just a matter of being able to sacrifice oneself to forage the farms, but hope was something else. It was needed to nurture aspirations in life. The American landing near Avella was not a total failure. They were able to set up a radio communication centered above the cave of San Michele. They communicated the location of German camps in Avella and German supply traffic to Salerno on Via Appia in Baiano.

As the battle for Salerno was raging, the paved road in Avella, from the camps to Via Appia in Baiano, was crammed with tanks, troop-carrying trucks and motorcycles. One could hear traffic night and day. Vehicles traveled on Via Appia to Nola, pivoting around Mount Vesuvius in a easterly direction and then South to Salerno. People in Avella were not allowed near the new paved road, only on the dirt road to the Cemetery, which ran parallel and close to the paved road. The war in Salerno reached the skies of Avella. German and Allied planes engaged in a dogfight above farmlands. One German plane was shot down very near the Roman Amphitheater and the new paved road. The area was cordoned off by soldiers for their entire stay in Avella. No one in town was allowed near the plane when scavenging for food on the farm, or for anything else edible, until soldiers left town.

The Piazza in Avella was nearly empty. All City Hall employees left their jobs. They refused to make records available to people snooping around City Hall, most likely Gestapo police and Fascists serving the Gestapo. Alvaro left the Magistrate Office, the mayor left town to places unknown. The Maresciallo dared not show his face for fear of providing information to strangers or being interrogated by the Gestapo. Don Nicola closed his studio but socialized with Sergio in the same building, and with Alvaro and Ramiro. Don Nicola was a marked man by the Fascist in the 1930s, but more so during the War. He was constantly reminded of that by the others. Sofia was frantic without Mario. As for the twin sisters, they still knitted sweaters at home to keep their hopes up as to the future of resuming their dressmaking business. The object was to lay low until something good might occur or, better yet, the soldiers left town. They all lived in Sergio's apartment building.

During this period, guards at internment camps were more confused than ever as to what to do. Should they leave or stay at internment camps, since its creator, Il Duce, was dwelling in jail someplace in the Abruzzo region (Central Italy). To make matters worse, Italian soldiers were being taken prisoners by German soldiers on Italian soil and sent to Germany to work in armament factories. Guards wondered: "Who is in charge of the internment program?" Most likely, they were not paid, since the new government was in Brindisi. Rome was occupied by the German Army and payments to the guards were their least concern. Like the locals and the internees in town, the guards had mouths to feed in the family. They shirked their duties and joined the rest of the people in town to search for food. Besides, no one at City Hall was going to hold them accountable, because, as city officials, they didn't want to be responsible for a Fascist program, especially when Fascism was obsolete then.

By then, most, if not all, Podestas (Fascist mayors) in Southern Italy left their posts. They moved to other towns and returned after the War. Few ever made it back, as Communist Partisans had them on their list to do away with after the War. In the interim period (July 25 to September 8, 1943), the registry of internees at the Magistrate Office was sloppily handled or filed away, never again to see daylight. However, records at Ferramonti di Tarsia and Campagna survived the war, but not in Potenza, Tito, and Brienza. Today, there is a museum commemorating the lives of internees at Ferramonti di Tarsia.

In Northern Italy, it was a whole different story. From Rome and North, internment camps were under the control of the German Army. Local administrations at City Hall were accountable to Nazi officials (see Chapter 8). In effect, Nazi officials replaced the Fascist infrastructure from the Minister of Interior to the perfect. As such, guards had no other choice but to acquiesce to Nazi demands. With the return of a "new" Fascist government at Salo (near Milan), Nazi officials still controlled the management of the internment camps in North Italy. There are very few records or stories about the disposition of guards or local administrators in Northern Italy but, clearly, they were under the watchful eyes of the SS troops or the like.

The former Interior Minister, Luigi Federzone, who was the Fascist official in charge of all the internment camps in Italy prior to July 25, 1943, voted together with eighteen others to oust Mussolini from the premiership. He was one of nineteen Ministers who put Il Duce in jail. Like Ciano, Il Duce's son-, he was running for his life from the Nazis after July 25th. This poses an interesting question, "Who was running the internment camps in Italy from July 25th to September 8th?" Certainly, not the prefects, since they were required to be apolitical. The next in line to run the internment camps in Southern Italy were City Hall officials, which meant the Podestas (Fascist mayors), but most of them left town. Thus, it was no surprise that guards left their posts in Campagna, Potenza, Tito, Brienza, and Ferramonti as well as other internment camps, where the Allies occupied that territory. Some guards decided to assist the internees in whatever their needs, including their own families. Both the guards and internees were in the same "boat rowing upstream," avoiding starvation. From the internees' perspective, they preferred to stay in the camps, since there was still a war North of the Alps. Hence, internees put their lives on hold through no fault of their own. They never lost hope that things would get better, knowing that local people cared about their plight.

The magistrate who was responsible for registering the internees at Potenza must have left City Hall, together with the mayor and other officials, well before German soldiers showed up in Potenza around the 15th of September. That may explain why there were no records of internees at the Magistrate's office, only birth and death certificates at City Hall. As such, future mayors and local historians were not aware of the existence of internees in Potenza. Like in Potenza, a small group of German soldiers also were stationed in Brienza, as witnessed by a German-speaking internee. The internee attracted the amorous attention of a German soldier which blossomed into a marriage after the War. This implied that there must have been German troops in Tito as well since it is located between Potenza and Brienza. Fortunately for the internees in those towns, they were able to mingle easily with the populace and hide among the locals. As such, in this case, they found it easier to weather the war than to escape into the hills. By then, Mario and the two Ukrainians escaped to Naples, eventually partaking in another battle there against German occupation.

In Campagna, near Salerno, the guards left the internment camp at the San Bartolomeo Convent on September 8th. The number of internees decreased by then from about 450 to 150. It is estimated that about 300 internees escaped to freedom during the confusion period (July 25 - September 8). On September 9th, the Convent again had a visitor from the German staff requesting a visit. This time, the remaining internees did not return to the Convent having escaped to the hillsides with the help of guards and locals. Besides, there was a major battle taking place, right about the time of that visit, at Battipaglia, a town only five miles away from Campagna. They stayed out on the hills for the duration of the War in Salerno, roughly two weeks. Ferramonti's internment camp was liberated on September 8th, as the guards left for good. Ferramonti was then under Allied control. However, some internees stayed there until 1945, when the War was finally over. From 1943 to 1945, the War was still raging in Europe and news about the atrocities at the extermination camps reached Ferramonti. No incentive to hurry home to Northern Europe. Ferramonti was a lot safer!

With the demise of the Fascist government, subsidies ceased. The fact that internees survived is attributable to their will for survival and the compassion of the locals throughout their stay in Italy. A story that illustrates the point is recounted in the book by Elizabeth Bettina *It Happened in Italy*. A mother from Potenza breastfed her child and a Jewish baby born in Potenza during the height of the battle in Potenza. The fact that the present mayor and local historians could not find the birth certificate of the Jewish child was inexcusable. Birth certificates at City Hall were issued regardless of nationality, even during the War. Most likely, records of the internees at the Magistrate office were destroyed. Some internees freed in Southern Italy found their way to Allied countries via Spain, Portugal, North Africa, the Middle East, etc., but not via Northern Europe, where the War was entering a critical stage.

At that time, Mario and the two deserters tried to appear as inconspicuous as possible to the German soldiers patrolling the streets of Naples. The fact that Mario was in Naples implies other internees were there as well since the islands (Capri, Ischia, etc.) offered some respite from the War. In Naples, anything was possible then with the Camorra operating freely. There was no City government to speak of then. In Naples, there were better possibilities for leaving the War altogether. It was just a question of money. German soldiers mostly concentrated their posting near the train station and the port of Naples, about two miles from the Naval station. The routine of the trio consisted of fishing there and Mario wandering up to the San Carlo Opera House with the hope of seeing Zi Nicola. By evening, they either got together with the scugnizzi to barter with them for food or to cook whatever the catch was for the day. By seven in the evening, a curfew was enforced.

On September 10, the Germans occupied Rome. Italian soldiers in Rome received no orders from Badoglio or the King in Brindisi and didn't know what to do. Germans captured many of them and sent them to German camps and/or armament factories. Some Italian soldiers stripped their clothes off in the streets of Rome and put on old trousers. About 60,000 soldiers wandered the streets begging for food in civilian clothes. German soldiers terrorized civilians in the streets, stole anything in sight, and many girls were violated. Major Herbert Kappler, head of the Gestapo in Rome, sequestered 120 tons of gold from the Bank of Italy and transferred it to Germany.

There was an "avalanche" of Romans taking English lessons and wanting to welcome and cheer the Allies when they would come to Rome. Roman men and allied prisoners were hiding in the city afraid of spending time in Italian or German labor camps. They hid in private homes, convents, seminaries, monasteries, and churches. Rome never had so many insanity cases in their history as some Italian soldiers, Allied prisoners, Roman and foreign Jews, OSS spies, etc. entered the Lunatic Asylum. Kappler forever chased these poor souls, as Romans pitched in to help in hiding them. (See the books, *Bitter Chicory to Sweet Espresso* and *The Battle for Rome.*)

Under Pope Pius XII's balcony, on October 16, 1943, Jewish residents of the Trastevere district of Rome were being transported by trucks to the railroad station in Tiburtina, and on their way to Auschwitz. Trucks stopped in front of Saint Peter Square so that soldiers could take pictures. How macabre that they should stop outside the "border" to the Vatican, a holy place! Those prisoners were more representative of Roman traditions than modern Romans. Roman Jews inhabited ancient Rome along the Tiber River long before Saint Peter appeared on the scene 2,000 years ago. Of 1023 deported, 16 of them made it back home.

Settimia Spizzichino was one of the 16. In 1995, she gave an interview to the BBC in London in which she said: "I came back from Auschwitz on my own. I lost my mother, two sisters, a niece and one brother. Pius XII could have warned us about what was going to happen. We might have escaped from Rome and joined the partisans. He played right into the Germans' hands. It all happened right under his nose. But he was an anti-Semitic Pope, a pro-German Pope. He didn't take a single risk. And when they say the Pope is like Jesus Christ, it is not true. He did not save a single child. Nothing." For more details, refer to the books, *Bitter Chicory to Sweet Espresso* (Carmine Vittoria), and *The Battle for Rome* (Robert Katz).

It is said that cats have nine lives. Mussolini must have had one extra life. On September 12, 1943, he escaped incarceration to torment the Italian people once again. He formed a new government under the banner of the Italian Socialist Republic (RSI) in Salo, near Milan.

THIRTEEN
An Unwanted Rescue

The signing of the Armistice on September 8th triggered several events that affected the warring countries as well as internees living among the populace in towns in Italy. Hitler was hell-bent to free Mussolini from prison, reinstating him, and starting a new Fascist government in North Italy. He justified to anyone who cared to listen that he was freeing a friend and a great modern-day Caesar. What bullshit! Those words were intended for Mussolini's ears and no one others. The real intent was to form a new Fascist government under Mussolini, ally with Germany for propaganda purposes, and legitimize the German occupation of Northern Italy. Eventually, Germany would annex part of Northern Italy bordering the Alps. He was still fighting WWI, when Italy took over the Dolomite Alps. In fact, the city of Bolzano was annexed during WWII and Mussolini did not resist that annexation. As such, Hitler assumed that there would be no resistance from anyone in the new Fascist government to his plan, annexation of the Dolomite Alps. Clearly, Hitler turned the tables on Mussolini. In their initial relationship, Mussolini was the "hunter" in squeezing his partner-in-crime for colonies at no cost. This time, Hitler was the predator looking to annex the Italian Alps. He was just returning the "favor." A con artist like Mussolini must have known then what Hitler was up to.

Since the main architects of internment camps in Italy, Mussolini, and former Fascist Interior Minister Federzone, were no longer in charge, local administrations took matters into their own hands. They released, with the approval of the Badoglio government, Carabinieri guards from internment camp duties and declared freedom for all internees in territories controlled by the new Italian government. Unfortunately, freedom did not come with a dish of spaghetti. It was no bargain to be free when internees had to scavenge for food much like the locals. What was the meaning of freedom, when all they could do was to walk out of their apartments, like anyone else in town, looking for food, and the war was all around them? They could not reclaim the lives they had before and the loss of material and other intangibles. They were stuck in a place for a while that they didn't want to be. At least, the guards or magistrates left them alone. In Northern Italy, they had a different worry, in their lives. With the establishment of a new Fascist government, once again Mussolini restored internment camps under the guidance of German "advisors" in the North. Thus, words from Badoglio about freedom were irrelevant to internees throughout Italy.

In summary, the following events took place in rapid succession and in more or less sequential order in Italy: July 25, Mussolini was incarcerated; September 8, the signing of Armistice; September 8, guards leave internment camps in the South of Italy; September 9, Badoglio and King leave Rome to form a new government: September 9, Allies invade Salerno; September 10, German troops occupy Rome; September 10, whereabouts of Mussolini discovered by Gestapo; September 11, German military staff plan to rescue Mussolini; September 12, Mussolini rescued. These events had significant impacts on the War effort, on the internment camps in Northern Italy, and on Mussolini himself.

Badoglio's government and the Allies also realized the relevance of a new Fascist government in the hands of the Germans. Strict measures to hide and secure Mussolini were taken by the Carabinieri; he was moved several times and guarded by almost a battalion of troops. On July 25, Mussolini was brought to the Carabinieri Headquarters in Trastevere, Rome; on July 27, he was transferred to the island of Ponza in the Tyrrhenian Sea. On August 7, he was transferred to the island of La Maddalena, near the island of Sardinia. Since August 28, he had been held at the Hotel Campo Imperatore, which was built on a remote and defensible mountain plateau 2,112 meters above sea level in the Gran

Sasso d'Italia mountain range, Abruzzo region. A ski station was located next to the hotel, linked by a cable car. He was guarded by forty-three Carabinieri officers and three undercover policemen, who protected their fortress with two heavy machine guns and rifles. One guard was always present in the apartment where Mussolini resided. However, the Chief of the Carabinieri, Senise, advised the guards to exercise "prudence," if the Germans attempted a rescue, contrary to Badoglio order to shoot Mussolini if Mussolini were to escape. In any case, the Carabinieri agreed among themselves that they would not put up a fight.

The three main summits of the Gran Sasso are Corno Grande, which, at 2,912 metres (9,554 feet) is the highest peak in the Apennines, *Corno Piccolo*, and *Pizzo d'Intermesoli*, which is separated from the other two peaks by Val Maone, a deep valley. Corno Grande and Corno Piccolo's ash coloration come from their limestone and dolomite composition. The peaks are snow-covered for much of the year; the snow cover appears to be less each decade. Corno Piccolo is referred to as, "The Sleeping Giant." This is due to the appearance of a profile of a reclined face. This view of Corno Piccolo is evident when viewing the mountain from Pietracamela, a small town near Prati di Tivo, on the north side of the mountain. Corno Grande and Corno Piccolo with their rough vertical walls provide challenges for serious rock climbers.

The mid-to-lower hills of the Gran Sasso are grazed in spring, summer, and autumn by large flocks of sheep guarded by Maremmano-Abruzzese sheepdogs, as well as herds of cattle and semi-wild horses. The pastures are covered with field grass and meadowland wildflowers. The park is also the habitat for diverse wildlife, from rare species such as the Apennine wolf, the Marsican bear, the European wildcat, and the Abruzzo chamois deer. These deer are a variety at the very edge of extinction but are now making a comeback in the park through the efforts of forest rangers and the park administration. Other species of wildlife include wild boar, foxes, grass snakes such as Orsini's viper, and a wide variety of bird life, including golden eagles, peregrine falcons, goshawks, rock sparrows, crested larks, red-backed shrikes, and downy pipits.

At the northern base of Corno Piccolo is Prati di Tivo, a ski village. To the east of Corno Grande and Corno Piccolo lies Campo Imperatore, a 27-kilometer-long (17-mile) and 8-kilometer-wide (5.0-mile) high plateau at about 2,000 meters (6,600 feet) height. Campo Imperatore is home to Italy's oldest continuously operating commercial ski area and is connected to Fonte Cerreto via cable cars. In summary, it was a very remote place to hide Mussolini and very difficult to reach on foot. The defenders had all the advantage of the view of the valley below them.

German intelligence intercepted a coded Italian report which indicated that Mussolini was imprisoned somewhere in the Abruzzo mountains. The Germans employed a ruse to confirm the exact location in which a German doctor pretended to establish a hospital at the hotel on the Grand Sasso. Major Herbert Kappler, in the Gestapo headquarters in Rome, (see the book, *Bitter Chicory to Sweet Espresso*) used counterfeit money to obtain crucial information from local informants. Hitler selected the man to personally escort Mussolini back to Germany: Otto Skozeny. The overall planner of the rescue attempt was General Kurt Student. Major Skorzeny was born in Vienna in 1908. He trained as an engineer and became the manager of a scaffolding business. In 1939, he joined the Luftwaffe and later transferred to a crack SS military formation.

On 12 September 1943, Skorzeny and 160 SS troopers rescued Mussolini in a high-risk glider mission. Ten gliders, each carrying nine soldiers and a pilot, towed planes started from the Pratica di Mare Air Base, near Rome. Meanwhile, the valley station of the funicular railway leading to the Campo Imperatore was captured at 2:00 pm in a ground attack by two paratrooper companies that cut all telephone lines. At 2:05, the airborne commandos landed their ten gliders on the mountain (Corno Piccolo) near the hotel. One crashed and caused injuries. Mussolini and a Carabiniere watched the landings from the little window of Il Duce's apartment. However, he looked worried and commented, "This was not (what I) wanted." After the gliders landed, parachutists climbed out, dropping to the ground. Italian General Fernando Soleti (of the Italian African Police, who flew in with Skorzeny), emerged, walking toward the Hotel Imperatore, where Mussolini resided. Soleti told the Carabinieri to stand down. Behind Soleti walked Skorzeny carrying a machine gun. Parachutists followed Skorzeny.

Approaching the hotel, Soleti shouted: "Don't shoot!" Skorzeny entered the radio room and kicked the chair from under the operator interrupting transmission. Then, he ran upstairs, with a pistol in hand, and burst into Mussolini's suite. "Il Duce, the Fuhrer sent me to free you," Skorzeny said. "I knew that my friend Adolf Hitler would not have abandoned me," Mussolini replied. Il Duce followed Skorzeny outside the hotel and turning to a Carabiniere said, "I would have preferred to be freed by Italians." It was clear to all who witnessed Il Duce, that he was pale and sickly in appearance. His great friend, SS Colonel Eugen Dollmann, who had often translated at Hitler-Mussolini meetings, said: "I believe that Mussolini would have preferred to remain on the Gran Sasso to admire the flight of eagles." According to the book, *Bitter Chicory to Sweet Espresso*, Dollmann may have been a double spy agent for the OSS (later, the CIA).

Mussolini was flown out by a plane that had arrived in the meantime. Although under the given circumstances the small plane was overloaded, Skorzeny insisted on accompanying Mussolini, which endangered the mission's success. After an extremely dangerous but successful takeoff, they flew to Pratica di Mare, Rome. They then immediately continued to fly to Vienna, where Mussolini stayed overnight at the Hotel Imperial. The next day he was flown to Munich, where his family had been waiting for him. On September 14, he met Hitler at Führer Headquarters, in Wolf's Lair, near Rastenburg. By then, Mussolini was a shadow of himself. He was a sick man.

German propaganda gave full credit for the rescue to Skorzeny. General Student, the main architect of the rescue, protested to Luftwaffe commander Hermann Goring about this, but Goring could do nothing because Hitler had accepted the story that Skorzeny was the principal hero. Goring suspected that SS Chief Heinrich Himmler maneuvered to make Skorzeny the hero to promote the SS over the Luftwaffe. This was an argument between the two whereby jealousy overruled rational exchanges between the two.

Once at Rastenburg, Hitler got down to business with a stern message. "I don't doubt that you will agree with me in believing that one of the first acts .... will be to sentence to death the traitors of the Grand Council...including Count Ciano. He is a traitor to his country, ...to Fascism... to Germany, and to his family... But I advise you: It is preferable that the death sentence be carried out in Italy." "But you're talking of the husband of the daughter (Edda) whom I adore, the father of my grandchildren," Mussolini protested. "All the more reason Count Ciano merits punishment in that not only has he failed in fidelity toward his country, but in fidelity to his family," Mussolini told Hitler that his only desire was to leave public life and rest due to his sickness. Finally, Hitler insisted that Mussolini return to Italy and head a new Fascist government. If Mussolini refused, he would...... destroy Milan, Genoa, and Turin just as he intended to destroy London.

The threat from Hitler was somewhat hypocritical. On one hand, Hitler was implying that Italy was going to be treated like any other European country colonized or terrorized by Germany, if Mussolini didn't do as told! On the other hand, Germany was already treating Italy as a colony, no different from other European countries occupied by Germany, raping its men, robbing material things, including priceless art, and indiscriminate killings all over Italy, including internees in Northern Italy. It could not have become any worse! Mussolini didn't realize that the threat did not carry any weight, since it made no difference to war conditions or impact on Italy. Mussolini didn't call his bluff and ask the question: "What is the difference between now and what you intend to do?" Perhaps, Mussolini was too sick to point out the absurdity of Hitler's threats or, perhaps, he was of the same kindred spirit. More likely, Il Duce was worried for himself at the hands of this madman. Finally, the clown was intimidated, and the gig was up!

Mussolini spent two weeks in Germany for medical exams, being reunited with his family and meeting Fascist Party and government officials who fled to safety in North Italy. Others fled to Spain. Mussolini, his wife Rachele, and their two youngest children, Romano and Anna Maria were secured in Hirschberg Castle, fifty miles South of Munich. Ciano and Edda had been in Munich about three weeks before Mussolini arrived. The Badoglio government placed Ciano under house arrest in Rome. Edda arranged, with Eugene Colonel Dollmann's help, for the couple and their three children to escape house arrest and fly to Spain on August 27th, 1943. Instead, they were flown to Munich by Skorzeny, and Ciano was placed under house arrest again. Obviously, the Cianos had no desire to go to Munich. The Ciano family was double-crossed. There is no information to clarify this story. However, this much can be said: Dollmann set it up for the couple to fly to Spain on a German plane. At the last minute, there was a switch of pilots. Skorzeny took over the flight and flew to Munich. The fact that Skorzeny was involved in this affair implies that Hitler must have heard of Ciano's plans. Let's examine this situation from reverse engineering on something that, perhaps, could have been arranged. Had Ciano's family reached Spain, a lot of heads would have rolled: the pilot and the person who instructed the pilot at minimum. Furthermore, If Doll-mann set it up through a third person, he, the pilot, and the third person would have been easily exposed and done away with by Hitler. The only possible way to have succeeded was for the pilot to remain in Spain. That was far-fetched unless Dollmann piloted the plane himself. Sooner or later the long arm of Hitler would have reached that pilot in Spain. Hence, the logical conclusion is that Dollmann was the double-crosser since he had direct connections to Hitler.

On September 18 in Munich, Mussolini made his first radio speech to the Italian people since the rescue. However, before the speech, Hitler had spoken to Mussolini about re-establishing an Italian Fascist state. Specifically, he suggested the name, Italian Fascist Republic, but Mussolini objected on the basis that the word Fascist might be a subject of discord among Italians. As of November 25, the new regime would be known as the Italian Social Republic (RSI). The name took him back to his past before he invented Fascism in the 1920s. In his speech, he contrasted Hitler's stable regime with the deceitfulness of the King. "It is not the Fascist regime that has betrayed...., it is the monarchy that has betrayed the regime," he said. " .... the state we want to establish will be national and social in the highest sense of the word............" he added.

Claretta Petacci heard the speech at an airfield near Bergamo, in Northern Italy, where she and her family had stopped en route to Merano, forty miles from Innsbruck and very near the Alps. She was so overcome with emotion that she fainted, according to her diary. Three days after the incarceration of Mussolini, the Petacci family left Rome for Northern Italy. On the night of August 12, 1943, the Petaccis were arrested on orders of the Badoglio government and imprisoned at Novara, a city west of Milan. This was an interesting development at that time. The Badoglio government was in Rome, well before the signing of the Armistice and still Allied with Germany. The government consisted of Badoglio, the King of Italy, and a handful of wannabe ministers. However, Novara was under German occupation, strange but true. One country occupying territories of its ally, no different than Italian soldiers under German command in Russia, Europe, North Africa, etc.! Let's put this in perspective. Badoglio did not have the time to warn Italian soldiers (more than a million of them) spread all over Europe to come home or hurry from the wrath of the German Army and, yet, he had the time to track down the Pettaccis all over Italy and prevail on the local Carabinieri to incarcerate her.

Undoubtedly, this operation must have been conducted by the Carabinieri secretly from the Nazis! So much energy was spent on one person at the expense of a million Italian soldiers. In fairness to Badoglio, there were no Carabinieri in Russia to warn Italian soldiers to come home, but there were other means to warn those poor souls, as Churchill did at Dunkirk. Obviously, Badoglio cared more about personal affairs than those soldiers stranded in faraway lands. On September 17, the Petaccis were freed in time for Clara to hear Mussolini's speech the next day.

Soon after the Petaccis settled in Marcello's (Clara's brother) villa, SS Commander General Karl Wolff arrived and told Clara that he needed help. He stated that Ciano must return to Italy. He told her that her influence could persuade Mussolini's government to issue extradition of Ciano from Germany. He added, so far, that hasn't been issued. She replied that she was not in the service of the Reich. After about two months, on October 28, Mussolini and Clara met, when he returned to Gargnano by the Garda Lake, Italy. When Clara returned to Merano, her mother pleaded with her to end her relationship with Mussolini. "....Our name has been compromised." "You are right, leave me alone," Clara replied.

From Merano, the Petacci family moved to Gardone Riviera, in the Villa Fiordaliso (lily), just six miles from the new Fascist government (RSI) at Gargnano. German and Japanese diplomats occupied the third and fourth floors of the villa and the Petaccis were on the first and second floors. Clara spent most of her time at the Villa Fiordaliso swimming and sunbathing in the daytime. In the evenings, she stayed in, awaiting Mussolini's phone calls. Mussolini arranged trysts with Clara in the tower of a building across the road that had belonged to his friend, the poet Gabriele D'Annunzio.

The new republic, essentially a Nazi puppet state, claimed sovereignty over all of Italy, though it only controlled those territories in German hands in Northern and Central Italy. Effectively, Germany legitimized the occupation of Italy. Secondly, German troops and the nasty SS soldiers could do as they wished in internment camps. On November 14, the RSI enacted 18 policy guidelines, formally legitimizing the extermination of Jews pursued by Nazism. In particular, RSI Interior Minister Guido Buffarini Guidi ordered the arrest of all Jews present in the territory controlled by the RSI and transferred them to "special" internment camps. In addition, RSI established the repossession of Jewish properties. With that order, the Nazi plans for extermination received crucial support. It is no coincidence that the German government hailed the Fascist anti-Jewish turn, as being very timely. Starting that December, the RSI and Nazis began a manhunt for Jews with thorough sweeps carried out in the Venice area. About 150 Venetian Jews were captured. That took place the night between December 5 and 6. Moreover, December 6 was the day that a deportation train departed for Auschwitz from Milan, where the city prison of San Vittore operated as a gathering point for Jews swept up in the North.

There were between 32,000 and 42,000 Jews in Italy in 1943. The Italian Social Republic (RSI), headquartered in Salò, on Lake Garda, was established. On November 1, RSI reinstituted internment camps in North Italy which had been abolished two months prior by the Badoglio government. On November 26, the RSI made available 1727 spaces for civilian internees; a capacity that would rise, in the early months of 1944 to 8,000 slots. Often German military command intervened on questions concerning internment, having its say on the fate of the camps, requisitioning personal files, requesting lists of Jews, and imposing sudden internment for security reasons.

With Mussolini back in power, at least in his mind, and the German Army in full retreat in Salerno, the War entered a new phase. No longer did the German Army dictate the pace of war to other combatants. The outcome of the war was inevitable, just a matter of time. Sooner or later, the Allies would occupy Italy, at least up to the Po River, which meant that the new Fascist government controlled very little territory. However, it exposed the diehards in the Fascist and Nazi movements, who refused to believe. As for the internees in Northern Italy, they still were stuck there waiting for the end of the war. Meanwhile, the Nazis were hell-bent on extermination. The lucky ones waited it out in Southern Italy.

FOURTEEN
Ghost of Masaniello

M ario and the two deserters (Vladimir and Dimitri) arrived in Naples about the same time as German troops, on about September 1, 1943. Upon arrival, the German Army secured the railroad station in Naples in order to facilitate the deployment of troops in the area and prevent deserters and other young men from leaving Naples. The trio (Mario and company) had no chance of making a run to the station on the way to Avella and escape the clutches of the German Army. By then, Naples had already suffered 105 bombings from Allied planes, resulting in over 25,000 dead, tens of thousands wounded, 100,000 apartments destroyed and incomparable cultural and artistic items, dear to Neapolitans, obliterated. The city was left smoldering in ruins, no water, no food and a populace composed of women, children, the wounded, and the elderly. The more able-bodied and young ones had either fled or were in some distant land. To add to the misery, Vesuvius had erupted, after having been dormant for a long time.

Neapolitans have seen invaders come and go for millennia in their cherished history. It appears everything and everyone was conspiring against the people of Naples. Not only was Vesuvius acting up, but the random bombings of the city in the ensuing days, and the uncertainty created by a military takeover of the city only rattled their nerves and added fear and trepidation. By nature, Neopolitans, do not frighten easily because of their ability to adapt and survive invaders. But these times were very different from the past. They were being hit from all sides: vagaries of nature, bombs from the skies and attacks on the ground. They made peace with temperamental Vesuvius long ago. In addition, Italian military generals, who were responsible for protecting Naples, abandoned it, having fled in civilian clothes. The city, left unprotected, was then at the mercy of a military force of 20,000 soldiers who were determined to follow Hitler's order to destroy it. The order was to reduce Naples to "cinders and mud" so that the arriving Allied forces could not use the port city as a strategic naval base. However, these invaders were different from the ones in the past; they were not about to "dilly-dally" with Neapolitans to accommodate the wishes of the natives.

Naples consists of relics of different cultures, as reflected in the architecture. One district may have narrow streets full of vendors selling everything imaginable, reminiscent of a street bazaar in an Arabic country. Right next to it there may be an avenue as wide as the Grand Canyon surrounded by buildings dating back to Spanish or French rule. In other districts, there may be a modern asphalt road leading to antique Roman Villas, etc. From the age of the buildings and their architecture, the streets, the music and the Neapolitan dialect, one could decipher the history of Naples from ancient to modern times. Each district is distinct from others in the sense that people living in a district have a unique characteristic different from the others, from the poor to the very rich and highly cultured.

It was inevitable that the street kids, the scugnizzi, would get themselves in trouble with the new invaders. Whereas scugnizzi strived for disorder in the streets to their advantage, the occupiers strived for the opposite. On September 10, the first bloody clash occurred. An Afrika Korp's jeep on patrol was stuck in one of those narrow streets full of vendors, detaining a scugnizzo in the back seat of the jeep. Obviously, the boy was in his territory and, most likely, had lured the jeep there, knowing full well that he would be rescued from the German soldiers. A scugnizzo is no one's child but, also, everybody's child in Naples. He was usually an "almost" orphan whose father died in war and who lived in the streets. The mothers threw them out of the house because they could not feed them. They begged, stole, bribed, and pimped to survive, and ranged from five to twenty years of age. Soon enough people gathered around the jeep to impede forward or reverse motion. Neapolitans blocked the path of the jeep, killing sailors and soldiers and freeing the scugnizzo. Thanks to a city official, who summoned his countrymen to surrender some of their hostages and all their weapons. Retaliation for the insurrection came quickly; the Germans set fire to the National Library and opened fire on the crowd gathered there.

On September 12, numerous German soldiers were killed on the streets of Naples, while about 4,000 Italian soldiers and civilians were deported to Germany for forced labor.

The populace refused to collaborate and rose to rebel. The same day, Colonel Walter Schöll assumed command of the military occupiers in the city, declaring a curfew and a state of siege, with orders to execute all those responsible for hostile actions against German troops, and up to 100 Neapolitans for every German killed. The following proclamations appeared on the walls of the city on September 13:

With immediate action from today, I assume the absolute control with full powers of the city of Naples and the surrounding areas.

1. **Every single citizen who behaves calmly will enjoy my protection. On the other hand, anyone who openly or surreptitiously acts against the German armed forces will be executed. Moreover, the home of the miscreant and its immediate surroundings will be destroyed and reduced to ruins. Every German soldier wounded or murdered will be avenged a hundred times.**
2. **I order a curfew from 8 pm to 6 am. Only in case of alarm will it be allowed to use the road in order to reach the nearest shelter.**
3. **A state of siege is proclaimed.**
4. **Within 24 hours all weapons and ammunition of any kind, including shotguns, hand grenades, etc., must be surrendered. Anyone who, after that period, is found**

**in possession of a weapon will be immediately
executed. The delivery of weapons and ammunition
shall be made to the German military patrols.**
5. **People must keep calm and act reasonably.**

**These orders and the already executed reprisals have been neces-
sary because of the large number of German soldiers and officers
who were vilely murdered or seriously wounded while fulfilling
their duties; indeed, in some cases the wounded have even been
insulted and abused in a manner unworthy of a civil population.**

The orders were followed with the shooting of eight prisoners of
war, while a tank opened fire against students who were beginning to
gather in the nearby University of Naples. A young Neapolitan sailor
was executed on the stairs of the German Military headquarters, while
thousands of people were forced by German troops to watch. On the
same day, 500 people were also forcibly deported to Germany, and again
forced to watch the execution of 14 Carabinieri policemen, who had
offered armed resistance to the occupying forces.

In other clashes, the people of Naples defended their city against the
systematic destruction and looting by German troops. Each day,
tensions were rising, with some of the most beloved and precious treasures of the city destroyed by fire at the University of Naples and the
National Historic Archives. These acts of brutality struck home with a
population battered, but still proud of their past. The straw that broke
the camel's back occurred on September 22, when a decree was issued
that all males between 18-33 years of age were to present themselves to
be deported and used for forced labor in Germany. Men were rounded
up and brought to the soccer stadium in the Vomero district to be
deported.

Meanwhile, people living within 300 meters of the coastline were
ordered to evacuate in 20 hours; 35,000 families were now filling the
streets while plans for blowing up the port were being finalized. This
meant that about 240,000 people were forced to leave their homes, take
refuge with other families, or in places such as caves and public buildings. Groups of citizens began to stock up on weapons stored in Cara-

binieri's barracks of the city and in various stores of arms and ammunition in view of the fighting that now seemed inevitable. A manifesto from the city's prefect called for compulsory work by all males in labor camps in Germany. However, only 150 Neapolitans (most likely Fascists) out of the planned 30,000 heeded the call, which led Schöll to send soldiers into the city to round up and immediately execute defaulting citizens.

This was the second and last incident that sparked the uprising; it was impossible to wait any longer. About 30,000 Neapolitans were ready to engage soldiers in the streets, parks, beaches, in their barracks, and anywhere else in Naples. On September 26, an unarmed and screaming crowd saved young men apprehended by German soldiers for deportation. In response to this, an unarmed crowd poured into the streets for the purpose of impeding or slowing the Nazi roundups of the young men. The rioters were joined by former Italian soldiers who had kept themselves hidden so far.

By then, German soldiers looted big department stores in the main streets of Naples, undercutting the scugnizzi. A group of scugnizzi was raiding a department store when German security police surrounded the store and demanded surrender. Masaniello, leader of the scugnizzi, showed up with 200-300 scugnizzi and counter-demanded that the Germans surrender.

What makes this story so remarkable was that Masaniello (a ficticious name) and a group of "children," scugnizzi, were staring right into two Tiger tanks. It was not clear whether Masaniello's response was an act of courage, foolishness, or simply a bluff. It was a life-or-death situation, and this teen-ager was the epitome of calm. The name Masaniello is derived from a Neapolitan fisherman who became a hero in the 1640s, in a revolt against Spanish rule. It was a classic stalemate leading to only one conclusion, a shootout. Every street in Naples was barricaded and the people rallied behind the scugnizzi. By this time, Neapolitans had enough of the invaders attacking their children.

The scugnizzi residing with Mario and the two deserters at the naval military station were itching to join their friends. There was determination in their eyes and hunger to prove themselves to their mothers and relatives. Mario surmised that there must have been a cache of arms and ammunition someplace in the station. They didn't have to search very hard; It was right under their noses. It was not a case of Mario leading the scugnizzi to the armory where the ammunition and rifles were located. The scugnizzi knew exactly where it was. That was survival course 101 for them, knowing the layout of the station. In the armory, there were rifles, pistols, hand grenades, assortments of small arms, and, most important, benzene containers.

The eyes of the two deserters lit up. They knew how to make the so-called Molotov cocktails (bombs), which were very effective against tanks. The Molotov bomb consists of a bottle half full of benzene or gasoline topped with a cloth rag. The object is to light the rag with a match when a tank's fuel is most exposed, and toss the bottle at it, hard enough to shatter the bottle resulting in an explosion. Russian soldiers used this technique during the battle of Stalingrad. Molotov was the name of the Russian Foreign Minister then, whose name became affiliated with the bomb.

The two Russian soldiers at the naval station taught the technique to a very receptive audience. The scugnizzi practiced and practiced until they ran out of bottles. They went to a department store and raided a month's supply of bottles. The two Russians joined their fight and led them in a hunt for Tiger tanks. Their spirits were sky-high. All of a sudden, they became the hunters rather than the hunted. All the while, Mario set up an intelligence network where barricades were to be in the city to maximize exposure of a tank to a Molotov bomb. Tanks became most vulnerable in riding over the barricades. He would set up a scugnizzo at each barricade. They in turn passed the location to others as to when and where a tank would be approaching. In addition, Molotov explosives were thrown from roofs, windows, and barricades. WWI rifles were the weapon of choice by the scugnizzi. Not a single scugnizzo died from tossing a Molotov cocktail, thanks to the training by the two Ukrainians.

The next four days, September 27 to 30, marked the turning point of the insurrection against German occupation. The defenders of Naples, composed mainly of women, scugnizzi, elderly, deserters, young men, and the wounded, would rise in a spontaneous act of defiance to rid themselves of the occupiers. There had been no meetings or action plans, but the air was charged with rebellion and Neapolitans grabbed the moment. Clashes sprang up randomly around the city. Everyone, from the young to the old, participated. After fierce fighting, they rose in unison, battled the occupiers, and drove them from the city. About fifteen Tiger tanks were destroyed. It was the first revolt in any big city in Europe against the German Army and the first city to expel the occupiers. It was an example of the subsequent actions in other big cities.

There was a deep-rooted reason for the Neapolitans to revolt. They have survived invasions for millennia. As a result of being "hit over the head" so many times, they have adopted a philosophy that can best be described as "Ci Arrangiamo" meaning that they will adapt to survive their credo. This is a philosophy of avoiding confrontations whereby they and the invaders can live together in harmony, although they may disagree politically, for example. In general, they are happy-go-lucky and easy-going people. Only once before, over a two-thousand-year span, in 1647, have they rebelled. It is not in their nature to resort to violence. They would rather talk their way out of a difficult situation and co-exist. In short, they are not born to be heroes. The fact that the German occupation provoked Neapolitans to their limit or to their threshold of what they considered humanly tolerable or adaptable speaks volumes about the brutality of the German occupation. Neapolitans reached a stage when dying was better than living with this occupation. The invaders didn't realize that the young Neapolitans, including the children, represented the heart and soul of the city, but the invaders were hell-bent on their mission to deport them. Thus, rebellion was inevitable. Without the young ones, Neapolitans felt that they had nothing to look forward to.

September 27, 1943

The rounding up of men continued, as Neapolitans were deported to Germany. The populace was furious. Meanwhile, the Germans commenced to raid the University of Naples for students to deport, but the streets of Naples found insurgent groups challenging the invaders every inch of the way. About 200 insurgents attacked the armory of Castel Sant'Elmo, near the Naval Station where Mario was hiding. They subdued German counterattacks, confiscating arms and ammunition. About 200 men, plus a reinforcement of another 50, attacked the soccer stadium in the Vomero district (near the San Carlo), where young Neapolitans were interned to be deported. It was defended by a large group of German soldiers. There were violent shootings carried out with machine guns that fired from above the surrounding buildings. The clash lasted several hours. German troops stationed in the stadium had no way out. In the evening the German commander came out with a white flag. Negotiations began which were also conducted at the German Headquarters in Corso Vittorio Emanuele. The soldiers were released from the bad predicament that they were in. Again, Neapolitans preferred to talk rather than to fight, and alleviate misery for all. As usual, the invaders learned nothing from the episode. They continued to search for young adults to deport.

Scugnizzi dove into the Gulf of Naples to retrieve guns of WWI vintage which had been dumped there by the Germans. Caches of weapons were distributed throughout the city by the scugnizzi network. Knives, broom handles, toilets, and furniture were tossed from balconies aimed at soldiers below to block roads, deterring passageways of motorized vehicles. Naples, having narrow and labyrinthine streets, was more easily defensible against large unwieldy tanks. The underground cave network also made it easy to get from one place to another, leading to successful surprise attacks.

September 28

Maddalena Cerasuolo, affectionately called Lenuccia, 23, was the eldest daughter of Carlo Cerasuolo, one of the leaders of the revolt in the Materdei district. She was tasked with procuring weapons for the insurgents in the Carabinieri stations and barracks in the neighborhood. The commander of the barracks, appreciating her courage and determination, proposed that she request surrender from Germans who were in the shoe factory on Trone Street. In exchange, the Maresciallo promised to give weapons to the insurgents. Lenuccia accepted. She did not want to consider the dangers that she might encounter. German soldiers could have killed her instantly.

The building was surrounded by insurgents. They prevented the German soldiers from leaving the factory where they had gone to steal leather hides and valuables that were in the building. Lenuccia knocked on the door and handed the request for surrender to the soldier who had appeared at the door. Again, a preference for talking. The soldier refused the surrender with a disgusting grin. Immediately a shooting started between the men surrounding the building and the Germans. Lenuccia barely had time to take shelter. Some insurgents and enemy soldiers died in that battle. The building occupants were forced to surrender.

On returning home Lenuccia saw a German patrol on a sidecar that had stopped to ask an old man where the Sanità bridge was. She immediately sensed that they intended to blow up the bridge. She ran at breakneck speed, reached her father Carlo, and told him of her fears. Carlo Cerasuolo gathered a few insurgents who were nearby and ran toward the bridge. Lenuccia ran through Via Santa Teresa to warn as many people as she could. She met a butcher in the neighborhood, a huge man in his bloody white coat because he had stopped halfway through a slaughter. He had two pistols, one in each hand, and ran to the bridge. He had just heard of the impending explosion of "his" bridge and wasted no time in giving his help.

Having gathered some insurgents, Lenuccia joined her father on one side of the Sanità bridge. Three German soldiers were under fire. They had already mined the bridge. Lenuccia also participated in the shooting with an old, but still effective, musket, WWI vintage. As the Germans were preparing to trigger the explosion, one of the insurgents bravely slipped inside the trap door, where the explosives had been placed, managing to tear the wires connected to the detonator, saving the bridge from destruction.

Gennarino and his companions had blown up a German truck with a grenade in via Toscanella. Soldiers on the truck were involved in a massacre in Miano, near Capodimonte. Then they blocked another truck, loaded with soldiers that followed a short distance away. Gennarino, with a hand grenade, stood in front of the vehicle blocking it. The Germans surrendered and were taken prisoner by that group of insurgents, made up of scugnizzi and other young people.

The fighting grew to a crescendo after more Neapolitans joined the rebellion. In the Materdei district, a German patrol, which had taken shelter in a city building, was surrounded and kept under siege for hours, until the arrival of reinforcements. In the end, three Neapolitans lost their lives in the battle. A group of 40 men, armed with rifles and machine guns, set up a roadblock, killing six German soldiers and capturing four, while other fighting broke out in other parts. The soldiers launched other raids in the Vomero district, amassing numerous prisoners inside the Campo Sportivo del Littorio. Scugnizzi and Italian deserters attacked the Vomero sports field, freeing prisoners who were earmarked to be deported to Germany. Even in the heat of battle, German soldiers were hell-bent to deport Neapolitans. Talking alone was not going to dissuade the occupiers from carrying out their mission, no matter the cost of lives. It was sheer madness, incredibly true. Neapolitans had no other choice but to fight.

September 29

On the third day of the riot, the streets of Naples witnessed fierce clashes. As no connection could be established with national anti-fascist organizations, the insurrection was still without central direction, operations being in the hands of local leaders. In Giuseppe Mazzini Square, a substantial German group reinforced by tanks attacked 50 rebels, killing 12 and injuring more than 15. The workers' quarter of Ponticelli suffered a heavy artillery bombardment, after which German units committed several indiscriminate massacres among the population. Other fighting took place near the Capodichino Airport in Piazza Otto-calli, in which three Italian airmen lost their lives.

In Santa Teresa, a group of scugnizzi armed with rifles and hand grenades opposed German tanks that advanced along the road. The most courageous boy was Gennarino Capuozzo. He was only 11 years old, a cousin of Lenuccia. Despite his young age, he already worked in the shop, since his father had enlisted and left for Libya in 1941. He had joined a group of scugnizzi who fled the reformatory to fight the Germans. The scugnizzi brigade had moved to Via Santa Teresa, the road that connected Via Toledo with Capodimonte, where they took up positions on the terrace of the building that housed the Istituto delle Maestre Pie Filippini, a hundred meters from the museum. The youths fired from the institute's terrace at German tanks that attempted to leave the city. Gennarino Capuozzo, in throwing hand grenades at the "panzers," leaned out of the institute's terrace. At that moment, a grenade, thrown by one of the tanks in the column, hit Gennarino in full, killing him instantly. The sacrifice of Gennarino Capuozzo, too early a hero, was one of the last casualties of the armed struggle since, that same evening, the Germans began negotiations with the insurgents to leave Naples before the arrival of the Allied Forces. Finally, the locals persuaded the invaders to talk, which had been their aim all along, consistent with their credo "Ci Arrangiamo."

September 30

In retreating, the Germans burned everything in sight: Museums, libraries, houses, etc. On October 1, the Allies entered Naples, welcomed by cheering people. The loss of life for the four days was 168 deaths among the 1,589 partisans and 159 among the civilians. However, cemetery records noted 562 deaths. The armed insurrection against the Germans prevented the occupiers from making Naples "ash and mud," as Adolf Hitler had explicitly asked, and the mass deportations of citizens of Naples were avoided as much as possible. To this day, it is not clear how many were deported to Germany but not the 30,000 initially planned by the Germans. It is estimated the number ranged between 4,000 and 5,000.

Although the Germans were about to leave Naples, some Fascists still resisted in the city. They shot treacherously from the windows at the civilian population. Some of these had barricaded themselves in a building in Materdei shooting wildly at passers-by. Lenuccia and other resistance men tried to flush them out of their lair. An American officer arrived with a jeep, replacing the insurgents with his soldiers. He disarmed them, breaking their rifles. Lenuccia said to the officer that she would have liked to keep her musket. The soldier with a smile told her to keep the rifle and added "Go home!"

The next day Lenuccia was invited to the royal palace where she met General Montgomery. He, having heard of her bravery, had wanted to meet her. Montgomery hugged and kissed her, thanking her for what she had done. The city of Naples was awarded the Gold Medal for Valor for this rebellion against German occupation. It is the highest honor of the Italian State. Also, four "scugnizzi," who lost their lives in the fighting, were awarded the Gold Medal for Valor: Gennaro (Gennarino) Capuozzo, 12, Filippo Illuminato, 13, Pasquale Formisano, 17 and Mario Menechini, 18.

Before the Germans left Naples, their demolition squads went around the city blowing up anything of value or in operation, including the telegraph building, central post office, department stores, etc. There was no water or electricity. Naples smelled of charred wood. People were experimenting with sea water for cooking and trying to distill it. Neapolitans were deprived of things that justify a city's existence and adapted themselves to a life in the Dark Ages. Even the upper class and royal families were suffering.

There was no food and Neapolitans went out to nearby farms in the valley to search for anything edible. Neapolitans fondly refer to the valley as their backyard. There were about fifteen different kinds of plants that were edible, but bitter in flavor, including the chicory plant.

Inexplicably, no boats were allowed to fish in the fall of 1943. Germans planted delayed-action explosive devices in Naples before departure. As a result, several buildings were pulverized in late October of 1943, about three weeks after they left. Colonel Scholl of the German army had mined buildings located 300 meters from the coastline. A million and a half people left their houses and crowded into the streets to avoid potential explosions in their respective buildings and streets. Fortunately, the bombs never exploded along the coastline, but they did at other places. In late fall, most restaurants in Naples were open but the clientele was mostly Allied officers.

Butcher shops displayed chicken heads for five lire (one dollar), chicken intestines for five lire, a gizzard for three lire, and a large piece of windpipe for seven lire. The cat and dog populations declined in the Naples area. Allied soldiers were charged with looting antique art objects. Officers of England's King's Dragoon Guards, who entered Naples first after the Germans left, removed paintings from frames in museums and made off with fine pottery collections. These items were crated and shipped to England, never to be returned!

The black market reigned supreme and prices were outrageous. At the famous restaurant Zi Teresa in Naples, the price for a fish dinner was priced at 10,000 Lire (about 5-10 dollars). That is equivalent to about $1000 today. The black market was controlled by the Camorra in collaboration with the local Maresciallo who wielded tyrannical power in towns as well as in cities like Naples. The Camorra was an organization of thieves, equivalent to the Mafia in Sicily. By this time things were returning to normal, except for telephone communications and electricity. People were stealing wires and selling the copper to small shops to melt. In the town of Cicciano, near Avella, the AMG (Allied Military Government) caught several wire cutters in the act of stealing copper wires, and they were sent to Military prison. At least, the prisoners had something to eat regularly. If there was plundered to be taken, the Camorra was first in line. They tolerated the Carabinieri, because the Carabinieri kept the brigands, small-time robbers, away from the big "spoils." The brigands operated mostly in the surrounding hill towns in the valley.

North of Naples, the Camorra, the local Mafia enterprise, was concentrated in towns like Afragola, Acerra, Aversa, and Casoria (Zona di Camorra), although they controlled all illicit trades or legal business throughout Naples and neighboring towns in the valley. Brigands offered the main competition to the Camorra. The Camorra lived by their own secret set of rules, whether Germans were in the city.

U.S. General Mark Clark came to Naples to take credit for "conquering" Naples. The fact that he was the youngest field general and declared himself as the liberator of Naples should tell you something about his ambition and vanity at the expense of the people of Southern Italy. The General had become the destroying angel, prone to panic, as at Paestum (Salerno), and then, to violent and vengeful reaction, occasioned by the sacrifice of the village of Altavilla. The town was shelled out of existence in the fear that it might have contained a few German soldiers! General Ulysses Grant of US Civil War fame would have been proud of General Clark had he lived then. He never acknowledged the role that the scugnizzi or anyone that played in the liberation of Naples, as Field Marshal Montgomery did. To General Clark's thinking, scugnizzi's efforts in war counted for naught! The historical fact remained that there was not a single German soldier in sight when General Clark entered Naples. The only thing that he captured was a destroyed city. Nevertheless, a celebration of the liberation was called for at the restaurant, "Zi Teresa," near where all the ships were sunk by Allied bombing. The problem with General Clark's visit to Zi Teresa was that there was no meat or fish to offer the general. One astute chef had a brilliant idea. He went to the aquarium located at City Hall in Naples, about a mile from the restaurant, and raided a large bass from the aquarium. He then cooked it with vegetables and, voila, dinner was served to General Clark. According to the General, it was the best fish meal that he ever had. The resourcefulness of the people of Naples in those starving days was truly remarkable. When the whole population was starving and the scugnizzi were pimping even their sisters and mothers, they produced a four-star meal for a three-star General! The General was so egocentric and pompous that he couldn't see the misery and starvation of the people all around Naples or try to do something about their plight. However, to General Clark's credit, his presence in Naples prevented a bloodbath. Without the Allied Army advancing to Naples, the German Army would have fought to the last soldier to carry out their mission and, unfortunately, the Neapolitans would have obliged. Yes, it was a confrontation of willpower.

SUMMARY

With roughly one Army Division and twenty Tiger tanks, the Germans tried to impose their will on the people of Naples. They took what little food there was, although Neapolitans were starving. They fraternized with local women, looted museums, specialized stores, and libraries, and enjoyed the scenery, the wine, and the music. But when it came to deporting their young men to Germany, Neapolitans reached a threshold where it was no longer tolerable or acceptable behavior. Neapolitans realized that the bullshit talk was not going to get anywhere with the invaders. They also realized that the ones deported might never return and the few deported never did. They rose spontaneously to oppose German occupation and deportation. In confronting the invaders, Neapolitans didn't see bullets and tanks coming their way. They saw a void in their lives without their young ones which spurred them to fight to the end. The confrontation was not about manpower, rifles, and bullets, but willpower. Those modern-day invaders underestimated the will of the locals because they misinterpreted the locals' laissez-faire* lifestyle as a weakness. It turned out to be just the opposite. To the Neapolitans, it was a way of life in which they were not willing to compromise and were more than willing to sacrifice themselves. It pitted Nazi oppressors against a populace that was drunk on that indomitable lifestyle of theirs or that spirit called freedom.

* This is a common expression in Naples dating from the Middle Ages, "Lasci-Fa," in Neapolitan dialect, meaning "let go." The ending ci is rarely pronounced. Today, the sentiment of the word has degenerated into the expression "Forget about it," or "Frigetz," as in some Italian communities in the USA. Most likely, the French adopted the original Neapolitan expression into their language, "Laissez-Faire," when they occupied Naples in the Middle Ages.

FIFTEEN
From Purgatory to Hell on Earth

A t Salerno, the German Army increased its strength from approximately two divisions to more than ten within two weeks, drawing strength from Army groups in occupied parts of Europe. By the beginning of October 1943, the German Army was in full retreat heading northward to Rome, well away from the beaches of Salerno and the city of Naples. One of the main escape routes was the old Via Appia built about 2000 years ago. There must have been at least 200 Tiger tanks on Via Appia passing through Baiano, heading north. Soldiers looked tired and distraught. A lot of them were injured, riding on trucks or other forms of transportation. Some still had sand on their faces from the beaches of Salerno. Residents of Sperone, Baiano, and Avella stood on the side of the highway staring at the soldiers, avoiding eye contact. The soldiers trudged along as though they were not there; their only concern was to get a ride.

Two of the ten German divisions consisted of veteran soldiers involved in the Russian and African campaigns. They were replaced by younger and younger inexperienced soldiers, barely out of high school. German troops retreated to form defensive positions from the Tyrrhenian to the Adriatic seas, referred to as the winter line, anchored at the San Pietro-Venafro area and later, the Gustav Line, anchored at Monte Cassino. The German Army maneuvered itself, under the stewardship of General Kesselring, to the high ground and forced the Allied Army to move in terribly soggy terrain along narrow uphill corridors in wet weather. In places, the mud was knee-high. In the fall, the rainy season is in full swing. The mostly dry Clanio Creek in Avella became a river, and it flooded the towns of Avella and Baiano. German soldiers left camps in Avella and Baiano just in time to avoid the monsoon rain of late October. They were prepared for that, as they bypassed the muddy road in front of the Cemetery and traveled on the paved one (built by them when they first arrived in Avella) to Via Appia in Baiano.

It seemed that the only reason people from Avella and Baiano went to Via Appia was that they wanted so much to believe that the German soldiers were finally leaving for good. They could not very well show delight or display the V sign but, for sure, they were gloating. The locals felt that they deserved a break after putting up with the occupation. At least, they could dream about what their lives could be like without soldiers all around town and the trash spread from the camps to the town. Stranded and charred trucks, jeeps, motor scooters, and benzene containers were spread all over the foothills near the camps. The farms were pockmarked with huge craters, due to Allied bombings, and the former lush greenery was charcoal black. Farms became useless for farming. The German plane shot down by Allied planes in a dogfight at the beginning of the Salerno invasion, was left behind. The dead pilot was buried in the Cemetery at Avella. Everyone in town pitched in to clean up the mess. People scavenged the camps for food but there was none to be had.

Back in Naples, Mario was happy, as his thoughts turned to Sofia, the children, family, and friends. Finally, he was going home and promised the Ukrainians a big welcome in Avella. As for the Ukrainians, they had seen enough of war in the two worst theaters, Tobruk, North Africa, and Stalingrad, Russia, to last a lifetime. They were more focused on making something of their lives. Going back to Ukraine (Russia at that time) was out of the question. There was still a war in Russia. Peasants in the farms had only one choice under the Stalin regime: to be happy with misery. That was the reason they left the Russian Army in the first place and joined the German Army. As it turned out, Hitler's regime was more despotic than Stalin's. At that time, there was still a war. Besides, they loved sunny Naples and the spirit of the Neapolitans. That spirit matched their desire to get away from the War and all that misery and live life to the fullest, like the Neapolitans. Also, the two liked the fact that when confronted, Neapolitans were not intimidated by the German Army. Their spirit rose to the occasion. They felt that they were going home, too. They recognized in Mario a special person who could be trusted to guide them in their endeavors in Avella. Mario distinguished himself in the insurrection in Naples as a master tactician in deploying scugnizzi in the streets hunting for tanks. As such, they had the greatest respect for him and vice versa. The Ukrainians instructed the scugnizzi on where to attack tanks when tossing the Molotov cocktails. The Ukrainians looked at Mario as a father figure.

Mario wanted to send word to Sofia as to when he would be home. The three of them headed to the post office where telephone and telegraph devices, mail deliveries, minor banking services, a coffee area, and an all-purpose room were located. He tried to get there just to let Sofia know that he was alive and well. However, German soldiers guarded the place night and day and censored all the mail. Only German soldiers could use the facility. As the three of them approached the entrance to the Post Office building, a tremendous explosion took place. The Ukrainians followed a step or two behind Mario. The Germans placed a delayed-action explosive device before they left town. They mined most of the functional buildings to facilitate their exit from Naples and to leave an imprint on the minds of Neapolitans. There was no love lost between Neapolitans and German soldiers.

As in most public buildings in Naples, the entrance was decorated with attractive glass figurines. Upon explosion, shards of glass flew in the air, as in a wave, toward the three, with Mario being closest to the entrance. Mario's face was unrecognizable and bloody. The two Ukrainians laid Mario on the ground protecting him with their lives. They wouldn't let anyone near Mario. As usual, scugnizzi showed up. Anytime there was a crowd, scugnizzi appeared. This time it was different. They quickly recognized their heroes, the Ukrainians, from past engagements against the German tanks. They cordoned off the crowd and secured a carriage from a fruit vendor. They didn't ask for permission. They just grabbed it from the vendor. The Ukrainians and the scugnizzi gently laid Mario onto the carriage and hurried to the nearest hospital, San Paolo Hospital, a short distance from the Naval Station.

Mario's face was bandaged by evening. For the entire time, as the doctors operated on Mario's face, removing small glass fragments, the Ukrainians refused to leave the surgery or the recovery room. That evening, Mario waved the two of them to his bedside. He asked, whispering, for them to go to Avella and contact his wife. He added that Erminio would take them to Sofia and that he could be found at the train station in Avella. Erminio's wine store was next to the station.

The brothers had no idea where the station in Naples was located. Again, they counted on the scugnizzi to take them there. However, they had no money. No problem, the scugnizzi absconded two tickets from the train master. They used the Ukrainians as the go-between to transfer the tickets from the master to them and, finally, steal the tickets from the hands of the Ukrainians scampering away, as if the scugnizzi were stealing from the Ukrainians. Hence, the Ukrainians appeared to be innocent bystanders. However, the station master had seen that stunt before at least a thousand times. So, he just handed two free tickets to the Ukrainians. On the way to Avella, they observed buildings nearly destroyed by Allied bombardments. Squatters all over those buildings appeared like rats running in and out of their broken balconies. Destroyed train wagons were pushed aside to make room for undamaged tracks. In Nola, a 1,000-pound unexploded bomb was pushed aside on top of a wooden plank. Only the USA built bombs that size. The devastation from those sized bombs was unfathomable.

On the train, there were no first-class wagons. First come, first served. Farmers, shepherds, women, and professional men were riding the train. Farmers and shepherds were returning home after setting up shop at the farmer's markets in various towns where a market was scheduled. Women were most likely returning home after spending time in houses of prostitution in Naples. Soldiers stationed in Naples were more concerned about syphilis than where they were going to be shipped for the next battle. About ten percent of the professional men on the train were peddling medicine (controlled by the Camorra) to cure syphilis. The remaining professional men were lawyers who represented women who petitioned the AMG (Allied Military Government) office for a license to marry an Allied soldier or petitioned allied consulates for immigration visas. The conductor never checked for the tickets. Most likely, he was rewarded by the farmers with food which he needed at that time. As such, farmers and shepherds never bought train tickets.

At the train station in Avella, the Ukrainians inquired about the wine store although all they had to do was to look to their right as soon as they got off the train. The winery was the only building near the station. Without Mario, they were panicking, but their confidence perked up as they saw a big sign, "Erminio's Winery" atop the building. They moseyed over there, as Erminio sat at a small table in the courtyard in awe as these two giants walked toward the winery. He was a short and swarthy guy. As they were approaching him, Erminio's mind wondered who they could be. For sure, they were not from the area. "Signore Erminio," they asked. At this point, Erminio panicked. "How did they know my name?" he wondered. The Ukrainians told him about Mario. That was the magic word. Erminio's ears perked up because the town hadn't heard a word from Mario for about a year and everyone worried about their beloved friend.

Erminio tried to strike up a conversation and his mind and words were coming out so fast that the Ukrainians couldn't possibly understand a word. They spoke some words in the Neapolitan dialect. For one thing, Erminio was wondering what the connection was between them and Mario. The two parties simply could not communicate until one of the Ukrainians mentioned the name Sofia. "Aha," said Erminio. He put two and two together and rationalized that he had better get Sofia, as it may be important. Erminio cupped his hand and gesticulated it toward his mouth, as if to say, "Are you hungry?" That much they understood and nodded "Yes." So, he told the two to sit there and have something to eat. He brought out local shepherd smoked cheese, salami, bread, tomatoes, and wine. Again, he used hand gestures to indicate that he would be back. Their eyes were fixated on the food, not noticing that Erminio left the winery.

Erminio drove to Sergio's building inquiring about the whereabouts of Sofia. In the courtyard, Erminio was telling Sergio about the two giants mentioning something about Mario. The tone of the conversation was excitement taken to the nth degree. Don Camillo ran down the steps from his apartment wanting to know more. They wanted so much to believe that Mario was alive. Everybody (Sergio, Don Camillo, Imalda, Felicia, and Alvaro) crammed into the car and they drove to the dress shop, where Sofia and the twin sisters worked. When the girls saw their parents and Zi Nicola, they panicked. The girls thought the worst possible outcome for Mario. Erminio reassured them and said that these two giants, who are now at his winery, have news about him. The girls jumped with joy and pleaded with Erminio to take them to those two men. Sofia turned to Sergio and company and said, "We will let you know."

By the time the car arrived at the winery, the two Ukrainians had finished eating everything on the table, including the crumbs. In Erminio's absence, Dimitri sketched a picture of Mario in bed with bandages on his face inscribing the word, vivo, meaning that Mario was alive. The girls were so happy that all three embraced them. Immediately, Sofia declared, "Let's go to Naples now and visit him. No reason to wait until tomorrow." Erminio interjected by asking the two Ukrainians if they wanted some fruits from the garden and to take some to Mario. Apples, pears, figs, and plums were there for the taking. Ramiro's Maserati 500 showed up with the two sets of parents and Zi Nicola. They, too, had heard the good news. Everyone in town seemed to be anxious to know, as they were standing in the streets asking each other about the whereabouts of Mario. Zi Nicola also insisted on coming along. In the late afternoon, Sofia, the twin sisters, Vladimir, Dimitri, and Zi Nicola boarded the train to Naples. Imalda and Felicia told their two grandchildren all about their papa and that he would be coming home soon. The children stood guard at the *portone* waiting for papa. Nothing in the world would have dislodged them from there.

Since the tracks for the tram rail line had been bombed by Allied planes during the German occupation of Naples, they walked to the San Paolo hospital, where they found Mario in very good spirits. He even suggested to Sofia that they pack up and go home. Although he was sensitive to anyone touching his face, he had no problem eating the figs or kissing Sofia. He didn't care how painful it was going to be. They told him that by now the whole town was aware of his ordeal. Even though neighbors didn't hear the full story, it didn't stop them from making up one or embellishing one. The girls wanted to know more about the two Ukrainians and how he got to know them. Mario recounted the whole episode that they went through and that, without them, he would never have made it alive. The two men knew that Mario was talking about them, and they blushed sheepishly toward the sisters. Although their body frames were huge, their behavior was akin to little boys wanting to be liked, especially by the sisters. Sofia, Mario, and Zi Nicola noticed the special attraction between the sisters and the two brothers.

Mario recovered after a couple of days in the hospital. In the meantime, the three girls stayed in the apartment in the San Carlo opera house with Zi Nicola. Maintenance people and stage managers welcomed him to San Carlo and told him that rumor had it that he was being considered as the orchestra conductor. He was expected at San Carlo well before the opening of the opera season on April 18, 1944. They added, "Now that you are here, Mario can stop coming here looking for you." Zi Nicola was deeply moved by Mario's devotion and loyalty to him. This also meant that Mario was getting his job back since the conductor would have a lot to say about the hiring of an accountant manager. The routine, while Mario was in the hospital, was the same as when he was at the Naval Station. The brothers went fishing and bartered for fruits and vegetables with the scugnizzi. Their favorite dish was fish soup and vegetables. The girls came in the evening to help with the cooking.

In the afternoon, Zi Nicola was the tour guide for the group. They would take a stroll to the Vomero Hills and overlook the bay of Naples and the valley to the mountains of Avella. Then, Zi Nicola would recount the historical background of the many invasions in the valley and the Bay. He would take them on a tour of San Carlo and show them his and Mario's former offices and pictures of the tenor, Enrico Caruso. The brothers were extremely interested in the history of Naples and of the Arab and Jewish influences on the Neapolitans, their songs, and their architecture. They couldn't ask for a better guide. Zi Nicola spoke a little Russian to keep the conversation going. The girls were impressed, especially the sisters. Vladimir asked the sisters if they could teach them

Italian. Scugnizzi taught them only swearing and dirty words in the Neapolitan dialect. Enough of that, he alluded. That was nothing more or less than an invitation for the four of them to be together. Before Serafina could answer, she whispered to Zi Nicola, "Are they Jewish?" There is one way of finding out," Zi Nicola whispered back with a smirk on his face. On the way back to cook for their dinner in the evening, Sofia could see out of the corner of her eye that the couple was holding hands.

The next day, Mario was up early in the morning, ready to go home. Stitches were removed and his face was full of scars. He was on a mission to make up for the lost time. He gathered the boys at the station and the rest of the group at San Carlo. Then, straight home. On the train, he noticed Serafina and Filomena cozying up to the two Ukrainians and asked Sofia, "What gives?" "Eh," shrugging her shoulders and smiling. After all, she was the architect of it all. In the old days, he and Zi Nicola would talk and talk, but not this time. He wanted to hear only from Sofia about everything: the children, the family, friends, etc. He had a lot to catch up on. Zi Nicola was beaming just like a conductor pleased with an orchestra's performance. Mario knew Zi Nicola well enough to know when he was up to something mischievous. That smile and that far-away look was a giveaway. But what? His mind started wondering about what it could be.

Erminio was nervous, as he looked at his watch every minute waiting for the train to arrive at the station in Avella. As the train appeared around the corner on the way to the station, Erminio rushed to his winery. No one was waiting for the train, but Zi Nicola suggested that the group stop at Erminio to get something to eat. All the while, Mario was suspicious. No one was around, "What is going on?" It was eerie. Usually, there were passengers at the station, especially in the morning. As the group approached the winery, the children darted to jump into the arms of Sofia and Mario. Then, Zi Nicola popped out of nowhere with a stick in his hand to conduct a chorus consisting of Erminio, Alvaro, Felicia, Sergio, Ramiro, Imalda, and friends singing the beautiful ballad, "Parlame D'Amore, Mariu." Mario and Sofia started to cry. So much love. No one noticed the scarred face. Love beautifies and forgives everything.

Serafina and Filomena introduced their new friends, Vladimir and Dimitri, to their parents, Alvaro and Felicia. Of course, the parents were pleased because there were very few bachelor's of eligible age in Avella or in any other town nearby. As with most parents, they wanted to know whether it was love or desperation. They didn't care what they did for a living, but they wanted good-hearted people in their midst.

Sergio took Vladimir under his wing, having him assist in patrolling the mountains. Many times, he helped with makeshift bridge repairs, tree removals from roads, land irrigation, etc. Sergio used Vladimir to do the heavy maintenance while he concentrated on the paperwork required by the central office of the Mountain police force in Naples. Vladimir mingled freely with the shepherds; philosophically and spiritually they were his kind of people. Dimitri was artistically inclined as the sisters realized when he sketched a portrait of Mario on the hospital bed. Paolo, Zi Nicola's son, was already a well-recognized artist and his reputation were growing by leaps and bounds. However, he was not cut out to build scaffolds in churches to paint from. Dimitri didn't mind doing that while learning from the master. Eventually, he branched out to become a great sculptor. The Ukrainians rented one of the empty apartments in Imalda's building. Lena and Imalda chaperoned the lovers in their passeggiata (social walk) on Main Street. That was the time for Italian lessons for the two Ukrainians. Most times Lena, Imalda's granddaughter, left the lovers alone to stop at a local cafe for gelato, and ice cream. Imalda loved to spoil her grandchildren and to incessantly talk to them about that special shepherd spirit.

The town was going through major changes politically and in many other ways. There was no Mayor. The last one left before the German Army arrived in town.

Alvaro resumed his duty as the Magistrate of City Hall and retrieved all records of people. The records had been hidden from the Germans in the cave of San Michele. Former employees returned and the bureaucracy was back in business. The Post Office resumed operation, delivering mail and providing telegraph and phone service. The Ramiro family, as always, was immune to war, since they belonged to the Colonna's vast empire, extending throughout Europe since the seventeenth century. It was financially and indirectly a political empire.

Whatever political activity was on Main Street, it was organized by the Communists. Partisans were busy chasing former Fascists, whose deaths were preordained. They visited Don Nicola in an attempt to obtain a list of Fascists who harassed him at the height of Fascism. Don Nicola did not comply for the simple fact that he was not equally sympathetic to Communist ideals and, also, he was not a revengeful person. He learned from the Ukrainians the plight of peasants in Russia. There was nothing to admire about the agricultural system deployed by their leaders. In many ways, Don Nicola was a naive dreamer as much as previous Socialists of the 1930s, like Carlo Levi and others. The Socialist Party in 1943 was allied with the Communist Party in Italy promising a better life for the peasants. Unfortunately, there will always be a peasant class, regardless of parties. It is in human nature.

Vladimir and Dimitri came to the dress shop for their Italian lessons. They were in love. Filomena and Vladimir formed one pair and the artist, Dimitri, and Serafina the other. They were soon married at City Hall, where Alvaro officiated at the weddings. For their honeymoons, they went to Posillipo, Naples. They loved to ride a horse-driven carriage where the driver sang Neapolitan songs.

The sisters were on a pilgrimage to visit the Naval Station since there was so much history of the family connected to the place. Mario and Sofia lived there before the War, and their husbands and Mario lived there during the insurrection in Naples. When they arrived, the station looked the same as before. The apartment where the trio had stayed was unoccupied and in total disarray. Scugnizzi still dominated the landscape, except for the older scugnizzo, Luigi, who was fishing on the dock using Vladimir's homemade fishing rod. Luigi jumped for joy as soon as he saw Vladimir. He couldn't stop talking to the sisters about the heroics of the two brothers during the insurrection.

The episode shed a whole new light on the brothers who hadn't been appreciated before by the sisters. The brothers were more Neapolitans than they appeared to be. They absorbed the spirit of Naples as if they were born there. There was no return to Odessa in their minds. It established a whole new relationship and understanding between the sisters and their husbands.

By the end of October or early November 1943, the rainy season reached its peak, lasting about a month. By then, the German occupation was long forgotten. However, the landscape was about to change soon. The British troops arrived in Avella just as the rains stopped. The locals in the East end of town could hear bagpipe music from a distance. "That's strange. Bagpipes music and not Christmas yet," they murmured to themselves. A contingent of the British Army was marching from a side street, past Saint Peter Church, led by Scottish soldiers playing the bagpipes. To the locals, it was a beautiful sight, because the town needed some levity. The soldiers were marching in an orderly fashion toward the foothills. No one paid attention to exactly where they were heading, as people were resigned to the worst. People assumed that the British troops were going to take over the German camp, well away from town. No such luck. The British camped very near the Roman amphitheater, about 100 meters from Sergio's building. The camp was accessible to some locals, as few farm owners from town received bread from the camp. The bread represented a form of payment for the rental of the farms by the British. It was truly tormenting to smell the aroma in town from the kitchens of the camping grounds. One could tell from the aroma what they were cooking.

Historically, Emperor Sulla of Rome (please see Anthony Everitt's book, Cicero) built this colosseum or amphitheater in 89 BC as a reward to the people of Abella (Avella) for being loyal to Rome in their battle against the Samnite tribe of Nola. It is interesting to note that, in one of the many museums in the Vatican, Abella is depicted in an ancient map of Roman territories as a colony of the Roman Empire. The capacity of the Colosseum in Rome was 50,000-80,000 spectators; the one in Avella seated 20,000-30,000. Besides colosseums in Avella and Rome, others were built in Verona, Pompeii, Naples, Pola, Nimes, Arles, and El Djeem (Carthage). The amphitheaters were adaptations of Greek theaters which were considerably smaller.

The amphitheater in Avella with Monte Avella in the background. The entrance to the amphitheater with the large portone (door) is shown at the opposite end. The British camp was about 50-70 yards to the left of the entrance beyond the trees. The town of Avella is on the left of the camp, ~100 meters. The cave of San Michele is above the gorge separating Monte Avella and the smaller hill. The German camps were located to the right of the portone on the small hills. Photo courtesy of Anmarie Vittoria, 1981.

Unbeknown to the locals the tranquility existing between the locals and the British soldiers was soon interrupted. In the middle of the night, colonial troops from North Africa came incognito and made camp on a farm located in between the British camp and Sergio's place. These troops first showed up in Avella circa mid-November 1943. The locals soon discovered what "Hell" must be like on this earth, not in Dante Alighieri's abstract world. These colonial troops were referred to as Goumiers. They were not allowed on French territory in the Allied invasion of France later, although they were part of the French Expedition Force, consisting of Algerian, Tunisian, and Moroccan soldiers. Their behavior gave a new meaning to the word atrocious. They raped anything on two legs. To them, young, old, male or female mattered none, purely democratic in their selection. Supposedly, they had uniforms, but they rarely used them. Besides the Goumiers, colonial troops from Australia and Canada camped in farms near the other two. Thus, different Allied camps brought different shades of misery to the people of Avella. The only remedial part of the unwanted visitors was the thought of a life without Fascism and Nazism.

The Goumiers appeared in town in bizarre uniforms – not like the British and German soldiers. The uniform looked like a loosely fit pajama with vertical brown and white streaks. However, their behavior was unlike that of the British and German soldiers. Typically, a group of Goumiers would enter a wine shop, consume all the wine in the store, and not pay. The British and German soldiers always paid. To add insult to injury, the Goumiers' payment consisted of raping the owner or clients who were on the premises. It was shocking behavior and defied all standards of civility. The reputation of these soldiers quickly circulated town and, of course, people tended to embellish the worst behavior.

Goumiers marched in the streets brandishing their knives. Often, they would come from the pool, built by the British, nude, and run up a farm road to their camp. Dante Alighieri described in his book *The Divine Comedy*, Heaven, Purgatory, and Hell as abstract concepts. People in Avella felt like they were in Purgatory with the presence of German and British troops, waiting for better times. Shepherds in the neighborhood were apprehensive that their matriarch lived next door to their camp. Once again, Sergio's residence was converted into a fortress whereby, besides the usual residents, the Da Alia family moved in with the newly married couples. The Ukrainians could have taken matters into their own hands, but they restrained themselves just to please their wives. Sergio locked the *portone* to the entrance of his building complex every night.

At the other end (west) of Main Street, everything seemed to be normal, where people were out and about shopping in the street or relaxing at a Cafe. However, Sofia, Filomena, and Serafina had seen enough in their neighborhood to shut their shop in the Piazza. They didn't want to be caught by the Goumiers on their way to the shop. Also, they didn't want to provoke any incidents involving their husbands and the Goumiers on the way to the shop, as the husbands would have escorted them there. For the same reason, Alvaro closed City

Hall to protect the workers until the Goumiers left town. Erminio was sitting pretty in his wine shop, as the soldiers didn't venture to that part of town or the train station. Whatever terror was generated by those soldiers it was localized near their camp.

However, it didn't stop the Goumiers from roaming around the high mountains. Sergio and Vladimir spotted them trying to domesticate wild horses at the base of the high mountains. It was clear to Sergio that the purpose of domesticating the horses was to ride them to their camp and then butcher them. That was sacrilegious not only to Sergio but to the whole shepherd community. Wild horses have been in that area of the mountains ever since the Stone Ages. It was useless to report to the Maresciallo as he was intimidated by the Goumiers. He told Imalda about it just as a matter of information but no more than that. Imalda was upset, to say the least. What she did with the information was not clear.

People complained to the local Maresciallo about the behavior of the Goumiers, since he represented the only authority in town. However, when he heard the nature or details of the complaints, he stopped taking his usual "prancing" walks in Main Street. Before the arrival of the Goumiers, he would walk around the Piazza like a peacock in heat. He fancied himself as a Don Juan or a predator. Suddenly, with the arrival of Goumiers, he thought of himself more of prey and avoided them. Thus, mentally, he was all fucked up for life! Never the same after the War.

Goumiers had no qualms about slaughtering sheep or goats or horses up on the mountains, where shepherds made their home during all the turmoil in the valley. Unfortunately for the Goumiers, they just awakened a sleeping giant, the shepherd community. A trap was laid out by the shepherds. Two Goumiers were enticed to visit a shepherd family in the hills for wine, roasted goat, and sex. The Goumiers were drugged as more shepherds joined the so-called festivities. The two Goumiers were tied onto the flat surface of the table and a shepherd performed surgery for the first time in their lives. The Goumiers were castrated and allowed to bleed to death. The bodies were carried back to the entrance of the Goumiers' camp. The message was delivered as both the shepherds and the Goumiers understood the same unwritten language of nomads.

Again, the Goumiers left in the middle of the night unnoticed by anyone. People were too stunned to realize what just happened. Once they recovered their equilibrium, they were in a hurry to get back to a normal life. To begin with, people began to assemble in the Piazza to socialize and see who survived the awful ordeal. The girls (Sofia, Filomena, and Serafina) wanted so badly to get back to their dress shop in the Piazza. They began to use pre-war fashion designs, with minor modifications, to make dresses. By then, Lena was becoming a beautiful young lady of fourteen and she modeled the dresses. However, most of their clients only needed alterations, a little tuck here or there, or more room here or there.

SIXTEEN
A Puppet Empty of Sawdust

I t was a bitterly cold winter in Avella in 1944. For anyone who couldn't remember, it snowed for the first time. Children ran out in the streets to grab a snowflake in the air for fear that if it touched the ground, it would melt. The War was effectively over in Avella as well as in the rest of Southern Italy. The German Army was entrenched at Monte Cassino, about one hundred miles north, holding the high ground next to the Abbey there. Allied planes bombed the Abbey of Monte Cassino, reducing it to rubble to prevent German soldiers from possibly hiding there. However, as in Avella, the soldiers hid in the caves within walking distance of the Abbey. Colonial and Polish soldiers of the Allied Army had an insurmountable task to gain the high ground by fighting uphill in muddy terrain. The Goumier troops were dispatched East of Monte Cassino to flush out German soldiers from the high ground by attacking from behind enemy lines. It didn't stop them from committing unspeakable atrocities in towns on the way to Monte Cassino. After the battle, the Goumiers regrouped in Cancello, a town ten miles north of Naples. This area was referred to then as the "Zona di Camorra," Camorra's headquarters. Again, their behavior was uncivilized in at least five towns nearby. It is not clear from historical books who was responsible for the castration of five Goumier soldiers, who were buried in a cabbage field [6-3]. That was the end of their escapades in Southern Italy and Europe. They were shipped back to their homes.

By 1944, the focus of the Allied Army shifted from the Italian campaign to the north of the Alps. This meant that the warring factions left enough soldiers and armaments in Italy to reach a stalemate. Also, the devastation remained the same as before in Italy for the rest of the War, resulting in more collateral damage than in any other country in Europe. Mussolini formed a new government stationed at Garda Lake. The Italian people were not surprised by another absurdity from the Duce. Badoglio and the King of Italy did the same by forming another government in Brindisi, Southern Italy. Both governments, supposedly, represented the Italian people, although neither was elected, as there was no national election in 1944. Neither government printed money to rev up the economy or brought their young men home from the War to work on the farms to produce food for the starving nation.

As for the shepherds in Avella, they were returning from the mountains to their neighborhood. The War was a long distance away and they felt safe to resume their lives. Carabinieri was not chasing them in the hills, as in the previous war for avoiding enlistment in the Army. Imalda and Sergio were happy to have them back, as some of them were related to the matriarch. Imalda was looking forward to getting back to the Farmer's Market in Nola. Another reason that the shepherds returned early was due to the inclement weather up in the high mountains of Avella. Sometimes, it is so cold that snow melts as late as July. Also, they wanted to take advantage of the wet season to replenish the pond with water so they could shear their sheep after dumping them in the pond. This was an annual ritual to rid them of ticks and fleas in the wool, except for the year before when soldiers of both armies occupied the lowlands during the rainy season. Water was rerouted temporarily in the foothills from Clanio Creek to the pond.

As for the farmers, they had a mess on their hands. All those Army vehicles from occupying armies dug trenches all over their farms. They had to replough furrows in ton farm to be ready to plant seeds. The most troublesome concern was to refill the large craters with dirt, and there were many of those. The craters were the result of the Allies bombing German camps in the foothills. In addition, German soldiers absconded their livestock and, whatever was leftover, Allied colonial troops pounced on. One major hurdle, at that time in early spring, was to sow seed in the farm fields to produce crops for the fall. However, there was no one around to help. Labor of any kind was short not only in Avella but all over Italy. Even if the farmer succeeded on his own to get the land ready for farming, there was protection from the brigands roaming the hills of Avella foraging for food. As such, farmers were just as content to plant corn seeds in a relatively small patch of land. Polenta (corn grits) was still the main meal of the day.

Lawlessness and corruption throughout Southern Italy didn't have to wait for spring to germinate like weeds. It was there all the time. The Maresciallo was as corrupt as the brigands and the Camorra (Mafia group in the Naples area). Italian and American deserters and common thieves made up the core of the brigands. Their favorite targets were bakeries, all-purpose stores, butcher shops, and pharmacies. In small towns like Avella, pharmacies were short on penicillin. But, somehow, brigands would show up every time there was a shipment of it. As such, it pitted the Camorra against the brigands, since the Camorra controlled the shipments of penicillin throughout the valley and the city of Naples. The Maresciallo was on the take from both sides.

Politically, the Communists were taking over the streets, as they paraded every so often in Main Street, carrying the hammer and sickle red flag everywhere. They were already politically campaigning by indoctrinating anyone in the streets about Communism for the next election, although no election was expected that year. Communists draped the statue of Garibaldi with the red flag in the Piazza. By then, Garibaldi must have been tired of being draped by all political parties with something or another, although he was still in a grave. When German soldiers first occupied the town, the mayor left and never returned to office. Alvaro ran City Hall in the absence of the mayor. By then, Zi Nicola abstained from politics so that he could concentrate on the coming opera season at the San Carlo starting in April 1944. He was promoted to the conductor of the orchestra. Mario returned to his former job as an accountant at the San Carlo.

Political confrontations in the streets of Avella between Communists and Fascists gave way to another form of conflict. With the establishment of a naval base in Naples by the US, the black market flourished not only in Naples but also in the valley. Approximately one-third of American goods at the base were sold in the black market.

American cigarettes were the most popular among the populace and the next popular thing was US Army-issued blankets. The thought that the locals didn't have to roll that harsh tobacco into a cigarette drove them to pure ecstasy. They saved whatever little money they had so that they could buy one measly American cigarette. It didn't matter what brand, but they preferred Camel cigarettes. Neapolitan housewives were very inventive in turning Army blankets into luxurious coats and jackets. The Camorra controlled the black market. However, Camorristi, members of the Camorra, were spread all over the valley, including Avella. The main competition of the Camorra was from the at-large brigand gangs roaming the hills in the valley.

The Camorra yielded tremendous political power over City Halls throughout the valley and Naples. Most, if not all, Podestas (Fascist mayors) of small and big towns were replaced by mayors appointed by the AMG (Allied Military Government). Vito Genovese, the former underboss of the New York City Mafia, made all the recommendations for those posts and, of course, the appointments were filled by Camorristi throughout Southern Italy. In Sicily mafiosi (members of the Sicilian Mafia) were appointed as mayors. Salvatore (Lucky) Luciano was then Mafia boss in NYC, although at that time he was incarcerated. Vito was born in Tufino*, very near Naples, and enjoyed protection from the US Army through the AMG. What a sweetheart arrangement! Only in Naples! (Appendix 2).

The ramifications of the appointments were far-reaching. For one thing, the Maresciallos had to toe the line to the appointed corrupt mayors and be subservient to them, i.e., both corrupt to the core. Their main role was to keep the brigands away from the spoils of corruption at all levels. The Camorra had the first pick of the spoils. Any murders of brigands in the streets were white washed by the local authorities, as, for example, in a town like Avella. With an abundance of soldiers and sailors in Naples, it attracted prostitutes as well from the valley. Thus, penicillin was in high demand. As such, the Camorra also controlled the distribution of penicillin and vaccine for smallpox. At that time, there was an outbreak of typhoid, smallpox, and influenza.

The fact that the Allies conquered Rome and that Mussolini was out of their hair, buoyed the hopes of people in Avella and in the valley that the War would be over soon, hopefully by Christmas of 1944. In that year, not a single Italian soldier returned home from any battlefront of the War, although a handful of ordinary Italian citizens showed up in Avella throughout the summer. These strangers had relatives in town and found a place to stay temporarily. Most likely, these strangers were former Fascist officials in towns north of Avella. They were escaping the wrath of Communists and Partisans, who were rounding them up for retribution.

As the Allied Army was advancing toward Rome more towns were liberated from the yoke of Fascism. Fascist officials crossed the battle-fronts into towns freed from German occupation. They would wait in liberated towns until it was safe to return to their former towns. In ancient Roman days, dictators, generals, and politicians escaped from Rome toward Greece or the Middle East to avoid the so-called "proscription list." Any Roman was welcome to murder the ones named on that list and derive the benefits of taking over all the material possessions of the deceased: villas, farms, sheep, etc. The escapees traveled on Via Appia to the city of Brindisi. From there, it was a short boat ride to Greece. They would return when another ruler, favorable to them, appeared on the scene in Rome. Apparently nothing in two thousand years.

With summer fast approaching, the shepherds, including Imalda, were itching to get back to their routine before the war. The wool generated in the spring was made available to Sofia, Filomena, and Serafina, enough to keep the dress shop open for that year. The Farmer's Market in Nola had been closed during the Allied bombing in the previous year. Imalda had a full assortment of cheeses to unload in the next couple of months. Sergio and Vladimir advised the shepherds to take their sheep grazing in the hills toward the town of Campagna in a Southerly direction around Vesuvius since the hills of Avella were infested with brigands. Both decided to lay low until the hills in Avella became safer. In the meantime, they cultivated the garden while growing more corn. As for Dimitri and Carlo, Zi Nicola's son, they were busy renovating paintings in churches. Churches had the financial means to pay them in those days. In the Communist section of town, commercial activity perked up as a new cafe opened in anticipation of the passeggiata resuming soon with Christmas approaching fast.

Between September 1943 and the end of 1944, Ferramonti was home to one of the largest and most active Jewish communities in liberated Italy. It was at this point that fragile Jewish self-governance first took shape during internment. It quickly developed into a vital infrastructure, including the set-up of all social and cultural services, media, education, small businesses, and, above all, a social fabric within which fostering entrepreneurship began. Many moved towards other camps located in better areas, especially in Puglia and Sicily. Others found their way to Africa, Palestine, and the United States.

On May 26th, 1944, 254 former internees left Ferramonti for Palestine on the first emigration transport authorized by the British mandatory government. On July 17th, 1944, a little over 1,000 Jews from Ferramonti, Campagna, Potenza, Tito and other internment towns in Southern Italy set sail from Naples for the United States. By the end of the Second World War, the facilities at Ferramonti had been abandoned. In the following decades its memory was kept alive solely through former internees and their families, and by some residents. There is little evidence in towns like Potenza and Tito that Jewish internees lived there, although in Campagna living quarters of internees have been preserved to this day.

The war was very much alive in people's minds in Northern Italy. The Germans wanted to keep Mussolini on a short leash. As such, they chose the headquarters of a new Italian Fascist government close to the German borders so that they could keep an eye on Mussolini and the new government. However, not so close that it would give an appearance of subjugation to the rest of the world. They chose a small town on Lake Garda, Gargnano, near the German Army Headquarters of Field Marshal Kesselring. Reluctantly, Mussolini accepted the town as his capital. He settled into the nineteenth-century Villa Feltrinelli, on the shores of the lake. It functioned as Mussolini's office and home, but the office was later transferred to lla delle Orsoline also in Gargnano. He never learned to like the 37 rooms in Villa Feltrinelli. According to him, it was too dark and hostile. The doorways to the Villa were guarded by one SS guard and one Blackshirt Fascist. However, SS men swarmed all over the grounds of Villa Feltrinelli.

Villa Feltrinelli, where Mussolini resided in Gargnano. German soldiers guarded the front and back of the Villa night and day. Courtesy of G. Vittoria.

Three days following Mussolini's rescue in the Gran Sasso raid, he was taken to Germany for a meeting in Hitler's headquarters in Rastenburg in East Prussia. While Mussolini was in poor health and wanted to retire, Hitler advised him to return to Italy and start a new Fascist State under the protection of the Wehrmacht, the unified armed forces of Nazi Germany. When Mussolini balked, tired of the responsibilities of the war and unwilling to retake power, Hitler told him the alternative would be a German military administration that would treat Italy no different from other occupied countries. Hitler also threatened to destroy Milan, Genoa, and Turin unless Mussolini agreed to set up a revived Fascist government. Reluctantly, Mussolini agreed to Hitler's demands. In retrospect, it was all a lie by Hitler, because Northern Italy was already treated as occupied territory like other European countries. Mussolini never saw through the bluff!

Hitler's motives were entirely different from what he expressed to

Mussolini. First, he wanted to legitimize Germany's occupation of Northern Italy with the eventual annexation of all the regions incorporating the Alps. He had already annexed Bolzano. Second, Hitler wanted direct access to internment camps in Northern and Central Italy to carry out his brutal extermination of Jewish internees. The new Fascist government would be held responsible for the extermination. This presented a cover-up in the future for his demonic deeds. Finally, Hitler had a personal message for Mussolini; he wanted to convey that the only buffoon between the two of them was Mussolini. Mussolini attempted to create an illusion in Hitler's mind that Italy, too, had internment camps. However, Hitler and other Nazi officials never bought that story. They felt that only clowns create illusions and that was Hitler's message. In effect, Hitler created a replica of an internment, camp, Italian style, in Gargnano, like the ones created in Southern Italy by Mussolini. For example, the Villa was guarded night and day and out of sight of anyone outside of it. The only time that he was free from the guards was when he went to the bathroom. Even when he visited his mistress, Clara Petacci, in town, he needed permission from the guards to escort him. Thus, Mussolini lived in a town setting where he was interned, much like internees in Tito or Potenza. Mussolini complained as much to his daughter (Edda) and wife (Donna Rachele), stating, "I am under house arrest."

The Fascist Party opened a Party Congress in Verona, Italy. The object was to draw up an eighteen-point political program for the new republic. On November 23, Mussolini announced the creation of the Republican Socialist Italian (RSI) Party with Mussolini as both chief of state and prime minister of the new government. The war was resumed by the RSI government alongside Germany and Japan. The Duce immediately announced the formation of a new Republican cabinet, although they came from a list chosen and appointed by Hitler himself. The RSI claimed Gargnano as its capital, but the *de facto* capital became the small town of Salò on Lake Garda, midway between Milan and Venice. Mussolini resided there along with the foreign office of the RSI. While Rome itself was still under Axis control at the time, given the city's proximity to Allied lines and the threat of civil unrest, neither the Germans nor Mussolini wanted to return to Rome.

The RSI had no constitution or organized economy, and its financing was dependent entirely on funding from Berlin. German forces themselves had little respect for Mussolini's failed Fascism and considered the regime merely a tool for maintaining order, such as repressing the Italian partisans. This work was also carried out by the infamous Pietro Koch and his group the Banda Koch on Germany's behalf. He pursued and tortured to death partisans, OSS (future CIA) officials, and citizens of Rome, Florence, and Milan, who assisted Jewish refugees in their escapes. He was born in Benevento, near Avella, to a German father and an Italian mother.

Journalists became accustomed to writing such phrases as "Salo has announced," or "Salo says," to report about the new government. Hence, the new government (RSI) was often referred to as the Salo government instead of Gargnano's. But some Italians insisted on calling the new government "Pinocchio's Republic." Just eight countries gave diplomatic recognition to the new Republic. Even Fascist Franco of Spain withheld recognition. The philosopher Benedetto Croce described Mussolini as such: "A patched puppet that has lost his sawdust and fallen limp." The town of Salo on the southern shore of Lake Garda housed only the Foreign Ministry and Ministry of Popular Culture (Propaganda). The Interior Ministry was at Maderno, Defense at Cremona, the Economy at Verona, and other ministries at Monza, Milan, Bergamo, Brescia, etc. The German's deliberate dispersion of the government ministries produced a crippling effect on the new government. According to Mussolini, "Distances divide us and this is the real reason they have put us in this hole."

The origins of the municipality of Salò are barely known: its autonomy from the city of Brescia dates to the end of the 13th century or the beginning of the next one. The most ancient statues conserved by the city authorities are dated to 1397. Before 1334, the town was part of a federation of town councils of the territory along the western lakeshore of Lake Garda. The federation did not want to form an alliance with Brescia or with Verona, deciding instead to request help from Venice. Due to the distance from Venice, this strategy did not guarantee the independence of the area and, after a short protectorate under the rule of Venice (from 1336 to 1349), Salò became a stronghold of the Milanese Visconti family. In 1377 Beatrice della Scala, the wife of Bernabò Visconti, wanted Salò to be the capital of the area, reducing the influence of Maderno; the city was provided with solid walls surrounding it. Today, Brescia is known to Italians as "Lionessa D'Italia", a lioness of Italy. This is because the city withstood the onslaught of Austrian and German troops in WWI.

The German political rulers of occupied Northern and Central Italy were Rudolf von Rahn (ambassador to the new Fascist government) and General Karl Wolff (SS Commander). Rahn became famous for his ruthless oppression. According to Mussolini's secretary, "He knows how to mask with courtesy the obvious hardness of his character." Mussolini was always agitated and nervous in Rahn's presence and, after meeting him, remained tired and in bad humor. He called Rahn "the Viceroy of Italy" and Wolff "the interior minister of Italy."

The German occupiers ruled through violence with the aid of the local Fascists. Throughout German-occupied Italy, Jews and political dissidents were rounded up and sent to detention camps or prisons. Many Jews were sent straight from Italy on trains to concentration and extermination camps in Poland and Germany. In all, nearly 9,000 Jews were deported by SS troops. Only 980 returned. The biggest deportation occurred in Rome in October 1943, when the Germans gathered more than 1,000 Jews from the city's ghetto and sent them to death camps. The Jewish community had been forced, early on, to give their gold (115 pounds) and money to the German Army. One concentration camp on Italian soil, near Trieste, also had an oven for burning bodies. Some 8,000 Italians, of whom 300 were Jews, were deported to Mauthausen in Austria. Only 850 came back.

The German Army responded to partisan activity with violence and reprisals. A series of massacres of civilians and partisans accompanied the German occupation and gradual retreat up the peninsula. In March 1944, after a partisan bomb attack killed 33 members of the occupying forces in Rome, the German Army shot 335 people (Jews, Communists, and others) in the Fosse Ardeatine, caves located outside the city. This massacre was one of the biggest of the war in Italy and has inspired controversy ever since. In the 1990s, a former Nazi captain, Erich Priebke, was arrested in Argentina and, after two dramatic trials, was convicted in Rome for his role in the massacre. He was incarcerated for a couple of years. Elsewhere, the German Army carried out frequent brutal and random massacres of civilians while retreating northward. In Tuscany and Emilia, German troops destroyed an entire village of some 1,800 people at Marzabotto in 1944. In addition, the Germans deported hundreds of thousands of young men to work as forced laborers in Germany and elsewhere. Many of those deported died en route.

After an absence of three months, Mussolini was reunited with Clara Petacci, his mistress. Mussolini sent a car driven by a German officer to take her from Merano to Villa Feltrinelli, Gargnano. His wife was still in Munich, Germany. Petacci planned to move to Gargnano soon after. Rachele Mussolini rejoined the Duce together with their two youngest children, Romano (16) and Anna Maria (14), soon after the mistress showed up in Gargnano. The police estimated that about 200 Mussolinis were living around Gargnano.

The return of Rachele and their children was not a happy one. Mussolini and Rachele often passed each other in their residence without speaking. Rachele took pride in her peasant background and her practical management of household affairs. She often ironed clothes, although the family had five servants. She was uncomfortable in public.

While Mussolini was busy setting up a new government, his son-in-law, Ciano, was languishing in jail in January 1944. Hitler had Ciano sent to jail in Verona after house arrest in Munich. The plan to go to Spain was not Ciano's idea, but Edda's (see Chapter 13). She was the oldest and favorite child of Mussolini. Also, she was in a good personal relationship with Hitler. She simply miscalculated her power to "influence" people at the top of both governments. The fact that Colonel Otto Skorzeny was responsible for flying the Cianos to Munich instead of Spain implicates Hitler in switching the two destinations because Skorzeny was extremely loyal (more like devoted) to Hitler. Dollmann was responsible for setting up and double-crossing the Ciano family to fly to Munich instead.

Dollmann had lived in Italy since 1927. His family had served the royal courts of Bavaria and Austria. He went to Italy to research Renaissance history; ad earned his living as a translator and writer. He moved in both Roman and German aristocratic and clerical circles and was not the type to become an SS officer. In 1937, Dollmann returned to Germany, with a group of Fascists, serving as an interpreter. When Hitler's interpreter fell ill, he was asked to substitute. The Nazi hierarchy was impressed with him, and Himmler made him his private SS interpreter. He seldom wore the SS uniform so as not to embarrass his Italian artistic friends. Dulles, Secretary of State, described him as "an intellectual, highly sophisticated, somewhat snobbish and cynical," and a man of almost effeminate gestures. An ideal double agent? See the book, *Bitter Chicory to Sweet Espresso*.

Bitler washed his hands of the whole affair by shipping Ciano to Verona and letting Mussolini do the dirty work. In a way, Il Duce had no choice. He was under house arrest. However, he did have many options, as Edda tried, in vain, to explain to him. Either he was too sick or cowardly to exercise any options. One straightforward option would have been to order the guards to release Ciano from jail or to demand a fair trial. Either way, Hitler would have done away with him. The only option was to leave the country altogether with the Cianos. However, he was too delusional to do that.

While Ciano considered how to leverage his diary to save himself, opportunity knocked on his door. The SS assigned an attractive young woman agent, Hildegard Burkhardt Beetz, to induce Ciano to reveal where he had hidden the diary. The Nazis were concerned about revelations of their demonic behavior. Ciano, a notorious womanizer, won her sympathy. She served as an interpreter for Ciano during discussions with German officials and already had developed a soft spot for him. Mrs. Beetz smuggled Ciano's letters out of prison and turned them over to Edda. On December 12, Emilio Pucci, a former lover of Edda, helped to smuggle the three Ciano children, Fabrizio (12), Raimonda (9), and Marzio (6), across the border into Switzerland. On December 18, Edda saw her father and he told her that there was nothing he could do to save her husband. She shouted at him, "You are all mad, you are all mad!" The final coup between the two came when she declared, "Between us, it is finished, finished forever...." Edda never saw her father thereafter.

Through Beetz, Ciano smuggled out a letter to Edda instructing her

225

to get a hold of the diary hidden in the train station in Milan. Edda and Pucci put in place a plan for Edda to escape to Switzerland. On January 8, Edda slipped out of the Ramiola clinic through a cellar door and walked across fields to join Pucci, who was waiting in his car. The next day, SS and Gestapo units discovered that Edda left the clinic. The race was on, with Edda having a day head start. In the early evening of January 9, Edda crossed into Switzerland with Pucci's help. With Germans in sight, he pushed Edda onto Swiss ground. Then he said, "Go now." She carried Ciano's diary in a pajama shirt under her dress, fashioned by Pucci so the bulge would make her look pregnant. Pucci later became one of the premier Italian fashion designers of women's clothing, rivaling the Dior house. The Swiss guards were shocked to see Edda and, the next day, she joined her children. Pucci was later discovered by the SS units only to be beaten almost to death. Somehow, he recovered from his skull being fractured in several places. In late 1944, he managed to join Edda. Mussolini was deeply hurt by Edda's estrangement, and he would later send an emissary to Switzerland, a priest who had known Edda for many years, to try to persuade her to return to no avail.

The trial of Ciano and his co-defendants began on January 8 in Verona, Italy. The trial lasted two days. It was a kangaroo court that found Count Ciano guilty of treason and the Judge condemned him and others to death by the firing squad: Giovanni Marinelli, Carlo Pareschi, Luciano Gottardi, Tullio Cianetti, and Emilio De Bono. Tullio Cianetti received a life sentence. That evening the condemned men signed a petition to Mussolini for pardon. They were all executed on 11 January 1944 in the fort of San Procolo in Verona. Each one was tied to a chair with their backs facing the shooters. At the very moment of the shooting, Ciano turned his face around shouting, "Viva L'Italia!" Mussolini never telephoned the prison to find out if pardon requests were en route to him, an omission that was no doubt deliberate.

New long-range rockets developed by Germany in 1944 had little effect on the war or the people when London was bombed. Rome and Paris were liberated, and the Russian Army was approaching the German border from the East and the Allies from the West. The Allies could see Ponte Vecchio, as they arrived in Florence. It was just a matter of time before the curtain came down on Nazi Germany. However, there was another war raging and it was in the Villa Feltrinelli. Rachele was fuming over the affair between her husband and Petacci. It was the talk of the town. There was no peace in the household. The constant bickering between Il Duce and Rachele about his affair dominated whatever conversation in the house. Finally, Rachele reached her threshold and decided to confront Petacci.

In November 1944, Rachele informed her husband that she was going to Villa Fiordaliso, Petacci's residence. She demanded that Buffarini (Interior Minister) accompany her. Mussolini phoned Clara to warn her of the storm that was about to break. "She is coming to you......Don't let her in.......she may be armed." Clara summoned an SS guard to close the gate, but Rachele began to climb over it with Buffarini tugging her skirt to hold her back. After the verbal confrontation between the two, and no resolution, Rachele returned to Villa Feltrinelli and swallowed bleach. She was sick, and Mussolini took care of her, patching up their differences.

By early, 1945, Mussolini broke free from house arrest. German troops were recalled home to defend their country. Russian and Allied troops broke through German defenses at the borders. Partisans were all over Northern Italy chasing Fascists. Mussolini was also trapped by the Partisans. South of the Po valley there was a stalemate by consent whereby Allied troops were facing enough German troops to force a stalemate. Partisans were getting brazen and roaming the hills surrounding main cities like Milan. Fascist territory shrank to areas around Milan. A meeting on April 24, 1945, was arranged by Cardinal Schuster, of the Milan diocese, between Mussolini, his associates, partisans, and aspirants to future governments. At that meeting, the Duce declared that he and 5,000 die-hard Fascists were ready to fight to the end. Cardinal Schuster asked, "And so you intend to continue the war in the mountains?" Mussolini replied, "Yet for a little while, but then I will surrender." Schuster shot back, "Don't deceive yourself, Duce, ... only three hundred....as you believe." Again, Il Duce was deluding himself. Only a handful of

Fascists followed him to the area of Lake Como. Forever delusional! He just couldn't help himself.

Discussions in the presence of the Cardinal pertained only to terms and conditions for surrender by the Fascists. The meeting broke up with Mussolini promising to respond to the terms of surrender offered by the Partisans. The next day, he left for the city of Como on Lake Como with a caravan of 20-30 Fascists. Arrangements were made to re-enforce the Mussolini group with 5,000 more Fascists. Those troops only existed in his mind. Mussolini arrived at a place near Lake Como, one to two miles from the Swiss border, but he never crossed the border. He didn't dare to cross it on foot. It cost him his life. He was caught by the partisans at Dongo, 25 miles north of Como, dressed as a regular German soldier. He and his mistress Clara Petacci were shot to death on April 28, 1945, by special, Communist agent Walter Audisio who had the explicit order from the Communist leadership to kill Mussolini. Two days later, Hitler heard the news and decided that he was not about to be taken alive by Russian troops like Mussolini had been by the Communists. He and Eva Braun decided to take cyanide pills and shoot themselves. Their bodies were never found in the underground bunker, where they committed suicide.

That historic day, May 1, 1945, was a beautiful sunny spring day with grape vines blooming that special sky-blue color all over town. People streamed toward the piazza in Avella. There was an enthusiastic celebration with the news that Mussolini was dead. No one showed any remorse. The same group of people, partisans and Communists parading a year before, were carrying their red flags all over the Piazza, and this time they had a loudspeaker blaring the news of Mussolini's death. Also, there was a two-man band playing a tambourine and trumpet and singing Communist revolutionary songs. The mood was jubilant and engaging. By this time a coffee shop/bar had opened at one corner of the Piazza. The aroma of sweet espresso could be smelled for the first time. Espresso coffee was brewed using roasted coffee beans rather than dried leaves and buds of chicory. People were waiting in line for an espresso and sat outside to take in the atmosphere and all the commotion around them. They sensed a truly historic moment. Everyone just wanted to turn the page and enter a new chapter in their lives. Their lives were no longer on hold. Although the food was still the main preoccupation, they were happy.

* The birthplace of Vito Genovese, as quoted in the literature in Tufino, near Nola and Avella, in Ricigliano, near Campagna and Vitigliano, near Catanzaro. We have assumed it to be Tufino for no believable reason. Most likely, he was born in Sicily, as he rose to a capo of the Mafia in New York City.

SEVENTEEN
Hidden Collateral Damage

There are two types of collateral damage in war: the visual kind (direct) and the non-visual one (hidden). Destruction of properties is an example of the former and the resurgence of crime syndicates in Italy, as well as globally, is one of many examples of the latter.

In 1946, Italians were finally free of dictatorship, tyranny, and occupation by foreign soldiers. Now, they could exercise their free wills and aspirations after many years of being harassed by Fascist thugs. It was the exhilaration of just letting it go to pursue one's dreams. Unfortunately, crooks and thieves felt the same way, but more so. Not only did they now enjoy the same liberty as everyone else, but they had the freedom to pick and choose illegal activities and to choose the victims to their hearts' content without consequences. They ran city halls in small and big towns. There was no law or public order. Simply put, there was no one running the local government to protect the people because the thieves oversaw City Halls. Before the outbreak of WWII, the Fascist government put a damper on organized crime, (Camorra) in Naples and the Mafia in Sicily. After WWII, the Camorra and the Mafia thrived as never before, and a new crime organization, equivalent to the Mafia or Camorra, emerged in the Calabria, Basilicata, and Puglia regions, called Ndrangheta. The evolution of these crime syndicates globally and the effects that they had on society is summarized.

SICILY

During prohibition times, the 1920s and 1930s, it was the turning point for mafiosi (members of the Mafia) in the USA. Mafiosi were no longer a bunch of misfit immigrants hustling here and there in small groups. Meyer Lansky organized and modeled these groups into one large crime syndicate in New York City, like an American corporation. Mafiosi emigrated to the USA from Sicily as early as the 1900s. Mussolini was about to clamp down later the Mafia in Sicily. Being a buffoon at heart, Mussolini could not stand the thought of being upstaged by a Capo Mafioso (Mafia boss) in Sicily during one of his many visits there. Mussolini employed Cesare Mori to eradicate the Mafia in Sicily.

Mori was born In Pavia (North Italy) and studied at the military academy in Turin. He had served two terms as police chief in Sicily before and after WWI. In 1924 he was appointed prefect of Trapani (Sicily) by the Fascist government and, in 1925, he was transferred to Palermo, the capital of Sicily. Mori was put in charge of the Carabinieri (local police), Publica Sicurezza (public security police), Polizia di Finanzia (police of finances), and other branches of the police department. The city of Trapani is in the western part of Sicily and Palermo falls between Trapani and the Strait of Messina. Most Mafia groups were concentrated in the western part of Sicily and the center of the island. The town of Corleone, as portrayed in the movie "The Godfather," is an example of the Mafia stronghold in that part of Sicily. The influence of the Mafia on local city officials was less in the eastern part of Sicily, but still significant. In the eastern part of the island, there are still Greek settlements from ancient times, like the town of Naxos. Sicily has maintained a steady export of olive oil and other produce to America for over a hundred years. The Mafia in Sicily and the USA has had strong control over these types of exports.

The mandate of the Fascist government to Mori was that the authority of the State must absre-established in Sicily and, accordingly, "If necessary, new laws would be adopted to force subjugation of the Mafia," according to Mussolini. In his first two months, Mori arrested five hundred Mafiosi, 450 in Palermo and more in the little hill town of Gangi, near the town of Corleone. In addition, Mori butchered all the cattle, sheep, and pigs in the town square of Gangi. This was the pattern for the next four years in areas controlled by the Mafia. Convicted Mafiosi were sent to islands near Sicily, like Lampadusa, Lipari, Stromboli, etc. The Fascist government wanted to isolate Mafiosi entirely from the people of Sicily. As Mori stated: "These people have not yet understood that brigands and the Mafia are two different things. We have hit the first ones, who are the most visible.... but not the most dangerous ones. The truly lethal blow to the Mafia will be given when we can roundup not only among prefectures, police headquarters, employers' mansions, and some ministries." By 1937 Mussolini believed that the Mafia was eradicated in Sicily and declared as much in public. Mori's comment implied that the Mafia cannot exist as a large organization, or crime syndicate, without a corrupt civil administration!

For Sicily, WWII was a total disaster compared with the rest of Italy. Ferry services to the mainland and elsewhere were disrupted and, as such, the export market of their farm products nearly vanished. Hence, the source of money was considerably reduced as well. The only thing that kept Sicilians from starvation was food produced locally on their farms. This meant that there was a glut of olive oil, wine, wheat flour, almond products, and fruits on the island. As such, it encouraged a barter system within the island, local bandits, and a black market for food products. This was an ideal setting for a Mafia comeback. Thus, by 1943 (after the Allied invasion) the Mafia came back stronger than ever to control the black market. Whatever Mussolini and Mori tried to achieve in six years or so disintegrated in less than a year.

American intelligence, being better informed than Il Duce, realized that for the invasion of Sicily to be successful it needed maps, photos of the beaches south of Sicily, and the cooperation of the Mafia. Navy and Army intelligence contacted Capo Mafiosi of crime families in the United States. In particular, the Navy contacted the Capo Mafioso in New York City, Salvatore "Lucky" Luciano, as he had already been in jail since 1936. He was jailed for running compulsory prostitution in the Midwest. Although he was incarcerated, he was still Capo, boss, in New York City. He was chased out of New York City and into jail by former New York Governor Dewey.

In return for the commutation of his jail sentence, Luciano ordered

Albert Anastasia to protect the USA waterfront from dock worker strikes for the duration of the war. Also, Luciano contacted other Capo Mafiosi in Sicily with the instructions to help with the incoming invasion by the Allies. Mafiosi provided intelligence information about German strength and layout of the beaches, troop concentration, and position, illumination of landing fields, tank positions of Germans, and radio operators. Albert Anastasia was the boss of the infamous Murder Inc. and controlled the American docks. He was killed after the war by a gang-style murder in a barber shop in NYC. Luciano's sentence was commuted to ten years in jail, and he was released in 1947. However, he was deported to Naples, Italy, in 1947 as an undesirable and returned to the USA in a casket, when he died in Naples in 1962. Interestingly, he was not welcomed by the Mafia to Sicily, although he was born there.

During the Allied invasion of Sicily, the US Navy employed special consultants to help the Allied Army in the invasion of Sicily, and Vito Genovese and similar organized crime figures? were employed. Genovese was *sottocapo*, underboss, to Lucky Luciano. His motive was to return to the USA, as he had been deported to Italy by the US Immigration Office as undesirable. He was charged with murder in New York City. After the war, he was allowed to return, as the star witness was murdered. While under police protection in prison, the witness was injected with enough sedatives to kill ten horses. The Allied Military Government (AMG) administration allowed him to come to Sicily to assist local city halls in running the towns (Appendix 3). This was like having the foxes guard the sheep. The only benefit, if one were to stretch it a bit, was that no bandits were running loose around the hills of Sicily as in the Naples area with Genovese in charge. The Mafia was not in the business of fostering competition with bandits not associated with the Mafia. Thus, they were hunted down by Mafiosi. That was good public relations. As a result, the Mafia returned to the former power it had before the Fascist government came to power in Italy.

Mafiosi had benefited greatly from their collusion with American intelligence. Vito Genovese was serving as an interpreter to the American Army in Sicily and later in Naples. He was issued an American Army uniform with the rank of sergeant, even though he was caught running a major black-market operation that involved stealing heavy trucks from American bases in Sicily. With the arrival of the Allies in Sicily, most of the Mafiosi exiled to small islands returned to Sicily with increased authority and tried to make up for the lost time. Mafia bosses were appointed by the AMG, with the assistance, more like a recommendation, of Genovese, to responsible positions in city halls, police headquarters, and security posts, since most Fascist administrators had been chased out of towns. Fascist mayors (Podestas) were replaced by Mafiosi.

Military administrators were not interested in running civil administrations in Sicilian cities. They had their hands full running. The German Army was building up then, although the Italian Army was deteriorating after the invasion of Sicily. Mafia became the establishment or was asked to provide law and order over the farms, peasants, and common people. In establishing a stable government and order over the people, the AMG didn't want to share power with the Communist or Socialist parties or brigands, which were active at that time.

In summary, the AMG created corrupt civilian administrations in Sicily and declared to the world that they restored these areas to normalcy, knowing full well that it was not the case at all. It was not until 1992 that magistrate detectives Giovanni Falcone and Paolo Borsellino, of the special investigative office in Sicily, discovered to what extent the Mafia had infiltrated government, police, and justice departments. Thus, Mori's fears were realized. The subtleties of this type of collateral damage due to WWII were never understood and reported. In short, it could not possibly have been seen before until the two investigators, Falcone and Borsellino, fifty years later! Hence, our terminology is hidden collateral damage. The hidden collateral damage caused by this crime syndicate, the Mafia, has caused more misery globally than the war itself. Perhaps, the AMG, at that time, might have not been aware of the predicament of local Sicilians.

After the war, Genovese consolidated his power in the Mafia by organizing the distribution of heroin and opium from Turkey to all parts of the world. These activities by him continued in New York City, resulting in a new order and gangland killing spree during the 1950s, as exemplified in the movie, *The Godfather*. Many of the killings were portrayed in the movie, although the storyline had nothing to do with the facts behind those murders. A new order was established.

NAPLES

The "sister" city to Palermo is Naples, Campania. Much like Sicily, Naples was settled by Greeks as far back as 800 BC, well before the Romans. Just as Sicilians, Neapolitans have seen invaders come and go for more than 2000 years; they have adapted to tyrannical invaders and survived them all. So, the mindset in Naples was, and is, not much different from Palermo. However, Naples has its brand of underworld organization, and it is often referred to as the Camorra. It has alluded that the Camorra and Mafia organizations may be a by-product of adapting to all those invasions. If so, those crime groups were localized to those two cities and were too small to expand in any other place. Invasions from WWII had a very different effect on these two crime organizations. It enhanced the power of the Mafia and the Camorra simultaneously, not only locally but also globally after the war. In addition, it created a whole new crime syndicate, called Ndrangheta, in Calabria, Basilicata, and Puglia, as it manifested itself later globally. Today, organized crime is prevalent globally, fashioned after the Mafia, Camorra, and Ndrangheta crime syndicates.

Camorristi (members of the Camorra) were jailed in Naples by Mussolini before the war. Trials were rigged by Fascist judges, and Camorristi were sent away to islands or resettled in other obscure places in Italy. In Sicily, bandits were looked upon by the Mafia as competitors; in Naples, bandits, and even scugnizzi, were looked upon by the Camorra as slave laborers to generate plunder. The Camorristi tolerated the local police if the police kept the small-time criminals and bandits in their place, especially those who did not cooperate with the Camorra. If there was plundered to be garnered, the Camorristi was first in line and shared the spoils with friends and local police. The purpose of the brigands or other thieves was to pave the way to the spoils for the Camorra, i.e., they were the slaves! The movie *Gomorrah*, directed by Matteo Garrone (2008), illustrates the point.

The Carabinieri did the best they could under these difficult circumstances and tried to stay neutral between Camorristi and small-time hustlers. Sooner or later, they too were corrupted, as their salaries didn't cover the basic needs of the family. In some cases, they were not even paid! Their main responsibility was whitewash any killing by the Camorra of "uncooperative" bandits. Allied Military administrators tried to do something about the lawless state of the occupied territories by deploying military officers throughout Southern Italy to maintain some form of civility. On average, one Allied Military administrator covered 10-20 small towns in trying to keep law and order. It helped in some places, but not in the Naples area (the valley) and Sicily. There were simply too many killings to investigate by one single administrator.

The so-called Zona di Camorra (Camorra territory) in 1946 was located about 20 miles north of Naples in the towns of Casoria, Afragola, and Aversa. However, the Camorristi were spread all over the valley, including Avella. Today, it is very difficult to pinpoint the area of concentration of Camorristi. It is like cancerous growth. Once the growth spreads in a body, it is difficult to track. Camorristi mingles among society much like growth in a body and is involved in legal and illegal businesses. They lived by their secret laws and recognized their secret courts, which imposed only one sentence on the enemy or betrayer – death. Before the war, there was some sort of moral authority and justice, but soon after there was only criminality.

Camorristi were appointed by the AMG to replace Fascist Podestas, near the end of the war and soon after. Again, Genovese, who was born in Tufino near Nola and Avella, was instrumental in those appointments (Appendix 3). Law and order were in the hands of poorly armed Carabinieri and Publica Sicurezza (security police) consisting of two or three men in each town. They were under constant threat of attack by well-armed criminals or brigands. Often Carabinieri walked through town with pistols drawn and cocked. Killings in small towns were reported to the Carabinieri but never investigated, either because they were understaffed, or the Camorra was involved in the killing. In either case, nothing was done about them.

The sale of contraband American cigarettes was a booming business. American cigarettes, shipped to the American base in Naples, disappeared as fast as they arrived in the port of Naples during and soon after WWII. There was inside collusion within the Naval base to do business at the scale in which it was conducted (Appendix 3). Contraband cigarettes were distributed from Naples by the Camorra throughout Southern Italy. After the war, the sale of contraband cigarettes extended throughout Europe. Certainly, scugnizzi and the local Camorristi were involved, to a large extent and yet, not a single internal collaborator in the Naples base was ever caught or brought to justice!

In addition, there was a black market for American goods normally not available in Northern Italy, such as blankets, medicine, soap, toothpaste, etc. Again, the source of these goods was the Naval base in Naples. Perhaps the introduction of American cigarettes and goods to Neapolitans may have been interpreted as a way of introducing capitalism to Italy. The American base in Naples was a "piece of cake" for Neapolitans to be able to tap into for survival. That is exactly what was needed at that time. In a very obtuse way, corruption at the base aided the locals. Everybody was starving before the Americans came. Most importantly, the locals survived because of the American base. However, the black market and the sale of cigarettes allowed the Camorra to operate beyond the confines of Naples for the first time after the War, all the way to Finland! That was the seed that blossomed into a crime syndicate organization.

Sixty-five percent of the per capita income of the Naples area was derived from transactions in stolen Allied supplies and one-third of all supplies and equipment imported continued to disappear into the black market. There were 42,000 women in Naples who engaged, either on a regular or occasional basis, in prostitution. The female population was about 150,000, and nine out of ten Italian women lost their men in battles, as prisoners of war, or as having vanished someplace in Europe never to return.

The black market operated under the protection of highly placed AMG officials. At the head of the AMG was Charles Polenti, and working with him was Vito Genovese (Appendix 3). The fact that "Lucky" Luciano was "exiled" to Naples by the US Immigration Office implied that he was unwanted by the Sicilian Mafia. Luciano was in Camorra territory, and as such, had very little leverage in the local operation, except for his underboss Genovese who was, supposedly, a native son of the area. The implications of such a snub in the Mafia portend a change in leadership. Indeed, there was such a change in New York City in the early 1950s. Genovese became Capo, although Lucky Luciano was floundering in Naples then.

The Camorristi went after bigger things, like all the tires from trucks stationed in large storage areas near Naples. An abandoned military tank in a town near Naples shrank to nothing slowly but surely over two months. Buses and trams came to a standstill when the departing Germans wrecked the generating station, which was carted away in a matter of a few days. Telegraph poles, vials of penicillin, and even unguarded small ships did not escape the Neapolitan kleptomania. Penicillin was then readily available in pharmacies, although these supplies were short at military hospitals. Don Nicola recounted an incident involving the San Carlo Opera house. The orchestra took a five-minute break only to return and discover all its instruments were missing. Nothing was outrageous for this new breed of robbers, scugnizzi, and Camorristi.

The Robin Hood tradition was as strong in the Zona di Camorra as it was in the vicinity of Naples. With the help of the AMG, bandits journeyed to the battle area in convoys of stolen cars to collect abandoned small arms, mortars, and metal scraps. Trains carrying supplies to the battlefront were hijacked and emptied of their contents. Bandits cultivated local sympathy by distributing a handful of thousand lire notes (five dollars) or a sack of stolen foods to the local peasantry. Tailors in Naples were cutting American military uniforms to pieces, dyeing the material, and turning it into smart civilian wear.

AVELLA

Brigands were made up of army deserters from various countries, Italian soldiers returning home, and thieves. They drove around in ex-German Army lorries and Allied vehicles stolen from storage. The police in most towns, including Avella, was corrupt and tyrannical and the civil population played a game with flexible rules that changed daily. The local police were involved in most of the spoils gathered by the brigands. There were open gunfights between rival gangs not affiliated with the Camorra in Baiano and other towns in the vicinity. In a town, on the other side of Monte Avella, Cervinara, gunfights were an almost daily occurrence. Matters were made even worse because ammunition in the police department was in short supply and pay for the officers was often delayed or not at all sometimes.

The Questore, equivalent to a Major-general in the police department, was paid $40 a month, a major $30 a month, and a postman $14 a month. Typically, the salary of the Chief of Police was $30 per month. The salaries of the Carabinieri were artificially low as they were expected to complement their pay by partaking in the "spoils" of the system. They tolerated the big racketeers of the Camorra and accepted protection money from them but were relentless in their pursuit of petty thieves. Southern Italians lived on bread dipped in olive oil. Bread bought on the black-market cost about 160 lire per kilogram (25 cents). Olive oil cost 450 lire per liter ($2-3 dollars), eggs 30 lire each and salt was not available at any price.

It was just a matter of time for street thugs, or simply brigands, to take over the hills, the farms, and the streets of Avella since the Maresciallo and the 2-3 guards at the barracks hadn't been paid in quite a while. Their focus was more on where to cash into the spoils of corruption in town. The only semblance of public order was provided by Alvaro, the Magistrate, and the postman, who also were not paid. The two old men, Badoglio and the King could not print money in Brindisi pretending to run a central government. In short, anarchy prevailed throughout Southern Italy. The political vacuum was taken over by brigands with guns. Different shades of anarchy existed in the valley as well as south of it.

Many Fascists were on the run. They were usually pursued by Communists and Partisans who had scores to settle. However, few of these Partisans were outright criminals. About 12,000 Fascists in Italy were killed without the benefit of a trial by jury after the war. Nothing had changed since the times of Cicero. The victors make the rules in the absence of law and public order. Two families in the east end of Main Street in Avella, and possibly more families who were Fascist sympathizers, left for South America never to return to avoid capture by Communist thugs. Others didn't travel as far and possibly paid heavy consequences. Only skeleton crews of previous administrations were in operation to conduct civil service, and they coped as best they could with the chaotic situation. They were not salaried employees and depended on bribes, much like the police in town.

Many towns in the valley were threatened by brigands. Some towns were taken over by them. That news reverberated in the soul of each person, young and old, in Avella. People were terrified. When things were nice and calm on one winter day, there was an ugly rumor circulating all over town; the "brigandi,", brigands, from the hills of Benevento were going to take over the town, including the police station. The unthinkable part of it was that chaos was going to be created in the part of the mountains where it had forever been peaceful. It was shepherd country. To say that the town was vulnerable was an understatement. People, in the east end of Main Street, put up barbed wires across the streets at every block. It looked like the British camp but in town. It was difficult to understand what good those wires were going to do! They were frantic and desperate times. Again, there were no Carabinieri around to supervise. Fear arrived with a vengeance.

Imalda couldn't believe that the rumor was true, and neither could Sergio. He had just been in that neck of the woods a couple of days before. He and Vladimir saw no human activity anywhere they went. Although the two were not paid to patrol the mountains, duty called. As for food, Imalda secured enough cheese to "last a lifetime" for them and the rest of the clan. Imalda begged Sergio to go back to the mountains of Cervinara and Benevento to see what was going on. Sergio was just as anxious to find out. He, Vladimir, and Dimitri began their journey very early in the morning. As for Dimitri, he wanted to be with his brother for the occasion.

However, Sergio told the boys that only he and Vladimir would carry a gun since Vladimir was then an employee without pay. Everything was peaceful on top of Monte Avella overlooking Cervinara and Benevento. The only "dangerous" sight was that of a wild boar charging

Dimitri, who climbed a tree to avoid it. As usual, they met shepherds camping there. The shepherds were surprised to hear about possible brigands in the mountains. The next day, the barbed wires were removed by the Carabinieri, since there was no danger in doing so. A sigh of relief could be heard in town.

Still, there was still a rash of robberies of bakeries, wine stores, supply stores, private homes, convenience stores, etc., in Avella. To what extent the Camorra was involved in those robberies was never investigated. Even if they were involved, the Carabinieri would never have investigated. It would have jeopardized bribe money from the Camorra. Most times, the Carabinieri didn't show up at the robbery sites. Serafina, Sofia, and Filomena worried that their dress shop would be next to be robbed since most of the robberies occurred in the Piazza area. Their three husbands, Mario, Vladimir, and Dimitri guarded the shop at night. The Carabinieri would have to be bribed to come over and do night guard duty. The wives would have to pay the Carabinieri to sleep over at the shop if they showed up at all. Thus, the men guarded for a couple of nights, until the threat subsided.

BASILICATA/CALABRIA/PUGLIA

As in the Naples area, brigands roamed in the hills and terrorized towns in the Basilicata, Puglia, and Calabria regions, more so than the valley in the Naples area. This tradition of brigands in the hills of Basilicata, etc. dates as far back as the Middle Ages. The regions were relatively poor and rampant with malaria for generations. Peasants made up the core of the populace there. Most of their land or farms were owned by wealthy barons and families who did not live in their town. The conflict there between the "haves and have not" was eternal. The existence of brigands in their midst was nothing new to peasants. In past generations, well before WWII, brigands were adored as heroes by the peasants, because they fought the establishment (the haves) on their behalf, as they liked to believe. Peasants recall those days as the golden era. The hate against the nobility and the rich were entrenched in their hearts. However, the new generation of brigands, of WWII vintage, was a nuisance to peasants. For one thing, the new brigands were not local, and peasants could not relate to them. In addition, these brigands stole whatever little they had from them. The wealthy ones were not around to be robbed. Nevertheless, peasants welcomed the new generation of brigands with the hope that they might get stuck in their farms as laborers. Some Russian deserters did settle in the Calabria area during the retreat from Sicily.

It didn't stop Genovese from appointing Camorristi and Mafiosi as mayors in towns of the Basilicata, Calabria, and Puglia regions where Fascist mayors left city halls. As the Allied Army advanced toward Northern Italy, these corrupt mayors exercised more control over the local economy as the black-market items from Naples and Sicily began to appear in those regions. For example, the Fascist mayor of Tito left town long before the Allied Army occupied the city of Potenza, near Tito. It didn't take very long for a Camorristi mayor to assume the office. A cafe owned by a nephew of the new mayor started selling American cigarettes on the premises. That was the beginning of many other items sold on the black market. As for Ottavio and Pasquale, it was like heaven on earth. They couldn't afford much, but American cigarettes were a must.

That was the beginning of organized crime in those regions. With the establishment of a black market and Camorristi mayors running city halls in those regions, it was only natural for organized crime operations in those towns to take place. However, corruption there took on a different flavor from the typical Neapolitan and/or Sicilian way of running the black market. For one thing, a new crime group called Ndrangheta was then in charge. The name of this criminal organization was not new. It was known during the reign of the Bourbons of Naples. In 1861, the prefect of Reggio Calabria already noticed the presence of a group of so-called *camorristi*, a term used at the time since there was no formal name for them in Calabria. Since the 1880s, there is ample evidence of Ndrangheta-type groups in police reports and sentences by local courts. At the time they were often referred to as *camorra* and *"Mana Nera," black hand, members*. In those days, the Mafia was also referred to as the Mana Nera. However, these groups were very localized to the area where they operated. For the lack of a better name, in the 1880s, they referred to these groups of thieves as Camorra or Mana Nera which already existed in Naples and Sicily, respectively. But these groups could not possibly be organized as syndicates of the modern days extending globally. They were an offshoot of the brigands of the past hustling in the hills. Since the 1950s, following wide-scale emigration from Calabria, the Ndrangheta organization had grown and established itself as a bona fide syndicate.

As of 1944, Carlo Levi wasn't aware of a global crime syndicate in Basilicata and Puglia by the name of Ndrangheta, when he wrote his book Christ Stopped at Eboli. However, he was aware of groups of brigands or thieves roaming the hills of Aliano, Basilicata! The word Ndrangheta was brought to a wider audience by the Calabrian writer Corrado Alvaro in the *Corriere della Sera, a* daily newspaper with circulation throughout Italy, in September 1955, because it had the appearance of a crime syndicate, for the first time, like the ones in NYC, for example. Thus, in a matter of ten years or so, the Ndrangheta had grown from a group of thieves to a crime syndicate operating throughout Europe.

The 'Ndrangheta is the only one of the mafia-type criminal organizations operating in Italy to have maintained the rites that distinguished it in the past, passing them down orally and through codes that, on rare occasions, have been discovered. It is characterized by a horizontal structure made up of autonomous clans known as *'ndrine,* based almost exclusively on blood ties. Its main activity is drug trafficking of which it has a monopoly in Europe, but it also deals with arms trafficking, money laundering, racketeering, extortion, loan sharking, and prostitution. The 'Ndrangheta has enjoyed, for decades, a privileged relationship with the main South American drug cartels, which consider it the most reliable European partner. It is capable of heavily influencing local and national politics and infiltrating large sectors of the legal economy. In 2013 they purportedly made 100 billion dollars according to a study from Demoskopika Research Institute. A US diplomat estimated that the organization's narcotics trafficking, extortion, and money laundering activities accounted for at least three percent of Italy's GDP in 2010.

The people of Southern Italy have survived, once again, another wave of invaders in WWII. They shed the yoke of Fascism to lead a normal life to recovery. However, the real beneficiary of the hidden collateral damage was the criminal element in Southern Italy that took over the political vacuum created with the help of the AMG, Allied Military Government. Hidden collateral damage started, as direct collateral damage ended, and, to this day, the whole world is still paying dearly for that blunder, more so than the cost of the War itself!

EIGHTEEN
Aftermath in Italy

The Union of Italian Jewish Communities reported that, in general, most confiscated assets were returned to their owners or next of kin, except in cases when the latter could not be identified. However, government institutions did not follow up in identifying survivors or their heirs entitled to unclaimed property. In December 1998, the Italian government created the Anselmi Commission, a technical body whose mandate was to investigate the confiscation and restitution of Jewish assets during the Holocaust. The Commission found evidence of at least 7,847 local and national government decrees expropriating Jewish assets during the Fascist era and analyzed 7,187 of them. The decrees affected approximately 8,000 individuals and 230 companies.

The Anselmi Commission released its final report and recommendations in April 2002. The report's findings show, in general, that assets were returned to deported survivors who submitted claims, but those survivors or heirs who did not submit claims were not proactively traced and compensated. The Commission recommended that Italian authorities investigate unclaimed assets to identify survivors and heirs who may not have filed claims and highlighted the need to investigate the unclaimed assets stored in the Italian investment bank, Cassa Depositi e Prestiti, which provides financing services for public-sector investments in Italy. Government institutions have not, in most cases, followed up on these recommendations. Furthermore, Italian Jews sold their assets at below-market value during the Holocaust due to dire and life-threatening circumstances. Post-war trauma and fear caused many Holocaust survivors and heirs not to pursue compensation for many years.

The Jewish community in Rome, which comprised almost half of the country's Jewish population before the war, successfully hid many historical artifacts, but some items in the community's archive were confiscated or destroyed. In 1943, the Nazis seized the contents of two libraries located in Rome in the same building: the library of Rome's Jewish community (4,728 books, 28 incunabula, and 183 books printed in the 16th century) and the library of the Italian Rabbinical College, a collection originally from Florence but later transferred to Rome (comprising 6,580 books and 1,760 booklets). The libraries contained prayer books, documents, prints, and manuscripts from all periods of Jewish history in Italy. The rabbinical library's collection was recovered in Germany after the war, but most of the contents of the Rome community library were lost.

The Jewish internees (about 200) at Tito disappeared just as they appeared in town before the War, incognito. They waited until after the War to leave Tito. From September 8, 1943, to May 1945, they were free to leave, but it was too dangerous to go home, North of the Alps. There was still a war. Some went home to conditions no better than those in Tito; others went to the newly declared state of Israel via Brindisi, the old Roman route to the Middle East. Most likely, internees in Campagna, Ferramonti, Potenza, and Brienza pursued the same route to Palestine. However, some stayed behind to return to their homes in central Europe or emigrated to the USA. All registration records of the internees at Tito's City Hall disappeared. How they disappeared is still a mystery. The only one who would have known, Pasquale, the Chief Magistrate, also disappeared after the War. He emigrated to the USA with Ottavio and his family. Most of the Italian American expatriates who were stuck in Tito and many other towns during the War returned to the USA after the war.

According to Elizabeth Bettina's book, *It Happened in Italy*, the only evidence supporting that Jewish internees lived in Tito during the War was traced to birth and death certificates at City Hall. This was not a unique situation in Tito. Most likely, towns like Tito purposely burned or got rid of in other ways, official records for fear that they might fall into the hands of SS officers, etc. During the battle of Potenza, German troops were all around the area surrounding Tito. This poses an interesting question: "What if there were no birth or death certificates discovered in Tito or Potenza or many other towns like them? Would the world forget or ignore the existence of Jewish internees in those towns? The mayor of Potenza denied, long after the war, the relevance of his town to Jewish internees until a birth certificate was shoved in his face!

As Bettina recounted in her book, the internees did return to those "internment" towns to thank the locals for making their plight much more tolerable and, most importantly, to help them survive the horrors of Nazism. Could the locals have done things differently to ameliorate the well-being of the internees? Probably not. Everyone in an "internment" town in Southern Italy was in survival mode until September 8, 1943. The local peasants were surprised to see educated and cultured visitors being subjected to such low indignity by their country. They could not comprehend why any country would get rid of its intelligentsia who had so much to offer. They could understand their plight, relative to Rome, but not that of the internees. It warranted much sympathy from the locals. The peasants highly respected education, because it was something denied to them for centuries. However, sympathy did not put food on the table, as everyone in town scavenged for food. They were shocked to see that internees preferred to stay longer in their towns even after they were told that they were free to go home in 1943.

In many ways, the internees and the locals had much in common. Both understood their special predicaments relative to their respective governments. As Carlo Levi pointed out in Aliano, Christ Stopped at Eboli, the local peasants had been ignored and neglected by the central government for centuries to the point of denying civilization not only for the peasants but also for the upper class. It didn't matter that many of the Jewish internees were well-educated, upper-class people. They were rejected, harassed, persecuted, and exterminated by the Nazi government. Both the townies and internees shared something in common: their governments rejected them. Whereas the central government of Rome turned a blind eye to the very existence of peasants in small towns, the Nazi regime hunted Jewish internees all over Europe to eradicate them. As far as their governments were concerned, they didn't exist. Hence, there was much empathy between the visiting Jewish internees and the local peasants. Besides, they were in the "same boat" to survive the war and resume their lives. Jewish internees, who came there as strangers, left with deep feelings of gratitude and friendship toward the locals on their return visit. They survived the Nazis, and the world recognized their existence.

The Wolf family was longing to get back to their beloved Vienna. By the end of the War, Werner was three and Beatrice seven years old and mingled easily with other children. The children didn't want to leave Tito and their friends. Mayor Bambolone and Magistrate Pasquale drove them to the Potenza train station instead of Tito only to spare them the uncomfortable ride in the local smaller wagon. At Potenza, they embraced, as if they had known each other forever. Retracing the train ride from Potenza to Vienna, they were shocked to see the devastation in Vienna. Whatever building was missed by Allied bombing was demolished by Russian tanks. The building where they had lived vanished.

Many survivors ended up in displaced persons (DP) camps set up in Western Europe under Allied military occupation at the sites of former concentration camps. There they waited to be admitted to places like the United States, South Africa, Palestine, and the Scandinavian countries. These countries needed skilled labor. Count Folke Bernadotte, who was chairman of the Swedish Red Cross and the Danish government sponsored 36 "white" buses to transport Jewish internees to their countries. In particular, the Wolf family arrived in Odense, Denmark, where they were provided with an apartment subsidized by the Danish government. Ehrlich was employed at an architecture firm owned by Mr. Herman Ricka, who was a former resident of Vienna. Ricka left Vienna soon after the occupation of Austria by Germany in 1938.

In addition to Jewish internees, many soldiers from various warring countries were dispersed all over Europe. An unaccountable number of Italian soldiers were imprisoned in concentration camps (Gulags) in Russia never to make it home. Some remained behind and started families and assumed a new life. For Fascist soldiers, it was too dangerous to return home with Communists lurking for them. Of the 600,000 Italian troops deployed in the Russian campaign, 5,000 to 10,000 soldiers returned to Italy after the war. There is no accountability for Italian youth deported to German factories and more than 600,000 Italian soldiers stranded in the battlefields of central Europe and the Balkans.

Besides Jews interned in Italy, soldiers throughout Europe, peasants, and gentry caught in the whirlpool of the war, and illustrious people, who were close to decision-makers, also hungered for a normal life. Edda Ciano escaped Switzerland January 9, 1944, disguised as a peasant. She managed to smuggle out her husband's wartime diaries, which had been hidden in her clothing by her confidant and lover Emilio Pucci. At that time, he was a lieutenant in the Italian Air Force but later found fame as a fashion designer. War correspondent Paul Ghali of the *Chicago Daily News* learned of her secret internment in a Swiss convent in Neggio and arranged for the publication of the diaries. They revealed much of the secret history of the Fascist regime between 1939 and 1943 and are considered a prime historical source.

The diaries are an account of the daily life of Count Galeazzo Ciano when he was Foreign Minister of the Fascist government. In it, he describes his dialogues and interpretations of the encounters with the Nazi and Fascist hierarchies including Hitler and Mussolini. It also contains personal observations of those leaders. After returning to Italy from Switzerland, Edda was arrested and held in detention on the island of Lipari. On 20 December 1945, she was sentenced to two years imprisonment for aiding Fascism. At that time Badoglio was still the prime minister of the new Italian government in Brindisi. It is noted that Captain Erich Priebke and Colonel Herbert Kappler of the Gestapo Headquarters in Rome were found guilty after the war of murdering 335 civilians during the German occupation. The killings were in retaliation for partisans killing 33 German security policemen. The irony of it all was that those policemen were Italian citizens (Bolzano) before the war. None of the remaining policemen took part in the retaliation! Yet, Priebke and Kappler did not spend one day in prison, because it was considered harsh punishment for them to endure. The British Military interfered with many of the court decisions of the Italian courts after the War.

An Italian film was dedicated to the incarceration of Edda in Lipari and her relationship with a young Communist guard. After the war, Mrs. Edda Ciano settled quietly in Rome. She broke her public silence on wartime events in a 1975 book *My Testimony,* and several years before her death, she attended a public mass in memory of her father. She is said never to have reconciled with her mother, Rachele, Mussolini's widow. Her mother blamed Mrs. Ciano's husband for being responsible for the fall of Benito Mussolini. Alessandra Mussolini, the wartime dictator's granddaughter who was a member of Parliament for the right-wing National Alliance, told Reuters: "My aunt was born a woman but lived like a man. Not only did she stand up to her father over the man she loved; she stood up to Il Duce, which is something altogether different."

Edda died in Rome in 1995. She forgave her father, Mussolini, just before she died for having her husband, Count Ciano, shot on January 11, 1944. Her relationship with her mother, Donna Rachele, was at best strained and uncomfortable. Italians referred to Rachele as "donna" (equivalent to a don in a man's world). Edda's love relationship with the fashion designer Emilio Pucci ceased soon after the War, as their lives and careers went separate ways.

During her husband's spectacular and bombastic political career, Donna Rachele remained in the background, caring for their five children and running her household. Mussolini and his mistress, Claretta Petacci, were executed in 1945 by Italian partisans/Communists. After the war, Donna Rachele spent most of her time on her farm in Predappio, a small town near the Adriatic Sea, in the Emilia region of Italy. It is in this district where she and Mussolini were born and where they first met. Despite the ruin spawned by Mussolini's public career and the infidelities that marked his private life, Donna Rachele honored his memory to the end of her days.

She insisted that his body be returned to her by the Italian government, and in 1956 it was. She saw to it that he received a Christian burial in the cemetery in Predappio. She insisted that part of his brain that had been taken to the United States be returned, and it was. She fought for the return of his personal belongings, all of which had been confiscated after the war, and many of them were given back. She insisted on her rights to a pension as the widow of a former soldier and government official. In 1968, the government capitulated and granted her a sum equal to $200 a month. A large portrait of "Il Duce" was displayed in her house. A smaller picture, taken when he was a young socialist newspaper editor, graced a table in her room.

Donna Rachele managed a restaurant at "La Caminate," the hilltop near her home where Mussolini once had a villa. It was popular with tourists, curiosity seekers, and neo-Fascists. It is said that the only one of her husband's belongings that she refused to accept was a large walnut bed. When the government offered it together with other furniture, she turned it down, reportedly saying, "Claretta used it." Donna Rachele often visited her husband's grave. Beside him lie the bodies of two of their children, Bruno, an Air Force pilot who was killed in a crash during World War II, and Anna Maria, who died in 1968. Donna Rachele had a granite coffin prepared for herself. That, too, lies next to the body of Mussolini. She professed little interest in politics. "I was sorry that Mussolini went into politics," she once said. "He had a newspaper; he was the editor. He should have stayed there. You can't be happy in politics, never, because one-day things go well, another day they go badly." Donna Rachele was survived by three children, Vittorio, who had a successful business career in Argentina before returning to Italy in 1968: Edda, the widow of Count Galeazzo Ciano, and Romano, one of Italy's leading jazz pianists and the former husband of Sophia Loren's younger sister. Donna Rachele died in 1979 at the age of 89.

Petacci's corpse and those of the other fifteen shot in April 1945 were taken to Milan. Her body was displayed in Piazzale Loreto on April 29th together with those of Mussolini and others, which were hung upside down. Around 3 pm, the American military command ordered the 19 bodies to be taken by lorry to the municipal morgue in Via Ronzo no. 1; Petacci's body was then taken to the Maggiore Cemetery and buried as unknown in a field of 16, where those of Mussolini and others already were. In March 1957 Clara was buried in the family tomb at the Verano Cemetery in Rome, thanks to permission given by Interior Minister Fernando Tambroni.

POLITICAL LANDSCAPE AFTER WWII

With all the scheming and make-believe by Mussolini, the modern-day Caesar, Italy lost all her colonies and Italian territories gained from its participation in WWI. In April and June 1946, the people of Italy were preoccupied with the coming election of the General Assembly on April 19, 1946, and the vote of a referendum on June 2, 1946, about the disposition of the Monarchy. The main purpose of the Assembly was to draft a new Constitution of a new government, and they had two years to do it. A "Yes" vote in the referendum implied that the Monarchy, or King Victor Emmanuel III, could form a post-war government similar to the British form of government. A "No" vote implied that the Monarchy or the King would be exiled from Italy. The Communist and Republican parties were actively against the King. The Communist Party in Avella was headquartered next to City Hall. They held a rally almost every day up and down Main Street and would carry their red flag, singing Communist revolutionary songs, and they had a trumpeter to get people's attention. Typically, the group consisted of 30-40 Communists.

In the belated hope of influencing public opinion ahead of the referendum on the continuation of the monarchy, King Victor Emmanuel formally abdicated in favor of Umberto II (his son) on 9 May 1946 and left for Egypt. The Catholic Church saw the continuation of the monarchy as the best way of keeping the Communists out of power. During the referendum campaign, Catholic priests used their pulpits to warn that "all the pains of hell" were reserved for those who voted for a republic. The Catholic Church presented the referendum not as a question of republic vs. monarchy but, instead, as a question of Communism vs. Catholicism; warning that to vote for a republic would be to vote for the Communists.

On the day before the referendum, June 1, 1946, Pope Pius XII, in a sermon on St. Peter's Square, said in what was widely seen as endorsing Umberto, "What is the problem? The problem is whether one or the other of those nations, of those two Latin sisters [elections were taking place in France on the same day] with several thousands of years of civilization, will continue to learn against the solid rock of Christianity...or, on the contrary, do they want to hand over the fate of their future to the impossible omnipotence of a material state without extraterrestrial ideals, without religion, and God. One of these two alternatives shall occur according to whether the names of the champions or the destroyers of Christian civilization emerge victorious from the urns."

King Victor Emanuel dressed in a toga. Courtesy of Enrico Albertis.

The Republican Party in Italy advocated a return to a democratic government and Constitution, like when Italy gained independence from France and Austria in the 1860s. The Republican Party in the USA represents different beliefs: the US Constitution and State's Rights. The King had mild support in Southern Italy only because he resided in the South, Brindisi, during the referendum. Northern Italy was solidly against the King. Members of the Monarchy Party in Avella plastered posters near the Café and along the passeggiata route on Main Street, supporting the King. It did not help, since the outcome was inevitable, and the referendum did not carry. In the referendum election, the "No" vote barely won in Southern Italy, but Northern Italy voted overwhelmingly against it. That was an unpredictable result because the house of Savoy (King) had come from near Turin (Northern Italy) since 1870.

The King and his wife, Queen Elena, were exiled to Egypt and he died on December 28, 1947, of pulmonary complications. Their son, Umberto II, was exiled to Cascais, Portugal. He reluctantly accepted the result of the referendum. People were afraid that he might incite a civil war. The following year, 1947, the new constitution was drafted and passed by the General Assembly with a vote of 452 to 63 against it.

The year in politics, 1948, started with the major parties inviting national politicians to come to Avella and give speeches at their rallies. Usually, the speeches were delivered on a temporary podium built on top of the water fountain in the piazza. The podium faced the entire Piazza near City Hall. The Communists brought their "big gun," Palmiro Togliatti, to give a speech. During WWII, he was exiled to Moscow. The Piazza was full to the limit. There were Communist groups from Baiano and Sperone as well as Avella. The towns of Baiano and Sperone had voted for the Communist party in local elections, in contrast to the town of Avella. Other politicians who came to Avella were DeGasperi (Christian Democrat) and Nenni (Socialist). For each of those speakers, the Piazza was full. Based on the capacity of the crowds it was clear that the two parties in contention for the next prime minister of Italy were the Communist and Christian Democratic Parties.

Italy was very much polarized politically for years to come and, as a result, the central government has not been stable since. There has been, on average, a change in the Prime Minister's office every 15-18 months. In most western countries, a change in leadership in the central government occurred every four years. The problem has been that a small change or perturbation of the electoral results, dramatically affected alliances needed to obtain a majority in parliament. For the fifty years since 1948, Italy has had the largest membership in the Communist Party of the Western Democratic countries.

General elections were held in Italy on Sunday, April 18, 1948, to decide members of parliament, the Chamber of Deputies, and Senators of the Republic. Italy was no longer reigned by a King, since the referendum of 1946. There were about 40 parties nationally. The major parties included the following: Christian Democracy, Communist, Socialist, Social Democracy, Social Communist, Monarchy, Liberal, Liberty, Leaf, Republican, and a few other minor ones. The National Fascist Party along with its successor, the Republican Fascist Party, were the only parties banned by the Constitution of Italy: "It shall be forbidden to reorganize, under any form whatsoever, the dissolved Fascist party." The elections were heavily influenced by the Cold War between the United States and the Soviet Union. The USA feared that if the Communist Party won, Italy would be drawn into the Soviet Union's sphere of interest (Appendix 2). It was a dirty and vicious political campaign.

The CIA gave two million dollars to centrist parties. The PCI was also funded by the Soviet Union and the Cominform. Ten million letters were sent by Italian Americans urging Italians not to vote Communist. The Christian Democrats won with 48.5% of the vote and 305 seats in the Chamber of Deputies and 131 seats in the Senate. Never again would the Christian Democratic Party poll as high. The total numbers of Deputies in the Chamber were 574 and 237 in the Senate. The Popular Democratic Front (FDP- Communist Party) under the leadership of Palmiro Togliatti and Pietro Nenni gathered 31% of the vote, 183 deputies, and 72 senators. Most of the support for the Communist party came from the so-called "Red Triangle" region of the Emilia, Liguria, and Savona area, which is still predominantly "red" or Communist.

The Marshall Plan derived its name from US Secretary of State, George C. Marshall, in President Truman's administration after the war. It was implemented in 1947 during the critical election year in Europe.

The fear at that time in countries like Italy, France, Greece, West Germany, etc., was that they might turn

Communist and, thereby, the Soviet Union would take over all of Europe. During the war, Marshall was a four-star General who was the main architect of the American war strategies in Europe and Asia. The plan was also referred to as the European Recovery Program or ERP. In three years, under this plan, the US gave away $12.4 billion, which was about 5% of its GDP at that time. In today's dollar value, it would amount to about one trillion dollars. The money was earmarked for the modernization of industries, bank systems, reconstruction of infrastructures, food, and minerals.

In Italy, most of the grants went into rebuilding the industrial base in Northern Italy. For example, the Fiat Company was able to modernize its plants and compete with German and French auto manufacturers. Once the domestic market was controlled by Fiat, they expanded to markets in Europe and the USA. As for Southern Italy, there was much infrastructure reconstruction, but no new investments in heavy industry activities or markets. Grant monies were spent on food supplies.

There were no matching funds to invest in heavy industries in Southern Italy as there were no new heavy industries. Before WWII, the disparity in industrial capacities and markets between Northern and Southern Italy was uneven. After the war, the disparity was even greater and Southern Italy has never recovered. In some sense, the Marshall Plan exacerbated a bad situation in Italy to make it even worse than before. It was not surprising that, after the war, there was a mass exodus of young people from Southern Italy to industrialized parts of Italy, Europe, and the USA.

The Marshall Plan accentuated the deep divide between Northern and Southern Italy. The industrial base was more and more concentrated in the North and the South was reverting to the Stone Age, comparatively speaking. The North looked at the South as a parasite, and the South viewed the North as the bully, hoarding all the industries. Whereas, in the past, the "haves and have-nots" were a local issue, in the late 1940s, it became a national issue, North versus South. In Italy, this contrast of classes has lasted for more than seventy-five years, since WWII.

Carlo Levi and other scholars dwelled on this disparity after the war. They proposed that the peasant class should have a parliamentary representation and, therefore, a voice in government decisions. Laws would then be enacted to benefit peasants and elevate them to the middle class, eliminating the peasantry in the South. That was utopia taken to the nth degree by those scholars. Still, it was an interesting proposal but not practical in terms of how to secure representation in parliament, exclusively for peasants. Besides, how does one classify a person as a peasant? Also, representation could be achieved only through the electoral process. Political parties for centuries have shunned the impact of the peasant vote as a bloc since peasants rarely voted. As a result, peasants in Southern Italy have been disenfranchised by the central government. Raising the standard of living of one peasant class would have generated another one to challenge the status quo; back to square one.

The clash between the classes is a result of the fact that natural resources in each country or region are finite, and the distribution of wealth, derived from it, is uneven. Thus, it comes down to the following: Are the people of Italy, or in any other country, willing to share the country's resources or wealth equally? The present electoral process is not able to do that, because it has been corrupt and flawed ever since its inception in Greek and Roman times. Thus, a different process from the electoral one needs to be devised to represent all and distribute wealth equally.

Nevertheless, in the 1950s, people in the South had the will to live life to the fullest and explore anything in their power. Tourism alleviated some of the unemployment woes in the South. In the post-war era, new technologies and gadgets, such as TV, jets, computers, cars, medicine, etc., became available to the world. Furthermore, there was the liberalization of old customs, as reflected in the music, the movies, and women's and men's fashions. The whole world conspired to get away from the dreary days of WWII. The coup d'etat finally came down on the chaperon escorting lovers in Southern Italy. The mind-set of the young called for a social revolution, which they won.

Hidden Governments

According to Cesare Mori (see chapter 17), ".... The truly lethal blow to the Mafia will be given when we can make roundups not only among prefectures, (but in) police headquarters, employers' mansions and some ministries". That was exactly what the Mafia, Camorra, and Ndrangheta were able to accomplish during and after the war. Vito Genovese planted seeds of Camorristi and Mafiosi in the "fields" of City Halls in Southern Italy. Soon after the war the "seeds" blossomed into crime syndicates. Corruption in the governments reached local as well as national levels. Today, corruption by organized crime syndicates has reached, Italy and the USA, South America, Europe, and even Asia. There is much cooperation between various syndicates in different parts of the world. The damage to societies globally caused by organized crime syndicates is far greater than all the world wars, flu pandemics, and natural disasters combined!

NINETEEN
Espresso, Please

A fter the war, the feeling among people of Avella was almost euphoric about the future without that monkey on their backs every minute of the day. They just wanted to forget about the nightmare and go on with their lives. For the first time in a long time, they had the freedom to pursue their dreams and aspirations. The new threat was the Communists marching up and down the streets of Avella, brandishing the Communist hammer and sickle red flag. Fascists were assassinated without trial since the acting government in Brindisi could not get their act together to replace Fascist judges. A mini-civil war was brewing in the streets of Italy in which Communists and former Fascists were at each other's throats. Newspapers shied away from reporting it for fear of inciting one. However, people were fed up with politics and in a hurry to catch up with the rest of the world, joining the twentieth century in exploring new ideas, fashion, and lifestyles. The USA was an exciting place to live and, for the most part, it was the first choice of where refugees wanted to emigrate.

Local and national elections were called throughout Italy. There were two candidates for mayor of Avella. The former apolitical mayor, who left the office when the Germans came to town, ran under the banner of the Christian Democratic Party. The other candidate, from the west end of Avella, ran under the Communist Party banner. Immediately, the local politics became nasty. The local Communist Party of Avella accused Imalda of taking bribes from the leaders of the Democratic Party. Like most shepherds, Imalda had no political leaning one way or another, but she felt that, with Communists in charge, the town would regress to the old days, and she had enough of that. It would have only generated more strife between the classes. Like her community of shepherds, she detested the Communist Party with a passion. She felt that, although her community might be poor, they worked hard to carve out a living; local Communists were forever looking for handouts from the church, government, business, the wealthy, etc. She decided to do something about the coming election. Imalda spent much time with shepherds teaching them to sign their names on the ballot which was a requirement to vote.

Partisans and Communists rounding up former Fascists in Naples. Courtesy of C. Vittoria.

The Catholic priests in Avella got involved in the election only because the church feared losing their extensive land holdings in town. Communists were campaigning on the promise to break up farms owned by the churches into smaller plots and distribute them to poor farm workers, mostly to loyal Communists. The Communists paraded in Main Street with a red bandanna around their necks like the one

Giuseppe Garibaldi wore during the revolutionary days of the 1850s, implying that Garibaldi was a founding father of the Communist Party. Of course, that was a false claim, as the party didn't exist until after the Russian revolution in 1918. That stunt garnered some votes, but not enough to win the election.

The Democratic candidate was elected with a majority of 56% versus 42% for the Communist candidate and 2% for other write-in candidates. This was a surprising result because towns surrounding Avella, Baiano, Sperone, Cervinara, and Cicciano, voted for Communist mayors. The surprising result was due mostly to Imalda's efforts in the shepherd community. The Communist Party put up a candidate who lived on the outskirts of town, near the Castle of Avella, and no one in town knew or was aware of him. Rumor had it that the Communist party of Avella brought in an outsider for the election. However, even if people knew who the man was, it would not have made any difference. The shepherd community is the largest one in Avella.

One of the first acts of the new mayor was to fund a road project toward the picnic grounds, the Fusaro area, which included the swimming pool built by the British Army. The rationale for the paved road was that, instead of a potential surge of visitors to the annual spring festival at the Fusaro, they would be ready for the large crowd. Before WWII, visitors from the city of Naples and towns in the valley made their pilgrimage to the picnic grounds and the Church of Montevergine on the high mountains. Imalda suggested that the mayor hire Dimitri and Paolo, Don Nicola's son since there was a shortage of construction workers in the valley and no one qualified as a civil engineer. The three of them, including the mayor, got together and planned the construction of the road. It was like "the three stooges" building something that they had no clue where to begin. The only clue was that they were aware that the Germans built a paved road near the Cemetery during the war. If only they could obtain those construction plans, they thought. However, the Communist mayor in Baiano had the road plans and he outright refused to release them to a Democratic mayor. How they got a hold of those plans is a mystery to this day. Everyone knew that they had them, as there were many road constructions in Baiano.

The mayor of Baiano let it be known that he would be happy to deal with a Socialist like Don Nicola since the two of them were orchestra members of the San Carlo. The two artists thrashed out a deal, a palatable bribe for both sides. Both being Neapolitans, it was a foregone conclusion that they would do so. Most of the laborers on the road construction were to be members of the Communist Party who had never worked on road construction and were unskilled residents of Baiano and Avella. The political implications were obvious. The day-to-day operation was handled by Dimitri. Paolo kept tabs on who should be paid on the project. The project to pave about two miles of road that ran from downtown Avella to the Fusaro picnic area was finished in a year. The mayor left office soon after the road was built as he was promoted to a judgeship position, replacing a Fascist judge.

An out-of-town person was installed as the new mayor. The people of Avella never knew where he came from and what his party affiliation was. The fact that there were not many crimes in Avella at that time, attested to his representing the Camorra's interests. The mayor kept to himself and didn't do much of anything for the rest of his term. In the following election for mayor, Imalda stayed out of the campaign. The local pharmacist ran for mayor against the Communist Party candidate. The pharmacist ran under the Republican Party. There was no candidate from the Democratic Party. The pharmacist easily won and was able to stay in office as mayor for four years. People wanted to be on good terms with the pharmacist, as they would need medicine in the future. By this time, Don Nicola also stayed out of politics and remained very busy with his studio and San Carlo. Whatever little time he had, he preferred to spend with his group of friends, the clan of old.

The picnic festival at the Fusaro fields resumed after a hiatus of seven or eight years, having been postponed during the war. A contingent of Neapolitan families made the pilgrimage to the Fusaro picnic grounds in Avella, located at the foothills of Mount Avella. Neapolitans have been fixated every spring on coming to the Fusaro area for a picnic, although there are many other similar places nearby. Neapolitans claim that they love the cool and clean mountain air, compared with the congested living conditions in Naples surrounded by charred buildings. This tradition goes back 600 years. Usually, Neapolitans and people in the valley came on the first Saturday in May and the people of Avella scheduled their picnic on the following Saturday.

The picnic was a two-day event. On the second day, mule, donkey, and horse-riders lined up for a race. If Hannibal's descendants could have been there, probably elephant and zebra riders would also have lined up for the race. Jockeys were ordinary people representing different districts of town, much like the "Palio" horse race in Siena. The mule was usually ridden by someone representing the farmers. The donkey was ridden by a bride pulled by the groom.

There were a few aficionados of the horse. This type of diversification in four-legged animals would not be allowed in Siena. Sergio and Vladimir served as the official timekeepers of the race; they also provided order and safety in the picnic area, which was part of their duties as mountain policemen. They walked up and down the foothills, all the way to the Church of Montevergine, Avellino, frequented mostly by Neapolitans. From the picnic grounds to Montevergine was straight uphill, through treacherous terrain. Surprisingly, city folks from Naples trekked through it all! And when they arrived at the church, they would get on their knees and struggle to get inside the church on their knees. Strange ritual!

On the outskirts of Avellino and the church, they followed a difficult and circuitous route to avoid stranded, charred and destroyed German tanks, cannons, trucks, jeeps, motor scooters, and benzene containers spread all over the road and this went on for a long distance. The destroyed vehicles appeared to be heading toward Salerno, probably as a supply convoy and were bombed by Allied planes. If Dante were there, he would have labeled the road as the "inferno" road. The smell of benzene was so powerful that it was difficult to breathe even two years later. Interestingly, a medical survey reported that thyroid cancer patients in old people are most pronounced in the Avellino area. The grass was charcoal black and did not grow back for a couple of years. Yet, Neapolitans were not fazed by the terrain and the terrible smell. They kept their pace to arrive at the church for the evening Mass. Sergio and Vladimir were happy that the Neapolitans headed back to Naples by bus the next day with everyone accounted for.

In some sense, those were the golden days for the people in the valley. Hope sprang up like the seeds in farms. It seemed like the whole world wanted to forget about the war and make up for a lost time. Europe was devastated by the war. Europeans looked to the USA for the latest diversions: movies, theaters, fashion, new appliances, television, etc. The most popular outlet for the people of Avella was the Cinema Theater, built in the winter of 1946. The Cinema in Avella was called Sala Azzurra (Blue Room). The people were enthralled by the new diversion. It played mainly "Cowboy and Indian" movies. Children sat on the ground in front of the first row, cheering for their heroes, Randolph Scott and Buster Crabbe, every time they appeared on the screen. Soon enough the kids made wooden pistols to use in gun duels out in the streets.

To appease the adults, sentimental Neapolitan movies, such as "Anema e Core" (Heart and Soul) were shown. The film industry was beginning to rise from the ashes in Italy then. Initially, favorite operas were filmed for the public. It was not until the early 1950s that the industry in Italy produced world-class directors and actors. Their theme was to inject more realism into the movies, and they began to replace American movies at the Cinema. Italian audiences were receptive to the new vision of films and so was the rest of the world. The comedian Toto (Antonio De Curtis) and actress Sofia Loren began to appear in slapstick movies about that time. Director Federico Fellini introduced escapism from realism with the famous movie, La Strada (The Road). People needed that diversion from all that destruction surrounding them.

In towns like Avella, people no longer wanted to be tied down to farming and shepherding. The world around them was moving faster than they liked. They wanted to be part of that evolution.

The dress shop, owned by the three women, began to expand its fashion line to a younger generation in addition to the older traditional clientele. The Pucci, and Dior fashion lines, and American casual clothes were popular with the young and old. The dress shop expanded to add apprentices to the shop while maintaining excellent rapport with their former mentor. Lena was as beautiful as ever modeling the new fashion designs. Her aspiration was beyond Avella. She had a dream of becoming a model in the USA.

As the dress-making business expanded, the "girls" were spending too much time together on the road to Nola to purchase various types of fabrics, as new dress fashions and fabrics were becoming available in local shops after the war. Sofia was designated to take over the role of purchasing fabrics and selecting new fashions since she could coordinate fabrics with styles. Besides, like her mother Imalda, she was the best negotiator! In a way, negotiations were another form of socializing. With the coming of summer, Sofia and Mario decided to buy an apartment in a building that also housed the dress-making shop. It was convenient for both Sofia and Mario to be closer to the train station and the dress shop. Their apartment was located within the common courtyard adjacent to the shop. Five residents shared that courtyard, and it was connected to the Piazza by a 60-foot-wide tunnel. Usually, tunnels were closed off by a large portone (front door), but not this one.

Sofia once rented an apartment at the Naval Station before the war near a well-to-do district of Naples, the Posillipo, and Vomero areas. When they lived there, they encountered people of the aristocracy. As the famous French writer Alexandre Dumas [18-1] discovered, most aristocrats in Naples were pretenders for wealth. Only a small percentage had access to real wealth and the means to afford the latest fashions. Sofia could discern whom to contact for future business. However, soon after the war, it wasn't safe for her to contact them. That district drew too much attention from scugnizzi, Communists, and prostitutes. Naples was "no man's land." Chaos and lawlessness reigned there as in other districts of Naples. The best option for Sofia was to bide her time until better days because the will to survive and live life to the fullest was and is inbred in every Neapolitan.

Sofia and the sisters would redesign or modify a style to fit the shape of a customer. They would cut the fabric based on the newly modified design. Lena, the teen-aged daughter of Sofia, would often model dresses after school. She blossomed into a beauty, like her mother. The boys in the neighborhood certainly took notice. As time went by, business improved steadily to the point that the women needed help from another dressmaker in town, their former teacher and mentor. The business was thriving in Avella, not because of the Marshall Plan, but because people escaped the yoke of Fascism and were free to express themselves in many ways. Shipments of food from the Marshall Plan and money from relatives in the USA spurred small businesses all over Southern Italy.

Cafes were open for business in the Piazza as well as in the poorer sections of town (East and West ends of town). The topic of conversation in the Piazza was who made it alive from the war and who was missing. In the east end of town, two soldiers made it home. One returned from the Russian front having been at the battle of Stalingrad. The other soldier was imprisoned in Libya by the British and released after the war. Often, he would sit in the piazza wanting to tell people his experience about the war, but no one wanted to hear him talk about it. People were afraid to get near him because his monkey, acquired in Libya, would attack anyone approaching the man. Overall, less than 2% returned to Avella from the war. Farm owners congregated in the piazza to recruit farmhands or anyone with two hands and legs to work on their farms. The shepherd community was unscathed by the war. However, more and more of them returned to their neighborhood in the east end of town.

A cafe and bar opened for business for the first time on the east end of Main Street. The new feature of this bar was the billiard room and spumoni gelato (ice cream). The bar was located across from Saint Anthony Church, and it was centrally located on the passeggiata route to the Piazza. Espresso aroma wafted to the Piazza, about two blocks away. In the morning, workers, on the way to the train station, would stop to buy a pastry and an espresso. In the afternoon, teenagers found a way of unwinding from schoolwork and socializing with their friends. The Giro D'Italia, the bicycle tour race of Italy, and the "Tour De France," were broadcast on the radio live. Teenagers were stuck to the radio listening to the outcome of each race. Their favorite riders were Gino Bartali and Fausto Coppi, who competed against each other for more than a decade. In the evening, teenagers were replaced by adults who played cards for serious money. However, there was a constant flow of people in and out of the bar, as people went for their passeggiata.

The Farmer's Market Day started in Avella in the winter of 1946. Before WWII, there was a similar market in Avella, but not during the war. There wasn't enough food to feed themselves. This type of market was equivalent to a combination of farmer and flea markets in the USA. The market was scheduled for each Monday except for holidays, such as Easter and Christmas. It extended from east to west of Main Street, for about ten blocks. Fruit and vegetables in season were sold, along with shoes, purses, bracelets, umbrellas, etc. However, it was more of a social gathering than a shopping day. Money was still a scarce commodity. Imalda welcomed the Market. It made life a lot easier for her since she could sell food items such as ricotta, hard and soft goat cheese, and goat milk, as well as cheesecloth, wool, and other things in Avella rather than in Nola. People from neighboring towns came to Avella to shop. Psychologically, they needed that outing and large gathering, just to confirm that this was real, not imagined, and to find out who came back from the war.

Beneath that veneer of aloofness or that aristocratic look Ramiro, was a soft-hearted sentimentalist, willing to take risks for others. During the German occupation, he offered Alvaro's family shelter in his Palazzo, but Alvaro refused because he didn't want to endanger his good friend. Thanks to Imalda, he was able to escape the Gestapo's entrapment of the whole family. Alvaro returned to City Hall once the British camped in town. However, Ramiro hid the mayor in his vast palazzo until after the war. The former mayor was in a strange predicament; when the Germans camped in Avella, the apolitical mayor feared that the local Fascists might have branded him a Socialist/Communist to the Gestapo police. However, when the British showed up, he feared that the Communists would brand him for being a Podesta (a Fascist mayor). Either way, he would have paid the price for being apolitical. Blame would have come from all directions. After the war, the former mayor became active politically in the Democratic party.

However, the most dangerous undertaking of Ramiro was to hide two American paratroopers of the 509th Battalion. During the Salerno invasion, the paratroopers were to be dropped in the city of Avellino to sabotage the German supply line through Avellino. However, the paratroopers were dropped from Avellino to Avella, thirty miles away from the intended target. Local partisans steered the two stranded American paratroopers to Ramiro's Palazzo where they wore the garments of farmers, just in time for the fall crop season. Coming from the Midwest of the USA, the paratroopers felt as though they were home.

Along Main Street, about a block from the Palazzo, a combination of pasta factory and bakery opened for business for the first time. It was managed by the two paratroopers who hid in the Palazzo. By then, they were fluent in the Neapolitan dialect and adopted the mannerisms of the locals. They had decided to stay, married local women, and assumed a new life in Avella. Pasta production occupied a large building and supplied dry pasta to all the grocery and pastry stores in Avella, Baiano, Sperone, Cicciano, and other towns in the vicinity. The pasta factory was owned by Ramiro. Besides these two businesses, he owned a factory that produced virgin olive oil which he shipped all over Italy and abroad. The farm was located immediately behind these three businesses and his residence and was surrounded by a 12 feet wall. The farm was cultivated for wheat, corn, and olives. In addition to these thriving businesses, the Count owned a cement and brick factory located near the creek. These factories are still in place in Avella. Before the brick factory, bricklayers made their own bricks and cement powder by heating rocks and pulverizing them.

The two Ukrainians were settling nicely in Avella. Dmitri branched out into sculpture, complementing the work of Paolo in churches. Paolo was a classical painter painting in churches. He regarded painting and repairing canvasses in churches as work that paid the rent. However, he saw an opportunity to spark the interest of churches in sculpture as well as paintings, as Dimitri loved sculpturing.

Paolo and Dimitri were impressed with the wave of impressionist paintings, but a Renoir painting would not have complemented any of their work in churches. Nevertheless, both were excited by expanding their repertoire in art by getting into impressionist works in their studio and the outdoors.

The team of Paolo and Dimitri was doing exceptionally well. They were getting church commissions, not only from local churches but also from churches in neighboring towns. Their reputations grew rapidly as artists who could repair famous paintings from the Middle Ages damaged by Allied bombing during the invasion of Salerno. Also, they were well-equipped to repair church building structures and install church bells. Dimitri became part owner of the local Cinema as well. They had no interest in going back to Ukraine and resuming farming there under the brutal Communist regime of Stalin. The same could be said of many Italian soldiers who started families in Russia and elsewhere in Europe. That may be considered another outcome of WWII, the intermixing of nationalities.

As for Vladimir, he felt at home being in the mountains with the shepherds. Sergio allowed him more and more responsibility in taking over the role of the inspector. As Sergio was getting older, he spent more time with paperwork, tax records of lands on the mountains, and presentations to Headquarters in Naples. By now, both Dmitri and Vladimir were fluent in Italian, but they preferred to speak in the Neapolitan dialect at home. Their size and light complexions indicated that they were not from the area. People didn't care. Both Serafina and Filomena gave birth to boys. Signore Alvaro resumed his post as Chief Magistrate at City Hall, ensuring that the bureaucracy was running at full capacity. Once a month, The Four Musketeers got together. Now the gatherings of the families grew bigger and bigger as Erminio's family joined the group. However, The Four Musketeers were able to enjoy their privacy by playing scopa, a card game, and sipping wine at Erminio's winery.

EPILOGUE

Quoting philosopher George Santayana: "Those who cannot remember the past are condemned to repeat it." This quotation has been repeated by many others in slightly different forms, but it has evolved into this often-quoted one: Those who do not learn history are doomed to repeat it.

Unfortunately, we haven't learned from Santayana's sage advice and have allowed two monstrous leaders, Mussolini and Hitler, to rise to positions that have had deleterious effects on the lives of millions. Those two tried to create empires that existed only in their warped minds. They initiated a calamity of major proportions, surpassing the death and destruction of previous wars and, even, some horrors described in all Bibles. The world is still recovering from the direct and hidden collateral damages, as well as the profound anguish of those times. In some instances, the pain remains so deep that it will never go away.

The personalities of Mussolini and Hitler were worlds apart. Mussolini was a coward; he wilted under pressure, had no principles, was unfaithful to women (including his wife), was one-dimensional in his aims, was highly opinionated and easily intimidated, had no clue as to how to wage wars (including being unaware of the Army's needs for warfare), and was completely disloyal to those around him. Though Mussolini aspired to be a current-day Caesar, that was merely his fantasy. Caesar was a courageous man, cool-headed in crisis, a man of principles, forever faithful to his wife, had a talent for improvisation, was rigorous in his analysis of a situation, was a man who feared nothing and was ready for everything, knew the proper time for waging war, was tireless and attentive to details, and had soldiers and generals loyal to him. Hitler's background was convoluted, and he suffered from an inferiority complex. He was influenced by outcasts and extreme characters who bolstered his battered self-image. As time went on and he gained a following in Germany, his intentions became more outlandish and harrowing. He had no imagination or complete awareness of how to start an original political movement, so copied the one Mussolini. Instead of one misguided political movement, there were two. The blind lead the blind. One blunder after another, which led to a predictable conclusion; Mussolini caved under pressure in the middle of WWII and Hitler held on until the end when he committed suicide, as did his paramour.

Among Hitler's preposterous and vicious acts was his passion for eliminating Jews, many of whom were cultured, professional elements of the warp and woof of German society. Mussolini followed this example, and Jews were placed, along with other internees, in facilities in small, remote towns in Southern Italy. Initially, residents of those small towns were not aware of the Jewish internees among them. They were all too involved in trying to survive the hardships of war. Besides, local Jews were part of the fabric of the town for centuries. Like any other resident of the town, no special attention was ever warranted toward the local Jews. As time went on and they recognized each other's needs, each group empathized with the other and helped when they could, even at the perils of the lives of the locals by the SS troops. All the Jewish internees in Southern Italy avoided the extermination camps.

The history of WWII has taught us that governments in the hands of weak and psychotic men can lead the world to a global catastrophe. We must learn from that lesson not to repeat it. Society can ill afford another global war because recovery may not be repeatable.

CHRONOLOGY

PIVOTAL TIMES: MAY - DECEMBER 1943

May 7 - Tunis falls to the British 7th Armored Division, and Bizerte, the last remaining port in North Africa in Axis hands, is taken by troops of the US II Army Corps.

May 13 - Axis forces in North Africa surrender to the Allies. Some 250,000 German and Italian soldiers are taken, prisoner.

July 9 - Operation *Husky*, the Allied invasion of Sicily, begins under the overall command of General Dwight D. Eisenhower.

July 19 - More than 500 Allied bombers strike Rome for the first time, hitting the San Lorenzo freight yard and steel factory, as well as the Littorio and Ciampino airports in the city.

July 22 - Troops of Patton's Seventh Army take Palermo.

July 24-25 - Most of the Fascist Grand Council approves (19 for, 7 against, 1 abstention) a motion of no confidence in Benito Mussolini.

July 25 - King Victor Emmanuel III meets with Mussolini, removes him from office, and has him arrested. Marshal Pietro Badoglio, former chief of the Italian general staff and member of the Fascist Party, replaces Mussolini as prime minister and declares on the radio that Italy will remain loyal to Germany.

August 1 - The hardest fighting of the entire campaign in Sicily sees the US 1st Infantry Division, "the Big Red One," under the command of Major General Terry de la Mesa Allen Sr., "Terrible Terry," as he is known to his men, battling the German Army for the town of Troina, centrally located in Sicily. With the Germans on the high ground and

US forces under enemy observation for the duration of the battle, US losses are heavy, but the Americans grind forward.

August 5 - First secret negotiations between Eisenhower and the Badoglio government take place to arrange an Italian unconditional surrender to the Allies.

August 6 - The US 1st Infantry Division takes Troina as German troops evacuate and continue their retreat to the northeast of Sicily (toward the Strait of Messina).

August 7 - Major General Allen relinquishes command of the US 1st Infantry Division to Major General Clarence R. Huebner. The August 9 issue of *Time* magazine features Allen.

August 11 - German soldiers begin evacuation at night from Sicily across the Straits of Messina. The bulk of the German force on Sicily escapes.

August 17 - Allies enter Messina, ending the conquest of Sicily.

September 3 - Field Marshal Montgomery's Eighth Army launches Operation *Baytown*, an amphibious operation at Reggio Calabria, the toe of the Italian peninsula. The Badoglio government secretly signs an armistice of unconditional surrender with the Allies.

September 8 - General Eisenhower announces that the Italian government under Badoglio agrees to an armistice with the Allies (General Giuseppe Castellano signed the armistice in Cassibile, Sicily)—and that Italy will have the status of a "co-belligerent" against Nazi Germany. German forces carry out Operation *Axis* (*Fall Achse*), occupying Italy using troops already in the country in conjunction with forces newly arriving via the Brenner Pass. Hitler orders that Italy be treated as an occupied country. Field Marshal Erwin Rommel is given responsibility for the occupation of Italy and for disarming the Italian armed forces. General Albert Kesselring was put in charge of central and southern Italy. He plans to take over Rome and organize the resistance to the Allied landing at Salerno. In addition, German forces moved to disarm Italian garrisons in France, Yugoslavia, Albania, and Greece.

September 9 - General Mark Clark, commander of the US Fifth Army, initiates Operation *Avalanche*, Allied landings on the Italian Peninsula at Salerno.

September 10 - German units, especially the 16th Panzer Division, launch fierce counterattacks at Salerno, which for a time threatened the integrity of General Clark's beachhead. Admiral Alberto da Zara surrenders the Italian fleet to British Admiral Andrew Cunningham, Commander-in-Chief, Mediterranean Fleet, in Malta.

September 10 - German troops occupy Rome.

September 11 - Germans begin to move troops from Sardinia to Corsica.

September 12 - German paratroopers and SS men, brought in by glider and led by SS-Hauptsturmführer, Otto Skorzeny, carries out a raid, freeing Mussolini from imprisonment in the Gran Sasso mountains of the Abruzzo region. Mussolini meets Adolf Hitler in Rastenburg, Germany, two days later.

September 13 - Italian 33rd Infantry Division ("Acqui") resists the Germans on the Greek island of Cephalonia. Fighting continues until September 21. More than 1,300 Italians were killed in battle. Over 5,100 were massacred. Some 3,000 members of the division perished when the German ships were sunk by Allied aircraft.

September 14 - Allied troops land on Sardinia.

September 15 - Allied Army secures the beachhead at Salerno, thanks to the skillful use of artillery and massive naval and air support.

September 16 - Canadian Troops of the British Eighth Army spearheads, moving from Calabria through Potenza, to meet troops of Clark's Fifth Army in the beachhead near Salerno.

September 19 - Confrontations between Italian partisans and German soldiers ensue.

September 23 - Mussolini is coerced by Hitler to form a new Fascist government.

September 25 - Reichsführer SS Heinrich Himmler notifies Herbert Kappler, head of the SD (the intelligence gathering branch of the SS) in Rome, to prepare for the immediate deportation of Jews from Rome.

September 26 - Without authorization from Himmler, Kappler orders Dante Almansi and Ugo Foà, two leaders of the Jewish community in Rome, to give him 50 kilograms of gold to save Rome's Jewish population from deportation. They comply with Kappler's demand.

September 27 - "Four Days of Naples," four days of the uprising in the city. On the first day, martial law by the Germans starts with the townspeople erecting barricades and attacking German soldiers. More than 660 Neapolitans perished during these four days.

October 1 - Allied troops enter Naples.

October 3 - German troops complete evacuation of Corsica, after battling Free French troops and resistance fighters.

October 6 - Adolf Eichmann's subordinate, Theodor Dannecker, arrives in Rome with a group of Waffen-SS personnel to organize the deportation of Roman Jews.

October 13 - Italy declares war on Germany. The declaration, signed by Victor Emmanuel III, is transmitted to Berlin through the Italian Embassy in Madrid.

October 16 - Dannecker's team, with support from Wehrmacht troops, arrests more than 1,200 Jews in Rome. Two days later 1,023 Jews, most of them women, and 200 of them children are deported to Auschwitz, where most of them are murdered immediately. Only 16 survive the war.

October 18 - The Allied Military Government (AMG) announces control over the zones of combat in Italy and the region of Naples, with its indispensable port.

November 6 - Hitler orders Field Marshal Rommel to leave Italy and go to France to prepare defenses there against an expected Allied invasion.

November 20 - Field Marshal Kesselring becomes supreme commander of German forces in Italy (from Rome to the Alps).

November 22 - British Eighth Army starts offensive on the Sangro River, Field Marshal Montgomery's final battle in the Mediterranean theater.

November 23 - Mussolini announces the creation of the Republican Socialist Italian (RSI) Party with Mussolini as both chief of state and prime minister of the new RSI government.

December 2 - At the Cairo Conference US President Franklin D. Roosevelt informs British Prime Minister Winston Churchill that he has chosen General Dwight D. Eisenhower to lead the Allied invasion of

France. Italy increasingly became a secondary theater of Allied operations.

December 24 - Lieutenant General Sir Oliver Leese succeeds Field Marshal Montgomery as commander of the British Eighth Army.

Jason Dawsey, Ph.D., Research Historian at The Institute for the Study of War and Democracy.

APPENDIX 1
Background on Internment Camps

Well before WWII, concentration camps were established in wars on three continents. They were used to exterminate undesirable populations through labor, to clear contested areas, to punish suspected rebel sympathizers, and as a cudgel against guerrilla fighters whose wives and children were interned. Most of all, concentration camps made civilians into proxies to get at combatants who had dared defy the ruling power. While these camps were widely viewed as a disgrace to modern society, this disgust was not sufficient to preclude their future use.

SPAIN

Before the 20th century had even begun, concentration camps found their first home in the cities and towns of Cuba. Battles had raged off and on for decades over Cuba's desire for independence from Spain. After years of fighting with Cuban rebels, Arsenio Martínez Campos of Spain believed the only path to victory lay in inflicting new cruelties on civilians and fighters alike. To isolate rebels from the peasants who sometimes fed or sheltered them, he thought it would be necessary to relocate hundreds of thousands of rural inhabitants into Spanish-held cities behind barbed wire, a strategy he called *reconcentración*. Britain With the sinking of the Lusitania in 1915 by a German submarine and the deaths of more than a thousand civilians, British prime minister Herbert Henry Asquith took revenge, locking up tens of thousands of

Germans and Austro-Hungarian "enemy aliens" in England. By the end of WWI, more than 800,000 civilians had been held in concentration camps, with hundreds of thousands more forced into exile in remote regions. Mental illness and shattered minority communities were just two of the tolls this long-term internment exacted on detainees.

GERMANY

Before the war, the Nazis were the only political party with paramilitary organizations at their disposal, the so-called SS and the SA, which had perpetrated surprise attacks on the offices and members of other parties throughout the 1920s. After the 1932 elections, it became clear to the Nazi leaders that they would never be able to secure a majority of the votes and that they would have to rely on other means to gain power. While gradually intensifying the acts of violence to wreak havoc among the opposition leading up to the 1933 elections, the Nazis set up concentration centers within Germany, many of which were established by local authorities, to hold, torture, or kill political prisoners and "undesirables" like outspoken journalists and Communists. These early prisons, usually basements and storehouses, were eventually consolidated into full-blown, centrally run camps outside of the cities and somewhat removed from the public eye.

The first German concentration camps were established in 1933 for the confinement of opponents of the Nazi Party, Communists, and Social Democrats. Political opposition soon included minority groups, chiefly Jewish people, but by the end of World War II, many gypsies, homosexuals, and anti-Nazi civilians from the occupied territories had also been liquidated. After the outbreak of World War II, the camp inmates were used as a supplementary labor force. Inmates were required to work for their wages in food; those unable to work usually died of starvation and those who did not starve often died of overwork. The most shocking extension of this system was the establishment, after 1940, of extermination camps, or "death camps." They were located primarily in Poland, which Adolf Hitler had selected as the setting for his "Final solution" to the "Jewish problem." The most notorious were Auschwitz, Majdanek, and Treblinka. At some camps, notably Buchenwald, medical experimentation was conducted. New toxins and anti-toxins were tried out, new surgical techniques devised, and studies were made of the effects of artificially induced diseases, all by experimenting on living human beings.

In 1938, the SS began to use the camps for forced labor at a profit. Many German companies used forced labor from these camps, especially during the subsequent war. Additionally, historians speculate that the Nazi regime utilized abandoned castles and similar existing structures to lock up the undesirable elements of society. The elderly, mentally ill, and handicapped were often confined in these makeshift camps where they were starved or gassed to death withdiesel engine exhaust. The Final Solution was, thus, initially tested upon German citizens.

After 1939, with the beginning of WWII, concentration camps increasingly became places where the enemies of the Nazis were killed, enslaved, starved, and tortured. During the war, concentration camps for "undesirables" were spread throughout Europe. New camps were created near centers of dense "undesirable" populations, often focusing on areas with large Jewish, Polish intelligentsia, Communist, or gypsy populations. Most of the camps were in occupied Poland for a simple logistical reason, millions of Jewish people lived in Poland.

Before and during World War II, Nazi Germany maintained concentration camps (*Konzentrationslager,* abbreviated KZ or KL) throughout the territories it controlled. In these camps, millions of prisoners were killed through mistreatment, disease, starvation, and overwork, or were executed as unfit for labor. The Nazis adopted the term euphemistically from the British concentration camps of the Second Boer War to conceal the deadly nature of the camps.

In most camps, prisoners were made to wear identifying overalls with colored badges according to their categorization: Red triangles for Communists and other political prisoners, green triangles for common criminals, pink for homosexual men, purple for Jehovah's Witnesses, black for gypsies and anti-socials, and yellow for Jews.

The transportation of prisoners was often carried out under horrifying conditions using rail freight cars, in which many died before they reached their destination. The prisoners were confined in these rail cars, often for days or weeks, without food or water. Many died in the intense heat of dehydration in summer or froze to death in the winter. Concentration camps for Jews and other "undesirables" also existed in Germany itself, and while not specifically designated for systematic extermination, many concentration camp prisoners died because of harsh conditions or were executed.

Starting in 1942, Nazi Germany established extermination or death camps for the sole purpose of carrying out the industrialized murder of the Jews of Europe. These camps were established in occupied Poland and Belarus. Millions of Jews would die in these extermination camps, primarily by poison gas, usually in gas chambers, although many prisoners were killed in mass shootings and by other means. These death camps, including Belzec, Sobibor, Treblinka, and Auschwitz-Birkenau, are commonly referred to as "concentration camps," but scholars of the Holocaust draw a distinction between concentration camps and death camps. After 1942, many small sub-camps were set up near factories to provide forced labor. IG Farben established a synthetic rubber plant in 1942 at Auschwitz III (Monowitz), and other camps was set up for airplane factories, coal mines, and rocket fuel factories. The conditions were brutal, and prisoners were often sent to the gas chambers or killed if they did not work fast enough.

RUSSIA

There are records of concentration camps by Soviet officials (including Lenin) as early as December 1917. While the primary purpose of Soviet camps was not mass extermination of prisoners, in many cases, the outcome was death or permanent disabilities. The total documentable deaths in the corrective-labor system from 1934 to 1953 amount to 1,054,000, including political and common prisoners; this does not include nearly 800,000 executions of "counterrevolutionaries" outside the camp system. From 1932 to 1940, at least 390,000 peasants died in places of peasant resettlement; this figure may overlap with the above, but, on the other hand, it does not include deaths outside the 1932-1940 period, or deaths among non-peasant internal exiles.

More than 14 million people passed through the *Gulags* from 1929 to 1953, with 6 to 7 million being deported and exiled to remote areas of the USSR (Russia). The death toll for this same period was 1,258,537, with an estimated 1.6 million casualties from 1929 to 1953. These estimates exclude those who died shortly after their release but whose deaths resulted from the harsh treatment in the camps, which was a common practice.

Political concentration camps instituted primarily to reinforce the state's control have been established in various forms under many totalitarian regimes, most extensively in Nazi Germany and the Soviet Union. To a considerable extent, the camps served as the special prisons of the secret police. Nazi concentration camps were under the administration of the SS; forced-labor camps of the Soviet Union were operated by a succession of organizations beginning in 1917 with the Cheka and ending in the early 1990s with the KGB (Soviet Spy Agency).

By 1922, there were 23 concentration camps for the incarceration of persons accused of political offenses as well as criminal offenses. Many corrective labor camps were established in northern Russia and Siberia, especially during the first Five-Year Plan, 1928–32, when millions of rich peasants were driven from their farms under the collectivization program. The Stalinist purges of 1936–38 brought additional millions into the camps—said to be essentially institutions of slavery.

The Soviet occupation of eastern Poland in 1939 and the absorption of the Baltic states in 1940 led to the incarceration of large numbers of non-Soviet citizens. By 1943, it included Italian soldiers captured at Stalingrad. Following the outbreak of war with Germany in 1941, the camps received Axis prisoners of war and Soviet nationals accused of collaboration with the enemy. After the death of Joseph Stalin in 1953, many prisoners were released, and the number of camps was drastically reduced.

USA

In the United States, more than 200,000 military prisoners were held in camps during the war. German-born conductor Karl Muck, a Swiss national, wound up in detention in Fort Oglethorpe, Georgia, after false rumors that he had refused to conduct "The Star-Spangled Banner."

Many camps during the First World War were hundreds or thousands of miles from the front lines, and life in them developed strange normalcy. Prisoners were assigned numbers that traveled with them as they moved from camp to camp. Letters could be sent to detainees, and packages received. In some cases, money was transferred, and accounts were kept. A bureaucracy of detention emerged, with Red Cross inspectors visiting and making reports.

On February 19, 1942, shortly after the bombing of Pearl Harbor by Japanese forces, President Roosevelt signed Executive Order 9066 with the stated intention of preventing espionage on American shores. Military zones were created in California, Washington, and Oregon—states with a large population of Japanese Americans. Then Roosevelt's executive order forcibly removed Americans of Japanese ancestry from their homes. The Order affected the lives of about 120,000 people, the majority of whom were American citizens. By 1944, there were 51,000 Italian prisoners of war spread throughout the USA. The POWs (prisoners of war) were moved around, depending on the needs of various civilian and industrial establishments. The number of German POWs far surpassed Italian and Japanese POWs.

APPENDIX 2
Aftermath in Europe and USA

For the Jewish survivors, returning home to Europe, as it had been before the Holocaust, was impossible. Jewish communities no longer existed in much of Europe after the war. When they tried to return to their homes from camps or hiding places, they found that, in many cases, those homes had been looted or taken over by others.

Returning home was also dangerous. After the war, anti-Jewish riots broke out in several Polish cities. The largest anti-Jewish pogrom took place in July 1946 in Kielce, a city in Southeastern Poland. When 150 Jews returned to the city, people living there feared that hundreds more would come back to reclaim their houses and belongings. Age-old anti-Semitic myths, such as Jewish ritual murders of Christians, arose once again. After an unfounded rumor spread that Jews had killed a Polish boy to use his blood in religious rituals, a mob attacked that group of survivors. The rioters killed 41 people and wounded 50 more. News of the Kielce pogrom spread rapidly, and Jews realized that there was no future for them in Poland.

Many survivors ended up in displaced persons (DP) camps set up in Western Europe under Allied military occupation at the sites of former concentration camps. There they waited to be admitted to places like the United States, South Africa, or Palestine. At first, many countries continued their old immigration policies, which greatly limited the number of refugees they would accept. The British government, which controlled Palestine, refused to let large numbers of Jews into the country. Many Jews tried to enter Palestine without legal papers and, when caught, some were held in camps on the island of Cyprus, while others were deported back to Germany. Great Britain's scandalous treatment of Jewish refugees added to international pressures for a homeland for the Jewish people. Early in 1948, the British began withdrawing from Palestine. On May 14, 1948, one of the leading voices for a Jewish homeland, David Ben-Gurion, announced the formation of the State of Israel. After this, Jewish refugee ships freely landed in the seaports of the new nation. The United States also changed its immigration policy to allow more Jewish refugees to enter.

Although many Jewish survivors were able to build new lives in their adopted countries, many non-Jewish victims of Nazi policies continued to be persecuted in Germany. Laws that discriminated against gypsies continued to be in effect until 1970 in some countries. The law used in Nazi Germany to imprison homosexuals remained in effect until 1969. US special envoy Earl Harrison headed a delegation to the displaced persons camps in Germany. Following World War II, several hundred thousand Jewish survivors were unable to return to their home countries and remained in Germany, Austria, or Italy. Most Jewish DPs preferred to emigrate to Palestine but many also sought entry into the United States. They remained in DP camps until they could leave Europe. Harrison's report underscored the plight of Jewish DPs and clamored for improved conditions in the camps. At the end of 1946, the number of Jewish DPs was estimated at 250,000.

On July 11, 1946, a refugee ship sailed for Palestine despite British restrictions. Many Jewish DPs sought to emigrate to Palestine, despite existing British emigration restrictions. Despite the restrictions, the refugee ship *Exodus* left Southern France for Palestine, carrying 4,500 Jewish refugees from DP camps in Germany. The British Navy intercepted the ship even before it entered territorial waters off the coast of Palestine. The passengers were forcibly transferred to British ships and deported back to their port of origin in France. For almost a month, the British held the refugees aboard the ship at anchor off the French coast. The French rejected the British demand to land the passengers. Ultimately, the British transported the refugees to Hamburg, Germany, and returned them to DP camps. The fate of the refugee ship *Exodus* dramatized the plight of Holocaust survivors thereby increasing international pressure on Great Britain to allow free Jewish immigration to Palestine.

On November 29, 1947, the United Nations voted to partition Palestine into two new states, one Jewish and the other Arab. Less than six months later, on May 14, 1948, the prominent Zionist leader David Ben-Gurion announced the establishment of the State of Israel and declared that Jewish immigration into the new state would be unrestricted. Between 1948 and 1951, almost 700,000 Jews immigrated to Israel, including more than two-thirds of the Jewish displaced people in Europe. Holocaust survivors, passengers from the *Exodus*, DPs from central Europe, and Jewish detainees from British detention camps in Cyprus were welcomed to the Jewish homeland.

GERMANY

On November 29, 1947, the United Nations voted to partition Palestine into two new states, one Jewish and the other Arab. Less than six months later, on May 14, 1948, the prominent Zionist leader David Ben-Gurion announced the establishment of the State of Israel and declared that Jewish immigration into the new state would be unrestricted. Between 1948 and 1951, almost 700,000 Jews immigrated to Israel, including more than two-thirds of the Jewish displaced people (DP) in Europe. Holocaust survivors, passengers from the ship *Exodus*, DPs throughout Europe, and Jewish detainees from British detention camps in Cyprus were welcomed to the Jewish homeland. Other DPs emigrated to South Africa and the USA.

The Communist Party in West Germany was never a threat to take over the government after the War. Even before the end of the War, a new political party was being formed, the German Christian Democratic Union (CDU), in which Roman Catholics and Protestants buried their long-standing differences to present a common front against Nazism and to promote Christian principles in government. Adenauer played an important role in the formation of this new party, and in 1946 he became its chairman in the British zone of occupation. Subsequently, the CDU expanded into the four zones of the Allied occupation. As the Soviet Union began to increasingly obstruct the Allied Control Council, the Western Allies decided to give their three occupation zones a federal-state organization. Adenauer became president of the Parliamentary Council, which produced a provisional constitution for the intended German Federal Republic. In 1949 Adenauer became chairman of the CDU for the whole of West Germany, and, in the first general elections under the new regime, his party and its regular ally, the Bavarian Christian Social Union (CSU), together won 139 of the 402 seats in the Bundestag, the lower house of the federal parliament. He managed to form a coalition government, but it was by a majority of only one vote that the Bundestag confirmed his appointment as chancellor on September 15, 1949.

Despite protests from many other European beneficiaries, the Marshall Plan was, in 1949, extended to also include the newly formed West Germany. The Allied forces worked heavily to remove Nazi influence from Germany in a process dubbed "denazification." By mid-1947, the success of denazification and the start of the Cold War had led to a reconsideration of policy, as the Germans were seen as possible allies in the contest, and it was becoming clear that the economic recovery of Europe was dependent on the reactivation of German industry. With the repudiation of the U.S. occupation directive in July 1947, the Western Allies were able to start planning for the introduction of a currency reform to halt rampant inflation. In the years 1949–1952, West Germany received loans that totaled $1.45 billion, equivalent to around $14.5 billion in 2006. The country subsequently began a slow but continuous improvement of its standard of living, with the export of local products, a reduction in unemployment, increased food production, and a reduced black market.

In 1948, the Deutsche Mark replaced the occupation currency as the currency of the Western occupation zones, leading to their eventual economic recovery. By 1950, the UK and France were finally induced to follow the U.S. lead and stop the dismantling of German heavy industry. The country's economic recovery under the newly formed democratic government was, once it was permitted, swift and effective. During the mid-1950s, the unemployment rate in Germany was so low that it led to the influx of Turkish immigrants into the country's labor force. Germany's economy continued to improve until the 1973 oil crisis.

Allied Countries

RUSSIA

During World War II, Stalin determined to acquire a buffer area against Germany, with pro-Soviet states on its border in an Eastern bloc. Stalin's aims led to strained relations at the Yalta Conference (February 1945) and the subsequent Potsdam Conference (July–August 1945). People in the West expressed opposition to Soviet domination over the buffer states, and the fear grew that the Soviets were building an empire that might be a threat to them and their interests.

Nonetheless, at the Potsdam Conference, the Allies assigned parts of Poland, Finland, Romania, Germany, and the Balkans to Soviet control or influence. In return, Stalin promised the Western Allies that he would allow those territories the right to national self-determination. Despite Soviet cooperation during the war, these concessions left many in the West uneasy. Churchill feared that the United States might return to its pre-war isolationism, leaving the exhausted European states unable to resist Soviet demands. President Franklin D. Roosevelt had announced at Yalta that after the defeat of Germany, U.S. forces would withdraw from Europe within two years.

Winston Churchill's "Sinews of Peace" address of March 5, 1946, at Westminster College in Fulton, Missouri, used the term "iron curtain" in the context of Soviet-dominated Eastern Europe: "From Stettin in the Baltic to Trieste in the Adriatic, an iron curtain has descended across the Continent. Behind that line lie all the capitals of the ancient states of Central and Eastern Europe. Warsaw, Berlin, Prague, Vienna, Budapest, Belgrade, Bucharest, and Sofia; all these famous cities and the populations around them lie in what I must call the Soviet sphere, and all are subject, in one form or another, not only to Soviet influence but to a very high and in some cases increasing measure of control from Moscow". Although not well received at the time, the phrase *iron curtain* gained popularity as a shorthand reference to the division of Europe as the Cold War strengthened. People throughout the West eventually came to accept and use the metaphor.

USA

Truman benefited from a honeymoon period from their success in defeating Nazi Germany in Europe and the nation celebrated V-E Day on May 8, 1945. Although Truman was told briefly on the afternoon of April 12 (the day that President Franklin D. Roosevelt died), that he had a new, highly destructive weapon, it was not until April 25 that Secretary of War Henry Stimson told him the details, "We have discovered the most terrible bomb in the history of the world. It may be the fire destruction prophesied in the Euphrates Valley Era, after Noah and his fabulous Ark."

Truman attended the Potsdam Conference with Stalin and Churchill. He was there when he learned the Trinity test—the first atomic bomb—on July 16 had been successful. He hinted to Stalin that he was about to use a new kind of weapon against the Japanese. Though this was the first time the Soviets had been officially given information about the atomic bomb, Stalin was already aware of the bomb project—having learned about it through atomic espionage long before Truman did.

In August, the Japanese government refused surrender demands as specifically outlined in the Potsdam Declaration. With the invasion of Japan imminent, Truman approved the schedule for dropping the two available bombs. Truman always said attacking Japan with atomic bombs saved many lives on both sides; military estimates for the invasion of Japan were that it could take a year and result in 250,000 to 500,000 Allied casualties. Hiroshima was bombed on August 6, and Nagasaki three days later, leaving 105,000 dead. The Soviet Union declared war on Japan on August 9 and invaded Manchuria. Japan agreed to surrender the following day.

Britain Winston Churchill's Conservative Party lost the July 1945 general election, forcing him to step down as Prime Minister of the United Kingdom. For six years he served as the Leader of the Opposition. During these years he continued to influence world affairs. In 1946 he gave his "Iron Curtain" speech which spoke of the expansionist policies of the Soviet Union and the creation of the Eastern Bloc; Churchill also argued strongly for British independence from the European Coal and Steel Community; he saw this as a Franco-German project and Britain still had an empire. In the General Election of 1951, The Labor Party was defeated.

Churchill became Prime Minister for a second time. He continued to lead Britain but was to suffer increasingly from health problems. Aware that he was slowing down both physically and mentally, he resigned in April 1955. He continued to sit as MP until he retired from politics in 1964. Churchill died in January 1965 and was granted the honor of a state funeral. He was buried in his family plot in St Martin's Church, Bladon, near where he was born at Blenheim Palace.

FRANCE

France emerged from World War II to face a series of new problems. After a short period of provisional government initially led by General Charles de Gaulle, a new constitution (October 13, 1946) established the Fourth Republic under a parliamentary form of government, controlled by a series of coalitions. The mixed nature of the coalitions and a consequent lack of agreement on measures for dealing with colonial wars in Indochina and Algeria caused successive cabinet crises and changes of government. The war in Indochina ended with French defeat and withdrawal in 1954. Algeria was no mere colony. With over a million European residents in Algeria, France refused to grant it independence, until a bloody colonial war (the Algerian War of Independence) had turned into a French political and civil crisis; Algeria was given its independence in 1962, unleashing a massive wave of immigration from the former colony back to France.

The threat of a coup d'état in May 1958 by French army units and French settlers opposed to concessions in the face of Arab nationalist insurrection led to the fall of the French government and a presidential invitation to de Gaulle to form an emergency government to forestall the threat of civil war. Swiftly replacing the existing constitution with one strengthening the powers of the presidency, he became the elected president in December of that year, inaugurating France's Fifth Republic.

APPENDIX 3
Vito Genovese in WWII

Underboss (sottocapo) Mafia Mobster Vito Genovese fled New York City in 1937 and settled in the Fascist regime in Italy. Supposedly, he was a friend of Mussolini, but there is no evidence of that. When the Allies invaded Italy, he swiftly changed sides and became close to the senior Allied administration. It would take a remarkable young CID (Criminal Investigation Division) officer by the name of Orange C. Dickey to hunt him down.

As the Allies entered Genovese's native area in Nola, near Naples, in the autumn of 1943, he offered to help the American Military as a translator and a guide to the region. U.S. Major E.N. Holmgreen, the civil affairs officer in Nola, was so impressed with Genovese that he wrote a letter of recommendation on Nov. 8, 1943. "The bearer (of the letter), Vito Genovese," wrote Holmgreen, "is an American citizen. When the undersigned arrived at Nola District as CAO (civil affairs officer), Mr. Genovese met me and acted as my interpreter for over a month. He would accept no pay; paid his expenses; worked day and night and rendered the most valuable assistance to the Allied Military Government (AMG). This statement is freely made to express my appreciation for the unselfish services of this man." The Major couldn't have known Genovese had already been in Sicily planting plenty of mafiosi (members of the Mafia) seeds in city halls.

Genovese could afford to appear unselfish, and it was no big surprise. He knew he had just struck a new criminal gold mine, the black market in American military goods. The FBI later quoted a U.S. attorney's report on his activities during this period. "During the war, he (Genovese) acted as a translator for numerous American military government officials, and, at the same time, was active in Black market activities. These activities consisted of stealing United States Army trucks, driving them to supply depots, and loading them up with flour, sugar, and other supplies. Then they were driven to a place of concealment and unloaded. The trucks were then destroyed."

Genovese continued to make a fortune from his mastery of the Black Market in wartime Italy until August 1944. Luke Monzelli, a lieutenant in the Carabinieri, claimed that a young Italian army sergeant investigated the discovery of a mysterious freight carriage full of cereal and salt parked in a siding near Nola. He revealed the link between Genovese and senior Sicilian Mafiosi but was told to forget about it. Supposedly, it was a secret military matter. He was later transferred out of the region, as was Monzelli.

It would be up to a fearless and determined 24-year-old U.S. Sgt. Orange C. Dickey to blow Genovese's cover. Dickey gave his testimony of his investigation regarding Genovese before three law officers in the Brooklyn office of District Attorney George Beldock on Sept. 1, 1945. "I arrived in Italy on or about the 19th day of December 1943," he reported. "My assignment was in the intelligence service squadron. I was appointed criminal investigation agent on the 2nd of February." He first came across the name of Genovese in late April 1944. At that time, he was investigating Black Market activities in olive oil and wheat in Italy between Foggia and Naples. Dickey had a lucky break in that a former senior gang member of the Camorra, the Neapolitan Mafia, had married an American girl and bought his way out of the organization. This man pointed the finger at Genovese, calling him the head of the Mafia in Southern Italy. During the first part of May, Dickey single-handedly began a thorough investigation of Genovese in the district of Nola.

"On or about the 2nd day of June, I proceeded to a vineyard located approximately seven miles from Nola proper in the Commune of San Gennaro, where I found several United States Army trucks which had been destroyed by fire. In tracing these trucks by serial numbers and other identification means, we found that the trucks had been stolen from docks in Naples and been driven to a quartermaster supply depot, where they were loaded principally with flour and sugar, after which they were driven to the area where they were found by myself, and the supplies unloaded onto cars and transported into nearby towns, for salt, after which the trucks were destroyed."

Shortly after this discovery, Dickey arrested two Canadian soldiers who had deserted their posts to serve as drivers of these stolen trucks. "The important part of their statements," said Dickey, "is the fact that they were told that when they reached the point of destination for these trucks, they were to say 'Genovese sent us'... And the truck was parked, and they were paid off and then left the area." Dickey continued to gather his evidence and then presented it to his superior officers. They gave him the okay to arrest Genovese. On the day that Genovese was arrested, a copy of a report from the Allied Provincial Public Safety Officer in Viterbo, north of Rome, was sent to the office of Col. Charles Poletti, then commissioner of the AMG in Italy. Getting wind of the mobster's imminent arrest, U.S. administrators wanted to clarify exactly what their relationship had been with Mr. Genovese. "Careful examination of the records and antecedents of the above-named (Genovese) has been made of all employees on the AMG. Payroll records show that such a person is not employed in this organization."

That was hardly surprising as Genovese operated way to the south of Viterbo, around Naples. The report then tried to identify the mobster with another bad character. "In the records of the Questore, a subject named Genovese di Giuseppe, born on 12/7/88, at Avignano, resident in America for many years, was charged on 9th July 1935, before a Military Tribunal in Naples for the offense of desertion, and was sentenced to one-year imprisonment in a Military Prison. He was known by the nickname of 'Mafrita,' and it would appear that this man was identical to the subject of the inquiry." However, Genovese was deported by the US Immigration Office to Italy in 1937, not in 1935. Therefore, something was amiss in the previous assertion. Also, his birthplace has been reported to be Tufino (near Nola), Ricigliano (near Potenza), and Avignano (near Potenza). Genovese reported different birthplaces, depending on where he was conducting the Black Market in Campania, Basilicata, Calabria, and Puglia regions. Most likely, he was born in Sicily, since he became the capo of the biggest crime syndicate in New York City. No Neapolitan Camorrista would have made it that far in the Mafia hierarchy. It is like a Jehovah's Witness person becoming a Pope. It would be interesting to note which birthplace Genovese adopted in Sicily.

Thus, the man described above was not the same Genovese. 'Mafrita' was almost a decade older than the gangster who had been running a criminal empire in the United States while he was in prison in Italy. The same report did, however, acknowledge that Genovese was employed by Maj. Holmgreen and three other U.S. officers. Now that was the real Genovese. Whether this report was a genuine attempt to identify the mobster or a smoke screen to distance the U.S. administration in Italy away from him, we will never know. It was dispatched on the exact day that Genovese was arrested.

On Aug. 27, 1944, Genovese arrived at the office of the Town mayor of Nola to request a travel permit. An armed chauffeur accompanied him. While the mafioso's bodyguard parked the car, Dickey made his move. "I approached Genovese, in the company of two English soldiers, and requested that he accompany me to the Military Police Office in Nola, which he did... Immediately after the arrest of Genovese, I proceeded to downtown Nola and confiscated the vehicle in which Genovese had been riding. This vehicle was an Italian civilian car, a Fiat model 1500.

"I searched the vehicle and in the compartment in the rear of the front seat. I mean the private front seat. I found two Italian weapons, one a 9mm Beretta and the other a 7.65 Victoria, both fully loaded." A few hours after the arrest of Genovese, Nicola Cutuli arrived at the AMG offices in Naples. He was Questore of Rome, the most senior investigating police officer in the country. He demanded that Genovese be released into his custody and taken to Rome. The Americans refused. Later, CID officers found a sheet of paper with Cutuli's name on it in Genovese's apartment.

While Dickey proceeded with the paperwork of his arrest, an informant in Nola gave him a copy of a book entitled *Gang Rule in New York City*, by Craig Thompson and Raymond Allen, published in 1940. In the book, he found a photograph of Genovese and it identified him as a former gangster associate of Lucky Luciano. Dickey showed his prisoner the picture. "Sure," said Genovese, "that's me when I was in New York City." When Dickey asked him about running the black Market in Italy, he denied some of the charges but accepted others. Dickey then contacted the FBI, and they informed him that Genovese was wanted for questioning over a murder in New York City.

Coincidentally, earlier in the month, a New York newspaper report on Aug. 9, 1944, said: "The whereabouts of all six (wanted for the murder of Ferdinand Boccia) were said to be unknown but an interesting sidelight on Genovese was that he was reported recently to have been in Italy acting as an interpreter for the Allied Military Government there." "The Army officials are going to bring him back," said Brooklyn D.A. Thomas Hughes. "How or when he will be brought back, I cannot say."

With Genovese safely under arrest, Dickey searched Genovese's apartment in Nola and found a bundle of documents. "Among these papers," remembered Dickey, "there was a small paper on which was written a number, easily identified as the number of a U.S. Army truck. Beneath this number was written, "The Shed." In a previous case, I had learned that the shed was a large underground storeroom and was used as a storage place for contraband wheat."

Dickey then went to Genovese's apartment in Naples where he found large quantities of PX supplies, such as soap, candy bars, and cigarettes. He also found a powerful radio receiver, used for receiving information on the arrival of valuable contraband. Among the documents found in Genovese's apartments were several business cards and other papers that linked him to prominent businessmen in the area as well as judges, the town mayor of Nola, the president of the Bank of Naples, and AMG officers.

There were nine official AMG travel passes, several just made out to the bearer, a sign of Genovese's influence within AMG. They even entitled the bearer to fill up with American gas. One was made out to a local leading dealer in olive oil. Two papers signed by AMG officers entitled Genovese to receive American food supplies, in violation of Army regulations. One business card belonged to Innocenza Monterisi, a mistress of Genovese who, according to Dickey, also supplied women for Allied officers.

But nowhere was found any significant stash of money. Dickey had his suspicions about a safe deposit vault in Banco del Lavoro in Nola. Genovese denied having a vault or a key for it. The bank records said the vault belonged to the gangster, but despite going before a Tribunal in Naples, a court order was refused to Dickey to force its opening. Dickey knew that one of Genovese's henchmen had visited it on the day he was arrested. A U.S. Army seal was put on the vault to prevent its opening. Genovese was still in military custody in November, as Dickey waited for an arrest warrant to arrive for him from the United States. But no one wanted to decide what to do with him. There was no suggestion even of putting him on trial for Black Market charges in Italy.

"At this time," said Dickey, "the Army did not seem very interested in returning this man to the States, and I was told that I was 'on my own, to do anything I cared to." It was an extraordinary situation, but clearly, Genovese's associates in and outside the U.S. Army were working their influence as best they could and stopped any fast action on Genovese in the hope that Dickey might get fed up with the procedure and let him go. That this might be the tactics of very highly placed U.S. officers was demonstrated when Dickey visited Rome to talk to Col. Charles Poletti, then commissioner of the (AMG) in Italy. "I wanted him to tell me whether I should try him by civilian authorities," said Dickey, "whether the AMG intended to try him, or whether the U.S. Army had control, or what I should do with him."

Dickey arrived at Poletti's headquarters at 10 a.m. and was told to go straight to his office and walk in. Excited at the prospect of finally getting some advice on what to do next with Genovese, Dickey pushed open the door of Poletti's room. "He seemed to be asleep," remembered Dickey. "He had his arms folded on the desk and his head down on his arms." Dickey returned two more times that day to see Poletti but did not get to speak to him. "On both of these occasions, his office was jammed with people... I was kept waiting on both occasions for long periods, and after making several attempts to talk to him, I left... (Poletti was) just walking around, giving orders to the girls; but it didn't seem to be essential business, just more or less enjoying himself."

It was outrageous behavior from Poletti who did not want to be dragged into the Genovese affair. Dickey then bumped into Brig. Gen. William O'Dwyer in the hall outside Poletti's office. O'Dwyer was on leave as district attorney from Brooklyn to serve in Italy. He knew all about the Genovese case but underlined the policy of his boss, Poletti, to steer well clear of it and advised Dickey to bypass his senior officers and deal directly with the Brooklyn D.A. Thomas Hughes. O'Dwyer would be later charged by a grand jury with incompetently failing to prosecute senior mobster Albert Anastasia.

Returning from Rome to Naples, Dickey reported Poletti's behavior to his immediate superior officer. "He took no particular notice of the information," recalled Dickey, "said that he had heard rumors to that effect previously, and with a few casual remarks it was dismissed. So that was the last that was said about Genovese up until the time I made an all-out effort for his extradition."

Dickey pressed on, but by now Genovese was getting desperate. The mobster offered Dickey $250,000 to forget about the whole matter and let him go. At the time, the U.S. sergeant was earning just $210 a month. "Now, look, you are young, and there are things you don't understand. This is the way it works. Take the money. You are set for the rest of your life. Nobody cares what you do. Why should you? Genovese told him.

When Dickey refused the money, the mobster turned nasty and threatened his life and that of his family. Dickey would not be intimidated. Finally, in January 1945, Dickey got the news he had been waiting for. With the help of the War Department, the Brooklyn D.A.'s office had set in motion extradition proceedings. The news traveled fast. Just seven days later, Genovese's American mobster friends swung into action. The one witness to his involvement in the murder of Boccia was Peter La Tempa, but he was in jail. No problem for Genovese's friends.

On Jan. 15, 1945, La Tempa awoke in his cell with acute gallstone pains. The valuable witness was then given sedatives strong enough "to kill eight horses." Luciano later claimed it was Frank Costello and his associates that set up the murder. With the only major witness against Genovese gone, the mobster no longer feared returning to the United States. He was glad of the free return journey.

"Kid," he said to Dickey, "you are doing me the biggest favor anyone has ever done to me. You are taking me home. You are taking me back to the USA." Dickey was designated as Genovese's guard on the voyage across the Atlantic. Handcuffed together they set sail on board the steamship *James Lykes* and arrived in New York on the morning of June 1, 1945.

No one met Dickey and his gangster prisoner at the port. He had to organize his own transport to arrive at the district attorney's office of Kings County in Brooklyn that afternoon. He presented himself to the policeman on duty and Asst. D.A. Edward A. Heffernan came down to greet them. When Heffernan recognized the mobster chained to Dickey's wrist, he whispered into the young man's ear. "Do you mind my saying," said Heffernan, "I am surprised. We never expected to see this boy back here." Heffernan would later be charged, alongside his boss O'Dwyer, of failing to successfully prosecute gangster Anastasia.

When Genovese finally appeared before a U.S. court in June 1946, all charges were dropped against him for lack of evidence. "By devious means," said the county judge, "among which were the terrorizing of witnesses, kidnapping them, yes, even murdering those who could give evidence against you, you have thwarted justice time and again." Dressed smartly in a double-breasted blue suit, white shirt, and maroon tie, Genovese smiled. He was now free to continue his career as one of the top Mafiosi in America and exploit his links with the old Mafia in Sicily. Dickey's heroic efforts had all been in vain.

Genovese went on to prosper as a top gangster in New York City, diminishing fellow Mafiosi, such as Frank Costello and Meyer Lansky. But in 1959, his luck ran out and he was nailed for narcotics deal and sentenced to 15 years in prison, where he died in 1969. Dickey became a legend to other CID agents in Italy, but little is known about his life after he left the army. A request to the CID archivist revealed little and they had no record of his later career or death.

Tim Newark is the author of the recently published book, *Mafia Allies: The True Story of America's Secret Alliance with the Mob* (Zenith Press), 2007.

ABOUT THE AUTHOR

Carmine Vittoria was born in Avella, a town located 20 km northeast of Naples, Italy, at the beginning of World War II. Unfortunately, Carmine's father passed away in Libya in 1941 which pushed the family to emigrate to Western Pennsylvania in 1953. This allowed Carmine to receive a formal education in the United States. Carmine ended up completing his undergraduate studies in electrical engineering at Toledo University. Later, he earned a Ph.D. in Applied Quantum Physics from Yale University, where he conducted theoretical research.

After completing his degree, Carmine was employed as a physicist at the Naval Research Laboratory in Washington, D.C., where he specialized in the physics of magnetism. He dedicated 20 years to this research before accepting a full professorship with tenure at Northeastern University, which was unusual at the time since universities rarely employed individuals from industry or government laboratories with tenure.

Throughout Carmine's 55-year career, he focused on researching new and artificial magnetic materials, earning numerous accolades and special memberships, such as the distinction of being a Fellow of both the American Physical Society (APS) and the Institute of Electrical and Electronic Engineering (IEEE). He has also published over 500 scientific papers and 25 patents, which have been cited over 10,000 times in top-rated journals. In addition, Carmine has written four scientific books, which have been distributed worldwide to universities and libraries.

Since retiring, he has also published six non-scientific books, including "Soccer USA," "Bitter Chicory to Sweet Espresso," "Dal Caffe di Cicoria al Caffe Espresso," "Once Upon a Hill," and "Hidden in Plain Sight."

Outside of his professional life, Carmine has a passion for playing bocce and has competed in tournaments with top-notch players for 25 years, winning first-place trophies. He also grows fig plants and runs a Bridge club, 3 times a week in Florida.

For more, Cvittoria.com

ACKNOWLEDGMENTS

Without these beautiful editors (Charlotte Frank, Isabella Braddish, and Rie Vittoria), I am like a sailor without a rudder, all over the place. Being avid readers, they are better than good at guiding me through this book. I needed that because the story in this book does not involve me. Writing memoirs was a lot easier, but thanks to them I believe I survived the ordeal. Most importantly, I learned a lot from them.

BIBLIOGRAPHY

The bibliography follows a time sequence of historical events consistent with the table of contents.

DESCENDANTS OF SOUTHERN ITALIANS

1. Chisholm, Hugh, "Avella", Encyclopedia Britannica (11th ed.), Cambridge University Press; Bunbury, Edward, "Abella", (https://books.google.com/books).
2. Kamen, Henry, The Spanish Inquisition: A Historical Revision, Yale University Press (1998). ISBN 9780300075229.
3. Colletta, Pietro, The History of the Kingdom of Naples, I. B. Tauris. ISBN 9781845118815.
4. Maltby, William S. Alba, A Biography of Fernando Alvarez de Toledo, Third Duke of Alba, University of California Press (1983). ISBN 0520046943.
5. Montanile, Nicola, The Baronial Palazzo: History, curiosities, nobles and benefactors, to be published and private communication.
6. Payne, Stanley G., Fascist Italy and Spain, 1922-45, Mediterranean Historical Review **13**, p. 99 (1998).
7. Leopold von Ranke, History of the Popes (Colonna) and State, Wellesley College Library Volume III, 2009.
8. Dodge, Theodore, Hannibal, Da Capo Press (1891), Cambridge, MA, ISBN 0306813629
9. Bradley, Keith R., Slavery and Rebellion in the Roman World, 140-70 BC, Indiana University Press (1989), ISBN 0253312590.

10. Gruen, Erich S., Jews Amidst Greeks and Romans, Harvard University Press (2009).

11. Gunther, R. T., Pausilypon, the Imperial villa near Naples, Oxford University Press (1913).

12. Isaia, Roberto, Marianelli, Paola and Sbrana, Alessandra, Caldera unrest before intense volcanism in Campi Flegrei at 4.0 ka B.P.: Implications for caldera dynamics and future eruptive scenarios, Geophysical Research Letters **36**, 2009.

13. E. T. Salmon, Samnium, and the Samnites, Cambridge University Press, Cambridge (2010).

14. A. Everitt, Cicero, Random House, Inc., New York (2001).

POST-WORLD WAR 1 POLITICAL EVENTS

1. Englestein, Laura, Russia in Flames: War, Revolution, and Civil War, 1914-1921, Oxford University Press (2018).

2. Morselli, Mario, Caporetto, 1917: Victory or Defeat? Routledge Pub. (2001), ISBN 0714650730.

3. Brundage, J. F. and Shanks, G. D., What really happened during the 1918 influenza pandemic? The importance of bacterial secondary infections, The Journal of Infectious Diseases **196**, p. 1717 (2007).

4. Taubenberger, J. K., 1918 Influenza: the mother of all pandemics, Emerging Infectious Diseases **2**, p.15 (2006).

5. Feldman, Gerald D., The great disorder politics, economics, and society in the German inflation, 1914-1924, Oxford University Press (1996). ISBN 0195101146.

6. Gregor, Jmes A., Young Mussolini and the Intellectual Origins of Fascism, University of California Press (1979). ISBN 9780520037991.

7. Bernardo, Francesco, Il Diavolo e L'Artista. Le passioni artistiche de giovani Mussolini, Stalin e Hitler (The devil and the artist. The artistic passions of young Mussolini, Stalin and Hitler), Tralerighe Pub. (2019). ISBN 978883287079.

8. Rieber, Alfred J., Stalin as Georgian: The Formative Years, Cambridge University Press (2005). ISBN 9781139446631.

9. Hafner, Sebastian, The meaning of Hitler, Harvard University Press, Cambridge (1979). IBSN 978067455778.

EVOLUTION OF FASCISM AND NAZISM

1. Shirer, William, The Rise, and Fall of the Third Reich, Simon & Schuster, New York (1960).
2. Young, Anthony J. G., Mussolini and the Intellectual Origins of Fascism, University of California Press. ISBN 9780520037991.
3. Ciano Galeazzo, Diary, 1937-1943, Enigma Books (2008). ISBN 9781929631025.
4. Mollo, Andrew, The Armed Forces of World War II, I. B. Tauris & Co. Ltd. ISBN 9780517544785.
5. Marino, James I., Italians on the Eastern Front: From Barbarossa to Stalingrad, Warfare History Network (Nov. 17, 2018).
6. Speer, Albert, Inside the Third Reich, Weidenfield & Nicholson (1995). ISBN 9781842127353.
7. Zimmerman, Joshua D., Jews in Italy Under Fascist and Nazi Rule, 1922-1945, Cambridge University Press (1980). ISBN 9780521841016.
8. Zuccotti, Susan, Italians and the Holocaust, Basic Books Inc., New York (1987). 326
9. Standenmeyer, Peter, Racial Ideology between Fascist Italy and Nazi Germany, Journal of Contemporary History **55**, p. 473 (2019).
10. Bosworth, R. J. B., Mussolini's Italy: Life Under the Dictatorship 1915-1945, Allen Lane, London (1998).
11. Moseley, Ray, Mussolini: The Last 600 Days of Il Duce, Taylor Trade Publishing, Dallas (2004).
12. Mussolini, Rachele, Mussolini: An Intimate Biography, Pocket Books (1970). ISBN 0671812726.
13. Puglese, Stanislao G., Fascism, Anti-Fascism and the Resistance in Italy: 1919 to Present, Rowan and Littlefield (2004). ISBN 0747531236.
14. Lyttelton, Adrian, The Seizure of Power: Fascism in Italy, 1919-1929, Routledge (2003). ISBN 0714654736.
15. Silvestri, Carlo, Matteotti, Mussolini e il Dramma Italiano, Ruffolo, Roma (1947). Translation: Matteotti, Mussolini and the Italian Drama.
16. Dornberg, John, Munich 1923: The Story of Hitler's First Grab for Power, Harper Row, New York (1982).

17. Gordon, Harold J. Jr., The Hitler Trial Before the People's Court in Munich, University Publications of America (1976).

18. Kershaw, Ian, Hitler: 1889-1936, Penguin Books, New York (2001).

19. Hitler, Adolf, Mein Kempf, Houghton Mifflin, New York (1999).

20. Pastore, Stephen R., The Art of Adolf Hitler, Grand Oaks Books (2013).

21. Fulda, Bernhard, Press Politics in the Weimar Republic, Oxford University Press. ISBN 9780199547784.

22. Goeschel, Christian, Mussolini and Hitler: The Forging of the Fascist Alliance, Yale University Press. ISBN 9780679446958.

POLITICAL DISSIDENTS AGAINST FASCISM

1. Levi, Carlo, Christ Stopped at Eboli, Farrar, Strauss and Giroux, New York (1974).

2. Casanova, Antonio G., Matteotti:Una Vita il Socialismo (A Life in Socialism), Bongianni Pub. (1974).

3. Canali, Mauro, Il delitto Matteotti (The Murder of Matteotti), Il Mulino (2004).

4. Moorehead, Caroline, A Bold and Dangerous Family:The Rosellis and the Fight Adainst Mussolini, Chatto and Windus (2000).

5. Amendola, Eva Kuhn, Life with Giovanni Amendola, Parenti (1960).

6. Colarizi, Simona, The Democrats in Opposition: Giovanni Amendola and the National Union, Il Mulino (1973).

7. Ward, David, Piero Gobetti's New World: Antifascism, Liberalism and Writing, University of Toronto Press (2010).

8. Ciano, Galeano, Diary, Ibid.

9. Moseley, Ray, Mussolini's Shadow:The Double Life of Count Galeano Ciano, Yale University Press, New Haven (1999). ISBN 97800300209563

RACIAL LAWS IN FASCIST ITALY

1. Sarfatti, Michael, Characteristics and Objectives of the Anti-Jewish Racial Lawsin Fascist Italy; Joshua D. Zimmerman, Jews in Italy Under

Fascist and Nazi Rule, 1922-1945, Cambridge University Press (2005). ISBN 0521841011.

2. Livingston, Michael A., The Fascists and the the Jews of Italy-Mussolini's Race Laws, 1938-1943, Cambridge University Press (2014). ISBN 0333760646.

3. Kertzer, David I., The Pope at War: The Secret History of Pope Pius XII, Mussolini and Hitler, Random House, New York (2022).

4. Kertzer, David I., The Secret History of Pope Pius XI and the Rise of Fascism in Europe, Random House, New York (2004).

5. Bradsher, Greg, The Nuremberg Racial Laws, Prologue Magazine, The National Archives and Records Administration **42**, (2010).

6. Burleigh, Michael, The Racial State: Germany 1933-1945, Cambridge University Press (2000). ISBN 9780521398022.

7. Longerich, Peter, Holocaust: The Nazi persecution and Murder of the Jews, Oxford University Press (2000). ISBN 9780192804365.

INTERNMENT CAMPS IN FASCIST ITALY

1. Capogreco, Carlo S., I Campi del Duce. L'Internamento Civili nell'Italia Fascista (Il Duce's Camps. Civil Internments in Fascist Italy) (1940-1943), Einaudi, Torino (1993).

2. Klinkhammer, Lutz, L' Occupazione Tedesca in Italia (German Occupation of Italy) 1943-1945, Bollati Boringhieri, Torino (1993).

3. Zuccoli, Susan, Holocaust Odysseys:The Jews of Saint-Martin-Vesubie and their Flight through France and Italy, Yale University Press, New Haven (2007).

4. Bettina, Elizabeth, It Happened in Italy, Thomas Nelson, Nashville (2009).

5. Freidberg, An Account of the S.S. Pentch and the Italian Internment Camps at
Rhodes and Ferramonti, The Israel Philatelist, **XV** (No. 8 and 9), p.112 (1964).

6. Watson, James, History and Memoryof the Italian Concentration Camps, Historical Journal **40** (#1), p. 169 (1997). Cambridge University Press.

7. Museum of Ferramont di Tarsia, (http://www.museoferrmonti.it).

8. Goeschel, Christian and Wachsmann, Nikolaus, The Nazi Concentration Camps 1933-1939: A Documentary History, University of Nebraska Press. ISBN 9780803227828.

9. Healey, Dan, Lives in the Balance: Weak and Disabled Prisoners and Biopolitics of the Gulag, Kritika **16** p. 3. (1980).

10. Blatman, Daniel, The Death Marches:The Final Phase of Nazi Genocide. Harvard University Press. ISBN 9780674059191.

11. Hinnershitz, Stephanie, Japanese American Incarceration, University of Pennsylvania Press. ISBN 9780812299953.

TURNING POINTS IN WORLD WAR 2

1. Wilhelm, Adam and Ruhle, Otto, With Paulus at Stalingrad, Penn Sword Books (2015). ISBN 9781473833869.

2. Bell, P. M. H., Twelve Turning Points of the Second World War, Yale University Press, New Haven (2011).

3. Craig, William, Enemy at the Gates: The Battle of Stalingrad, Penguin Books, New York (2000).

4. Ban, Niall, Pendulum of War: The Three Battles of El Alamein, Overlook Press, Woodstock (2000). ISBN 9781585617382.

5. Greene, Jack and Massignani, Alessandro, Rommel'd North African Campaign: September 190-November 1942, Da Capo, Cambridge (1994). ISBN 97815809970181.

6. Blumenson, Martin, Kasserine Pass, Houghton Mifflin, Boston (1966).

7. Badoglio, Pietro, Italy in The Second World War, Memories and Documents, Oxford University Press (1948).

8. Badoglio, Pietro, The War in Abyssinia, Methuen Publishers, London (1937). 330

9. Smith, Dennis M., Italy and Its Monarchy, Yale University Press, New Haven (1989).

10. Bastianini, Giuseppe, Memoirs, Vitigliano, Rome (1959); "Volevo Fermare Mussolini" ("I wanted to stop Mussolini), BUR Saggi, Rome (2005).

11. Guderian Heinz, "Hitler's Momentous Order to Stop", Panzer Group Leader, Da Capo Press (1952, 2001). ISBN 9780306811012.

12. Lord, Walter, The Miracle of Dunkirk, Allen Lane, London (1983).

13. Thompson, Julian, Dunkirk: Retreat to Victory, Acade, New York (2011).

14. Richardso, Mathew, Tigers at Dunkirk and the Fall of France, Pen Sword, Barnsley (2010). ISBN 9781848842106.

GLOBALLY ORGANIZED CRIME SYNDICATES

1. Vittoria, Carmine, Once Upon a Hill, Purpo, Inc., Key Biscayne (2022). ISBN 9780578320014.

2. Nicasio, Antonio and Lamothe, Lee, The Global Mafia: The New Order of Organized Crime, MacMillan of Canada (1995). ISBN 0771573111.

3. Saviano, R., Gomorrah, Arnoldo Mondatori Editore, Milan (2008).

4. Frasca, D., Vito Genovese: King of Crime, Avon Books. New York (1963).

5. Gosch, M. A. and Hammer, R., Lucky Luciano, Little Brown and Company, Boston (1975).

6. Raab, S., Five Families, Saint Martin Press, New York (2005).

7. Reavill, G., Mafia Summit, Thomas Dunne Books, New York (2013).

8. Dickie, John, Mafia Republic: Italy's Criminal Curse. Cosa Nostra, Ndrangheta and Camorra from 1946 to the present, Hodder and Stoughton, New York (2013). ISBN 97814444726435.

9. Behau, Tom, The Camorra, Routledge (1996). ISBN 0415099870.

10. Letizia, Paoli, Mafia Brotherhoods: Organized Crime, Italian Style, Oxford University Press, New York (2003).

11. Varese, Federico, How Mafias Migrate: The Case of Ndrangheta in Northern Italy, Law and Society Review, June 2006.

RELEVANT LITERATURE

1. Atkinson, R. A., The Day Battle in Sicily and Italy, 1943-1944, Henry Holt, New York (2007).

2. Bertoldi, S., Badoglio, Rizzoli, Milan (1982).

3. Branko, B., Spy in the Vatican, Vita, London (1973).

4. Hapgood D. and Richardson D., Monte Cassino, Congdon & Weed, Inc., New York (1984).

5. Katz, R., The Battle for Rome, Simon & Schuster, New York (2003).

6. Posner, G., God's Bankers (A History of Money and Power at the Vatican), Simon & Schuster, New York (2015).

7. Stille, A., Benevolence and Betrayal (Five Jewish Families under Fascism), Summit Books, New York (1991).

8. Tompkins, Peter, Una Spia a Roma (A spy in Rome), Il Saggiatore, Milan (2002).

9. LaFarge, John, Interracial Justice as a Principle of Order Catholic University of America Press, Washington D. C. (1937).

10. Goldhagen, D. J., What Would Jesus Have Done? The New Republic, New York (2002).

11. Castellano, Giuseppe, How I Signed the Armistice of Cassabile, Mondatori, Milan (1945).

12. Churchill, Winston, Closing the Ring, Houghton Mifflin, Boston (1951).

13. Mikolashek J. B., General Mark Clark, Casemate, New York (2013).

14. Falconi, Carlo, The Silence of Pius XII, Little Brown, Boston (1970).

15. Dollman, E., Roma Nazista, Longanesi, Milan (1949); Call me Coward, William Kimber, London (1956); The Interpreter, Hutchison, London (1967).

16. Harris C. R. S., Allied Military Administration of Italy, 1943-1945 (HMSO, 1957).

17. Croce, Benedetto, The King and the Allies, Allen & Unwin, London (1950).

18. Everitt, Anthony, Cicero, Random House, New York (2001).

19. Bimberg, E. L., The Moroccan Goums: Tribal Warriors in a Modern War, Greenwood Press, Westport (1999).

20. Carter, R. S., Those Devils in Baggy Pants, Signet, New York (1999).

21. Montgomery, B. L., The Memoirs of Field Marshal the Viscount Montgomery of Alamein, K. G. the Companion Book Club, London (1958).

22. Clark, M. W., Calculated Risk, Harper & Brothers, New York (1950).

23. Newark, T., The Mafia at War: Allied Collusion with the Mob, Greenhill Books, New York 2007).

24. Passelecq, G. and Suchecky B., The Hidden Encyclical of Pius XI, Harcourt Brace, New York (1997).

25. Kesselring, A., A Soldier's Record, Morrow, New York (1954).

26. Casanova, A.G., Matteotti, Bombiani, Milan (1974).

27. Battistelli, Pier Paolo, Tobruk 1941, The History Press, New York (2012). 28. Hellbeck, J., Stalingrad, Public Affairs, New York (2015).

29. Patton, G. S. and Harkins, P. D., War as I Knew It, Houghton Mifflin, Boston, (1995).

30. Newness G., Appian Way, Chambers' Encyclopedia, **1**, p.149, London (1961).

31. Eisenhower D. D., A Crusade in Europe, Doubleday, New York (1948).

32. Smith R. H., OSS, Lyons Press, New York (1972).

33. Stalin Joseph, The Road to Power, University Press of the Pacific, New York (2003).

34. Cawthorne W., The History of the Mafia, Arcturus, New York (2011).

35. Hogan Michael J., The Marshall Plan, Cambridge University Press, Cambridge (1987).

36. Orlando L., Fighting the Mafia, Encounter Books, San Francisco (2001). 37. Stille Alexander, Excellent Cadavers, Random House, New York (1995).

Made in the USA
Coppell, TX
15 July 2023

19243187R00184